PENGU

COLLEC

Graham Greene was born in
School, where his father was the headmaster.
from Balliol College, Oxford, where he published a book of verse,
he worked for four years as a sub-editor on *The Times*. He established his reputation with his fourth novel, *Stamboul Train*, which
he classed as an 'entertainment' in order to distinguish it from
more serious work. In 1935 he made a journey across Liberia,
described in *Journey Without Maps*, and on his return was appointed film critic of the *Spectator*. In 1926 he had been received
into the Roman Catholic Church and was commissioned to visit
Mexico in 1938, and report on the religious persecution there. As
a result he wrote *The Lawless Roads* and, later, *The Power and the
Glory*.

Brighton Rock was published in 1938, and in 1940 he became
literary editor of the *Spectator*. The next year he undertook work
for the Foreign Office and was sent out to Sierra Leone in 1941–3.
One of his major post-war novels, *The Heart of the Matter*, is set
in West Africa and is considered by many to be his finest book.
This was followed by *The End of the Affair*, *The Quiet American*,
a story set in Vietnam, *Our Man in Havana*, and *A Burnt-Out
Case*. Many of his novels and short stories have been filmed and
The Third Man was first written as a film. In 1967 he published a
collection of short stories under the title: *May We Borrow Your
Husband?* His later publications include his autobiography, *A
Sort of Life* (1971), *The Honorary Consul* (1973), *Lord Rochester's
Monkey* (1974), *An Impossible Woman: the Memories of
Dottoressa Moor of Capri* (edited 1975) and *Doctor Fischer of
Geneva or The Bomb Party* (1980).

In all, Graham Greene has written some thirty novels, many of
which have been published in Penguins, 'entertainments', plays,
children's books, travel books, and collections of essays and short
stories. He was made a Companion of Honour in 1966.

GRAHAM GREENE

COLLECTED ESSAYS

PENGUIN BOOKS

in association with The Bodley Head

Penguin Books Ltd, Harmondsworth, Middlesex, England
Penguin Books, 625 Madison Avenue, New York, New York 10022, U.S.A.
Penguin Books Australia Ltd, Ringwood, Victoria, Australia
Penguin Books Canada Ltd, 2801 John Street, Markham, Ontario, Canada L3R 1B4
Penguin Books (N.Z.) Ltd, 182-190 Wairau Road, Auckland 10, New Zealand

—

First published in Great Britain by The Bodley Head 1969
First published in the United States of America by The Viking Press 1969
Published in Penguin Books 1970
Reprinted 1977, 1978, 1981

—

—

Made and printed in Great Britain by
Hazell Watson & Viney Ltd,
Aylesbury, Bucks
Set in Linotype Times Roman

CONTENTS

CONTENTS

PART III: SOME CHARACTERS

[1]

[2]

CONTENTS

[3]

[4]

PART IV: PERSONAL POSTSCRIPT

AUTHOR'S NOTE

In selecting what essays to reprint over a period of more than thirty years I have made it a principle to include nothing of which I can say that, if I were writing today, I would write in a different sense. The principle applies as much to my hatreds as to my loves. Some of these attacks, reprinted after so many years, are directed at what might seem now rather diminished objects, but I would feel a serious lack in the book if they were omitted. A man should be judged by his enmities as well as by his friendships.

Acknowledgements

ACKNOWLEDGEMENTS are due to the following publishers for permission to reprint essays contained in this volume:

Chatto & Windus for 'Henry James: The Private Universe'; Elkin Matthews for 'Henry James: The Religious Aspect'; Oxford University Press for the introduction to *The Portrait of a Lady*; Hamish Hamilton for 'The Young Dickens' and for 'Edgar Wallace'; Cassells for 'Fielding and Sterne'; The Bodley Head for 'The Burden of Childhood'; Faber & Faber for 'Walter de la Mare's Short Stories'; Librairie Plon for 'Bernanos, the Beginner'; Methuen for 'The Town of Malgudi'; Heinemann for 'Norman Douglas'; and McGibbon & Kee for 'The Spy'.

Acknowledgements are also made to editors of the following periodicals:

New Statesman, Spectator, Time & Tide, the *London Mercury, Night and Day, France Libre, Horizon*, the *Month*, the *Tablet*, the *Listener*, the *Observer*, the *Sunday Times, London Magazine, Life*, and the *Daily Telegraph Magazine*.

'The Spy' was first published in *Esquire* under the title 'Reflections on the Character of Kim Philby'.

PART I

Personal Prologue

THE LOST CHILDHOOD

PERHAPS it is only in childhood that books have any deep influence on our lives. In later life we admire, we are entertained, we may modify some views we already hold, but we are more likely to find in books merely a confirmation of what is in our minds already: as in a love affair it is our own features that we see reflected flatteringly back.

But in childhood all books are books of divination, telling us about the future, and like the fortune-teller who sees a long journey in the cards or death by water they influence the future. I suppose that is why books excited us so much. What do we ever get nowadays from reading to equal the excitement and the revelation in those first fourteen years? Of course I should be interested to hear that a new novel by Mr E. M. Forster was going to appear this spring, but I could never compare that mild expectation of civilized pleasure with the missed heart-beat, the appalled glee I felt when I found on a library shelf a novel by Rider Haggard, Percy Westerman, Captain Brereton or Stanley Weyman which I had not read before. It is in those early years that I would look for the crisis, the moment when life took a new slant in its journey towards death.

I remember distinctly the suddenness with which a key turned in a lock and I found I could read – not just the sentences in a reading book with the syllables coupled like railway carriages, but a real book. It was paper-covered with the picture of a boy, bound and gagged, dangling at the end of a rope inside a well with the water rising above his waist – an adventure of Dixon Brett, detective. All a long summer holiday I kept my secret, as I believed: I did not want anybody to know that I could read. I suppose I half consciously realized even then that this was the dangerous moment. I was safe so long as I could not read – the wheels had not begun to turn, but now the future stood around on bookshelves everywhere

waiting for the child to choose – the life of a chartered accountant perhaps, a colonial civil servant, a planter in China, a
steady job in a bank, happiness and misery, eventually one
particular form of death, for surely we choose our death much
as we choose our job. It grows out of our acts and our evasions,
out of our fears and out of our moments of courage. I suppose
my mother must have discovered my secret, for on the journey
home I was presented for the train with another real book, a
copy of Ballantyne's *Coral Island* with only a single picture to
look at, a coloured frontispiece. But I would admit nothing. All
the long journey I stared at the one picture and never opened
the book.

But there on the shelves at home (so many shelves for we
were a large family) the books waited – one book in particular,
but before I reach that one down let me take a few others at
random from the shelf. Each was a crystal in which the child
dreamed that he saw life moving. Here in a cover stamped
dramatically in several colours was Captain Gilson's *The Pirate
Aeroplane*. I must have read that book six times at least – the
story of a lost civilization in the Sahara and of a villainous
Yankee pirate with an aeroplane like a box kite and bombs
the size of tennis balls who held the golden city to ransom. It was saved by the hero, a young subaltern who crept
up to the pirate camp to put the aeroplane out of action. He
was captured and watched his enemies dig his grave. He was to
be shot at dawn, and to pass the time and keep his mind from
uncomfortable thoughts the amiable Yankee pirate played
cards with him – the mild nursery game of Kuhn Kan. The
memory of that nocturnal game on the edge of life haunted
me for years, until I set it to rest at last in one of my own novels
with a game of poker played in remotely similar circumstances.

And here is *Sophy of Kravonia* by Anthony Hope – the
story of a kitchen-maid who became a queen. One of the
first films I ever saw, about 1911, was made from that book,
and I can hear still the rumble of the Queen's guns crossing
the high Kravonian pass beaten hollowly out on a single piano.
Then there was Stanley Weyman's *The Story of Francis*

Cludde, and above all other books at that time of my life *King Solomon's Mines.*

This book did not perhaps provide the crisis, but it certainly influenced the future. If it had not been for that romantic tale of Allan Quatermain, Sir Henry Curtis, Captain Good, and, above all, the ancient witch Gagool, would I at nineteen have studied the appointments list of the Colonial Office and very nearly picked on the Nigerian Navy for a career? And later, when surely I ought to have known better, the odd African fixation remained. In 1935 I found myself sick with fever on a camp bed in a Liberian native's hut with a candle going out in an empty whisky bottle and a rat moving in the shadows. Wasn't it the incurable fascination of Gagool with her bare yellow skull, the wrinkled scalp that moved and contracted like the hood of a cobra, that led me to work all through 1942 in a little stuffy office in Freetown, Sierra Leone? There is not much in common between the land of the Kukuanas, behind the desert and the mountain range of Sheba's Breast, and a tin-roofed house on a bit of swamp where the vultures moved like domestic turkeys and the pi-dogs kept me awake on moonlit nights with their wailing, and the white women yellowed by atebrin drove by to the club; but the two belonged at any rate to the same continent, and, however distantly, to the same region of the imagination – the region of uncertainty, of not knowing the way out. Once I came a little nearer to Gagool and her witch-hunters, one night in Zigita on the Liberian side of the French Guinea border, when my servants sat in their shuttered hut with their hands over their eyes and someone beat a drum and a whole town stayed behind closed doors while the big bush devil – whom it would mean blindness to see – moved between the huts.

But *King Solomon's Mines* could not finally satisfy. It was not the right answer. The key did not quite fit. Gagool I could recognize – didn't she wait for me in dreams every night, in the passage by the linen cupboard, near the nursery door? and she continues to wait, when the mind is sick or tired, though now she is dressed in the theological garments of Despair and speaks in Spenser's accents:

The longer life, I wote the greater sin,
The greater sin, the greater punishment.

Gagool has remained a permanent part of the imagination, but Quatermain and Curtis – weren't they, even when I was only ten years old, a little too good to be true? They were men of such unyielding integrity (they would only admit to a fault in order to show how it might be overcome) that the wavering personality of a child could not rest for long against those monumental shoulders. A child, after all, knows most of the game – it is only an attitude to it that he lacks. He is quite well aware of cowardice, shame, deception, disappointment. Sir Henry Curtis perched upon a rock bleeding from a dozen wounds but fighting on with the remnant of the Greys against the hordes of Twala was too heroic. These men were like Platonic ideas: they were not life as one had already begun to know it.

But when – perhaps I was fourteen by that time – I took Miss Marjorie Bowen's *The Viper of Milan* from the library shelf, the future for better or worse really struck. From that moment I began to write. All the other possible futures slid away: the potential civil servant, the don, the clerk had to look for other incarnations. Imitation after imitation of Miss Bowen's magnificent novel went into exercise-books – stories of sixteenth-century Italy or twelfth-century England marked with enormous brutality and a despairing romanticism. It was as if I had been supplied once and for all with a subject.

Why? On the surface *The Viper of Milan* is only the story of a war between Gian Galeazzo Visconti, Duke of Milan, and Mastino della Scala, Duke of Verona, told with zest and cunning and an amazing pictorial sense. Why did it creep in and colour and explain the terrible living world of the stone stairs and the never quiet dormitory? It was no good in that real world to dream that one would ever be a Sir Henry Curtis, but della Scala who at last turned from an honesty that never paid and betrayed his friends and died dishonoured and a failure even at treachery – it was easier for a child to escape behind his mask. As for Visconti, with his beauty, his patience,

16

and his genius for evil, I had watched him pass by many a time in his black Sunday suit smelling of mothballs. His name was Carter. He exercised terror from a distance like a snow-cloud over the young fields. Goodness has only once found a perfect incarnation in a human body and never will again, but evil can always find a home there. Human nature is not black and white but black and grey. I read all that in *The Viper of Milan* and I looked round and I saw that it was so.

There was another theme I found there. At the end of *The Viper of Milan* – you will remember if you have once read it – comes the great scene of complete success – della Scala is dead, Ferrara, Verona, Novara, Mantua have all fallen, the messengers pour in with news of fresh victories, the whole world outside is cracking up, and Visconti sits and jokes in the wine-light. I was not on the classical side or I would have discovered I suppose, in Greek literature instead of in Miss Bowen's novel the sense of doom that lies over success – the feeling that the pendulum is about to swing. That too made sense; one looked around and saw the doomed everywhere – the champion runner who one day would sag over the tape; the head of the school who would atone, poor devil, during forty dreary undistin-guished years; the scholar ... and when success began to touch oneself too, however mildly, one could only pray that failure would not be held off for too long.

One had lived for fourteen years in a wild jungle country without a map, but now the paths had been traced and naturally one had to follow them. But I think it was Miss Bowen's apparent zest that made me want to write. One could not read her without believing that to write was to live and to enjoy, and before one had discovered one's mistake it was too late – the first book one does enjoy. Anyway she had given me my pattern – religion might later explain it to me in other terms, but the pattern was already there – perfect evil walking the world where perfect good can never walk again, and only the pendulum ensures that after all in the end justice is done. Man is never satisfied, and often I have wished that my hand had not moved further than *King Solomon's Mines*, and that the future I had taken down from the nursery shelf had been a district office in Sierra Leone and twelve tours of malarial duty and a finishing dose of blackwater fever when the danger of retirement approached. What is the good of wishing? The books are always there, the moment of crisis waits, and now our children in their turn are taking down the future and opening the pages. In his poem 'Germinal' A. E. wrote:

> In ancient shadows and twilights
> Where childhood had strayed,
> The world's great sorrows were born
> And its heroes were made.
> In the lost boyhood of Judas
> Christ was betrayed.

1947

PART II

Novels and Novelists

HENRY JAMES: THE PRIVATE UNIVERSE

THE technical qualities of Henry James's novels have been so often and so satisfactorily explored, notably by Mr Percy Lubbock, that perhaps I may be forgiven for ignoring James as the fully conscious craftsman in order to try to track the instinctive, the poetic writer back to the source of his fantasies. In all writers there occurs a moment of crystallization when the dominant theme is plainly expressed, when the private universe becomes visible even to the least sensitive reader. Such a crystallization is Hardy's often-quoted phrase: 'The President of the Immortals ... had ended his sport with Tess', or that passage in his preface to *Jude the Obscure*, when he writes of 'the fret and fever, derision and disaster, that may press in the wake of the strongest passion known to humanity'. It is less easy to find such a crystallization in the works of James, whose chief aim was always to dramatize, who was more than usually careful to exclude the personal statement, but I think we may take the sentence in the scenario of *The Ivory Tower*, in which James speaks of 'the black and merciless things that are behind great possessions', as an expression of the ruling fantasy which drove him to write: a sense of evil religious in its intensity.

'Art itself', Conrad wrote, 'may be defined as a single-minded attempt to render the highest kind of justice to the visible universe', and no definition in his own prefaces better describes the object Henry James so passionately pursued, if the word visible does not exclude the private vision. If there are times when we feel, in *The Sacred Fount*, even in the exquisite *Golden Bowl*, that the judge is taking too much into consideration, that he could have passed his sentence on less evidence, we have always to admit, as the long record of human corruption unrolls, that he has never allowed us to lose sight of the main case; and because his mind is bent on rendering even evil 'the highest kind of justice', the symmetry of his

21

thought lends the whole body of his work the importance of a system.

No writer has left a series of novels more of one moral piece. The differences between James's first works and his last are only differences of art as Conrad defined it. In his early work, perhaps, he rendered a little less than the highest kind of justice; the progress from *The American* to *The Golden Bowl* is a progress from a rather crude and inexperienced symbolization of truth itself: a progress from evil represented rather obviously in terms of murder to evil *in propria persona*, walking down Bond Street, charming, cultured, sensitive – evil to be distinguished from good chiefly in the complete egotism of its outlook. They are complete anarchists, these later Jamesian characters, they form the immoral background to that extraordinary period of haphazard violence which anticipated the first world war: the attempt on Greenwich Observatory, the siege of Sidney Street. They lent the tone which made possible the cruder manifestations presented by Conrad in *The Secret Agent.* Merton Densher, who planned to marry the dying Milly Theale for her money, plotting with his mistress who was her best friend; Prince Amerigo, who betrayed his wife with her friend, her father's wife; Horton, who swindled his friend Gray of his money: the last twist (it is always the friend, the intimate who betrays) is given to these studies of moral corruption. They represent an attitude which had been James's from very far back; they are not the slow painful fruit of experience. The attitude never varied from the time of *The American* onwards. Mme de Bellegarde, who murdered her husband and sold her daughter, is only the first crude presentation of a woman gradually subtilized, by way of Mme Merle in *The Portrait of a Lady*, into the incomparable figures of evil, Kate Croy and Charlotte Stant.

This point is of importance. James has been too often regarded as a novelist of superficial experience, as a painter of social types, who was cut off by exile from the deepest roots of experience (as if there were something superior in the Sussex or Shropshire of the localized talent to James's international scene). But James was not in that sense an exile; he could have dispensed with the international scene as easily as he dispensed with all the world of Wall Street finance. For the roots were not in Venice, Paris, London; they were in himself. Densher, the Prince, just as much as the redhaired valet Quint and the adulterous governess, were rooted in his own character. They were there when he wrote *The American* in 1876; all he needed afterwards to perfect his work to his own impeccable standard was technical subtlety and that other subtlety which comes from superficial observation, the ability to construct convincing masks for his own personality.

I do not use superficial in any disparaging sense. If his practice-pieces, from *The Europeans* to *The Tragic Muse*, didn't engage his full powers, and were certainly not the vehicle for his most urgent fantasies, they were examples of sharp observation, the fruits of a direct objective experience, unsurpassed in their kind. He never again proved himself capable of drawing a portrait so directly, with such command of relevant detail. We know Charlotte Stant, of course, more thoroughly than we know Miss Birdseye in *The Bostonians*, but she emerges gradually through that long book, we don't 'see' her with the immediacy that we see Miss Birdseye:

She was a little old lady with an enormous head; that was the first thing Ransom noticed – the vast, fair, protuberant, candid, ungarnished brow, surmounting a pair of weak, kind, tired-looking eyes. ... The long practice of philanthropy had not given accent to her features; it had rubbed out their transitions, their meanings. ... In her large countenance her dim little smile scarcely showed. It was a mere sketch of a smile, a kind of instalment, or payment on account; it seemed to say that she would smile more if she had time, but that you could see, without this, that she was gentle and easy to beguile. ... She looked as if she had spent her life on platforms, in audiences, in conventions, in phalansteries, in seances; in her faded face there was a kind of reflexion of ugly lecture-lamps.

No writer's apprentice-work contains so wide and brilliant a range of portraits from this very early Miss Birdseye to Mrs Brookenham in *The Awkward Age*:

Mrs Brookenham was, in her forty-first year, still charmingly pretty, and the nearest approach she made at this moment to meeting her son's description of her was by looking beautifully desperate. She had about her the pure light of youth – would always have it; her head, her figure, her flexibility, her flickering colour, her lovely, silly eyes, her natural, quavering tone, all played together towards this effect by some trick that had never yet been exposed. It was at the same time remarkable that – at least in the bosom of her family – she rarely wore an appearance of gaiety less qualified than at the present juncture; she suggested for the most part the luxury, the novelty of woe, the excitement of strange sorrows and the cultivation of fine indifferencies. This was her special sign – an innocence dimly tragic. It gave immense effect to her other resources ...

The Awkward Age stands formidably between the two halves of James's achievement. It marks his decision to develop finally from *The American* rather than from *The Europeans*. It is the surrender of experience to fantasy. He hadn't found his method, but he had definitely found his theme. One may regret, in some moods, that his more superficial books had so few successors (English literature has too little that is light, lucid, and witty), but one cannot be surprised that he discarded many of them from the collected edition while retaining so crude a fiction as *The American*, discarded even the delicate, feline *Washington Square*, perhaps the only novel in which a man has successfully invaded the feminine field and produced work comparable to Jane Austen's.

How could he have done otherwise if he was to be faithful to his deeper personal fantasy? He wrote of 'poor Flaubert' that

he stopped too short. He hovered for ever at the public door, in the outer court, the splendour of which very properly beguiled him, and in which he seems still to stand as upright as a sentinel and as shapely as a statue. But that immobility and even that erectness were paid too dear. The shining arms were meant to carry further, the outer doors were meant to open. He should at least have listened at the chamber of the soul. This would have floated him on a deeper tide; above all it would have calmed his nerves.

His early novels, except *The American*, certainly belonged to the outer court. They had served their purpose, he had improved his masks, he was never to be more witty; but when he emerged from them again to take up his main study of corruption in *The Wings of the Dove* he had amazingly advanced: instead of murder, the more agonizing mental violence; instead of Mme de Bellegarde, Kate Croy; instead of the melodramatic heroine Mme de Cintré, the deeply felt subjective study of Milly Theale.

For to render the highest justice to corruption you must retain your innocence: you have to be conscious all the time within yourself of treachery to something valuable. If Peter Quint is to be rooted in you, so must the child his ghost corrupts: if Osmond, Isabel Archer too. These centres of innocence, these objects of treachery, are nearly always women: the lovely daring Isabel Archer, who goes out in her high-handed, wealthy way to meet life and falls to Osmond; Nanda, the young girl 'coming out', who is hemmed in by a vicious social set; Milly Theale, sick to death just at the time when life has most to offer, surrendering to Merton Densher and Kate Croy (apart from Quint and the Governess the most driven and 'damned' of all James's characters); Maggie Verver, the unsophisticated 'good' young American who encounters her particular corruption in the Prince and Charlotte Stant; the child Maisie tossed about among grown-up adulteries. These are the points of purity in the dark picture.

The attitude of mind which dictated these situations was a permanent one. Henry James had a marvellous facility for covering up his tracks (can we be blamed if we assume he had a reason?). In his magnificent prefaces he describes the geneses of his stories, where they were written, the method he adopted, the problems he faced: he seems, like the conjurer with rolled sleeves, to show everything. But you have to go further back than the anecdote at the dinner-table to trace the origin of such urgent fantasies. In this exploration his prefaces, even his autobiographies, offer very little help. Certainly they give his model for goodness; he is less careful to obliterate *that* trail back into youth (if one can speak of care in connexion with a design which was probably only half-conscious if it was conscious at all). His cousin, Mary Temple, was the model, a model in her deadly sickness and her high courage, above all in her hungry grip on life, for Milly Theale in particular.

She had [James wrote of her] beyond any equally young creature I have known a sense for verity of character and play of life in others, for their acting out of their force or their weakness, whatever either might be, at no matter what cost to herself. ... Life claimed her and used her and beset her – made her range in her groping: her naturally immature and unlighted way from end to end of the scale. ... She was absolutely afraid of nothing she might come to by living with enough sincerity and enough wonder; and I think it is because one was to see her launched on that adventure in such bedimmed, such almost tragically compromised conditions that one is caught by her title to the heroic and pathetic mask.

Mary Temple then, whatever mask she wore, was always the point of purity, but again one must seek further if one is to trace the source of James's passionate distrust in human nature, his sense of evil. Mary Temple was experience, but that other sense, one feels, was born in him, was his inheritance.

It cannot but seem odd how little in his volumes of reminiscence, *A Small Boy and Others* and *Notes of a Son and Brother*, Henry James really touches the subject of his family. His style is at its most complex: the beauty of the books is very like the beauty of Turner's later pictures: they are all air and light: you have to look a long while into their glow before you discern the most tenuous outline of their subjects. Certainly of the two main figures, Henry James, Senior, and William James, you learn nothing of what must have been to them of painful importance: their sense of daemonic possession.

James was to draw the figure of Peter Quint with his little red whiskers and his white damned face, he was to show Densher and Kate writhing in their hopeless infernal sundering success; evil was overwhelmingly part of his visible universe; but the sense (we got no indication of it in his reminiscences) was a family sense. He shared it with his father and brother

26

and sister. One may find the dark source of his deepest fantasy concealed in a family life which for sensitive boys must have been almost ideally free from compulsions, a tolerant cultured life led between Concord and Geneva. For nearly two years his father was intermittently attacked by a sense of 'perfectly insane and abject terror' (his own words); a damned shape seemed to squat beside him raying out 'a fetid influence'. Henry James's sister, Alice, was a prey to suicidal tendencies, and William James suffered in much the same way as his father.

I went one evening into a dressing-room in the twilight to procure some article that was there; when suddenly there fell upon me without any warning, just as if it came out of the darkness, a horrible fear of my own existence. Simultaneously there arose in my mind the image of an epileptic patient whom I had seen in the asylum, a black-haired youth the greenish skin, entirely idiotic, who used to sit all day on one of the benches, or rather shelves against the wall, with his knees drawn up against his chin, and the coarse grey undershirt, which was his only garment, drawn over them enclosing his entire figure. ...This image and my fear entered into a species of combination with each other. *That shape am I*, I felt potentially. Nothing that I possess can defend me against that fate, if the hour for it should strike for me as it struck for him. There was such a horror of him, and such a perception of my own merely momentary discrepancy from him, that it was as if something hitherto solid within my breast gave way entirely, and I became a mass of quivering fear. After this the universe was changed for me altogether. I awoke morning after morning with a horrible dread at the pit of my stomach, and with a sense of the insecurity of life, that I never knew before. ... It gradually faded, but for months I was unable to go out into the dark alone.

This epileptic idiot, this urge towards death, the damned shape, are a more important background to Henry James's novels than Grosvenor House and late Victorian society. It is true that the moral anarchy of the age gave him his material, but he would not have treated it with such intensity if it had not corresponded with his private fantasy. They were materialists, his characters, but you cannot read far in Henry

27

James's novels without realizing that their creator was not a materialist. If ever a man's imagination was clouded by the Pit, it was James's. When he touches this nerve, the fear of spiritual evil, he treats the reader with less than his usual frankness: 'a fairy-tale pure and simple', something seasonable for Christmas, is a disingenuous description of *The Turn of the Screw*. One cannot avoid a conviction that here he touched and recoiled from an important inhibition.

To a biographer the early formative years of a writer must always have a special fascination: the innocent eye dwelling frankly on a new unexplored world, the vistas of future experience at the end of the laurel walk, the voices of older people, like 'Viziers nodding together in some Arabian night', the strange accidents that seem to decide not only that this child shall be a writer but what kind of a writer this child shall be.

The eleven-year-old Conrad prepares his school work in the big old Cracow house where his father, the patriot Korzeniowski, lies dying:

There, in a large drawing room, panelled and bare, with heavy cornices and a lofty ceiling, in a little oasis of light made by two candles in a desert of dusk, I sat at a little table to worry and ink myself all over till the task of my preparation was done. The table of my toil faced a tall white door, which was kept closed; now and then it would come ajar and a nun in a white coif would squeeze herself through the crack, glide across the room, and disappear. There were two of these noiseless nursing nuns. Their voices were seldom heard. For, indeed, what could they have had to say? When they did speak to me it was with their lips hardly moving, in a cloistral clear whisper. Our domestic matters were ordered by the elderly housekeeper of our emergency. She, too, spoke but seldom. She wore a black dress with a cross hanging by a chain on her ample bosom. And though when she spoke she moved her lips more than the nuns, she never let her voice rise above a peacefully murmuring note. The air around me was all piety, resignation and silence.

Stevenson is scared into Calvinism at three years old by his nurse Cummy: 'I remember repeatedly awaking from a dream of Hell, clinging to the horizontal bar of my bed, with my knees and chin together, my soul shaken, my body convulsed with agony.'

The young James at thirteen finds himself 'overwhelmed and bewildered' in the Galerie d'Apollon with its frescoes by Lebrun and the great mythological paintings of Delacroix:

I shall never forget how – speaking, that is, for my own sense – they filled those vast halls with the influence rather of some complicated sound, diffused and reverberant, than of such visibilities as one could directly deal with. To distinguish among these, in the charged and coloured and confounding air, was difficult – it discouraged and defied; which was doubtless why my impression originally best entertained was that of those magnificent parts of the great gallery simply not inviting us to distinguish. They only arched over us in the wonder of their endless golden riot and relief, figured and flourished in perpetual revolution, breaking into great high-hung circles and symmetries of squandered picture, opening into deep outward embrasures that threw off the rest of monumental Paris somehow as a told story, a sort of wrought effect or bold ambiguity for a vista, and yet held it there, at every point, as a vast bright gage, even at moments a felt adventure, of experience.

It is impossible not to hear in such memories the opening of the door: in some such moment of 'piety, resignation and silence' Conrad's brooding note of sombre dignity and laconic heroism was first struck; the Master of Ballantrae may have been buried alive in Stevenson's nightmare as years later in the Canadian wastes, while the great wide air of glory and possessions and 'bold ambiguity' was breathed into James like a holy ghost at Pentecost in the great Paris gallery, where the spoils of Poynton gathered round the schoolboy and Madame Vionnet bloomed from the ceiling, a naked Venus.

It was just because the visible universe which he was so careful to treat with the highest kind of justice was determined for him at an early age that his family background is of such interest. There are two other odd gaps in his autobiographies; his two brothers, Wilky and Bob, play in them an infinitesimal part. To Miss Burr, the editor of Alice James's Journal, we owe most of our knowledge of these almost commonplace, almost low-brow members of a family intellectual even to excess. To Wilky 'the act of reading was inhuman and repugnant'; he wrote from his brigade, 'Tell Harry that I am waiting anxiously for his "next". I can find a large sale for any blood-and-thunder tale among the darks.' From his brigade: that was the point. It was the two failures, Wilky and Bob, who at eighteen and seventeen represented the family on the battlefields of the Civil War. William's eyesight was always bad, and Henry escaped because of an accident, the exact nature of which has always remained a mystery. One is glad, of course, that he escaped the obvious effects of war: Wilky was ruined physically, Bob nervously; both drifted in the manner of war-time heroes from farming in Florida to petty business careers in Milwaukee; and it is not improbable that the presence of these ruined heroes helped to keep Henry James out of America.

It is possible that through Wilky and Bob we can trace the source of James's main fantasy, the idea of treachery which was always attached to his sense of evil. James had not, so far as we know, been betrayed, like Monteith, like Gray, like Milly Theale and Maggie Verver and Isabel Archer, by his best friend, and it would have taken surely a very deep betrayal to explain an impulse which dictated *The American* in 1876 and *The Golden Bowl* in 1905, which attached itself to the family sense of supernatural evil and produced his great gallery of the damned. It takes some form of self-betrayal to dip so deep, and one need not go, like some modern critics, to a 'castration complex' to find the reason. There are psychological clues which point to James having evaded military service with insufficient excuse. A civil war is not a continental squabble; its motives are usually deeper, represent less superficial beliefs on the part of the ordinary combatant, and the James family at Concord were at the very spot where the motives of the North sounded at their noblest. His accident has an air of mystery about it (that is why some of his critics have imagined a literal castration), and one needs some explanation of his almost hysterical participation in the Great War on the side of a civilization about which he had no illusions, over whose corruption he had swapped amusing anecdotes with Alice. It will be remembered that in his magnificent study of treachery, *A Round of Visits*, Monteith's Betrayer, like all the others, was a very near friend. 'To live thus with his unremoved undestroyed, engaging, treacherous face, had been, as our traveller desired, to live with all of the felt pang.' His unremoved face, the felt pang: it is not hard to believe that James suffered from a long subconscious uneasiness about a personal failure.

This, then, was his visible universe: visible indeed if it faced him daily in his glass: the treachery of friends, the meanest kind of lies, 'the black and merciless things', as he wrote in the scenario of *The Ivory Tower*, 'that are behind great possessions'. But it is perhaps the measure of his greatness, of the wideness and justice of his view, that critics of an older generation, Mr Desmond MacCarthy among them, have seen him primarily as a friendly, rather covetous follower of the 'best' society. The sense of evil never obsessed him, as it obsessed Dostoevsky; he never ceased to be primarily an artist, unlike those driven geniuses, Lawrence and Tolstoy, and he could always throw off from the superfluity of his talent such exquisite amiable fragments as *Daisy Miller* and *The Pension Beaurepas*: satire so gentle, even while so witty, that it has the quality of nostalgia, a looking back towards a way of life simple and unreflecting, with a kind of innocence even in its greed. 'Common she might be,' he wrote of Daisy Miller, 'yet what provision was made by that epithet for her queer little native grace.' It is in these diversions, these lovely little marginalia, that the Marxist critic, just as much as Mr MacCarthy, finds his material. He was a social critic only when he was not a religious one. No writer was more conscious that he was at the end of a period, at the end of the society he knew. It was a revolution he quite explicitly foresaw; he spoke of

the class, as I seemed to see it, that had had the longest and happiest innings in history ... and for whom the future wasn't going to be, by most signs, anything like so bland and benedictory as the past ... I cannot say how vivid I felt the drama so preparing might become – that of the lapse of immemorial protection, that of the finally complete exposure of the immemorially protected.

But the Marxists, just as much as the older critics, are dwelling on the marginalia. Wealth may have been almost invariably connected with the treacheries he described, but so was passion. When he was floating on his fullest tide, 'listening' as he put it, 'at the chamber of the soul', the evil of capitalist society is an altogether inadequate explanation of his theme. It was not the desire for money alone which united Densher and Kate, and the author of *The Spoils of Poynton* would no more have condemned passion than the author of *The Ambassadors* would have condemned private wealth. His lot and his experience happened to lie among the great possessions, but 'the black and merciless things' were no more intrinsically part of a capitalist than of a socialist system: they belonged to human nature. They amounted really to this: an egotism so complete that you could believe that something inhuman, supernatural, was working there through the poor devils it had chosen.

In *The Jolly Corner* Brydon, the cultured American expatriate, returned to his New York home and found it haunted. He hunted the ghost down. It was afraid of him (the origin of that twist is known to us. In *A Small Boy* James had described the childish dream he built his story on). He drove it to bay in its evening dress under the skylight in the hall, discovered in the 'evil, odious, blatant, vulgar' features the reflection of himself. This is what he would have been if he had stayed and joined the Wall Street racket and prospered. It is easy to take the mere social criticism implied, but I have yet to find socialist or conservative who can feel any pity for the evil he denounces, and the final beauty of James's stories lies in their pity: 'The poetry is in the pity.' His egotists, poor souls, are as pitiable as Lucifer. The woman Brydon loved had also seen the ghost; he had not appeared less blatant, less vulgar to her with his ruined sight and maimed hand and his million a year, but the emotion she chiefly felt was pity.

'He has been unhappy, he has been ravaged,' she said.

'And haven't I been unhappy? Am not I – you've only to look at me! – ravaged?'

'Ah, I don't say I like him *better*,' she granted after a thought. 'But he's grim, he's worn – and things have happened to him. He doesn't make shift, for sight, with your charming monocle.'

James wasn't a prophet, he hadn't a didactic purpose; he wished only to render the highest kind of justice, and you cannot render the highest kind of justice if you hate. He was a realist: he had to show the triumphs of egotism; he was a realist: he had to show that a damned soul has its chains. Milly Theale, Maggie Verver, these 'good' people had their escapes, they were lucky in that they loved, could sacrifice themselves like Wilky and Bob, they were never quite alone on the bench of desolation. But the egotists had no escape, there was no tenderness in their passion, and their pursuit of money was often no more than an interest, a hobby: they were, inescapably, themselves. Kate and Merton Densher get the money for which they'd schemed; they don't get each other. Charlotte Stant and the Prince satisfy their passion at the expense of a lifetime of separation.

This is not 'poetic justice'; it was not as a moralist that James designed his stories, but as a realist. His family background, his personal failure, determined his view of the visible universe when he first began to write, and there was nothing in the society of his time to make him reconsider his view. He had always been strictly just to the truth as he saw it, and all that his deepening experience had done for him was to alter a murder to an adultery, but while in *The American* he had not pitied the murderer, in *The Golden Bowl* he had certainly learned to pity the adulterers. There was no victory for human beings, that was his conclusion; you were punished in your own way, whether you were of God's or the Devil's party. James believed in the supernatural, but he saw evil as an equal force with good. Humanity was cannon fodder in a war too balanced ever to be concluded. If he had been guilty himself of the supreme egotism of preserving his own existence, he left the material, in his profound unsparing analysis, for rendering even egotism the highest kind of justice, of giving the devil his due.

It brought Spencer Brydon to his feet. 'You "like" that horror –?'
'I *could* have liked him. And to me,' she said, 'he was no horror, I had accepted him.'

'I had accepted him.' James, who had never taken a great interest in his father's Swedenborgianism, had gathered enough to strengthen his own older more traditional heresy. For his father believed, in his own words, that 'the evil or hellish element in our nature, even when out of divine order ... is yet not only no less vigorous than the latter, but on the contrary much more vigorous, sagacious, and productive of eminent earthly uses' (so one might describe the acquisition of Milly Theale's money). The difference, of course, was greater than the resemblance. The son was not an optimist, he didn't share his father's hopes of the hellish element, he only pitied those who were immersed in it; and it is in the final justice of his pity, the completeness of an analysis which enabled him to pity the most shabby, the most corrupt, of his human actors, that he ranks with the greatest of creative writers. He is as solitary in the history of the novel as Shakespeare in the history of poetry.

1936

HENRY JAMES: THE RELIGIOUS ASPECT

IT is possible for an author's friends to know him too well. His books are hidden behind the façade of his public life, and his friends remember his conversations when they have forgotten his characters. It is a situation which by its irony appealed to Henry James. At the time of his own siege of London, he took note of Robert Browning, the veteran victor seen at every dinner table.

I have never ceased to ask myself [James wrote], in this particular loud, sound, normal hearty presence, all so assertive and so whole, all bristling with prompt responses and expected opinions and usual views ... I never ceased, I say, to ask myself what lodgement, on such premises, the rich proud genius one adored could ever have contrived, what domestic commerce the subtlety that was its prime ornament and the world's wonder have enjoyed, under what shelter the obscurity that was its luckless drawback and the world's despair have flourished.

It is a double irony that James himself should have so disappeared behind the public life. There are times when those who met him at Grosvenor House, those who dined with him at Chelsea, even the favoured few who visited him at Rye, seem, while they have remembered his presence (that great bald brow, those soothing and reassuring gestures) and the curiosity of his conversation (the voice ponderously refining and refining on his meaning), to have forgotten his books. This, at any rate, is a possible explanation of Mr MacCarthy's statement in a delightful and deceptive essay on 'The World of Henry James': 'The universe and religion are so completely excluded from his books as if he had been an eighteenth-century writer. The sky above his people, the earth beneath them, contain no mysteries for them', and in the same essay that the religious sense 'is singularly absent from his work'.

It would indeed be singular if the religious sense were absent. Consider the father, the son of a Presbyterian and intended for the ministry, who travelling in England was possessed (during a nervous disorder) by the teaching of Swedenborg and devoted the rest of his life to writing theological books which no one read. His inspiration was the same as William Blake's and it was not less strong because its expression was chilled within the icy limits of Boston. It is difficult to believe that a child brought up by Henry James senior did not inherit a few of his father's perplexities if not his beliefs. Certainly he inherited a suspicion of organized religion, although that suspicion conflicted with his deepest instinct, his passion for Europe and tradition.

It is a platitude that in all his novels one is aware of James's deep love of age; not one generation had tended the lawns of his country houses, but centuries of taste had smoothed the grass and weathered the stone, 'the warm, weary brickwork'.

This love of age and tradition, even without his love of Italy, was enough to draw him towards the Catholic Church as, in his own words, 'the most impressive convention in all history'. As early as 1869, in a letter from Rome, he noted its aesthetic appeal.

> In St Peter's I stayed some time. It's even beyond its reputation. It was filled with foreign ecclesiastics – great armies encamped in prayer on the marble plains of its pavement – an inexhaustible physiognomical study. To crown my day, on my way home, I met his Holiness in person – driving in prodigious purple state – sitting dim within the shadows of his coach with two uplifted benedictory fingers – like some dusky Hindoo idol in the depths of its shrine. ... From the high tribune of a great chapel of St Peter's I have heard in the Papal choir a strange old man sing in a shrill unpleasant soprano. I've seen troops of little tortured neophytes clad in scarlet, marching and counter-marching and ducking and flopping, like poor little raw recruits for the heavenly host.

But no one can long fail to discover how superficial is the purely aesthetic appeal of Catholicism; it is more accidental than the closeness of turf. The pageantry may be well done and excite the cultured visitor or it may be ill done and repel him. The Catholic Church has never hesitated to indulge in the lowest forms of popular 'art'; it has never used beauty for the sake of beauty. Any little junk shop of statues and holy pictures beside a cathedral is an example of what I mean. 'The Catholic Church, as churches go today,' James wrote in *A Little Tour in France*, 'is certainly the most spectacular; but it must feel that it has a great fund of impressiveness to draw upon when it opens such sordid little shops of sanctity as this.' If it had been true that Henry James had no religious sense and that Catholicism spoke only to his aesthetic sense, Catholicism and Henry James at this point would finally have parted company; or if his religious sense had been sufficiently vague and 'numinous', he would then surely have approached the Anglican Church to discover whether he could find there satisfaction for the sense of awe and reverence, whether he could build within it his system of 'make-believe'. If the Anglican Church did not offer to his love of age so unbroken a tradition, it offered to an Englishman or an American a purer literary appeal. Crashaw's style, if it occasionally has the beauty of those 'marble plains', is more often the poetical equivalent of the shop for holy statues; it has neither the purity nor the emotional integrity of Herbert's and Vaughan's; nor as literature can the Douai Bible be compared with the Authorized Version. And yet the Anglican Church never gained the least hold on James's interest, while the Catholic Church seems to have retained its appeal to the end. He never even felt the possibility of choice; it was membership of the Catholic Church or nothing. Rowland Mallet wondered 'whether it be that one tacitly concedes to the Roman Church the monopoly of a guarantee of immortality, so that if one is indisposed to bargain with her for the precious gift one must do without it altogether'.

In James's first novel, *Roderick Hudson*, published in 1875, six years after his first sight of the high tribune and the tortured neophytes, the hero 'pushed into St Peter's, in whose vast clear element the hardest particle of thought ever infallibly entered into solution. From a heartache to a Roman rain there were few contrarieties the great church did not help him to forget.' The same emotion was later expressed in novel after novel. In times of mental weariness, at moments of crisis, his characters inevitably find their way into some dim nave, to some lit altar; Merton Densher, haunted by his own treachery, enters the Brompton Oratory, 'on the edge of a splendid service – the flocking crowd told of it – which glittered and resounded, from distant depths, in the blaze of altar lights and the swell of organ and choir. It didn't match his own day, but it was much less of a discord than some other things actual and possible.'

It is a rather lukewarm tribute to a religious system, but Strether in *The Ambassadors*, published in 1903, enters Notre-Dame for a more significant purpose.

He was aware of having no errand in such a place but the desire not to be, for the hour, in certain other places; a sense of safety, of simplification, which each time he yielded to it he amused himself by thinking of as a private concession to cowardice. The great church had no altar for his worship, no direct voice for his soul; but it was none the less soothing even to sanctity; for he could feel while there what he couldn't elsewhere, that he was a plain tired man taking the holiday he had earned. He was tired, but he wasn't plain – that was the pity and the trouble of it; he was able, however, to drop his problem at the door very much as if it had been the copper piece that he deposited, on the threshold, in the receptacle of the inveterate blind beggar. He trod the long dim nave, sat in the splendid choir, paused before the clustered chapels of the east end, and the mighty monument laid upon him its spell. ... This form of sacrifice did at any rate for the occasion as well as another; it made him quite sufficiently understand how, within the precinct, for the real refugee, the things of the world could fall into abeyance. That was the cowardice, probably – to dodge them, to beg the question, not to deal with it in the hard outer light; but his own oblivions were too brief, too vain, to hurt anyone but himself, and he had a vague and fanciful kindness of certain persons whom he met, figures of mystery and anxiety, and whom, with observation for his pastime, he ranked with those who were fleeing from justice. Justice was outside, in the hard light, and injustice too; but one was as absent as the other from the air of the long aisles and the brightness of the many altars.

It is worth noting, in connexion with Mr MacCarthy's criticism, that this was not Strether's first visit to Notre-Dame:

he had lately made the pilgrimage more than once by himself – had quite stolen off, taking an unnoticed chance and making no point of speaking of the adventure when restored to his friends.

In 1875, Rowland Mallet found in St Peter's relief for most contrarieties 'from a heartache to a Roman rain'; in 1903 Strether found in Notre-Dame 'a sense of safety, of simplification'; the difference is remarkably small, and almost equally small the difference between Strether's feelings and those of the 'real refugee', whom he watches 'from a respectable distance, remarking some note of behaviour, of penitence, of prostration, of the absolved, relieved state'. Strether wondered whether the attitude of a woman who sat without prayer 'were some congruous fruit of absolution, of 'indulgence'. He knew but dimly what indulgence, in such a place, might mean; yet he had, as with a soft sweep, a vision of how it might indeed add to the zest of active rights.' It would have been a more astonishing avowal if Strether's knowledge had been less dim, and it must be admitted that the vagueness of James's knowledge, which led him sometimes ludicrously astray, may have contributed to the emotional appeal.

But it would be unfair to attribute this constant intrusion of the Catholic Church merely to the unreasoning emotions. There were dogmas in Catholic teaching, avoided by the Anglican Church, which attracted James, and one of these dealt with prayers for the dead.

Mr MacCarthy mentions James's horror of 'the brutality and rushing confusion of the world, where the dead are forgotten', and James himself, trying to trace the genesis of that beautiful and ridiculous story *The Altar of the Dead*, came to the conclusion that the idea embodied in it 'had always, or from ever so far back, been there'. This is not to say that he was conscious of how fully Catholic teaching might have satisfied his desire not merely to commemorate but to share life with the dead. Commemoration – there is as much acreage of marble monuments in the London churches as any man can need; James wanted something more living, something symbolized in his mind, in the story to which I refer, by candles on an altar. It was not exactly prayer, but how close it was to prayer, how near James was to believing that the dead have need of prayer, may be seen in the case of George Stransom.

He had not had more losses than most men, but he had counted his losses more; he hadn't seen death more closely, but had in a manner felt it more deeply. He had formed little by little the habit of numbering his Dead: it had come to him early in life that there was something one had to do for them. They were there in their simplified intensified essence, their conscious absence and expressive patience, as personally there as if they had only been stricken dumb. When all sense of them failed, all sound of them ceased, it was as if their purgatory were really still on earth: they asked so little that they got, poor things, even less, and died again, died every day, of the hard usage of life. They had no organized service, no reserved place, no honour, no shelter, no safety.

The Altar of the Dead I have called ridiculous as well as beautiful, and it is ridiculous because James never understood that his desire to help the dead was not a personal passion, that it did not require secret subjective rites. Haunted by this idea of the neglected dead, 'the general black truth that London was a terrible place to die in', by the phrase of his foreign friend, as they watched a funeral train 'bound merrily by' on its way to Kensal Green, *'Mourir à Londres, c'est être bien mort'*, James was literally driven into a church. Stransom leaves the grey foggy afternoon for 'a temple of the old persuasion, and there had evidently been a function – perhaps a service for the dead; the high altar was still a blaze of candles. This was an exhibition he always liked, and he dropped into a seat with relief. More than it had ever yet come home to him it struck him as good there should be churches.' This one might expect to be the end of Stransom's search. He had only to kneel, to pray, to remember. But again the subjective beauty of the story is caricatured by the objective action. Stransom buys an altar for one of the chapels: 'the altar and the sacred shell that half encircled it, consecrated to an ostensible and customary worship, were to be splendidly maintained; all that Stransom reserved to himself was the number of his lights, and the free enjoyment of his intentions'. Surely no one so near in spirit, at any rate in this one particular, to the Catholic Church was ever so ignorant of its rules. How was it that a writer as careful as James to secure the fullest authenticity for his subjects could mar in this way one of his most important stories? It cannot be said that he had not the time to study Catholicism: there was no limit to the time which James would devote to anything remotely connected with his art. Was it perhaps that the son of the old Swedenborgian was afraid of capture? A friend of James once spoke to him of a lady who had been converted to Catholicism. James was silent for a long while; then he remarked that he envied her.

The second point which may have attracted James to the Church was its treatment of supernatural evil. The Anglican Church had almost relinquished Hell. It smoked and burned on Sundays only in obscure provincial pulpits, but no day passed in a Catholic Church without prayers for deliverance from evil spirits 'wandering through the world for the ruin of souls'. This savage elementary belief found an echo in James's sophisticated mind, to which the evil of the world was very present. He faced it in his work with a religious intensity. The man was sensitive, a lover of privacy, but it is absurd for Mr MacCarthy to picture the writer 'flying with frightened eyes and stopped ears from that City of Destruction till the terrified bang of his sanctuary door leaves him palpitating but safe'.

If he fled from London to Rye, it was the better to turn at bay. This imaginary world, which according to Mr MacCarthy he created, peopled with 'beings who had leisure and the finest faculties for comprehending and appreciating each other, where the reward of goodness was the recognition of its beauty', comes not from James's imagination but from Mr MacCarthy's; the world of Henry James's novels is a world of treachery and deceit, a realist's world in which Osmond is victorious, Isabel Archer defeated, Densher gains his end and Milly Theale dies disillusioned. The novels are only saved from the deepest cynicism by the religious sense; the struggle between the beautiful and the treacherous is lent, as in Hardy's novels, the importance of the supernatural, human nature is not despicable in Osmond or Densher, for they are both capable of damnation. 'It is true to say', Mr Eliot has written in an essay on Baudelaire, 'that the glory of man is his capacity for salvation; it is also true to say that his glory is his capacity for damnation. The worst that can be said of most malefactors, from statesmen to thieves, is that they are not men enough to be damned.' This worst cannot be said of James's characters: both Densher and the Prince have on their faces the flush of the flames.

One remembers in this context the poor damned ghost of Brydon's other self, Brydon, the American expatriate and cultured failure, who returns after many years and in his New York house becomes aware of another presence, the self he might have been, unhappy and ravaged with a million a year and ruined sight and crippled hand. Through the great house

41

he hunts the ghost, until it turns at bay under the fanlight in the entrance hall.

Rigid and conscious, spectral yet human, a man of his own substance and stature waited there to measure himself with his power to dismay. This only could it be – this only till he recognized, with his advance, that what made the face dim was the pair of raised hands that covered it and in which, so far from being offered in defiance, it was buried as for dark deprecation. So Brydon, before him, took him in; with every fact of him now, in the higher light, hard and acute – his planted stillness, his vivid truth, his grizzled bent head and white masking hands, his queer actuality of evening dress, of dangling double eyeglass, of gleaming silk lappet and white linen, of pearl button and gold watchguard and polished shoe. ... He could but gape at his other self in this other anguish, gape as a proof that *he*, standing there for the achieved, the enjoyed, the triumphant life, couldn't be faced in his triumph. Wasn't the proof in the splendid covering hands, strong and completely spread? – so spread and so intentional that, in spite of a special verity that surpassed every other, the fact that one of these hands had lost two fingers which were reduced to stumps, as if accidentally shot away, the face was effectually guarded and saved.

When the hands drop they disclose a face of horror, evil, odious, blatant, vulgar, and as the ghost advances, Brydon falls back 'as under the hot breath and the roused passion of a life larger than his own, a rage of personality before which his own collapsed'.

The story has been quoted by an American critic as an example of the fascination and repulsion James felt for his country. The idea that he should have stayed and faced his native scene never left him; he never ceased to wonder whether he had not cut himself off from the source of deepest inspiration. This the story reveals on one level of consciousness; on a deeper level it is not too fanciful to see in it an expression of faith in man's ability to damn himself. A rage of personality – it is a quality of the religious sense, a spiritual quality which the materialist writer can never convey, not even Dickens, by the most adept use of exaggeration.

It is tempting to reinforce this point – James's belief in supernatural evil – with *The Turn of the Screw*. Here in the two evil spirits – Peter Quint, the dead valet, with his ginger hair and his little whiskers and his air of an actor and 'his white face of damnation', and Miss Jessel 'dark as midnight in her black dress, her haggard beauty, and her unutterable woe' – is the explicit breath of Hell. They declare themselves in every attitude and glance, with everything but voice, to be suffering the torments of the damned, the torments which they intend the two children to share. It is tempting to point to the scene of Miles's confession, which frees him from the possession of Peter Quint. But James himself has uttered too clear a warning. The story is, in his own words, 'a fairy-tale pure and simple', something seasonable for Christmas, 'a piece of ingenuity pure and simple, of cold artistic calculation, an amusette to catch those not easily caught . . . the jaded, the disillusioned, the fastidious'. So a valuable ally must be relinquished, not without a mental reservation that no one by mere calculation could have made the situation so 'reek with the air of Evil' and amazement that such a story should have been thought seasonable for Christmas.

Hell and Purgatory, James came very close to a direct statement of his belief in both of these. What personal experience of treachery and death stood between the author of *Washington Square* and *The Bostonians* and the author of *The Wings of the Dove* and *The Golden Bowl* is not known. The younger author might have developed into the gentle urbane social critic of Mr MacCarthy's imagination, the latter writer is only just prevented from being as explicitly religious as Dostoevsky by the fact that neither a philosophy nor a creed ever emerged from his religious sense. His religion was always a mirror of his experience. Experience taught him to believe in supernatural evil, but not in supernatural good. Milly Theale is all human; her courage has not the supernatural support which holds Kate Croy and Charlotte Stant in a strong coil. The rage of personality is all the devil's. The good and the beautiful meet betrayal with patience and forgiveness, but without sublimity, and their death is at best a guarantee of no more pain. Ralph Touchett dying at Gardencourt only offers himself the consolation that pain is passing. 'I don't know why we should suffer so much. Perhaps I shall find out.'

It would be wrong to leave the impression that James's religious sense ever brought him nearer than hailing distance to an organized system, even to a system organized by himself. The organizing ability exhausted itself in his father and elder brother. James never tried to state a philosophy and this reluctance to trespass outside his art may have led Mr Mac-Carthy astray. But no one, with the example of Hardy before them, can deny that James was right. The novelist depends preponderantly on his personal experience, the philosopher on correlating the experience of others, and the novelist's philosophy will always be a little lop-sided. There is much in common between the pessimism of Hardy and of James; both had a stronger belief in supernatural evil than in supernatural good, and if James had, like Hardy, tried to systematize his ideas, his novels too would have lurched with the same one-sided gait. They retain their beautiful symmetry at a price, the price which Turgenev paid and Dostoevsky refused to pay, the price of refraining from adding to the novelist's distinction that of a philosopher or a religious teacher of the second rank.

1933

THE PORTRAIT OF A LADY

'THE conception of a certain young lady affronting her destiny' – that is how Henry James described the subject of this book, for which he felt, next to *The Ambassadors*, the greatest personal tenderness. In his wonderful preface (for no other book in the collected edition of his works did he write a preface so rich in revelations and memories) he compares *The Portrait of a Lady* several times to a building, and it is as a great, leisurely built cathedral that one thinks of it, with immense smooth pillars, side-chapels and aisles, and a dark crypt where Ralph Touchett lies in marble like a crusader with his feet crossed to show that he has seen the Holy Land; sometimes, indeed, it may seem to us too ample a shrine for one portrait until we remember that this master-craftsman always has his reasons: those huge pillars are required to bear the weight of Time (that dark backward and abysm that is the novelist's abiding problem): the succession of side-chapels are all designed to cast their particular light upon the high altar: no vista is without its ambiguous purpose. The whole building, indeed, is a triumph of architectural planning: the prentice hand which had already produced some works – *Roderick Hudson* and *The American* – impressive if clumsy, and others – *The Europeans* and *Washington Square* – graceful if slight, had at last learnt the whole secret of planning for permanence. And the subject? 'A certain young woman affronting her destiny.' Does it perhaps still, at first thought, seem a little inadequate?

The answer, of course, is that it all depends on the destiny, and about the destiny Henry James has in his preface nothing to tell us. He is always something of a conjurer in these prefaces; he seems ready to disclose everything – the source of his story: the technique of its writing: even the room in which he settles down to work and the noises of the street outside. Sometimes he blinds the reader with a bold sleight of hand, calling, for example, *The Turn of the Screw* 'a fairy-tale pure and simple'. We must always remain on our guard while reading these prefaces, for at a certain level no writer has really disclosed less.

The plot in the case of this novel is far from being an original one: it is as if James, looking round for the events which were to bring his young woman, Isabel Archer, into play, had taken the first to hand: a fortune-hunter, the fortune-hunter's unscrupulous mistress, and a young American heiress caught in the meshes of a loveless marriage. (He was to use almost identically the same plot but with deeper implications and more elaborate undertones in *The Wings of the Dove*.) We can almost see the young James laying down some popular three-decker of the period in his Roman or Venetian lodgings and wondering, 'What could I do with even that story?' For a plot after all is only the machinery – the machinery which will show the young woman (what young woman?) affronting her destiny (but what destiny?). In his preface, apparently so revealing, James has no answer to these questions. Nor is there anything there which will help us to guess what element it was in the melodramatic plot that attracted the young writer at this moment when he came first into his full powers as a novelist, and again years later when as an old man he set to work to crown his career with the three poetic masterpieces, *The Wings of the Dove*, *The Ambassadors*, and *The Golden Bowl*.

The first question is the least important and we have the answer in Isabel Archer's relationship to Milly Theale in *The Wings of the Dove*. It is not only their predicament which is the same, or nearly so (Milly's fortune-hunter, Merton Densher, was enriched by the later James with a conscience, a depth of character, a dignity in his corruption that Gilbert Osmond lacks: indeed in the later book it is the fortune-hunter who steals the tragedy, for Milly dies and it is the living whom we pity): the two women are identical. Milly Theale, if it had not been for her fatal sickness, would have affronted the same destiny and met the same fate as Isabel Archer: the courage, the generosity, the confidence and inexperience belong to the same character, and James has disclosed to us the source of the later portrait – his young and much-loved cousin Mary Temple who died of tuberculosis at twenty-four. This girl of infinite potentiality, whose gay sad troubled letters can be read in *Notes of a Son and Brother*, haunted his memory like a legend; it was as if her image stood for everything that had been graceful, charming, happy in youth – 'the whole world of the old New York, that of the earlier dancing years' – everything that was to be betrayed by life. We have only to compare these pages of his autobiography, full of air and space and light, in which the figures of the son and brother, the Albany uncles, the beloved cousin, move like the pastoral figures in a Poussin landscape, with his description of America when he revisited the States in his middle age, to see how far he had travelled, how life had closed in. In his fiction he travelled even farther. In his magnificent last short story, Brydon, the returned expatriate, finds his old New York house haunted by the ghost of himself, the self he would have become if he had remained in America. At that moment one remembers what James also remembered: 'the springtime of '65 as it breathed through Denton streets', the summer twilight sailing back from Newport, Mary Temple.

In none of the company was the note so clear as in this rarest, though at the same time symptomatically or ominously palest, flower of the stem; who was natural at more points and about more things, with a greater sense of freedom and ease and reach of horizon than any of the others dreamed of. They had that way, delightfully, with the small, after all, and the common matters – while she had it with those too, but with the great and rare ones over and above; so that she was to remain for us the very figure and image of a felt interest in life, an interest as magnanimously far spread, or as familiarly and exquisitely fixed, as her splendid shifting sensibility, moral, personal, nervous and having at once such noble flights and such touchingly discouraged drops, such graces of indifference and inconsequence, might at any moment determine. She was really to remain, for our appreciation, the supreme case of a taste for life as life, as personal living, of an endlessly active and yet somehow a careless, an illusionless, a sublimely forewarned curiosity about it; something that made her, slim and fair and quick, all straightness and charming tossed head, with long and yet almost sliding steps and a large light postponing, renouncing laugh, the very muse or amateur priestess of rash speculation.

Even if we had not James's own word for it, we could never doubt that here is the source: the fork of his imagination was struck and went on sounding. Mary Temple, of course, never affronted her destiny: she was betrayed quite simply by her body, and James uses words of her that he could as well have used of Milly Theale dying in her Venetian palace – 'death at the last was dreadful to her; she would have given anything to live', but isn't it significant that whenever an imaginary future is conceived for this brave spontaneous young woman it always ends in betrayal? Milly Theale escapes from her betrayal simply by dying; Isabel Archer, tied for life to Gilbert Osmond – that precious vulgarian, cold as a fishmonger's slab – is deserted even by her creator. For how are we to understand the ambiguity of the closing pages when Isabel's friend, Henrietta Stackpole, tries to comfort the faithful and despairing 'follower' (this word surely best describes Caspar Goodwood's relationship to Isabel)?

> 'Look here, Mr Goodwood,' she said, 'just you wait!'
> On which he looked up at her – but only to guess, from her face, with a revulsion, that she simply meant he was young. She stood shining at him with that cheap comfort, and it added, on the spot, thirty years to his life. She walked him away with her, however, as if she had given him now the key to patience.

It is as if James, too, were handing his more casual readers the key to patience, while at the same time asserting between the lines that there is no way out of the inevitable betrayal except the way that Milly Theale and Mary Temple took involuntarily. There is no possibility of a happy ending: this is surely what James always tells us, not with the despairing larger-than-life gesture of a romantic novelist but with a kind of bitter precision. He presents us with a theorem, but it is we who have to work out the meaning of x and discover that x equals no-way-out. It is part of the permanent fascination of his style that he never does all the work for us, and there will always be careless mathematicians prepared to argue the meaning of that other ambiguous ending, when Merton Densher, having gained a fortune with Milly Theale's death, is left alone with his mistress, Kate Croy, who had planned it all, just as Mme Merle had planned Isabel's betrayal.

> 'He heard her out in stillness, watching her face but not moving. Then he only said: 'I'll marry you, mind you, in an hour.'
> 'As we were?'
> 'As we were.'
> But she turned to the door, and her headshake was now the end. 'We shall never be again as we were!'

Some of James's critics have preferred to ignore the real destiny of his characters, and they can produce many of his false revealing statements to support them; he has been multitudinously discussed as a social novelist primarily concerned with the international scene, with the impact of the Old World on the New. It is true the innocent figure is nearly always American (Roderick Hudson, Newman, Isabel and Milly, Maggie Verver and her father), but the corrupted characters – the vehicles for a sense of evil unsurpassed by the theological novelists of our day, M. Mauriac or M. Bernanos – are also American: Mme Merle, Gilbert Osmond, Kate Croy, Merton Densher, Charlotte Stant. His characters are mainly American, simply because James himself was American.

No, it was only on the superficial level of plot, one feels, that James was interested in the American visitor; what deeply interested him, what was indeed his ruling passion, was the idea of treachery, the 'Judas complex'. In a very early novel which he never reprinted, *Watch and Ward*, James dealt with the blackmailer, the man enabled to betray because of his intimate knowledge. As he proceeded in his career he shed the more obvious melodramatic trappings of betrayal, and in *The Portrait of a Lady*, melodrama is at the point of vanishing. What was to follow was only to be the turning of the screw. Isabel Archer was betrayed by little more than an acquaintance; Milly Theale by her dearest friend; until we reach the complicated culmination of treacheries in *The Golden Bowl*. But how many turns and twists of betrayal we could follow, had we space and time, between *Watch and Ward* and that grand climax!

This then is the destiny that not only the young women affront – you must betray or, more fortunately perhaps, you must be betrayed. A few – James himself, Ralph Touchett in this novel, Mrs Assingham in *The Golden Bowl* – will simply sadly watch. We shall never know what it was at the very start of life that so deeply impressed on the young James's mind this sense of treachery; but when we remember how patiently and faithfully throughout his life he drew the portrait of one young woman who died, one wonders whether it was just simply a death that opened his eyes to the inherent disappointment of existence, the betrayal of hope. The eyes once open, the material need never fail him. He could sit there, an ageing honoured man in Lamb House, Rye, and hear the footsteps of the traitors and their victims going endlessly by on the pavement. It is of James himself that we think when we read in *The Portrait of a Lady* of Ralph Touchett's melancholy vigil in the big house in Winchester Square:

> The square was still, the house was still, when he raised one of the windows of the dining-room to let in the air he heard the slow creak of the boots of a lone constable. His own step, in the empty place, seemed loud and sonorous; some of the carpets had been raised, and whenever he moved he roused a melancholy echo. He sat down in one of the armchairs; the big dark dining table twinkled here and there in the small candle-light; the pictures on the wall, all of them very brown, looked vague and incoherent. There was a ghostly presence as of dinners long since digested, of table-talk that had lost its actuality. This hint of the supernatural perhaps had something to do with the fact that his imagination took a flight and that he remained in his chair a long time beyond the hour at which he should have been in bed; doing nothing, not even reading the evening paper. I say he did nothing, and I maintain the phrase in the face of the fact that he thought at these moments of Isabel.

1947

THE PLAYS OF HENRY JAMES

THERE had always been – let us face it – a suspicion of vulgarity about the Old Master. Just as the tiny colloquialism was sometimes hidden unnoticeably away in the intricate convolutions of his sentences, so one was sometimes fleetingly aware of small clouds – difficult to detach in the bland wide sunlit air of his later world – of something closely akin to the vulgar. Was it sometimes his aesthetic approach to the human problem, his use of the word 'beautiful' in connexion with an emotional situation? Was it sometimes a touch of aesthetic exclusiveness as in the reference to Poynton and its treasures, 'there were places much grander and richer, but no such complete work of art, nothing that would appeal so to those really informed'? Was it sometimes a hidden craving for the mere treasures themselves, for the cash value? We must do James justice. He would not have altered a sentence of a novel or a story for the sake of popularity or monetary reward, but the craving was there, disguised by references to financial problems that did not really exist – his private income was adequate, even comfortable. But if only, it surely occurred to him, there were some literary Tom Tiddler's ground he could enter as a stranger, where he would not be compromised if observed in the act of stooping to pick up the gold and silver; in that case he was ready for a while to put integrity in the drawer and turn the key. Fate was kind to him: other artists have had the same intention and have been caught by success. James found neither cash nor credit on the stage and returned enriched by his failure.

Of course it would be wrong to suggest that the appeal of the theatre to James was purely commercial. He was challenged, as any artist, by a new method of expression; the pride and interest in attempting the difficult and the new possessed him. He wrote to his brother:

I feel at last as if I had found my real form, which I am capable of carrying far, and for which the pale little art of fiction, as I have practised it, has been, for me, but a limited and restricted substitute. The strange thing is that I always, universally, knew *this* was my more characteristic form – but was kept away from it by a half-modest, half-exaggerated sense of the difficulty (that is, I mean the practical odiousness) of the conditions. But now that I have accepted them and met them, I see that one isn't at all, needfully, their victim, but is, from the moment one *is* anything, one's self, worth speaking of, their *master*: and may use them, command them, squeeze them, lift them up and better them. As for the form *itself*, its honour and inspiration are (*à défaut d'autres*) in its difficulty. If it were easy to write a good play I couldn't and wouldn't think of it; but it is in fact damnably hard (to this truth the paucity of the article – in the English-speaking world – testifies), and that constitutes a solid respectability – guarantees one's *intellectual* self-respect.

But even in this mood is not the self-respect a little too underlined, the protest purposely loud to drown another note,

51

which was to be repeated again and again? 'I am very impatient to get to work writing for the stage – a project I have long had. I am ... certain I should succeed and it would be an open gate to money making,' and later he turned with some ignobility on Wilde, when *The Importance of Being Earnest* had followed his own catastrophic failure *Guy Domville* at the St James's Theatre: 'There is nothing fortunately so dead as a dead play – unless it be sometimes a living one. Oscar Wilde's farce ... is, I believe, a great success – and with his two roaring successes running now at once he must be raking in the profits.' The ring of the counter is in the phrase.

Until Mr Edel published this huge volume* (over 800 pages, the greater part in double column) we had no idea how completely James had failed. The two volumes of *Theatricals* published in his lifetime were slight affairs. The theatre of his time was so bad, we had wondered whether it was not possible that his contemporaries had simply failed to recognize his genius as a playwright. We knew the sad story of the production of *Guy Domville*, the successful first act, the laughter in the second, the storm of catcalls at the close; we had heard how the critics had defended it, how the prose was praised by the young Bernard Shaw, and yet there existed, so far as one could discover, only a typewritten copy in the Lord Chamberlain's office. Yes, one had expectations and excitement. Now the picture has been filled in, and reading the deplorable results of 'the theatrical years' we need to bear always in mind James's recovery. This is unmistakably trash, but it is not the end of a great writer: out of the experience and failure with another technique came the three great novels *The Wings of the Dove, The Ambassadors, The Golden Bowl.* He was never so much of a dramatist as when he had ceased to have theatrical ambitions.

Mr Edel has done a magnificent editorial work. Why should the word 'painstaking' carry implications of dullness? Here every pain has been taken and every pain has had its reward. Each play has a separate factual preface of extreme readability; particularly fascinating is the long preface to *Guy*

* *The Complete Plays of Henry James,* edited by Leon Edel.

Domville which traces the disastrous first night almost hour by hour: the early afternoon when two unknown ladies sent a telegram from Sloane Street Post Office to George Alexander, 'With hearty wishes for a complete failure'; James sitting in the Haymarket listening to Wilde's epigrams and unaware of the applause at his own first curtain; the disastrous laughable hat in the second act; the first mutter from the gallery in the third, when Alexander began to deliver the speech, 'I am the last, my lord of the Domvilles,' to be answered, 'It's a bloody good thing y'are'; the pandemonium at the close when this too sensitive author, who had anticipated failure but not this savage public execration, was flung helplessly into the turmoil from the peace of the night in St James's Square and fled into the wings, his face 'green with dismay'; the grim first night supper party which took place 'as arranged'.

It is easier now to understand the public than the critics who were perhaps influenced by horror of the Roman holiday. H. G. Wells found the play 'finely conceived and beautifully written': Shaw wrote, 'Line after line comes with such a delicate turn and fall that I unhesitatingly challenge any of our popular dramatists to write a scene in verse with half the beauty of Mr James's prose. ... *Guy Domville* is a story and not a mere situation hung out on a gallows of plot. And it is a story of fine sentiment and delicate manners, with an entirely worthy and touching ending.' To us today the story of *Guy Domville* seems singularly unconvincing, one more example of the not always fortunate fascination exercised on James by the Christian faith and by Catholicism in particular. It stands beside *The Altar of the Dead* and *The Great Good Place* as an example of how completely James could miss the point. Mr Edel writes truly of James's interest in Catholicism being mainly an interest in a refuge and a retreat; when James wrote in that mood from the outside he conveyed a genuine and moving sense of nostalgia. But in *Guy Domville* he was rashly attempting to convey the sense of Catholicism from within: his characters are Catholics, his hero a young man brought up to become a priest. Domville is on the eve of leaving England to enter a seminary when he becomes heir to a fortune and estate (money again!) and is tempted temporarily by a mistaken sense of duty to his family to re-enter the world. The story is set in the eighteenth century, and the period falls like a dead hand over the prose. Unlike the hero of *The Sense of the Past* we never really go back. Can we believe in a young man who speaks of a girl as 'attached to our Holy Church'? There is really more truth to the religious life in the novels of Mrs Humphrey Ward. Here for example is *Guy Domville's* first reply to temptation:

Break with all the past, and break with it this minute? – turn back from the threshold, take my hand from the plough? – the hour is too troubled, your news too strange, your summons too sudden!

Strangely enough the failure of *Guy Domville* was not the end. Now that he had given up any hopes of stage success, perhaps he felt a certain freedom in his relations with that 'insufferable little art'. The love affair was at an end and he need no longer try to please. 'The hard meagreness inherent in the theatrical form' could be ignored. One critic had observed of his early plays, 'We wish very much that Mr James would write some farces to please himself, and not to please the stage', and right at the close with *The Outcry* – a thin amusing story of how a picture was saved for the nation against the will of the owner, an individualistic peer who wanted to sell it for sheer cussedness to an American dealer – he very nearly succeeded in producing an actable comedy. A comedy, for the author of *The Turn of the Screw* and *The Wings of the Dove* strangely failed when he tried on the stage to express the horrors or tragedies of the human situation. 'You don't know – but we're abysses,' one of the characters cried in his creaking melodrama, *The Other House*, but it was just the sense of the abyss that he failed on those flat boards ever to convey. Turn to his ghost story of *Owen Wingrave*, the story of a young man who refused to continue the military tradition of his family and died bravely facing the supernatural in his own home ('Owen Wingrave, dressed as he had last seen him, lay dead on the spot on which his ancestor had been found. He was

54

all the young soldier on the gained field') and compare the dignity of this story, which does indeed convey a sense of the abyss, with the complicated and unspeakable prattle of the stage adaptation.

That proud old Sir Philip, and that wonderful Miss Wingrave, Deputy Governor, herself, of the Family Fortress – that they with their immense Military Tradition, and with their particular responsibility to his gallant Father, the Soldier Son, the Soldier Brother sacrificed on an Egyptian battlefield, and whose example – as that of his dead Mother's, of so warlike a race too – it had been their religion to keep before him; that *they* should take sudden startling action hard is a fact I indeed understand and appreciate. But – I maintain it to you – I should deny my own intelligence if I didn't find our young man, at our crisis, and certainly at *his*, more interesting, perhaps than ever!

Unwillingly we have to condemn the Master for a fault we had previously never suspected the possibility of his possessing – incompetence.

1950

THE DARK BACKWARD: A FOOTNOTE

'THIS eternal time-question is ... for the novelist always there and always formidable; always insisting on the *effect* of the great lapse and passage, of the "dark backward and abysm", by the terms of truth, and on the effect of compression, of composition and form, by the terms of literary arrangement. It is really a business to terrify all but stout hearts....' So Henry James in the preface to his first novel, written at the end of his career when he could see all the difficulties.

The moment comes to every writer worth consideration when he faces for the first time something which he *knows* he cannot do. It is the moment by which he will be judged, the moment when his individual technique will be evolved. For technique is more than anything else a means of evading the personally impossible, of disguising a deficiency. The whole magnificent achievement of James's prefaces is from this point of view like a confession of failure. He is telling how he hid the traces of the botched line.

The consciousness of what he cannot do – and it is sometimes something so apparently simple that a more popular writer never gives it a thought – is a mark of the good novelist. The second-rate novelists never know: nothing is beyond their sublimely foolish confidence as they turn out their great epics of European turmoil or industrial unrest, their family sagas. The Lake novelists, the Severn novelists, the Yorkshire novelists, the Jewish novelists, they stream by, like recruits in the first month of a war, with a *folie de grandeur* on their march to oblivion. Not for them the plan of campaign, the recognition of impenetrable enemy lines which cannot be taken by direct assault, which must be turned or for which new instruments of war must be invented. And they have their uses as cannon fodder. They are the lives lost in proving the ineffectiveness of the frontal assault. (There is irony, of course, in the fact that the technique an original writer used to cover his personal difficulties will later be taken over by other writers who may not share his difficulties and who believe that his value has lain in his method.)

It is from this point of view that I want to touch on three admirable novelists, whose works I have lately been reading or re-reading: Mr Ford Madox Ford, Miss Elizabeth Bowen, and Mr Calder-Marshall. One cannot in a short essay study all the inabilities which have gone to the making of their methods, but the quotation from James's preface to *Roderick Hudson* does indicate one inability they have in common.

I suppose even the popular writer, little given as he usually is to self-criticism, feels *that* supreme difficulty. We need not be so uncharitable as to believe that he writes long books only because long books pay. He is trying to give significance to the individual story by extending it in time. Mrs Soames Forsyte may not seem significant, nor her little adulterous drama, but if we write as well about Mr Forsyte's parents and his children, surely, he thinks, we shall get *somewhere*. Length becomes a substitute for sensitivity, and the long book is the obvious, the frontal assault on the sense of time. The method is invariably dull, but certainly, by its accumulation of trivialities, its digressions, it does achieve an effect, though it is an effect which has more in common with a club bore than with art. The popular novelist rushes in where even the angels. ... Henry James never wrote a novel which covered a quarter of the period of Mr Brett Young's *White Ladies*.

But though we may not want to follow a family's fortunes through three generations, we are not less faced with time. Our characters have lived outside the story, and even if within the story they have only a month to spend, that month makes demands it is not easy to meet.

I suspect that this 'time' problem is one of Mr Calder-Marshall's main difficulties, for since his first novel when he attempted to convey the passage of time quite conventionally, he has tried to avoid it altogether inside the story and outside the story. One can see very clearly here how the individual writer has been born of his deficiencies. *About Levy* took place during the few days of a murder trial, *At Sea* during the twenty-four hours when a young honeymooning couple were adrift in an open boat in the Channel, his novel, *Dead Centre*, has more than sixty characters belonging to a public school who are each allowed to express themselves for no more than a page or two, to describe an incident, to give a quick impression of their personalities *at the moment* with hardly any reference at all to the 'dark backward'. Here Mr Calder-Marshall, by his choice of theme as well as method, has disguised his inability to convey the sense of time. He has made a virtue, the virtue of things seen by a lightning flash vivid and *there* and gone again, out of a deficiency. But there *is* weakness if the deficiency continues to dictate the theme as well as the method; that is to make things easy and an individual technique thrives on difficulty.

Miss Bowen certainly does not let *her* inability to describe the passage of time dictate the theme. Her novel, *The House in Paris*, covers a period from before the birth of an illegitimate child until he has reached the age of nine. The popular novelist would have described every one of those years, however dull to the reader the accumulation of trivialities. Miss Bowen has simply left them out with the merest glance backward; we may believe that she has been forced to omit, but she has made of her omissions a completely individual method, she has dramatized ignorance. How with so little known of the 'backward and abysm' can she convey her characters with any clearness? It is impossible, but her consciousness of that impossibility proves her great value as a novelist. She makes it the virtue of her characters that they are three parts mystery; the darkness which hides their past makes the cerebrations which we are allowed to follow the more vivid, as vivid as the exchanges of people overheard talking on a platform before a train goes out. It is an exquisite sleight of hand: the egg was in the hat, now it is being removed from the tip of a robust woman's nose. We must fill in for ourselves what happened between; the burden of that problem is passed to the reader. To the author remains the task of making the characters understand each other without our losing the sense of mystery: they must be able to tell all from a gesture, a whisper, a written sentence: they have to be endowed with an inhuman intuition as James's characters were endowed with an inhuman intelligence, and no writer since James has proved capable of a more cunning evasion. Unable to convey the passage of time, she has made capital out of the gap in the records; how can we doubt the existence of a past which these characters can so easily convey to each other?

When one finds Mr Ford Madox Ford, the most able of these novelists, devising a technique more complicated than Conrad's to disguise the same time-problem, one begins to wonder whether any novelist has found it possible to express the passage of time directly. Has every technical trick since the novel became conscious of itself with *Tristram Shandy* been directed mainly to this end to convey enough of the dark backward for verisimilitude without losing the advantage of compression – compression which will leave in relief the novelist's best quality: the nervous vibrations and intuitions with which Miss Bowen endows her characters, the contrast in Mr Calder-Marshall's novels between thought and expression,

Mr Ford's dramatic dialogue? Mr Ford's novels are novels of dramatic situations, situations of often wildly complicated irony. It would take a long while to record the complicated misunderstandings, gossiping, and malice which in *Some Do Not* and the succeeding novels ruin the reputation and career of Christopher Tietjens, a centre point of purity and honour in a hopelessly corrupt society. The novel covers more than ten years; the narrative does not proceed chronologically but leaps back and forth in time with an agility unknown to Conrad. Indeed the reviewers of the Sunday Press have frequently criticized Mr Ford's method for what they consider its unnecessary complexity. They grant him vividness in his 'big scenes'; they cannot understand that the vividness owes everything to the method. Mr Ford is unable to write narrative; he is conscious of his inability to write, as it were, along the line of time. How slipshod and perfunctory the joins between his dramatic scenes would seem if they were not put into the minds of the characters and their perfunctory nature 'naturalized'. The memory *is* perfunctory: you do not lose verisimilitude by such a bare record as this if you are looking back to events which have become history. The trouble in a novel which follows the chronological sequence is that your events are never history. You are condemned to write of a perpetual present and to convey the shrillness of its emotions.

Poverty invaded them. The police raided the house in search of her brother and his friends. Then her brother went to prison somewhere in the Midlands. The friendliness of their former neighbours turned to surly suspicion. They could get no milk. Food became almost unprocurable without going to long distances. For three days Mrs Wannop was clean out of her mind. Then she grew better and began to write a new book . . .

Mr Ford does not, like Miss Bowen, simply leave out; he puts in the links in his own good time, but they are properly subordinated to what he can do supremely well, dialogue and the dramatic scene.

And now – if this were more than a footnote – one would have to consider James himself. *There* would be the most exciting, the most baffling search. What defects was he hiding behind the strict rules he invented for the novel? Undoubtedly they are there, but no novelist has so successfully disguised them with what he called 'delightful dissimulation'. The completeness of the dissimulation is the measure of his genius; but it remains a pleasantly ironic thought that the magnificent structure of his last novels, the complexity of his 'points of view', are arranged to the same end, to evade something which even he could not do, something which may be taken in the easy regardless stride of the latest Book Society choice.

1935

TWO FRIENDS

No smaller distance than that between Samoa and De Vere Gardens, Kensington, you might have guessed, separated these two characters, Henry James and Robert Louis Stevenson. On the one side that great domed brow, that reputable beard which evoked incongruously in the mind of some acquaintances a resemblance to the Prince of Wales, broad shoulders that seemed perpetually a little bent by crouching too long over a precious flame, fanning it one moment, guarding it with protective hand another, never relaxing vigilance whether at a dinner party or at a desk in the small hours: on the other, the man with the hollow nervous face, the thin gangling legs, the over-publicized moustache, splashing through fords at midnight, risking a bullet in parochial politics, endangering his life every day he lived for no apparent purpose except perhaps a desperate desire to prove that he could be something other than a writer. On what was this odd friendship based?

Miss Janet Adam Smith, the author of the most perceptive life of Stevenson, has put us further in her debt by compiling this record of friendship.* Most of the letters printed here are known to us already, though in the case of Steven-

* *Henry James and Robert Louis Stevenson. A Record of Friendship and Criticism*, edited by Janet Adam Smith.

son in garbled Colvin versions, but how seldom it is that we can read both sides of a correspondence together. A letter gains by its reply: the mirror in De Vere Gardens gains in depth when we see the answering flash from Samoa. Miss Adam Smith sees in the friendship the aesthetic appeal to James of Stevenson's situation:

The man living under the daily threat of a fatal haemorrhage, yet with such an appetite for the active life; the novelist who could only gain the health and energy for writing at the risk of dissipating them on other ends; the writer who had to spur his talent to earn more and more money to pay for the life of action that kept him alive; the continual tug between the claims of life and literature – here was a situation not unlike those which had provided James with the germ of a novel or story.

This is understandable; Stevenson's friendship for James is perhaps more unexpected. The literary character is not noted for generosity and Stevenson was well aware that James was the superior artist. In the public controversy on the art of the novel with which this collection and their friendship open, Stevenson scored some good debating points against James in the argument whether or not art could 'compete' with life, and the readers of *Longman's Magazine* preferred, no doubt, his cleverly varied cadences and sudden metaphors to the weighty seriousness of the older writer. 'These phantom reproductions of experience, even at their most acute, convey decided pleasure; while experience itself, in the cockpit of life, can torture and slay'; 'catching the very note and trick, the strange irregular rhythm of life, that is the attempt whose strenuous force keeps Fiction upon her feet'. The first metaphor startles, like a handful of pebbles flung against a window; the other imperceptibly, invincibly, flows like a sea.

At this period James was selling less and less and Stevenson more and more – a difficult period for the more successful man. 'There must be something wrong in me, or I would not be popular' – the doomed Calvinistic conscience directed at his own work saved Stevenson from self-justification as well as from pride. 'What the public likes is work (of any kind) a little loosely executed; so long as it is a little wordy, a little slack, a little dim and knotless, the dear public likes it; it should (if possible) be a little dull into the bargain.' He was never deceived by acclamation – not even by the acclamation of Gosse or Colvin, for he had learned in childhood that salvation is always for the other man. In the years of adolescence he had rebelled, but he had never regarded himself as innocent and his father as guilty. So now perhaps it was easier for him than it would have been for a less scrupulous character to maintain his devotion to a greater man. Criticism from James never came amiss. He would defend, but he would never resent.

The only thing I miss in the book is the note of *visibility* – it subjects my visual sense, my *seeing* imagination, to an almost painful underfeeding. The *hearing* imagination, as it were, is nourished like an alderman, and the loud audibility seems a slight the more on the baffled lust of the eyes –

So James on *Catriona* and Stevenson replies:

Your jubilation over *Catriona* did me good, and still more the subtlety and truth of your remark on the starving of the visual sense of that book. 'Tis true, and unless I make the greater effort – and am, as a step to that, convinced of its necessity – it will be more true I fear in the future. I *hear* people talking, and I *feel* them acting, and that seems to me to be fiction, My two aims may be described as –

1st. War to the adjective.

2nd. Death to the optic nerve.

Admitted we live in an age of the optic nerve in literature. For how many centuries did literature get along without a sign of it?

This book will appeal to all interested in the technique of the novelist, and it should do much to raise Stevenson's unjustly fallen reputation. Who today can afford to patronize a novelist to whom James wrote with a copy of *The Tragic Muse* that he was 'the sole and single Anglo-Saxon capable of perceiving . . . how well it is written'? James was capable of oriental courtesy to his inferiors, but the praise he gives to Stevenson has the directness and warmth of equality. 'He lighted up one whole side of the globe, and was in himself a whole province of one's imagination.'

1948

STEVENSON'S reputation has suffered perhaps more from his early death than from any other cause. He was only forty-four when he died, and he left behind him what mainly amounts to a mass of Juvenilia. Gay, bright, and perennially attractive though much of his work may be, it has a spurious maturity which hides the fact that, like other men, he was developing. Indeed it was only in the last six years of his life – the Samoan years – that his fine dandified talent began to shed its disguising graces, the granite to show through. And how rich those last years were; *The Wrong Box*, *The Master of Ballantrae*, *The Island Nights' Entertainments*, *The Ebb Tide*, and *Weir of Hermiston*. Could he have kept it up? Henry James wondered of the last unfinished book and added with gracious pessimism,

the reason for which he didn't reads itself back into his text as a kind of beautiful rash divination in him that he mightn't have to. Among prose fragments it stands quite alone, with the particular grace and sanctity of mutilation worn by the marble morsels of masterwork in another art.

Unfortunately Stevenson's reputation was not left in the hands of so cautious and subtle a critic. The early affected books of travel by canoe and donkey, the too personal letters full of 'rot about a fellow's behaviour', with a slang that rings falsely on the page like an obscenity in a parson's mouth, the immature musings on his craft ('Fiction is to the grown man what play is to the child'), the early ethical essays of *Virginibus Puerisque*, all these were thrust into the foreground by the appearance of collected edition after collected edition: his youthful thoughts still sprinkle the commercial calendars with quotations. His comparatively uneventful life (adventurous only to the sedate Civil Service minds of Colvin and Gosse) was magnified into a saga: early indiscretions were carefully obliterated from the record, until at last his friends had their reward – that pale hollow stuffed figure in a velvet jacket with a Lang moustache, kneeling by a chair of native wood, with the pokerwork mottoes just behind the head – 'to travel hopefully is a better thing than to arrive', etc., etc. Did it never occur to these industrious champions that as an adventurer, as a man of religion, as a traveller, as a friend of the 'coloured races' he must wither into insignificance beside that other Scotsman, with the name rather like his own but the letters reshuffled into a stronger pattern, Livingstone? If he is to survive for us today, it will not be as Tusitala or the rather absurd lover collapsing at Monterrey or the dandy of Davos, but as the tired disheartened writer of the last eight years, pegging desperately away at what he failed to recognize as his masterworks.

Miss Cooper in her short biography * has followed conventionally the well-worn tracks which James noticed had been laid carefully by the hero himself. 'Stevenson never covered his tracks,' James wrote. 'We follow them here, from year to year and from stage to stage, with the same charmed sense with which he has made us follow some hunted hero in the heather.' As an interpreter of his work she is incomparably less sensitive than Miss Janet Adam Smith who has already written to my mind the best possible book on Stevenson of this length. One cannot really dismiss *The Wrong Box* as '*a tour de force* sometimes enlivened by a faintly ghoulish humour, but with no breath of reality in the characters', and criticism such as this (Miss Cooper is dealing with *The Master of Ballantrae*) has too much of the common touch even for a popular series: 'The reader feels Henry's unhappiness, even when he finds it difficult to care very much about Henry, who is, it must be confessed, a dull dog.' Of *The Ebb Tide* the ignorant reader will learn only that it is 'a grim study of shady characters in the South Seas'.

However, here for those who want it (though insufficiently charted with dates) is the obvious trail: we can watch Stevenson scatter his scraps of paper across the clearings for his pursuers to spy. His immense correspondence was mainly written with an eye on his pursuers – he encouraged Colvin

* *Robert Louis Stevenson*, by Lettice Cooper.

to arrange it for publication. Miss Emily Dickinson wrote with some lack of wisdom in one of her poems, 'I like a look of agony because I know it's true', but we are never, before the last years, quite sure of the agony. Compare his Davos letters – 'Here a sheer hulk lies poor Tom Bowling and aspires, yes, C.B., with tears after the past' or doing his courageous act, 'I am better. I begin to hope that I may, if not outlive this wolverine on my shoulder, at least carry him bravely', with the letters of his last year (for suffering like literature has its juvenilia – men mature and graduate in suffering):

The truth is I am nearly useless at literature, and I will ask you to spare *St Ives* when it goes to you. ... No toil has been spared over the ungrateful canvas: and it *will not* come together, and I must live, and my family. Were it not for my health, which made it impossible, I could not find it in my heart to forgive myself that I did not stick to an honest commonplace trade when I was young, which might have now supported me during these ill years. ... It was a very little dose of inspiration, and a pretty little trick of style, long lost, improved by the most heroic industry. So far I have managed to please the journalists. But I am a fictitious article and have long known it.

A month before this he had written to his friend Baxter, admitting his life-long attempt to turn 'Bald Conduct' into an emotional religion and comparing with the dreariness of his own creed the new spirit of the anarchists in Europe, men who 'commit dastardly murders very basely, die like saints, and leave beautiful letters behind 'em ... people whose conduct is inexplicable to me, and yet their spiritual life higher than that of most'. '*Si vieillesse pouvait*', he quoted, while Colvin supplied the asterisks. He was on the eve of *Weir*: the old trim surface was cracking up: the granite was coming painfully through. It is at that point, where the spade strikes the edge of the stone, that the biographer should begin to dig.

1948

[2]

FIELDING AND STERNE

> All, all, of a piece throughout:
>   Thy Chase had a Beast in View;
> Thy Wars brought nothing about;
>   Thy Lovers were all untrue.
> 'Tis well an Old Age is out,
>   And time to begin a New.

So Dryden, looking back from the turn of the century on the muddle of hopes and disappointments, revolution and counter-revolution, and revolution again. The age had been kept busily spinning, but to the poet in 1700 it seemed to have amounted to little: what Cromwell had overthrown, Charles had rebuilt: what James would have established, William had destroyed. But literature may thrive on political disturbance, if the disturbance goes deep enough and arouses a sufficiently passionate agreement or denial. One remembers Trotsky's account of the first meeting of the Soviet after the October days of 1917: 'Among their number were completely grey soldiers, shell-shocked as it were by the insurrection, and still hardly in control of their tongues. But they were just the ones who found the words which no orator could find. That was one of the most moving scenes of the revolution, now first feeling its power, feeling the unnumbered masses it has aroused, the colossal tasks, the pride in success, the joyful failing of the heart at the thought of the morrow which is to be more beautiful than today.'

These terms can be transposed to fit the seventeenth century as they cannot to fit the eighteenth, the century to which Fielding was born in 1707 and Sterne six years later. Bunyan, Fox, the Quakers, and Levellers, those were the grey, the shell-shocked soldiers who found the words which no official orator of the Established Church could find, and one cannot question some of the poets who welcomed the return of Charles a genuine

66

thankfulness for a morrow which they believed was to be still more beautiful. The great figure of Dryden comprises the whole of the late seventeenth-century scene: like some infinitely subtle meteorological instrument, he was open to every wind: he registered the triumph of Cromwell, the hopes of the Restoration, the Catholicism of James, the final disillusionment. When he died, in 1700, he left the new age, the quieter, more rational age, curiously empty. Not until the romantics at the end of the century was politics again to be of importance to the creative, the recording mind, not until Newman and Hopkins orthodox religion. All that was left was the personal sensibility or the superficial social panorama, from the highwayman in the cart and the debtor in gaol to the lascivious lord at Vauxhall and the virtuous heroine bent over the admirable, unenthusiastic works of Bishop Burnet.

One cannot separate literature and life. If an age appears creatively, poetically, empty, it is fair to assume that life too had its emptiness, was carried on at a lower, less passionate level. I use the word poetry in the widest sense, in the sense that Henry James was a poet and Defoe was not. When Fielding published his first novel, *Joseph Andrews*, in 1742, Swift was on the verge of death and Pope as well, Cowper was ten years old and Blake unborn. Dramatic poetry, which had survived Dryden's death only in such feeble hands as Addison's and Rowe's, was to all intents a finished form.

But fiction is one of the prime needs of human nature, and someone in that empty world had got to begin building again. One cannot in such a period expect the greatest literature: the old forms are seen to be old when the fine excitement is over, and all the best minds can do is to construct new forms in which the poetic imagination may eventually find itself a home. Something in the eighteenth century had got to take the place of dramatic poetry (perhaps it is not too fanciful to see in the innumerable translations of Homer, Virgil, Lucan a popular hunger for the lost poetic fiction), and it was Fielding who for the first time since the Elizabethan age directed the poetic imagination into prose fiction. That he began as a parodist of Richardson may indicate that he recognized the inadequacy of *Pamela*, of the epistolary novel, to satisfy the hunger of the age.

In the previous century the distinction between prose fiction and poetic fiction had been a very simple one: one might almost say that prose fiction had been pornographic fiction, in the sense that it had been confined to a more or less flippant study of sexual relations (whether you take the plays of Wycherley, the prose comedies of Dryden, the novels of Aphra Behn, the huge picaresque novel of Richard Head and Francis Kirkman, the generalization remains true almost without exception), while poetic fiction had meant heroic drama, a distinction underlined in plays like *Marriage à la Mode* which contained both poetry and prose – the heroic and the pornographic. Nowhere during the Restoration period, except perhaps in Cowley's great comedy, does one find prose used in fiction as Webster and other Jacobean playwrights used it, as a medium of equal dignity and intensity to poetry with the rhythm of ordinary speech. It was from the traditional ideal of prose fiction that Defoe's novels were derived: *Moll Flanders* is only a more concise *English Rogue*, and it was left to Fielding, who had not himself the poetic mind (he declared roundly: 'I should have honoured and loved Homer more had he written a true history of his own times in humble prose'), to construct a fictional form which could attract the poetic imagination. *Tom Jones* was to prove the archetype not only of the picaresque novelists. James and Joyce owe as much to it as Dickens.

Today, when we have seen in the novels of Henry James the metaphysical poet working in the medium of prose fiction, in Lawrence's and Conrad's novels the romantic, we cannot easily recognize the revolutionary nature of *Tom Jones* and *Amelia*. Sterne who came later – the first volumes of *Tristram Shandy* were published five years after Fielding's death – bears so much more the obvious marks of a revolutionary, simply because he remains, in essentials, a revolutionary still. Even today he continues magnificently to upset all our notions of what a novel's form should be; it is his least valuable qualities which have been passed on. His sensibility founded a whole school of Bages and Bancrofts and Blowers (I cannot remember who it was who wrote: 'Great G—d, unless I have greatly offended Thee, grant me the luxury sometimes to slip a bit of silver, though no bigger than a shilling, into the clammy-cold hand of the decayed wife of a baronet', but it was to the author of the *Sentimental Journey* that he owed his sensibility), while his whimsicality was inherited by the essayists, by Lamb in particular. But his form no one has ever tried to imitate, for what would be the good? An imitation could do nothing but recall the original. *Tristram Shandy* exists, a lovely sterile eccentricity, the last word in literary egotism. Even the fact that Sterne was – sometimes – a poet is less important to practitioners of his art than that Fielding – sometimes – tried to be one.

Sterne, the sly, uneasy, unhappily married cleric, the son of an elderly ensign who never had the means or the influence to buy promotion, had suffered so many humiliations from the world that he had to erect defences of sentiment and of small indecencies between him and it (he admired Rabelais, but how timidly, how 'naughtily', his chapter on Noses reflects the author of *The Heroic Deeds of Gargantua and Pantagruel*), so that he has nothing to offer us on our side of the barrier but his genius, his genius for expressing the personal emotions of the sly, uneasy, the unhappily married. The appalling conceit of this genius, one protests, who claimed Posterity for his book without troubling himself a hang over the value of its contents: 'for what has this book done more than the Legation of Moses, or *The Tale of a Tub*, that it may not swim down the gutter of Time along with them?' The nearest that this shrinking sentimental man came to the ordinary run of life was Hall-Stevenson's pornographic circle, the nearest to passion his journals to Eliza who was safely separated from him by the Indian Ocean as well as by the difference in their years. There is nothing he can tell us about anyone, we feel, but himself, and that self has been so tidied and idealized that it would be unrecognizable, one imagines, to his wife.

Compare his position in the life of his time with that of Fielding, Fielding the rake, Fielding the country gentleman,

Fielding the hack dramatist, and finally Fielding the Westminster magistrate who knew all the outcast side of life, from the thief and the cut-throat to the seedy genteel and the half-pay officer in the debtor's court, as no other man of his time. Compare the careful architecture of *Tom Jones*: the introductory essays which enable the author to put his point of view and to leave the characters to go their way untainted by the uncharacteristic moralizing of Defoe's; the introduction of parody in the same way and for the same purpose as Joyce's in *Ulysses*; the innumerable sub-plots which give the book the proportions of life, the personal story of Jones taking its place in the general orchestration; the movement back and forth in time as the characters meet each other and recount the past in much the same way as Conrad's, a craftsman's bluff by which we seem to get a glimpse of that 'dark backward and abysm' that challenges the ingenuity of every novelist. Compare all this careful architecture with the schoolboy squibs – the blank, the blackened, and the marbled leaves, the asterisks – of *Tristram Shandy*. We cannot help but feel ungrateful when we think of the work that Fielding put into his books, the importance of his technical innovations, and realize that Sterne, who contributed nothing, can still give more pleasure because of what we call his genius, his skill at self-portraiture (even Uncle Toby is only another example of his colossal egotism: the only outside character he ever really drew – and all the time we are aware of the author preening himself at the tender insight of his admiration).

The man Sterne is unbearable, even the emotions he displayed with such amazing mastery were cheap emotions. Dryden is dead: the great days are over: Cavaliers and Roundheads have become Whigs and Tories: Cumberland has slaughtered the Stuart hopes at Culloden: the whole age cannot produce a respectable passion. So anyone must feel to whom the change, say, from the essays of Bacon and his true descendant Cowley to the essays of Lamb is a change for the worse in human dignity: a change from 'Revenge is a kind of wild justice' or 'It was the Funeral day of the late man who made himself to be called Protector' to 'I have no ear – Mistake me not, reader – nor imagine that I am by nature destitute of those exterior twin appendages or hanging ornaments ...' or to the latest little weekly essay on 'Rising Early' or on 'Losing a Collar Stud'. The personal emotion, personal sensibility, the whim, in Sterne's day crept into our literature. It is impossible not to feel a faint disgust at this man, officially a man of God, who in the *Sentimental Journey* found in his own tearful reaction to the mad girl of Moulines the satisfactory conclusion: 'I am positive I have a soul; nor can all the books with which materialists have pester'd the world ever convince me of the contrary.'

It is a little galling to find the conceit of such a man justified. However much we hate the man, or hate rather his coy whimsical defences, he is more 'readable' than Fielding by virtue of that most musical style, the day-dream conversation of a man with a stutter in a world of his imagination where tongue and teeth havè no problems to overcome, where no syllables are harsh, where mind speaks softly to mind with infinite subtlety of tone.

The various accidents which befell a very worthy couple, after their uniting in the state of matrimony, will be the subject of the following history. The distresses which they waded through were some of them so exquisite, and the incidents which produced them so extraordinary that they seem to require not only the utmost malice, but the utmost invention which superstition hath ever attributed to Fortune.

So Fielding begins his most mature – if not his greatest – novel. How this book, one wants to protest, should appeal to the craftsman: the *tour de force* with which for half the long novel he unfolds the story of Booth and Amelia without abandoning the absolute unity of his scene, the prison where Booth is confined. It is quite as remarkable as the designed confusion of *Tristram Shandy*, but there is no answer to a reader who replies: 'I read to be entertained and how heavily this style of Fielding's weighs beside Sterne's impudent opening. "I wish either my father or my mother, or indeed both of them, as they were in duty both equally bound to it, had minded what they were about when they begot me ..."'

71

No, one must surrender to Sterne most of the graces. What Fielding possessed, and Sterne did not, was something quite as new to the novel as Sterne's lightness and sensibility, moral seriousness. He was not a poet – and Sterne was at any rate a minor one – but this moral seriousness enabled him to construct a form which would later satisfy the requirements of major poets as Defoe's plain narrative could not. When we admire Tom Jones as being the first portrait of 'a whole man' (a description which perhaps fits only Bloom in later fiction), it is Fielding's seriousness to which we are paying tribute, his power of discriminating between immorality and vice. He had no high opinion of human nature: the small sensualities of Tom Jones, the incorrigible propensities of Booth, his own direct statement, when he heard his poor dying body, ugly with the dropsy, mocked by the watermen at Rother-hithe ('it was a lively picture of that cruelty and inhumanity in the nature of men which I have often contemplated with concern, and which leads the mind into a train of very uncomfortable and melancholy thoughts'), prove it no more certainly than his quite incredible pictures of virtue, the rectitude of Mr Allworthy, the heroic nature of the patient Amelia. Experience had supplied him with many a Booth and Tom Jones (indeed someone of the latter name appeared before him at Bow Street), but for examples of virtue he had to call on his imagination, and one cannot agree with Saintsbury who remarked quaintly and uncritically of his heroines: 'There is no more touching portrait in the whole of fiction than this heroic and immortal one of feminine goodness and forbearance.'

It is impossible to use these immoderate terms of Fielding without absurdity: to compare the kept woman, Miss Mathews, in *Amelia*, as Dobson did, with a character of Balzac's. He belonged to the wrong century for this kind of greatness. His heroic characters are derived from Dryden – unsuccessfully (the relation between Amelia and a character like Almeyda is obvious). But what puts us so supremely in his debt is this: that he had gathered up in his novels the two divided strands of Restoration fiction: he had combined on

72

his own lower level the flippant prose fictions of the dramatists
and the heroic drama of the poets.

On the lower, the unreligious level. His virtues are natural
virtues, his despair a natural despair, endured with as much
courage as Dryden's but without the supernatural reason.

> Brutus and Cato might discharge their Souls,
> And give them Furlo's for another World:
> But we like Centries are oblig'd to stand
> In Starless Nights, and wait th' appointed hour.

So Dryden, and here more lovably perhaps, with purely natural
virtue, Fielding faces death – death in the shape of a last hard
piece of work for public order, undertaken in his final sickness
with intention of winning from the government some pension
for his wife and children: 'And though I disclaim all pretence
to that Spartan or Roman patriotism which loved the public
so well that it was always ready to become a voluntary sacrifice to the public good I do solemnly declare I have that
love for my family.'

He hated iniquity and he certainly died in exile: his books
do represent a moral struggle, but they completely lack the
sense of supernatural evil or supernatural good. Mr Eliot has
suggested that 'with the disappearance of the idea of Original
Sin, with the disappearance of the idea of intense moral struggle
the human beings presented to us both in poetry and in prose
fiction ... tend to become less and less real', and it is the intensity of the struggle which is lacking in Fielding. Evil is
always a purely sexual matter: the struggle seems invariably
to take the form of whether or not the 'noble lord' or colonel
James will succeed in raping or seducing Amelia, and the
characters in this superficial struggle, carried out with quite
as much ingenuity as Uncle Toby employed on his fortifica-
tions, do tend to become less and less real. How can one take
seriously Mrs Heartfree's five escapes from ravishment in
twenty pages? One can only say in favour of this conception
that it is at least expressed with more dignity than in the
Sentimental Journey where Sterne himself has stolen the part
of Pamela, of Amelia, and Mrs Heartfree, and asks us to be

breathlessly concerned for *his* virtue ('The foot of the bed was within a yard and a half of the place where we were standing – I had still hold of her hands – and how it happened I can give no account, but I neither ask'd her – nor drew her – nor did I think of the bed –'). But the moral life in Fielding is apt to resemble one of those pictorial games of Snakes and Ladders. If the player's counter should happen to fall on a Masquerade or a ticket to Vauxhall Gardens, down it slides by way of the longest snake.

It would be ungrateful to end on this carping note. There had been picaresque novels before Fielding – from the days of Nashe to the days of Defoe – but the picaresque had not before in English been raised to an art, given the form, the arrangement, which separates art from mere realistic reporting however vivid. Fielding lifted life out of its setting and arranged it for the delight of all who love symmetry. He can afford to leave Sterne his graceful play with the emotions, his amusing little indecencies: the man who created Partridge had a distant kinship to the creator of Falstaff. 'Nothing', Jones remarks, 'can be more likely to happen than death to men who go into battle. Perhaps we shall both fall in it – and what then?' 'What then?' replied Partridge; 'why then there is an end of us, is there not? When I am gone, all is over with me. What matters the cause to me, or who gets the victory, if I am killed? I shall never enjoy any advantage from it. What are all the ringing of bells, and bonfires, to one that is six foot under ground? there will be an end of poor Partridge.'

Fielding had tried to make the novel poetic, even though he himself had not the poetic mind, only a fair, a generous and a courageous mind, and the conventions which he established for the novel enabled it in a more passionate age to become a poetic art, to fill the gap in literature left when Dryden died and the seventeenth century was over. He was the best product of his age, the post-revolutionary age when politics for the first time ceased to represent any deep issues and religion excited only the shallowest feeling. His material was underpaid officers, highwaymen, debtors, noblemen who had nothing better to do than pursue sexual adventures, clergymen

like Parson Adams whose virtues are as much pagan as
Christian. 'At the moment when one writes,' to quote Mr Eliot
again, 'one is what one is, and the damage of a lifetime ...
cannot be repaired at the moment of composition.' We
should not complain; rather we should be amazed at what
so unpoetic a mind accomplished in such an age.

1937

SERVANTS OF THE NOVEL

ROBERT BAGE, Edward Bancroft, Elizabeth Blower – like
the names on country tombs they are deeply forgotten, but now
a new scroll has been beautifully cut for them. They deserve
their new memorial, for they held the fort. When Richardson,
Smollett, Fielding, and Sterne were dead, these kept their public
ready for Jane Austen and Scott. Without a novel-reading
public, Scott would have remained an inferior poet, and even
the self-sufficient and solitary genius of Jane Austen owed a
debt to the innumerable female novelists of this dead period,
who persuaded the critics that it was respectable for a woman
to write.

'There was, in the period that followed the masterpieces
of the four great novelists, a real conviction that the novel
was played out.' Miss Tompkins* might be referring to the
1930s as easily as to the 1770s. We, too, have our four great
dead, Hardy and Lawrence, James and Conrad, and Miss
Tompkins's sketch of the novel market bears many resemb-
lances to the noisier modern trade. In the 1770s new editions
were faked, being announced long before the first had been sold,
a method of advertisement with a familiar ring. To give them
a longer life books were post-dated (a custom adopted today
by women's magazines); reviewers complained of the flood of
novels and were abused in their turn for high-handedness;
there were schoolboy novelists; and women, always women,

---

*The Popular Novel in England, 1770–1800, by J. M. S. Tompkins.

writing with 'a dry intolerance of phrase', 'an irritated fastidiousness'.

'Dead books', Miss Tompkins remarks in her preface 'can provide little information when exposed on the gibbet of scorn.' It would have been too easy to guy the novel of sensibility with its voluptuous enjoyment of charity or the Gothic romance; it is far more valuable to discover the aim of the author. The popular writer of today will be fortunate if in a hundred and fifty years he is disinterred by a critic so sensitive to shades of intention, who responds so quickly to the faintest sign of originality, cutting away from the dead the quick wood, the 'real things seen and heard, dresses and street-cries and smoking puddings and the talk of the servants' hall'; who is alive in Charles Jenner to the first lyric quickening of prose when a character tells how, as a boy of nineteen, he was drowsing all night in a dark stage coach and at last opened the wooden shutter to see if it was light: 'I had better have left it alone; it was light; and by that light I saw over against me a face, which several years' experience of its deceit has hardly been able to reconcile me to consigning to oblivion.'

There are passages in Miss Tompkins's chapter on 'Theory and Technique' which should modify the criticism of the novel. She is discussing the accepted view that the novel of her period suffered from laxity of structure.

It is abundantly clear that careful articulation of plot and due regard for proportion, even in a simple story, were not among the principles of composition current in the 'seventies and 'eighties. But principles of composition there must have been; and we shall appreciate them more easily if, remembering the *Sentimental Journey* and the *Man of Feeling*, we discard the term structure, with its architectural suggestions, and think of these books rather in terms of colour. What their authors aimed at – at least the best of them – was delicacy and variety of emotional hue. The novel was to be a sort of artificial rainbow, woven of tears and glinting sunshine, but allowing, at times, of more violent contrasts.

This was the excuse for the episode unconnected with the main plot and for the apparently unnecessary character.

A technical device is practised by the novelist half-consciously a long while before the critic analyses it. Henry James did not invent the 'point of view', but his prefaces gave the method a general importance it lacked as long as it was practised unconsciously. No novelist now can fail to take the 'point of view' into account. For this reason Miss Tompkins's study of eighteenth-century technique is of far wider importance than the novelists she discusses.

1932

ROMANCE IN PIMLICO

THIS entertaining volume * is a by-product of the author's reading while she was engaged on her fascinating study, *The Popular Novel in England*, and the reviewer who criticizes it can only do so on material supplied him by Dr Tompkins, for I doubt if there is any other living authority on the Bristol Milkwoman, Dr Downman, the author of *Infancy*, a poem published with the wish 'that even in hostile America mothers might be the better for his advice', Mary Hays, Philosophess, James White, the author of burlesque medieval romances, the Griffiths who publicized their happy marriage with the reckless confidence of modern film-stars, and, best of all to my mind, the ingenuous and disreputable author of *The Scotch Parents*. For once the reviewer is also the general reader, and as a general reader let us leave behind all nonsense about literary influences and the like and consider a *character* – John Ramble, whom we should certainly have never encountered without Dr Tompkins's aid, and his cunning, emotional and heartless pursuit of Nell Macpherson, a milliner's apprentice.

The most fascinating feature of this autobiographical novel – written apparently with the idea of blackmailing Nell's stubborn parents into returning his mistress whom they had rather roughly taken from him – is a pink ribbon. Nell gave him this to tie round his guitar, and in a fit of jealousy he

---

* *The Polite Marriage and Other 18th Century Essays*, by J. M. S. Tompkins.

removed it and substituted a white one, 'which hung over Nell', in Dr Tompkins's words, 'like a sign of wrath and estrangement, to be removed only by an abasement of devotion'. How we keep our eyes on that guitar! 'When will the ribbon be changed? how far must she go?' The answer is – a very long way; every man in that rational and rather lubricious age felt that he had a right to life, liberties, and the pursuit of happiness. An Act and Deed signed and dated by Nell guaranteed Ramble's sole possession of her body: but the white ribbon remained on the guitar. One day, overcome by a violent fit of toothache when he was walking with Nell, Ramble sought an inn. 'There was a bed in the room. ... Situations at *times* are so critical that it is not in the power of us mortals to resist.' Nevertheless the pink ribbon was not restored, and as the suspense grows the ribbons become identified in our mind with the black and the white sails for which Tristram waited; but this is life – grotesque and comic – not fiction. The ribbon remained white even after her attempted suicide in the Serpentine, after she had scalded her hand to prove the resolution of her love, and after she had borne unflinchingly his murderous assault with a tea knife. Only when she had deserted her parents and deceived her mother did the white ribbon give place to the pink. 'I made her no answer, but got up directly, and then put the exiled ribbon on my guitar, and showing it to her, I said, look here. – You remember the token.' But they didn't marry: as Ramble put it to Mrs Macpherson, 'Call to mind the delicacy of marrying a Girl too soon after the loss of her honour.' There is an odd realistic charm about this transparent romance: it emerges from the vivid and surprising 'properties' – toothache and Hyde Park, the Serpentine and Pimlico and the pink ribbon and a kettle of boiling water, Nell's uncle called McClack who was too much for not very brave Ramble, and a poor relation called Mrs Drulin; and like most of the romances in this book it is conveyed to us by Dr Tompkins with elegance and wit.

Indeed we have so much reason for gratitude that it seems surly to complain that the volume has *longueurs*; that there are occasions when Dr Tompkins seems to take a little too seriously the *literary* interest of the Bristol Milkwoman or Mary Hays. She puts as her epigraph a rather unwise remark of G. K. Chesterton, 'It is too often forgotten that just as a bad man is nevertheless a man, so a bad poet is nevertheless a poet', and sometimes her investigation of these obscure works becomes too whimsical-serious. The real interest in the bad poet is not literary but psychological – the twist in Dr Downman's character which induced him to put into blank verse his advice to mothers on 'rickets, regular meals and a fruit diet', and we feel Dr Tompkins has struck a wrong note when she observes: 'A nerve thrilled in him. He has directness of attack – a resonant simplicity in the opening line of a poem, that recalls Sidney.' And occasionally she is guilty of such a phrase as 'Downman zealously inverting the garden-mould with his new-found strength.' It is as though she had been temporarily possessed by her curious by-way writers, with their strenuous euphuism – she will really have to be careful of Ramble.

1938

THE YOUNG DICKENS

A CRITIC must try to avoid being a prisoner of his time, and if we are to appreciate *Oliver Twist* at its full value we must forget that long shelf-load of books, all the stifling importance of a great author, the scandals and the controversies of the private life; it would be well too if we could forget the Phiz and the Cruikshank illustrations that have frozen the excited, excitable world of Dickens into a hall of waxworks, where Mr Mantalini's whiskers have always the same trim, where Mr Pickwick perpetually turns up the tails of his coat, and in the Chamber of Horrors Fagin crouches over an undying fire. His illustrators, brilliant craftsmen though they were, did Dickens a disservice, for no character any more will walk for the first time into our memory as we ourselves imagine him and *our* imagination after all has just as much claim to truth as Cruikshank's.

Nevertheless the effort to go back is well worth while. The journey is only a little more than a hundred years long, and at the other end of the road is a young author whose sole claim to renown in 1836 had been the publication of some journalistic sketches and a number of comic operettas: *The Strange Gentleman, The Village Coquette, Is She His Wife?* I doubt whether any literary Cortez at that date would have yet stood them upon his shelves. Then suddenly with *The Pickwick Papers* came popularity and fame. Fame falls like a dead hand on an author's shoulder, and it is well for him when it falls only in later life. How many in Dickens's place would have withstood what James called 'the great corrupting contact of the public', the popularity founded, as it almost always is, on the weakness and not the strength of an author?

The young Dickens, at the age of twenty-five, had hit on a mine that paid him a tremendous dividend. Fielding and Smollett, tidied and refined for the new industrial bourgeoisie, had both salted it; Goldsmith had contributed sentimentality and Monk Lewis horror. The book was enormous, shapeless, familiar (that important recipe for popularity). What Henry James wrote of a long-forgotten French critic applies well to the young Dickens: 'He is homely, familiar and colloquial; he leans his elbows on his desk and does up his weekly budget into a parcel the reverse of compact. You can fancy him a grocer retailing tapioca and hominy full weight for the price; his style seems a sort of integument of brown paper.'

This is, of course, unfair to *The Pickwick Papers*. The driest critic could not have quite blinkered his eyes to those sudden wide illuminations of comic genius that flap across the waste of words like sheet lightning, but could he have foreseen the second novel, not a repetition of this great loose popular holdall, but a short melodrama, tight in construction, almost entirely lacking in broad comedy, and possessing only the sad twisted humour of the orphan's asylum?

'You'll make your fortune, Mr Sowerberry,' said the beadle, as he thrust his thumb and forefinger into the proffered snuff-box of the undertaker: which was an ingenious little model of a patent coffin.

Such a development was as inconceivable as the gradual transformation of that thick boggy prose into the delicate and exact poetic cadences, the music of memory, that so influenced Proust.

We are too inclined to take Dickens as a whole and to treat his juvenilia with the same kindness or harshness as his later work. *Oliver Twist* is still juvenilia – magnificent juvenilia: it is the first step on the road that led from *Pickwick* to *Great Expectations*, and we condone the faults of taste in the early book the more readily if we recognize the distance Dickens had to travel. These two typical didactic passages can act as the first two milestones at the opening of the journey, the first from *Pickwick*, the second from *Oliver Twist*.

And numerous indeed are the hearts to which Christmas brings a brief season of happiness and enjoyment. How many families, whose members have been dispersed and scattered far and wide, in the restless struggles of life, are then reunited, and meet once again in that happy state of companionship and mutual goodwill, which is a source of such pure and unalloyed delight, and one so incompatible with the cares and sorrows of the world, that the religious belief of the most civilized nations, and the rude traditions of the roughest savages, alike number it among the first joys of a future condition of existence, provided for the blest and happy.

The boy stirred and smiled in his sleep, as though these marks of pity and compassion had awakened some pleasant dream of a love and affection he had never known. Thus, a strain of gentle music, or the rippling of water in a silent place, or the odour of a flower, or the mention of a familiar word, will sometimes call up sudden dim remembrances of scenes that never were in this life; which vanish like a breath; which some brief memory of a happier existence, long gone by, would seem to have awakened; which no voluntary exertion of the mind can ever recall.

The first is certainly brown paper: what it wraps has been chosen by the grocer to suit his clients' tastes, but cannot we detect already in the second passage the tone of Dickens's secret prose, that sense of a mind speaking to itself with no one there to listen, as we find it in *Great Expectations*?

It was fine summer weather again, and, as I walked along, the times when I was a little helpless creature, and my sister did not spare me, vividly returned. But they returned with a gentle tone upon them that softened even the edge of Tickler. For now, the very breath of the beans and clover whispered to my heart that the day must come when it would be well for my memory that others walking in the sunshine should be softened as they thought of me.

It is a mistake to think of *Oliver Twist* as a realistic story: only late in his career did Dickens learn to write realistically of human beings; at the beginning he invented life and we no more believe in the temporal existence of Fagin or Bill Sikes than we believe in the existence of that Giant whom Jack slew as he bellowed his Fee Fi Fo Fum. There were real Fagins and Bill Sikes and real Bumbles in the England of his day, but he had not drawn them, as he was later to draw the convict Magwitch; these characters in *Oliver Twist* are simply parts of one huge invented scene, what Dickens in his own preface called 'the cold wet shelterless midnight streets of London'. How the phrase goes echoing on through the books of Dickens until we meet it again so many years later in 'the weary western streets of London on a cold dusty spring night' which were so melancholy to Pip. But Pip was to be as real as the weary streets, while Oliver was as unrealistic as the cold wet midnight of which he formed a part.

This is not to criticize the book so much as to describe it. For what an imagination this youth of twenty-six had that he could invent so monstrous and complete a legend! We are not lost with Oliver Twist round Saffron Hill: we are lost in the interstices of one young, angry, gloomy brain, and the oppressive images stand out along the track like the lit figures in a Ghost Train tunnel.

Against the wall were ranged, in regular array, a long row of elm boards cut into the same shape, looking in the dim light, like high shouldered ghosts with their hands in their breeches pockets.

We have most of us seen those nineteenth-century prints where the bodies of naked women form the face of a character,

82

the Diplomat, the Miser, and the like. So the crouching figure of Fagin seems to form the mouth, Sikes with his bludgeon the jutting features, and the sad lost Oliver the eyes of one man as lost as Oliver.

Chesterton, in a fine imaginative passage, has described the mystery behind Dickens's plots, the sense that even the author was unaware of what was really going on, so that when the explanations come and we reach, huddled into the last pages of *Oliver Twist*, a naked complex narrative of illegitimacy and burnt wills and destroyed evidence, we simply do not believe.

The secrecy is sensational; the secret is tame. The surface of the thing seems more awful than the core of it. It seems almost as if these grisly figures, Mrs Chadband and Mrs Clennam, Miss Havisham and Miss Flite, Nemo and Sally Brass, were keeping something back from the author as well as from the reader. When the book closes we do not know their real secret, They soothed the optimistic Dickens with something less terrible than the truth.

What strikes the attention most in this closed Fagin universe are the different levels of unreality. If, as one is inclined to believe, the creative writer perceives his world once and for all in childhood and adolescence, and his whole career is an effort to illustrate his private world in terms of the great public world we all share, we can understand why Fagin and Sikes in their most extreme exaggerations move us more than the benevolence of Mr Brownlow or the sweetness of Mrs Maylie – they touch with fear as the others never really touch with love. It was not that the unhappy child, with his hurt pride and his sense of hopeless insecurity, had not encountered human goodness – he had simply failed to recognize it in those streets between Gadshill and Hungerford Market which had been as narrowly enclosed as Oliver Twist's. When Dickens at this early period tried to describe goodness he seems to have remembered the small stationers' shops on the way to the blacking factory with their coloured paper scraps of angels and virgins, or perhaps the face of some old gentleman who had spoken kindly to him outside Warren's factory. He had swum up towards goodness from the deepest world of his experience, and on this shallow level the conscious brain has taken a hand, trying to construct characters to represent virtue and, because his age demanded it, triumphant virtue, but all he can produce are powdered wigs and gleaming spectacles and a lot of bustle with bowls of broth and a pale angelic face. Compare the way in which we first meet evil with his introduction of goodness.

The walls and ceiling of the room were perfectly black with age and dirt. There was a deal table before the fire: upon which were a candle, stuck in a ginger-beer bottle, two or three pewter pots, a loaf and butter, and a plate. In a frying pan, which was on the fire, and which was secured to the mantel-shelf by a string, some sausages were cooking; and standing over them, with a toasting-fork in his hand, was a very old shrivelled Jew, whose villainous-looking and repulsive face was obscured by a quantity of matted red hair. He was dressed in a greasy flannel gown, with his throat bare ... 'This is him, Fagin,' said Jack Dawkins: 'my friend Oliver Twist.' The Jew grinned; and, making a low obeisance to Oliver, took him by the hand, and hoped he should have the honour of his intimate acquaintance.

Fagin has always about him this quality of darkness and nightmare. He never appears on the daylight streets. Even when we see him last in the condemned cell, it is in the hours before the dawn. In the Fagin darkness Dickens's hand seldom fumbles. Hear him turning the screw of horror when Nancy speaks of the thoughts of death that have haunted her:

'Imagination,' said the gentleman, soothing her.
'No imagination,' replied the girl in a hoarse voice. 'I'll swear I saw "coffin" written in every page of the book in large black letters, – aye, and they carried one close to me, in the streets tonight.'
'There is nothing unusual in that,' said the gentleman. 'They have passed me often.'
'Real ones,' rejoined the girl. 'This was not.'

Now turn to the daylight world and our first sight of Rose:

The younger lady was in the lovely bloom and springtime of womanhood; at that age, when, if ever angels be for God's good purposes enthroned in mortal forms, they may be, without impiety, supposed to abide in such as hers. She was not past seventeen. Cast in so slight and exquisite a mould; so mild and gentle; so pure and beautiful; that earth seemed not her element, nor its rough creatures her fit companions.

Or Mr Brownlow as he first appeared to Oliver:

Now, the old gentleman came in as brisk as need be; but he had no sooner raised his spectacles on his forehead, and thrust his hands behind the skirts of his dressing-gown to take a good long look at Oliver, than his countenance underwent a very great variety of odd contortions ... The fact is, if the truth must be told, that Mr Brownlow's heart, being large enough for any six ordinary old gentlemen of humane disposition, forced a supply of tears into his eyes by some hydraulic process which we are not sufficiently philosophical to be in a condition to explain.

How can we really believe that these inadequate ghosts of goodness can triumph over Fagin, Monks, and Sikes? And the answer, of course, is that they never could have triumphed without the elaborate machinery of the plot disclosed in the last pages. This world of Dickens is a world without God; and as a substitute for the power and the glory of the omnipotent and omniscient are a few sentimental references to heaven, angels, the sweet faces of the dead, and Oliver saying, 'Heaven is a long way off, and they are too happy there to come down to the bedside of a poor boy.' In this Manichaean world we can believe in evil-doing, but goodness wilts into philanthropy, kindness, and those strange vague sicknesses into which Dickens's young women so frequently fall and which seem in his eyes a kind of badge of virtue, as though there were a merit in death.

But how instinctively Dickens's genius recognized the flaw and made a virtue out of it. We cannot believe in the power of Mr Brownlow, but nor did Dickens, and from his inability to believe in his own good character springs the real tension of his novel. The boy Oliver may not lodge in our brain like David Copperfield, and though many of Mr Bumble's phrases have become and deserve to have become familiar quotations we can feel he was manufactured: he never breathes like Mr Dorrit; yet Oliver's predicament, the nightmare fight between the darkness, where the demons walk, and the sunlight, where ineffective goodness makes its last stand in a condemned world, will remain part of our imaginations forever. We read of the defeat of Monks, and of Fagin screaming in the condemned cell, and of Sikes dangling from his self-made noose, but we don't believe. We have witnessed Oliver's temporary escapes too often and his inevitable recapture: *there* is the truth and the creative experience. We know that when Oliver leaves Mr Brownlow's house to walk a few hundred yards to the book-seller, his friends will wait in vain for his return. All London outside the quiet shady street in Pentonville belongs to his pursuers; and when he escapes again into the house of Mrs Maylie in the fields beyond Shepperton, we know his security is false. The seasons may pass, but safety depends not on time but on daylight. As children we all knew that: how all day we could forget the dark and the journey to bed. It is with a sense of relief that at last in twilight we see the faces of the Jew and Monks peer into the cottage window between the sprays of jessamine. At that moment we realize how the whole world, and not London only, belongs to these two after dark. Dickens, dealing out his happy endings and his unreal re-tributions, can never ruin the validity and dignity of that moment. 'They had recognized him, and he them; and their look was as firmly impressed upon his memory, as if it had been deeply carved in stone, and set before him from his birth.'

'From his birth' – Dickens may have intended that phrase to refer to the complicated imbroglios of the plot that lie out-side the novel, 'something less terrible than the truth'. As for the truth, is it too fantastic to imagine that in this novel, as in many of his later books, creeps in, unrecognized by the author, the eternal and alluring taint of the Manichee, with its simple and terrible explanation of our plight, how the world was made by Satan and not by God, lulling us with the music of despair?

1950

THERE are men whose lives seem arguments for the existence of a conscious providence, lives fashioned as it were deliberately for one purpose with a cruelty that has deprived them of any obscure and friendly retreat. Hans Andersen is one of these, and there is a sense of unusual brutality in the ingenuity which providence expended for so small a result, a few volumes of children's stories and a shelf of poetic dramas without merit.

To fashion this writer what was required? First and foremost a raw sensibility, a bundle of shrieking nerves which barred the possessor hopelessly from any easy comfort. The son of a cobbler of unbalanced mind, the grandson of a lunatic, Andersen might as easily have become a madman as an artist. When he was a child, his parents tried to cure his nerves at the holy well of St Regisse on St John's Eve; but during the night which he spent by the spring he was woken by a thunderstorm and the screams of a lunatic girl who had been sleeping at his feet. It is possible that one thought saved the boy and the man from madness: 'I am going to be famous. First you suffer the most awful things, and *then* you get to be famous.' The same idea is expressed again and again in his work. 'All who see you,' the witch says to the mermaid who seeks a human form, 'will say that you are the most beautiful child of man they have ever seen. You will keep your gliding gait, no dancer will rival you, but every step you take will be as if you were treading upon sharp knives, so sharp as to draw blood. If you are willing to suffer all this I am ready to help you.' And in the story of *The Wild Swans* the heroine to save her brothers has to weave eleven shirts from stinging-nettles. 'The sea is indeed softer than your hands, and it moulds the hardest stone, but it does not feel the pain your fingers will feel. It has no heart and does not suffer the pain and anguish you must feel.'

Andersen has been held up as an example of supreme egotism, because everything which he and those he loved suffered he related to his own future, wondering of his family's early bitter disappointment at a failure to find a livelihood on a country estate whether God had not ruined their hopes to save him from becoming a mere farmer. But this was not egotism; it was an artist's parallel to the Catholic ideal of the acceptance of pain for a spiritual benefit. If he had not found a reason to accept pain, his mind might well have broken; he might have been happy in the manner of his grandfather who wandered singing and wreathed in flowers through the streets of Odense or of his father who imagined himself on his deathbed one of Napoleon's captains, instead of the broken private that he was, and cried aloud, 'Hats off, you whelps, when the Emperor rides by.'

His nerves, too, supplied what fate next demanded in completing the artist – persistence, an inability to find happiness even when he had won his fame. In Sweden, when the students of Lund marched in a body to acclaim him, he could not believe in their sincerity; he thought they were making game of him and searched their faces for smiles. When he left Odense for Copenhagen, at the age of fourteen, without work or friends, a wise woman had declared that one day his native place would be illuminated in his honour, so that when, 48 years later, he returned to receive the freedom of the city, it might have been expected that he would enjoy a few moments of unmixed happiness. But at night, as he watched from the City Hall the torches and the lamps and the crowd singing in his honour in the square, the cold wind touched a tooth into almost unbearable pain, so that he could only count the verses still remaining and long for the programme to end. It is impossible, at times, not be convinced of the actuality of this purposeful fate; for it was an extraordinary coincidence, if it was not a malignant providence, which caused him to overhear, as he stood at his window in Copenhagen, just returned from his triumphal visit to England, a man say to his companion: 'Look, there is our orang-outang who is so famous abroad.'

Most men have one earth into which they can creep to rest the nerves, but for Andersen it was stopped. He was deprived even of the satisfaction of sex. Again his life was curiously of a piece, as if no opportunity was to be wasted to warp his nature to the required shape. As a boy alone in Copenhagen, chance found him lodgings in a street of red lights. His surroundings must have continually aroused desires which he had not the money to satisfy. And they were never satisfied. He was as passionate as most men, three times he tried to marry, but he retained the exhausting innocence which, to quote Miss Toksvig,* 'he described himself as the kind which reads the Bible and always finds the Song of Songs; the innocence that ruins sleep'.

There remained for fate to limit and define his range as an artist. The son of a washerwoman and a cobbler Andersen inherited the folk tradition; his earliest fairy stories were transcripts of tales he had heard as a child. Witches were part of his everyday life; they were called in by his mother to foretell his future, to heal his father's sickness, and the little medieval court of Odense supplied one of the commonest ingredients of his tales, the ease with which a poor child can talk with royalty. Odense had only 7,000 inhabitants, but it had a palace and a governor and a regiment of dragoons, and the cobbler's son was admitted to audience. But Andersen did not submit easily to the claims of this environment. It was his ambition to be a dramatic poet; with extraordinary persistence he followed this aim to the end of his life, and because his plays almost invariably failed he was convinced that he was not appreciated in his own country.

Miss Toksvig's is a most satisfying biography of this unhappy man in all his curious glassy transparency. She writes with sympathy and without sentimentality; and it is a pleasure to watch her masterly choice and arrangement of incident into a story which is always exciting. One can only wish that she had not confined herself to Andersen's life. She throws off suggestions for a new estimate of his work, which I should like to have seen pursued. 'In Hans Christian,' Miss Toksvig writes, 'the Unconscious was made flesh and dwelt unashamed and bewildered among men,' and perhaps the chief importance of Hans Andersen today to adult readers lies in the frequency with

* *Hans Christian Andersen*, by Signe Toksvig.

which he allowed his unconscious mind to take control of his pen. There are passages in *The Snow Queen* which anticipate the method of the Surréalistes. His contemporaries complained that his stories contained no moral, but it is in their occasional passages of pure fantasy, as when the flowers speak their irrelevant messages to Gerda, that his stories have their greatest importance for the contemporaries of M. Philippe Soupault.

1933

[3]

FRANÇOIS MAURIAC

AFTER the death of Henry James a disaster overtook the
English novel; indeed long before his death one can picture
that quiet, impressive, rather complacent figure, like the last
survivor on a raft, gazing out over a sea scattered with wreck-
age. He even recorded his impressions in an article in the
Times Literary Supplement, recorded his hope – but was it
really hope or only a form of his unconquerable oriental
politeness? – in such young novelists as Mr Compton Mackenzie and Mr David Herbert Lawrence, and we who have
lived after the disaster can realize the futility of those hopes.

For with the death of James the religious sense was lost to
the English novel, and with the religious sense went the
sense of the importance of the human act. It was as if the
world of fiction had lost a dimension: the characters of such
distinguished writers as Mrs Virginia Woolf and Mr E. M.
Forster wandered like cardboard symbols through a world that
was paper-thin. Even in one of the most materialistic of our
great novelists – in Trollope – we are aware of another world
against which the actions of the characters are thrown into
relief. The ungainly clergyman picking his black-booted way
through the mud, handling so awkwardly his umbrella, speaking of his miserable income and stumbling through a proposal
of marriage, exists in a way that Mrs Woolf's Mr Ramsay
never does, because we are aware that he exists not only to the
woman he is addressing but also in a God's eye. His unimportance in the world of the senses is only matched by his enormous importance in another world.

The novelist, perhaps unconsciously aware of his predicament, took refuge in the subjective novel. It was as if he
thought that by mining into layers of personality hitherto un-
touched he could unearth the secret of 'importance', but in
these mining operations he lost yet another dimension. The
visible world for him ceased to exist as completely as the

spiritual. Mrs Dalloway walking down Regent Street was aware of the glitter of shop windows, the smooth passage of cars, the conversation of shoppers, but it was only a Regent Street seen by Mrs Dalloway that was conveyed to the reader: a charming whimsical rather sentimental prose poem was what Regent Street had become: a current of air, a touch of scent, a sparkle of glass. But, we protest, Regent Street too has a right to exist; it is more real than Mrs Dalloway, and we look back with nostalgia towards the chop houses, the mean courts, the still Sunday streets of Dickens. Dickens's characters were of immortal importance, and the houses in which they loved, the mews in which they damned themselves were lent importance by their presence. They were given the right to exist as they were, distorted, if at all, only by their observer's eye – not further distorted at a second remove by an imagined character.

M. Mauriac's first importance to an English reader, therefore, is that he belongs to the company of the great traditional novelists: he is a writer for whom the visible world has not ceased to exist, whose characters have the solidity and importance of men with souls to save or lose, and a writer who claims the traditional and essential right of a novelist, to comment, to express his views. For how tired we have become of the dogmatically 'pure' novel, the tradition founded by Flaubert and reaching its magnificent tortuous climax in England in the works of Henry James. One is reminded of those puzzles in children's papers which take the form of a maze. The child is encouraged to trace with his pencil a path to the centre of the maze. But in the pure novel the reader begins at the centre and has to find his way to the gate. He runs his pencil down avenues which must surely go straight to the circumference, the world outside the maze, where moral judgements and acts of supernatural importance can be found (even the writing of a novel indeed can be regarded as a more important action, expressing an intention of more vital importance, than the adultery of the main character or the murder in chapter three), but the printed channels slip and twist and slide, landing him back where he began, and he finds on close examination that the designer of the maze has in fact overprinted the only exit.

I am not denying the greatness of either Flaubert or James. The novel was ceasing to be an aesthetic form and they recalled it to the artistic conscience. It was the later writers who by accepting the technical dogma blindly made the novel the dull devitalized form (form it retained) that it has become. The exclusion of the author can go too far. Even the author, poor devil, has a right to exist, and M. Mauriac reaffirms that right. It is true that the Flaubertian form is not so completely abandoned in this novel* as in *Le Baiser au lépreux*; the 'I' of the story plays a part in the action; any commentary there is can be attributed by purists to this fictional 'I', but the pretence is thin – 'I' is dominated by I. Let me quote two passages:

– Et puis, tellement beau, tu ne trouves pas?

Non, je ne le trouvais pas beau. Qu'est-ce que la beauté pour un enfant? Sans doute, est-il surtout sensible à la force, à la puissance. Mais cette question dut me frapper puisque je me souviens encore, après toute une vie, de cet endroit de l'allée où Michèle m'interrogea ainsi, à propos de Jean. Saurais-je mieux définir aujourd'hui, ce que j'appelle beauté? saurais-je dire à quel signe je la reconnais, qu'il s'agisse d'un visage de chair, d'un horizon, d'un ciel, d'une couleur, d'une parole, d'un chant? A ce tressaillement charnel et qui, pourtant, intéresse l'âme, à cette joie désespérée à cette contemplation sans issue et que ne récompense aucune étreinte ...

Ce jour-là, j'ai vu pour la première fois à visage découvert, ma vieille ennemie la solitude, avec qui je fais bon ménage aujourd'hui. Nous nous connaissons: elle m'a asséné tous les coups imaginables, et il n'y a plus de place où frapper. Je ne crois avoir évité aucun de ses pièges. Maintenant elle a fini de me torturer. Nous tisonnons face à face, durant ces soirs d'hiver où la chute d'une 'pigne', un sanglot de nocturne ont autant d'intérêt pour mon coeur qu'une voix humaine.

In such passages one is aware, as in Shakespeare's plays, of a sudden tensing, a hush seems to fall on the spirit – this is something more important than the king, Lear, or the general,

* *La Pharisienne.*

Othello, something which is unconfined and unconditioned by plot. 'I' has ceased to speak, I is speaking.

One is never tempted to consider in detail M. Mauriac's plots. Who can describe six months afterwards the order of events, say in *Ce qui était perdu*? One remembers the simple outlines of *Le Baiser au lépreux*, but the less simple the events of the novel the more they disappear from the mind, leaving in our memory only the characters, whom we have known so intimately that the events at the one period of their lives chosen by the novelist can be forgotten without forgetting them. (The first lines of *La Pharisienne* create completely the horrible Comte de Mirbel: ' "Approche ici, garçon!" Je me retournai, croyant qu'il s'adressait à un de mes camarades. Mais non, c'était bien moi qu'appelait l'ancien zouave pontifical, souriant. La cicatrice de sa lèvre supérieure rendait le sourire hideux.') M. Mauriac's characters exist with extraordinary physical completeness (he has affinities here we feel to Dickens), but their particular acts are less important than the force, whether God or Devil, that compels them, and though M. Mauriac rises to dramatic heights in his great 'scenes', as when Jean de Mirbel, the boy whose soul is in such danger (a kind of unhappy tortured Grand Meaulnes), is the silent, witness outside the country hotel of his beloved mother's vulgar adultery, the 'joins' of his plot, the events which should make a plausible progression from one scene to another, are often oddly lacking. Described as plots his novels would sometimes seem to flicker like an early film. But who would attempt to describe them as plots? Wipe out the whole progression of events and we would be left still with the characters in a way I can compare with no other novelist. Take away Mrs Dalloway's capability of self-expression and there is not merely no novel but no Mrs Dalloway: take away the plot from Dickens and the characters who have lived so vividly from event to event would dissolve. But if the Comtesse de Mirbel had not committed adultery, if Jean's guardian, the evil Papal Zouave, had never lifted a hand against him: if the clumsy well-meaning saintly priest, the Abbé Calou, had never been put in charge of the boy, the characters, we feel, would have continued to exist in identically the same way. We are saved or damned by our thoughts, not by our actions.

The events of M. Mauriac's novels are used not to change characters (how little in truth are we changed by events: how romantic and false in comparison is a book such as Conrad's *Lord Jim*) but to reveal characters – reveal them gradually with an incomparable subtlety. His moral and religious insight is the reverse of the obvious: you will seldom find the easy false assumption, the stock figure in M. Mauriac. Take for example the poor pious usher M. Puybaraud. He is what we call in England a creeping Jesus, but M. Mauriac shows how in truth the creeping Jesus may creep towards Jesus. La Pharisienne herself under her layer of destructive egotism and false pity is disclosed sympathetically to the religious core. She learns through hypocrisy. The hypocrite cannot live insulated for ever against the beliefs she professes. There is irony but no satire in M. Mauriac's work.

I am conscious of having scattered too many names and comparisons in this short and superficial essay, but one name – the greatest – cannot be left out of any consideration of M. Mauriac's work, Pascal. This modern novelist, who allows himself the freedom to comment, comments, whether through his characters or in his own 'I', again in the very accents of Pascal.

Les êtres ne changent pas, c'est là une vérité dont on ne doute plus à mon âge; mais ils retournent souvent à l'inclination que durant une vie ils se sont épuisés à combattre. Ce qui ne signifie point qu'ils finissent toujours par céder au pire d'eux-mêmes: Dieu est la bonne tentation à laquelle beaucoup d'hommes succombent à la fin.

Il y a des êtres qui tendent leurs toiles et peuvent jeûner longtemps avant qu'aucune proie s'y laisse prendre: la patience du vice est infinie.

Il ne faut pas essayer d'entrer dans la vie des êtres malgré eux: retiens cette leçon, mon petit. Il ne faut pas pousser la porte de cette seconde ni de cette troisième vie que Dieu seul connaît. Il ne faut jamais tourner la tête vers la ville secrète, vers la cité maudite des autres, si on ne veut pas être changé en statue de sel . . .

Notre-Seigneur exige que nous aimions nos ennemis; c'est plus facile souvent que de ne pas haïr ceux que nous aimons.

If Pascal had been a novelist, we feel, this is the method and the tone he would have used.

1945

BERNANOS, THE BEGINNER

Sous Le Soleil de Satan, the first novel of Bernanos, is stamped in deep wax with the very personal seal which he never lost. Technically it is full of faults, faults many of them that he never troubled to amend in his later books. He was a writer rather than a novelist; in the impatience and even the fury of his creation he seems to have snatched at fiction because it was nearest to his hand. He belongs in the company of Leon Bloy rather than of François Mauriac, who has patiently through the years pruned and perfected his style and learned his method. Bernanos belongs to the world of angry men, to a tradition of religious writing that stretches back to Dante, 'who loved well because he hated'.

Bloy wrote in an essay on the Danish writer Joergensen, 'It will always be known that he wrote for the glory of God ... and I know it well, that terrible profession.' Bernanos could have made the same claim. There is no catharsis in his work; his stories are open wounds which refuse, like the stigmata, to heal. The curé of Lumbres dies standing upright in pain pressed against the back wall of his confessional in the empty church where he is discovered by the illustrious member of the Académie Française (like Bloy, Bernanos is ready to spit in the face of his own profession, for literature only exists for him as a means to an end: sanctification):

Toute belle vie, Seigneur, témoigne pour vous; mais le témoignage du saint est comme arraché par le fer.

Telle fut sans doute, ici-bas, la plainte suprême du curé de Lumbres, élevée vers le Juge, et son reproche amoureux. Mais, à l'homme illustre qui l'est venu chercher si loin, il a autre chose à dire. Et si la bouche noire, dans l'ombre, qui resemble à une plaie ouverte par l'explosion d'un cri, ne profère aucun son, le corps tout entier mime un affreux défi :

TU VOULAIS MA PAIX, S'ÉCRIE LE SAINT, VEINS LA PRENDRE! ...

In this, his first novel, Bernanos too seems to cry defiantly to all the readers of the latest literary prizes, to the readers of feuilletons, even to the *avant-garde* of his own day, 'Come and read me if you dare', expecting no more response than did the curé of Lumbres. What astonishment he must have felt when he saw his great world-wide audience assembling.

We musn't ignore his faults, because they were part of the man, as much as the disordered clothes were part of the curé when we meet him first through the critical eyes of the Abbé Menou-Segrais:

Le désordre, ou plutôt l'aspect presque sordide de ses vêtements journaliers, était rendu plus remarquable encore par la singulière opposition d'une douillette neuve, raide d'apprêt, qu'il avait glissée avec tant d'émotion qu'une des manches se retroussait risiblement sur un poignet noueux comme un cep.

The story, which is written in the form of three linking *nouvelles* (the only form which Bernanos up till then had tried) begins with the history of Mouchette, the country girl seduced by the aristocratic landowner whom she murders. Only in the second *nouvelle* do we encounter the curé, who is tempted to despair by the diabolic horse-dealer on his way to assist at a retreat in a neighbouring parish and is afterwards concerned, to the public scandal, in the suicide of Mouchette. In the final *nouvelle* he has been appointed, after a disciplinary period in a monastery, to the parish of Lumbres, and like the Curé d'Ars he is a saint accepted in his lifetime by all but himself – an object of pilgrimage, even to curious literary men.

It is a weakness, I think, in the novel that it begins with the story of Mouchette, a melodramatic nineteenth-century plot even though seen through Bernanos's timeless eyes, and if we judge a book strictly as a novel, we have to deplore the intrusions of the author who occasionally mounts the pulpit to draw a lesson which we would have preferred to discover for ourselves. There is even a hint of old-fashioned hagiology:

C'était l'heure de la nuit où cet homme intrépide, soutien de tant d'âmes, chancelait sous le poids de son magnifique fardeau.

Perhaps only in *Journal d'un Curé*, where a stricter method was imposed by his use of the first person, did Bernanos allow his characters to speak for themselves without explanation or annotation by the author. He never discovered the cunning method of disguised commentary employed by Mauriac who conceals the author's voice in a simile or an unexpected adjective, like a film director who makes his personal comment with a camera angle.

And yet ... are we, when all this has been said, only trying to impose arbitrary laws which have no authority higher than Flaubert's? Even what sometimes seem to be clumsy or undramatized interventions by the author are the very characteristics which give the story of the curé of Lumbres its odd authenticity. It is as though Bernanos were a biographer rather than a novelist. True that on occasion he takes on the tone of a hagiographer, but a work of hagiology has been written about a real saint, and the very faults of Bernanos's first novel become virtues and authenticate the character of the curé – this is not fiction, we tell ourselves: the curé exists in the same historic world as the Curé d'Ars and his parish with him. Surely, just as at Ars, the pilgrims debouch in Lumbres daily from their motor-coaches to examine the rough confessional where the curé died.

And would we for the sake of a stricter discipline sacrifice the *pensées*, like Mauriac's not unworthy of Pascal?

Il est naturel à l'homme de haïr sa propre souffrance dans la souffrance d'autrui.

Quand l'homme se lève pour le maudire, c'est Lui seul qui soutient cette main débile.

L'enfer aussi a ses cloîtres.

An author, when his greatness is accepted, loses a great deal of his impact; he becomes the reading of the lycées, part of a course in literature; he is taught and not enjoyed. How I wish I could have been one of those who read *Sous Le Soleil de*

Satan for the first time when it appeared in 1926. With what astonishment, in this novel unlike all novels hitherto, they must have encountered *le tueur d'âmes* when he intercepted the curé on the dark road to Boulaincourt in the guise of a little lubricious horse-dealer with his sinister gaiety and his horrible affection and his grotesque playfulness.

This is surely one of the great scenes in literature, the scenes which suddenly enlarge the whole scope of fiction and like new discoveries in science alter the future and correct the past. Never again will it be possible to write off the infantile devils of *Doctor Faustus* with their fire-crackers and conjuring tricks. They are more understandable now, masks of the horse-dealer who made his own kind of Host with childish malice out of a pebble. '*Un jeu d'enfants*', he called it in proud mockery, for infantility, if the inferno exists at all, must surely be a mark of that Hell which is the home of the eternally undeveloped.

1968

THE BURDEN OF CHILDHOOD

THERE are certain writers, as different as Dickens from Kipling, who never shake off the burden of their childhood. The abandonment to the blacking factory in Dickens's case and in Kipling's to the cruel Aunt Rosa living in the sandy suburban road were never forgotten. All later experience seems to have been related to those months or years of un-happiness. Life which turns its cruel side to most of us at an age when we have begun to learn the arts of self-protection took these two writers by surprise during the defencelessness of early childhood. How differently they reacted. Dickens learnt sympathy, Kipling cruelty – Dickens developed a style so easy and natural that it seems capable of including the whole human race in its understanding: Kipling designed a machine, the cogwheels perfectly fashioned, for exclusion. The charac-ters sometimes seem to rattle down a conveyor-belt like match-boxes.

There are great similarities in the early life of Kipling and

Saki, and Saki's reaction to misery was nearer Kipling's than Dickens's. Kipling was born in India. H. H. Munro (I would like to drop that rather meaningless mask of the pen name) in Burma. Family life for such children is always broken – the miseries recorded by Kipling and Munro must be experienced by many mute inglorious children born to the civil servant or the colonial officer in the East: the arrival of the cab at the strange relative's house, the unpacking of the boxes, the unfamiliar improvised nursery, the terrible departure of the parents, a four years' absence from affection that in child-time can be as long as a generation (at four one is a small child, at eight a boy). Kipling described the horror of that time in *Baa Baa Black Sheep* – a story in spite of its sentimentality almost unbearable to read: Aunt Rosa's prayers, the beatings, the card with the word L I A R pinned upon the back, the growing and neglected blindness, until at last came the moment of rebellion.

'If you make me do that,' said Black Sheep very quietly, 'I shall burn this house down and perhaps I will kill you. I don't know whether I *can* kill you – you are so bony, but I will try.'

No punishment followed this blasphemy, though Black Sheep held himself ready to work his way to Auntie Rosa's withered throat and grip there till he was beaten off.

In the last sentence we can hear something very much like the tones of Munro's voice as we hear them in one of his finest stories *Sredni Vashtar*. Neither his Aunt Augusta nor his Aunt Charlotte with whom he was left near Barnstaple after his mother's death, while his father served in Burma, had the fiendish cruelty of Aunt Rosa, but Augusta ('a woman', Munro's sister wrote, 'of ungovernable temper, of fierce likes and dislikes, imperious, a moral coward, possessing no brains worth speaking of, and a primitive disposition') was quite capable of making a child's life miserable. Munro was not himself beaten, Augusta preferred his younger brother for that exercise, but we can measure the hatred he felt for her in his story of the small boy Conradin who prayed so successfully for vengeance to his tame ferret. ' "Whoever will break it to the poor child? I couldn't for the life of me!", exclaimed a shrill voice, and while they debated the matter among themselves Conradin made himself another piece of toast.' Unhappiness wonderfully aids the memory, and the best stories of Munro are all of childhood, its humour and its anarchy as well as its cruelty and unhappiness.

For Munro reacted to those years rather differently from Kipling. He, too, developed a style like a machine in self-protection, but what sparks this machine gave off. He did not protect himself like Kipling with manliness, knowingness, imaginary adventures of soldiers and Empire Builders (though a certain nostalgia for such a life can be read into *The Unbearable Bassington*): he protected himself with epigrams as closely set as currants in an old-fashioned Dundee cake. As a young man trying to make a career with his father's help in the Burma Police, he wrote to his sister in 1893 complaining that she had made no effort to see *A Woman of No Importance*. Reginald and Clovis are children of Wilde: the epigrams, the absurdities fly unremittingly back and forth, they dazzle and delight, but we are aware of a harsher, less kindly mind behind them than Wilde's. Clovis and Reginald are not creatures of fairy tale, they belong nearer to the visible world than Ernest Moncrieff. While Ernest floats airily like a Rubens cupid among the over-blue clouds, Clovis and Reginald belong to the Park, the tea-parties of Kensington, and evenings at Covent Garden – they even sometimes date, like the suffragettes. They cannot quite disguise, in spite of the glint and the sparkle, the loneliness of the Barnstaple years – they are quick to hurt first, before they can be hurt, and the witty and devastating asides cut like Aunt Augusta's cane. How often these stories are stories of practical jokes. The victims with their weird names are sufficiently foolish to awaken no sympathy – they are the middle-aged, the people with power; it is right that they should suffer temporary humiliation because the world is always on their side in the long run. Munro, like a chivalrous highwayman, only robs the rich: behind all these stories is an exacting sense of justice. In this they are to be distinguished from Kipling's stories in the same genre – *The Village That Voted The Earth Was Flat* and others where the joke is carried too far. With Kipling revenge rather than justice seems to be the motive (Aunt Rosa had established herself in the mind of her victim and corrupted it).

Perhaps I have gone a little too far in emphasizing the cruelty of Munro's work, for there are times when it seems to remind us only of the sunniness of the Edwardian scene, young men in boaters, the box at the Opera, long lazy afternoons in the Park, tea out of the thinnest porcelain with cucumber sandwiches, the easy irresponsible prattle.

Never be a pioneer. It's the Early Christian that gets the fattest lion.

There's Marion Mulciber, who *would* think she could ride down a hill on a bicycle; on that occasion she went to a hospital, now she's gone into a Sisterhood – lost all she had you know, and gave the rest to Heaven.

Her frocks are built in Paris, but she wears them with a strong English accent.

It requires a great deal of moral courage to leave in a marked manner in the middle of the second Act when your carriage is not ordered till twelve.

Sad to think that this sunniness and this prattle could not go on for ever, but the worst and cruellest practical joke was left to the end. Munro's witty cynical hero, Comus Bassington, died incongruously of fever in a West African village, and in the early morning of 13 November 1916, from a shallow crater near Beaumont Hamel, Munro was heard to shout 'Put out that bloody cigarette.' They were the unpredictable last words of Clovis and Reginald.

1950

MAN MADE ANGRY

IT is a waste of time criticizing Léon Bloy as a novelist: he hadn't the creative instinct – he was busy all the time being created himself, created by his own angers and hatreds and humiliations. Those who meet him first in this grotesque and ill-made novel* need go no further than the dedication to Brigand-Kaire, Ocean Captain, to feel the angry quality of his mind. 'God keep you safe from fire and steel and contemporary literature and the malevolence of the evil dead.' He was a religious man but without humility, a social reformer without disinterestedness, he hated the world as a saint might have done, but only because of what it did to him and not because of what it did to others. He never made the mistake by worldly standards of treating his enemies with tolerance – and in that he resembled the members of the literary cliques he most despised. Unlike his contemporary Péguy, he would never have risked damnation himself in order to save another soul, and though again and again we are surprised by sentences in his work of nobility or penetration, they are contradicted by the savage and selfish core of his intelligence. 'I must stop now, my beloved,' he wrote to his fiancée, 'to go and suffer for another day'; he had prayed for suffering, and yet he never ceased to complain that he had been granted more of it than most men; it made him at the same time boastful and bitter.

He wrote in another letter:

I am forty-three years old, and I have published some literary works of considerable importance. Even my enemies can see that I am a great artist. Also, I have suffered much for the truth, whereas I could have prostituted my pen, like so many others, and lived on the fat of the land. I have had plenty of opportunities, but I have not chosen to betray justice and I have preferred misery, obscurity and indescribable agony. It is obvious that these things ought to merit respect.

It is obvious too that these things would have been better claimed for him by others. It is the self-pity of this attitude, the luxurious bitterness that prevents Bloy from being more than an interesting eccentric of the Catholic religion. He reminds us – in our own literature – a little of Patmore, and sometimes of Corvo. He is near Patmore in his brand of pious and uxorious sexuality which makes him describe the character of Clotilde, the heroine of his novel, as 'chaste as a Visitationist Sister's

* *The Woman Who Was Poor.*

103

rosary', and near Corvo in the furious zest with which he takes sides against his characters: 'She bellowed, if the comparison may be permitted, like a cow that has been forgotten in a railway truck.' Indeed the hatred he feels for the characters he has himself created (surely in itself a mark of limited imagination) leads him to pile on the violence to a comic extent – 'a scandalous roar of cachinnation ... like a bellowing of cattle from some goitred valley colonized by murderers'.

No, one reads this novel of Bloy not for his characters, who are painted only deformity-deep, not for his story, but for the occasional flashes of his poetic sense, for images like 'upright souls are reserved for rectilinear torments'; for passages with a nervous nightmare vision which reminds us of Rilke:

A little middleclass township, with a pretension to the possession of gardens, such as are to be found in the quarters colonized by eccentrics, where murderous landlords hold out the bait of horticulture to trap those condemned to die.

We read him with pleasure to just the extent that we share the hatred of life which prevented him from being a novelist or a mystic of the first order (he might have taken as his motto Gauguin's great phrase – 'Life being what it is, one dreams of revenge') and because of a certain indestructible honesty and self-knowledge which in the long run always enables him to turn his fury on himself, as when in one of his letters he recognizes the presence of 'that bitch literature' penetrating 'even the most *naïf* stirrings of my heart'.

1939

G. K. CHESTERTON

1

I T is possible to argue that the best biographies have been the result of conflict and not of surrender. One pictures the biographer, however cheerfully he may have undertaken his task, glowering with sullen determination and resentment at the huge mass of intractable material any life must represent.

A man lives for seventy years: to make sense of this is a worse labour than reducing to order the record of a mere four-years' war. To simplify is essential: so we see Boswell brushing aside in a few pages more than half his subject's lifetime, or Lytton Strachey choosing one characteristic sentence and holding it like a thread of cotton through the maze.

Mrs Ward, however, is too fond of her subject and too close to it to reduce her material into a portrait for strangers. Her biography* is often of great interest: it is a useful and sometimes explicit corrective to Mrs Cecil Chesterton's vulgar and inaccurate study of the Chesterton family; but it is too long for its material, too cumbered with affectionate trivialities. When we love we hoard a scrap of dialogue, a picture postcard, a foreign coin, but 'these foolish things' must be excluded from a biography which is written for strangers. Mrs Ward has amiably supposed her readers to be all friends of her subject: her book would have been better if she had realized – as Stevenson's biographers also failed to realize – that in the case of a great writer the years inevitably produce enemies. One wishes, too, that she had remembered more frequently her non-Catholic audience. Remarks such as 'the "holier bread" came perhaps to his [Chesterton's] mind from the fact that the average of Daily Communion is unusually high at Notre Dame' display the embarrassing parochialism which haunts so much Catholic writing in England.

Chesterton's bibliography consists of one hundred volumes, the 'quiet resolute practice of the liberty of a free mind', as Mrs Ward admirably expresses it. Out of this enormous output time will choose. Time often chooses oddly, or so it seems to us, though it is more reasonable to suppose that it is we ourselves who are erratic in our judgements. We are already proving our eccentricity in the case of Chesterton: a generation that appreciates Joyce finds for some reason Chesterton's equally fanatical play on words exhausting. Perhaps it is that he is still suspected of levity, and the generation now reaching middle age has been a peculiarly serious one. Mrs Ward should at least alter that opinion: she dwells at great length on

* *Gilbert Keith Chesterton*, by Maisie Ward.

Chesterton's political opinions. He cared passionately for individual liberty and for local patriotism, but the party which he largely inspired has an art-and-crafty air about it today. He was too good a man for politics: he never, one feels, penetrated far enough into the murky intricacies of political thought. To be a politician a man needs to be a psychologist, and Chesterton was no psychologist, as his novels prove. He saw things in absolute terms of good and evil, and his immense charity prevented him admitting the amount of ordinary shabby deception in human life. At their worst our politicians were fallen angels.

For the same reason that he failed as a political writer he succeeded as a religious one, for religion is simple, dogma is simple. Much of the difficulty of theology arises from the efforts of men who are not primarily writers to distinguish a quite simple idea with the utmost accuracy. He restated the original thought with the freshness, simplicity, and excitement of discovery. In fact, it was discovery: he unearthed the defined from beneath the definitions, and the reader wondered why the definitions had ever been thought necessary. *Orthodoxy*, *The Thing* and *The Everlasting Man* are among the great books of the age. Much else, of course, it will be disappointing if time does not preserve out of that weight of work: *The Ballad of the White Horse*, the satirical poems, such prose fantasies as *The Man Who Was Thursday* and *The Napoleon of Notting Hill*, the early critical books on Browning and Dickens; but in these three religious books, inspired by a cosmic optimism, the passionately held belief that 'it is good to be here', he contributed what another great religious writer closely akin to him in political ideas, and even in style, saw was most lacking in our age. Péguy put these lines on man into the mouth of his Creator:

> On peut lui demander beaucoup de coeur, beaucoup de
> charité, beaucoup de sacrifice.
> Il a beaucoup de foi et beaucoup de charité.
> Mais ce qu'on ne peut pas lui demander, sacredié, c'est
> un peu d'espérance.

1944

2

A man's enemies are not always deserved. He has not chosen his in-laws. The most obvious feature of Mrs Cecil Chesterton's book* is the steady undercurrent of rather petty dislike: dislike of her sister-in-law, who took G. K. Chesterton away from London, from the convivial Fleet Street nights, to the quiet of Beaconsfield. Mrs Chesterton paints – from her personal angle – the picture of an unhappy man cut off from the companionship of his peers, his mind dulled and his work ruined. But it is possible to doubt whether in fact those noisy pub-crawling Fleet Street friends, Crosland and the rest, were his peers, and whether he ever wrote better books than *The Everlasting Man*, *The Thing* and the *Autobiography* – all completed at Beaconsfield. Dislike may produce a good book, but not when it is expressed so covertly as here – the sneer between the lines, from the first page, when we read that Chesterton 'was a striking figure in those days' (the days, Mrs Chesterton means, before his marriage, but when was he not a striking figure?) to almost the last, when she complains that there was not enough to eat and drink after G. K.'s funeral. On p. 26 we are introduced to Frances Chesterton: 'She looked charming in blue or green, but she rarely wore those shades, and usually effected dim browns and greys'; on p. 70, 'a tragedy fell on the Blogg family which hit Frances cruelly hard. She had an engrossing affection for her people; they were indeed the altar of sacrifice, both for her and her husband'; on p. 72, 'She did not like food, except cakes, chocolate and similar flim-flams, and her appreciation of liquor stopped short at tea'; on p. 69, 'Frances disliked the Press as such, and really only cared for small journals and parish magazines, to which she contributed her quite charming verse.' So they go on, the little gibes against the dead woman who did not care for Fleet Street, harmless and silly enough if it were not for the culminating passage of staggering vulgarity which purports to describe – in the melodramatic and sensational terms of the novelettes the author used to write – Chesterton's wedding night. Chesterton is sup-

* *The Chestertons*, by Mrs Cecil Chesterton.

107

posed to have confided this to his brother, and one can only say that in that case he trusted someone who was not to be trusted. Mrs Cecil Chesterton may consider that this passage of her book disposes of Frances Chesterton once and for all; it disposes far more destructively of the author who is ready to print it.

It must be admitted that it is not only her enemies who suffer from Mrs Cecil Chesterton's tastelessness. Her own honeymoon is thus described:

> In honour of the occasion I wore a dress of green and gold – a favourite combination of Cecil's. I was all ready when he emerged from his bedroom, astonishingly well groomed. He looked at me from the door, and his face lit up, almost ecstatically, as though he had glimpsed some sort of vision. '. . . For mine is the kingdom, the power and the glory, sweetheart,' he said softly, and I wondered at the worship in his eyes.

One is reminded again and again of a song called 'Literary Widows' in one of Mr Farjeon's early revues which had a refrain something like this:

> Shovel the dust on the old man's coffin,
> Then pick up your pen and write.

One is left contrasting these badly-written, expansive, discretionless memoirs with the silence of Frances Chesterton, the wife of the greater brother, who will be remembered in her husband's verse long after these spiteful anecdotes are forgotten.

> With leaves below and leaves above,
> And groping under tree and tree,
> I found the home of my true love
> Who is a wandering home for me.

1941

WALTER DE LA MARE'S SHORT STORIES

EVERY creative writer worth our consideration, every writer who can be called in the wide eighteenth-century use of the term a poet, is a victim: a man given over to an obsession.

Was it not the obsessive fear of treachery which dictated not only James's plots but also his elaborate conceits (behind the barbed network of his style he could feel really secure himself), and was it not another obsession, a terrible pity for human beings, which drove Hardy to write novels that are like desperate acts of rebellion in a lost cause? What obsession then do we find in Mr de la Mare – one of the few living writers who can survive in this company?

The obsession is perhaps most easily detected in the symbols an author uses, and it would not be far from the truth – odd as it may seem on the face of it – to say that the dominant symbol in Mr de la Mare's short stories is the railway station or the railway journey: sometimes the small country railway station, all but deserted except by a couple of travellers chance met and an aged porter, at dusk or bathed in the quiet meditative light of a harvest afternoon: sometimes the waiting room of a great junction with its dying dusty fire and its garrulous occupant. But if not the dominant symbol at least this symbol – or rather group of symbols – occurs almost as frequently as do the ghosts of his poems – the ghosts that listen to the mother as she reads to her children, the lamenting ghosts that rattle the door like wind or moisten the glass like rain. Prose is a more intractable medium than verse. In prose we must be gently lured outside the boundaries of our experience. The symbol must in a favourable sense of the word be prosaic.

One hasty glance around him showed that he was the sole traveller to alight on the frosted timbers of the obscure little station. A faint rosiness in the west foretold the decline of the still wintry day. The firs that flanked the dreary passenger-shed of the platform stood burdened already with the blackness of coming night. (*The Tree*)

When murky winter dusk begins to settle over the railway station at Crewe its first-class waiting-room grows steadily more stagnant. Particularly if one is alone in it. The long grimed windows do little more than sift the failing light that slopes in on them from the glass roof outside and is too feeble to penetrate into the recesses beyond. And the grained massive black-leathered furniture becomes less and less inviting. It appears to have been made for a scene of extreme and diabolical violence that one may hope will never occur. One can hardly at any rate imagine it to have been designed by a really *good* man! (*Crewe*)

... at this instant the sad neutral winter landscape, already scarcely perceptible beneath a thin grey skin of frozen snow and a steadily descending veil of tiny flakes from the heavens above it, was suddenly blotted out. The train lights had come on, and the small cabin in which the two of them sat together had become a cage of radiance. How Lavinia hated too much light. (*A Froward Child*)

She was standing at the open window [of the train], looking out, but not as if she had ever entirely desisted from looking in – an oval face with highish cheekbones, and eyes and mouth from which a remote smile was now vanishing as softly and secretly as a bird enters and vanishes into its nest. (*A Nest of Singing Birds*)

The noonday express with a wildly soaring crescendo of lamentation came sweeping in sheer magnificence of onset round the curve, soared through the little green empty station – its windows a long broken faceless glint of sunlit glass – and that too vanished. Vanished! A swirl of dust and an unutterable stillness followed after it. The skin of a banana on the platform was the only proof that it had come and gone. Its shattering clamour had left for contrast an almost helpless sense of peace. 'Yes, yes!' we all seemed to be whispering – from the Cedar of Lebanon to the little hyssop in the wall – 'here we all are; and still, thank heaven, safe. *Safe!*' (*Ding Dong Bell*)

It is surely impossible not to feel ourselves in the presence of an obsession – the same obsession that haunts the melancholy subtle cadences of Mr de la Mare's poetry. Such trite phrases as 'ships that pass', 'travellers through life', 'journey's end' are the way in which for centuries the common man has taken a sidelong glance at the common fate (to be here, and there, and gone) – and looked away again. But every once in a while, perhaps only once or twice in a century, a man finds he cannot so easily dismiss with a regulation phrase what meets his eyes: the eyes linger: the obsession is born – in an Emily Brontë, a Beddoes, a James Thomson, in Mr de la Mare.

'*Mors*. And what does *Mors* mean?' enquired that oddly indolent voice in the quiet. 'Was it his name, or his initials, or is it a charm?' 'It means – well, sleep,' I said, 'Or nightmare, or dawn, or nothing, or – it might mean everything.' I confess, though, that to my ear it had the sound at that moment of an enormous breaker, bursting on the shore of some unspeakably remote island and we two marooned. (*Ding Dong Bell*)

One thing, it will be noticed in all these stories, *Mors* does not mean; it does not mean Hell – or Heaven. That obsession with death that fills Mr de la Mare's poetry with the whisper of ghosts, that expresses itself over and over again in the short story in the form of *revenants*, has never led him to accept – or even to speculate on – the Christian answer. Christianity when it figures in these stories is like a dead religion of which we see only the enormous stone memorials. Churches do occur – in *All Hallows, The Trumpet, Strangers and Pilgrims*, but they are empty haunted buildings.

At this moment of the afternoon the great church almost cheated one into the belief that it was possessed of a life of its own. It lay, as I say, couched in its natural hollow, basking under the dark dome of the heavens like some half-fossilized monster that might at any moment stir and awaken out of the swoon to which the wand of the enchanter had committed it. (*All Hallows*)

What an odd world, to those of us with traditional Christian beliefs, is this world of Mr de la Mare's: the world where the terrible Seaton's Aunt absorbs the living as a spider does and remains alive herself in the company of the dead. 'I don't look to flesh and blood for my company. When you've got to be my age, Mr Smithers (which God forbid), you'll find life a very different affair from what you seem to think it is now. You won't seek company then, I'll be bound. It's thrust on you'; the world of the recluse Mr Bloom, that spiritualist who had pressed on too far ignoring the advice that the poet would have given him.

> Bethink thee: every enticing league thou wend
> Beyond the mark where life its bound hath set
> Will lead thee at length where human pathways end
> And the dark enemy spreads his maddening net.

How wrong, however, it would be to give the impression that Mr de la Mare is just another, however accomplished, writer of ghost stories, yet what is it that divides this world of Mr Kempe and Mr Bloom and Seaton's Aunt, the dubious fellow-passenger with Lavinia in the train, the stranger in Crewe waiting room from the world of the late M. R. James's creation – told by the antiquary? M. R. James with admirable skill invented ghosts to make the flesh creep; astutely he used the image which would best convey horror; he was concerned with truth only in the sense that his stories must ring true – while they were being read. But Mr de la Mare is concerned, like his own Mr Bloom, to find out: his stories are true in the sense that the author believes – and conveys his belief – that this is the real world, but only in so far as he has yet discovered it. They are tentative. His use of prose reminds us frequently of a blind man trying to describe an object from the touch only – 'this thing is circular, or nearly circular, oddly dinted, too hard to be a ball: it might be, yes it might be, a human skull'. At any moment we expect a complete discovery, but the discovery is delayed. We, as well as the author, are this side of Lethe. When I was a child I used to be horrified by Carroll's poem *The Hunting of the Snark*. The danger that the snark might prove to be a boojum haunted me from the first page, and sometimes reading Mr de la Mare's stories, I fear that the author in his strange fumbling at the invisible curtain may suddenly come on the inescapable boojum truth, and just as quickly vanish away.

For how they continually seek their snark, his characters – in railway trains, in deserted churches, even in the bars of village inns. Listen to them speaking, and see how all the time they ignore what is at least a fact – that an answer to their question has been proposed: how intent they are to find an alternative, personal explanation: how they hover and debate and touch and withdraw, while the boojum waits.

There's Free Will, for example: there's Moral Responsibility; and such little riddles as where we all come from and where we are going to, why, we don't even know what we are – in ourselves, I mean. And how many of us have tried to find out? (*Mr Kempe*)

112

'The points as I take it, sir, are these. First,' he laid forefinger on forefinger, 'the number of those gone as compared with ourselves who are still waiting. Next, there being no warrant that what is seen – if seen at all – is wraiths of the departed, and not from elsewhere. The very waterspouts outside are said to be demonstrations of that belief. Third and last, another question: What purpose could call so small a sprinkling of them back – a few grains of sand out of the wilderness, unless, it may be, some festering grievance; or hunger for the living, sir; or duty left undone? In which case, mark you, which of any of us is safe?' (*Strangers and Pilgrims*)

'My dream was only – *after*; the state after death, as they call it ...' Mr Eaves leaned forward, and all but whispered the curious tidings into her ear. 'It's – it's just the same,' he said. (*The Three Friends*)

There is no space in an essay of this length to study the technique which does occasionally creak with other than the tread of visitants; nor to dwell on the minor defects – the occasional archness, whimsicality, playfulness, especially when Mr de la Mare is unwise enough to dress his narrator up in women's clothes (as he did in *The Memoirs of a Midget*). Perhaps we could surrender without too much regret one third of his short stories, but what a volume would be left. *The Almond Tree, Seaton's Aunt, The Three Friends, The Count's Courtship, Miss Duveen, A Recluse, Willows, Crewe, An Ideal Craftsman, A Froward Child, A Revenant, The Trumpet, Strangers and Pilgrims, Mr Kempe, Missing, Disillusioned, All Hallows* – here is one man's choice of what he could not, under any circumstances, spare.

In all these stories we have a prose unequalled in its richness since the death of James, or dare one, at this date, say Robert Louis Stevenson. Stevenson comes particularly to mind because he played with so wide a vocabulary – the colloquial and the literary phrase, incorporating even the dialect word and naturalizing it. So Mr de la Mare will play consciously with clichés (hemmed like James's between inverted commas), turning them under-side as it were to the reader, and showing what other meanings lie there hidden: he will suddenly enrich a colloquial conversation with a literary phrase out of the

common tongue, or enrich on the contrary a conscious literary description with a turn of country phrase – 'destiny was
spudding at his tap root'.

With these resources at his command no one can bring the
natural visible world more sharply to the eye: from the railway
carriage window we watch the landscape unfold, the sparkle
of frost and rain, the glare of summer sunlight, the lights in
evening windows; we are wooed and lulled sometimes to the
verge of sleep by the beauty of the prose, until suddenly without warning a sentence breaks in mid-breath and we look up
and see the terrified eyes of our fellow-passenger, appealing,
hungry, scared, as he watches what we cannot see – 'the sedi-
ment of an unspeakable possession', and a certain glibness
would seem to surround our easy conscious Christian answers
to all that wild speculation, if we could ever trust ourselves to
urge that cold comfort upon this stranger travelling 'our way'.

1948

THE SARATOGA TRUNK

THE long trainload * draws by our platform, passes us with
an inimical flash of female eyes, and proceeds on into how
many more dry and gritty years. It set out in 1915 with some
acclamation, carrying its embarrassing cargo – the stream of
consciousness – saluted by many prominent bystanders – Miss
West and Mrs Woolf, Mr Wells, Mr Beresford, Mr Swinnerton,
and Mr Hugh Walpole:

Miriam left the gaslit hall and went slowly upstairs. The March
twilight lay upon the landings, but the staircase was almost dark.
The top landing was quite dark and silent. There was no one
about. It would be quiet in her room. She could sit by the fire and
be quiet and think things over until Eve and Harriet came back
with the parcels. She would have time to think about the journey
and decide what she was going to say to the Fraulein. Her new
Saratoga trunk stood solid and gleaming in the firelight.

Who could have foreseen in those first ordinary phrases
* *Pilgrimage*, by Dorothy M. Richardson.

this gigantic work which has now reached its two thousandth page, without any indication of a close? The Saratoga trunk becomes progressively more worn and labelled. There is no reason why the pilgrimage should ever end, except with the author's life, for she is attempting to represent the whole effect of every experience – friendship, politics, tea-parties, books, weather, what you will – on a woman's sensibility.

I am uncertain of my dates, but I should imagine Miss Richardson in her ponderous unwitty way has had an immense influence on such writers as Mrs Woolf and Miss Stein, and through them on their disciples. Her novel, therefore, has something in common with Bowles's Sonnets. She herself became influenced about halfway through these four volumes (comprising twelve novels or instalments) by the later novels of Henry James – the result, though it increased the obscurity of her sensibility, was to the good, for she began to shed the adjectives which in the first volume disguise any muscles her prose may possess – 'large soft fresh pink full-blown roses' is only one phrase in a paragraph containing 41 adjectives qualifying 15 nouns. Or was it simply that Miriam became a little older, unhappier, less lyrical? In the monstrous subjectivity of this novel the author is absorbed into her character. There is no longer a Miss Richardson: only Miriam – Miriam off to teach English in a German School, off again to be a teacher in North London, a governess in the country, a dental secretary in Wimpole Street: a flotsam of female friendships piling up, descriptions of clothes, lodgings, encounters at the Fabian Society: Miriam taking to reviewing, among the first bicyclists, Miriam enlightened about socialism and women's rights, reading Zola from Mudie's (surely this is inaccurate) and later Ibsen, losing her virginity tardily and ineffectually on page 218 of volume 4. When the book pauses we have not yet reached the Great War.

There are passages of admirable description, characters do sometimes emerge clearly from the stream of consciousness – the Russian Jew, Mr Shatov, waiting at the end of the street with a rose, patronizing the British Museum, an embarrassing and pathetic companion, and the ex-nurse Eleanor

115

Dear, the lower middle-class consumptive clawing her unscrupulous petty acquisitive way through other people's lives. There are passages, too, where Miriam's thought, in its Jacobean dress, takes on her master's wide impressionist poetry among the dental surroundings, as in this description of the frightened peer who has cancelled all his appointments:

Through his staccato incoherencies – as he stood shamed and suppliant, and sociable down to the very movement of his eyelashes, and looking so much as if he had come straight from a racecourse that her mind's eye saw the diagonal from shoulder to hip of the strap of his binoculars and upon his head the grey topper that would complete his dress, and the gay rose in his buttonhole – she saw his pleasant life, saw its coming weeks, the best and brightest of the spring season, broken up by appointments to sit every few days for an indefinite time enduring discomfort and sometimes acute pain, and facing the intimate reminder that the body doesn't last, facing and feeling the certainty of death.

But the final effect, I fear, is one of weariness (that may be a tribute to Miss Richardson's integrity), the weariness of the best years of life shared with an earnest, rather sentimental, and complacent woman. For one of the drawbacks of Miss Richardson's unironic, undetached method is that the compliments paid so frequently to the wit or intellect of Miriam seem addressed to the author herself. (We are reminded of those American women who remark to strangers, 'They simply worshipped me.') And as for the method – it must have seemed in 1915 a revivifying change from the tyranny of the 'plot'. But time has taken its revenge: after twenty years of subjectivity, we are turning back with relief to the old dictatorship, to the detached and objective treatment, while this novel, ignoring all signals, just ploughs on and on, the Saratoga trunk, labelled this time for Switzerland, for Austria, shaking on the rack, and Miriam still sensitively on the alert, reading far too much significance into a cup of coffee, a flower in a vase, a fog, or a sunset.

1938

ONE opens the new novel by Mr Conrad Aiken * with all the excitement that comes from complete confidence in the author. One is satisfied beforehand of the impregnable front he will offer to the details of criticism, the contemporary nature of his thought, the subtlety and exactitude of his style, his technical ability which never allows a value to escape. One can surrender at once to appreciation, to the deep interest of his psychological exploration. One of the characters in *Great Circle* described the map of a brain as being like an imaginary map of Mars. 'Full of Arabia Desertas. Canals, seas, mountains, glaciers, extinct volcanoes, or ulcers ... And all that strange congregation of scars, that record of wounds and fissures, is what speaks and acts.' That is the region in which Mr Aiken moves.

King Coffin is a study in madness. The Arabia Deserta of Jasper Ammen's brain lies much further from the ordinary trade routes than the brain Mr Aiken mapped in *Great Circle* of the damned-to-be-cuckolded dweller in polite Cambridge, Mass., further, I think, than many previous novelists have gone. Jasper Ammen is an egocentric; one sees him always from inside his brain, trying to get free in a crazy superman pride from life, from the little circle of theoretical anarchists he has supported with his money, from the woman who loves him, from every friend in turn, by deliberate acts of rudeness, by mystifications, asserting his superiority by small social immoralities such as reading other people's letters and diaries. The last stage of that assertion, of course, must be to destroy life. But the crime must be a pure one; if he murders a friend, too many impure motives, of irritation, boredom, jealousy, may play their part. So Ammen chooses a complete stranger, a little man he happens to notice in the subway.

To satisfy his sense of power Ammen sets himself to learn all the details of the life he proposes to end; he speaks to Jones on the telephone, sends him theatre tickets anonymously

* *King Coffin.*

the better to watch him, shadows him to his office and his home in its mean villa-ed street, he even makes his way into the cellar of his house when all above are occupied with childbirth. All interests but Jones, the chosen stranger, and his own sense of power fade out of Ammen's brain: ordinary life reaches him only in snatches of overheard conversation, married people talking on stairways, girls in the street, two students starting a car.

Ammen's madness is not of merely specialized interest, for it is a form of self-consciousness, not of derangement. He has carried consciousness of himself, the mapping of his own brain, to a point that excludes the world, but it is an accurate, not a crazily drawn map. The pathos of his situation is that so complete a self-consciousness must inevitably recognize its own defeat. The moment of cutting himself loose, the moment when he made his decision to destroy, is the only real moment of detachment, of complete superiority:

It seemed very remote, a long time ago, very remote and oddly bright and innocent: it had been spring; and although it was *still* spring, somehow now it seemed as if he was looking back to it from another season, another year. The plan had then been formless, of course, and this had given it the charm and vagueness of all new things, new undertakings – the stranger had not yet been discovered or his strangeness identified, the whole problem still remained metaphysical – a mere formula – and it was now possible to recognize that at that stage there had been an unmistakable sense of *freedom* which had, at once, with the actual selection of Jones disappeared.

The values of this story could not have been conveyed through any other mind than Ammen's, but Mr Aiken, of course, by keeping his story inside the egocentric consciousness, has had to sacrifice all the usual enticements of the novel in the way of vivid objective characterization. I wish I could convey with what poetry and subtle drama, with what pathos in the climax when hopeless defeated Ammen watches Jones put away his still-born child in the hideous marble necropolis, Mr Aiken has compensated the reader. Mr Herbert Read once wrote of the psychological complexity of James's world that 'it was obviously the real world, the only world worth describing, once your course is set that way. Henry James went ahead, fearlessly, irretrievably, into regions where few are found who care to follow him.' Mr Aiken is one of the few – which is only another way of saying that he is perhaps the most exciting, the most finally satisfying of living novelists.

1935

THE POKER-FACE

ONE has seen that face over a hundred bar counters – the lick of hair over the broad white brow, the heavy moustache with pointed ends, the firm, good-humoured eyes, the man who is a cause of conviviality in other men but knows exactly when the fun should cease. He is wearing a dark suit (the jacket has four buttons) and well-polished boots. Could Sherlock Holmes have deduced from this magnificently open appearance anything at all resembling the bizarre truth?

Mr Hesketh Pearson tells this far from ordinary story * with his admirable accustomed forthrightness: Mr Pearson as a biographer has some of the qualities of Dr Johnson – a plainness, an honesty, a sense of ordinary life going on all the time. A dull biographer would never have got behind that poker-face; an excited biographer would have made us disbelieve the story, which wanders from whaling in the Arctic to fever on the West Coast of Africa, a practice in Portsea to ghost-hunting in Sussex. But from Mr Pearson we are able to accept it. Conan Doyle has too often been compared with Dr Watson: in this biography it is Mr Pearson who plays Watson to the odd enigmatic product of a Jesuit education, the Sherlock-hearted Doyle.

It is an exciting story admirably told, and it is one of Mr Pearson's virtues that he drives us to champion the subject against his biographer (Johnson has the same effect on the reader). For example, this reviewer would like to put in a

---

* *Conan Doyle: His Life and Art*, by Hesketh Pearson.

word which Mr Pearson omits for the poetic quality in Doyle, the quality which gives life to his work far more surely than does his wit. Think of the sense of horror which hangs over the laurelled drive of Upper Norwood and behind the curtains of Lower Camberwell: the dead body of Bartholomew Sholto swinging to and fro in Pondicherri Lodge, the 'bristle of red hair', 'the ghastly inscrutable smile', and in contrast Watson and Miss Mortsan hand in hand like children among the strange rubbish heaps: he made Plumstead Marshes and the Barking Level as vivid and unfamiliar as a lesser writer would have made the mangrove swamps of the West Coast which he had also known and of which he did not bother to write.

And, unlike most great writers, he remained so honest and pleasant a man. The child who wrote with careful necessary economy to his mother from Stonyhurst: 'I have been to the Taylor, and I showed him your letter, explaining to him that you wanted something that would wear well and at the same time look well. He told me that the blue cloth he had was meant especially for Coats, but that none of it would suit well as Fresson. He showed me a dark sort of cloth which he said would suit a coat better than any other cloth he has and would wear well as trousers. On his recommendation I took this cloth. I think you will like it; it does not show dirt and looks very well; it is a sort of black and white very dark cloth'; this child had obviously the same character as the middle-aged man who wrote chivalrously and violently against Shaw in defence of the *Titanic* officers (he was probably wrong, but, as Mr Pearson nearly says, most of us would have preferred to be wrong with Doyle than right with Shaw).

It isn't easy for an author to remain a pleasant human being: both success and failure are usually of a crippling kind. There are so many opportunities for histrionics, hysterics, waywardness, self-importance; within very wide limits a writer can do what he likes and go where he likes, and a human being has seldom stood up so well to such a test of freedom as Doyle did. The eccentric figure of his partner, Dr Budd, may stride like a giant through the early pages of his biography, but in memory he dwindles into the far distance, and in the foreground we see the large, sturdy, working shoulders, a face so commonplace that it has the effect of a time-worn sculpture representing some abstract quality like Kindness or Patience, but never, one would mistakenly have said, Imagination or Poetry.

1943

FORD MADOX FORD

1

THE death of Ford Madox Ford was like the obscure death of a veteran – an impossibly Napoleonic veteran, say, whose immense memory spanned the period from Jena to Sedan: he belonged to the heroic age of English fiction and outlived it – yet he was only sixty-six. In one of his many volumes of reminiscence – those magnificent books where in an atmosphere of casual talk outrageous story jostles outrageous story – he quoted Mr Wells as saying some years ago that in the southern counties a number of foreigners were conspiring against the form of the English novel. There was James at Lamb House, Crane at Brede Manor, Conrad at The Pent, and he might have added his own name, Hueffer at Aldington, for he was a quarter German (and just before the first world war made an odd extravagant effort to naturalize himself as a citizen of his grandfather's country). The conspiracy, of course, failed: the big loose middlebrow novel goes on its happy way unconscious of James's 'point of view': Conrad is regarded again as the writer of romantic sea stories and purple passages: nobody reads Crane, and Ford – well, an anonymous writer in the *Times Literary Supplement* remarked in an obituary notice that his novels began to date twenty years ago. Conservatism among English critics is extraordinarily tenacious, and they hasten, on a man's death, to wipe out any disturbance he has caused.

The son of Francis Hueffer, the musical critic of *The Times*, and grandson, on his mother's side, of Ford Madox Brown, 'Fordie' Hueffer emerges into history at the age of three offering a chair to Turgenev, and again, a little later, dressed in a suit of yellow velveteen with gold buttons, wearing one red stocking and one green one, and with long golden hair, having his chair stolen from him at a concert by the Abbé Liszt. I say emerges into history, but it is never possible to say where history ends and the hilarious imagination begins. He was always an atmospheric writer, whether he was describing the confused Armistice night when Tietjens found himself back with his mistress, Valentine Wannop, among a horde of grotesque and inexplicable strangers, or just recounting a literary anecdote of dubious origin – the drunk writer who thought himself a Bengal tiger trying to tear out the throat of the blind poet Marston, or Henry James getting hopelessly entangled in the long lead of his dachshund Maximilian. Nobody ever wrote more about himself than Ford, but the figure he presented was just as dubious as his anecdotes – the figure of a Tory country gentleman who liked to grow his own food and had sturdy independent views on politics: it all seems a long way from the yellow velveteen. He even, at the end of his life, a little plump and a little pink, looked the part – and all the while he had been turning out the immense number of books which stand to his name: memoirs, criticism, poetry, sociology, novels. And in between, if one can so put it, he found time to be the best literary editor England has ever had: what Masefield, Hudson, Conrad, even Hardy owed to the *English Review* is well known, and after the war in *the Transatlantic Review* he bridged the great gap, publishing the early Hemingway, Cocteau, Stein, Pound, the music of Antheil, and the drawings of Braque.

He had the advantage – or the disadvantage – of being brought up in pre-Raphaelite circles, and although he made a tentative effort to break away into the Indian Civil Service, he was pushed steadily by his father towards art – any kind of art was better than any kind of profession. He published his first book at the age of sixteen, and his first novel, *The Shifting of the Fire*, in 1892, when he was only nineteen – three years before Conrad had published anything and only two years after the serial appearance of *The Tragic Muse*, long before

James had matured his method and his style. It wasn't, of course, a good book, but neither was it an 'arty' book – there was nothing of the 'nineties about it except its elegant period binding, and it already bore the unmistakable Hueffer stamp – the outrageous fancy, the pessimistic high spirits, and an abominable hero called Kasker-Ryves. Human nature in his books was usually phosphorescent – varying from the daemonic malice of Sylvia Tietjens to the painstaking, rather hopeless will-to-be-good of Captain Ashburnham, 'the good soldier'. The little virtue that existed only attracted evil. But to Mr Ford, a Catholic in theory though not for long in practice, this was neither surprising nor depressing: it was just what one expected.

The long roll of novels ended with *Vive le Roy* in 1937. A few deserve to be forgotten, but I doubt whether the accusation of dating can be brought against even such minor work as *Mr Apollo*, *The Marsden Case*, *When the Wicked Man*: there were the historical novels, too, with their enormous vigour and authenticity – *The Fifth Queen* and its sequels: but the novels which stand as high as any fiction written since the death of James are *The Good Soldier* with its magnificent claim in the first line, 'This is the saddest story I have ever heard' – the study of an averagely good man of a conventional class driven, divided and destroyed by unconventional passion – and the Tietjens series, that appalling examination of how private malice goes on during public disaster – no escape even in the trenches from the secret gossip and the lawyers' papers. It is dangerous in this country to talk about technique or a long essay could be written on his method in these later books, the method Conrad followed more stiffly and less skilfully, having learnt it perhaps from Ford when they collaborated on *Romance*: James's point of view was carried a step further, so that a book took place not only from the point of view but in the brain of a character and events were remembered not in chronological order, but as free association brought them to mind.

When Ford died he had passed through a period of neglect and was re-emerging. His latest books were not his best, but they were hailed as if they were. The first war had ruined him. He had volunteered, though he was over military age and was fighting a country he loved; his health was broken, and he came back to a new literary world which had carefully eliminated him. For some of his later work he could not even find a publisher in England. No wonder he preferred to live abroad – in Provence or New York. But I don't suppose failure disturbed him much: he had never really believed in human happiness, his middle life had been made miserable by passion, and he had come through – with his humour intact, his stock of unreliable anecdotes, the kind of enemies a man ought to have, and a half-belief in a posterity which would care for good writing.

2

How seldom a novelist chooses the material nearest to his hand; it is almost as if he were driven to earn experience the hard way. Ford, whom we might have expected to become a novelist of artistic bohemia, a kind of English Murger, did indeed employ the material of Fitzroy Square incomparably well in his volumes of reminiscence – and some people might regard those as his finest novels, for he brought to his drama-tizations of people he had known the same astonishing knack he showed with his historical figures. Most writers dealing with real people find their invention confined, but that was not so with Ford. 'When it has seemed expedient to me I have altered episodes that I have witnessed, but I have been careful never to distort the character of the episode. *The accuracies I deal in are the accuracies of my impressions.* If you want factual accuracies you must go to ... but no, no, don't go to anyone, stay with me.' (The italics are mine: it is a phrase worth bear-ing in mind in reading all his works.)

In fact as a novelist Ford began to move further and further from bohemia for his material. His first period as an historical novelist, which he began by collaborating with Conrad in that underrated novel *Romance*, virtually closed with his Tudor trilogy. There were to be two or three more historical novels, until in *Ladies Whose Bright Eyes* ... he came half out into the contemporary world and began to find his true subject. It could even be argued that in *The Fifth Queen* he was nearest as a novelist to Fitzroy Square. There is the sense of saturation: something is always happening on the stairs, in the passages the servants come and go on half explained errands, and the great King may at any moment erupt upon the scene, half kindly, half malevolent, rather as we feel the presence of Madox Brown in the gas-lit interstices of No. 37.

Most historical novelists use real characters only for purposes of local colour – Lord Nelson passes up a Portsmouth street or Doctor Johnson enters ponderously to close a chapter, but in *The Fifth Queen* we have virtually no fictional characters – the King, Thomas Cromwell, Catherine Howard, they are the principals; we are nearer to the historical plays of Shakespeare than to the fictions of such historical writers as Miss Irwin or Miss Heyer.

'The accuracies I deal in are the accuracies of my impressions.' In *The Fifth Queen* Ford tries out the impressionist method which he was later to employ with triumphant ease in the great confused armistice-day scene of *A Man Could Stand Up*. The whole story of the struggle between Catherine and Cromwell for the King seems told in shadows – shadows which flicker with the flames of a log-fire, diminished suddenly as a torch recedes, stand calm awhile in the candlelight of a chapel: a cresset flares and all the shadows leap together. Has a novel ever before been lit as carefully as a stage production? Nicolas Udal's lies, which play so important a part in the first volume, take their substance from the lighting: they are monstrously elongated or suddenly shrivel: one can believe anything by torchlight. (The power of a lie – that too was a subject he was to pursue through all his later books: the lies of Sylvia Tietjens which ruined her husband's army-career and the monstrous lie of 'poor Florence' in *The Good Soldier* which brought death to three people and madness to a fourth.)

If *The Fifth Queen* is a magnificent bravura piece – and you could say that it was a better painting than ever came out of Fitzroy Square with all the mingled talents there of Madox Brown and Morris, Rossetti and Burne-Jones – in *The Good*

Soldier Ford triumphantly found his true subject and oddly enough, for a child of the Pre-Raphaelites, his subject was the English 'gentleman', the 'black and merciless things' which lie behind that façade.

Edward Ashburnham was the cleanest looking sort of chap; – an excellent magistrate, a first rate soldier, one of the best landlords, so they said, in Hampshire, England. To the poor and to hopeless drunkards, as I myself have witnessed, he was like a painstaking guardian. And he never told a story that couldn't have gone into the columns of the *Field* more than once or twice in all the nine years of my knowing him. He didn't even like hearing them; he would fidget and get up and go out to buy a cigar or something of that sort. You would have said he was just exactly the sort of chap that you could have trusted your wife with. And I trusted mine and it was madness.

The Good Soldier, which Ford had wished to call *The Saddest Story*, concerns the ravages wrought by a passionate man who had all the virtues but continence. The narrator is the betrayed husband, and it is through his eyes alone that we watch the complications and involvements left by Ashburnham's blind urge towards satisfaction. Technically the story is undoubtedly Ford's masterpiece. The time-shifts are valuable not merely for purposes of suspense – they lend veracity to the appalling events. This is just how memory works, and we become involved with the narrator's memory as though it were our own. Ford's apprenticeship with Conrad had borne its fruit, but he improved on the Master.

I have, I am aware, told this story in a very rambling way so that it may be difficult for anyone to find their path through what may be a sort of maze. I cannot help it. I have stuck to my idea of being in a country cottage with a silent listener, hearing between the gusts of the wind and amidst the noises of the distant sea, the story as it comes. And when one discusses an affair – a long sad affair – one goes back, one goes forward. One remembers points that one has forgotten and one explains them all the more minutely since one recognizes that one has forgotten to mention them in their proper places and that one may have given, by omitting them, a false impression. I console myself with thinking that this is a real story and that, after all, real stories are probably told best in the way a person telling a story would tell them. They will then seem most real.

A short enough book it is to contain two suicides, two ruined lives, a death, and a girl driven insane: it may seem odd to find the keynote of the book is restraint, a restraint which is given it by the gentle character of the narrator ('I am only an ageing American with very little knowledge of life') who never loses his love and compassion for the characters concerned. 'Here were two noble people – for I am convinced that both Edward and Leonara had noble natures – here, then, were two noble natures, drifting down life, like fireships afloat on a lagoon and causing miseries, heartaches, agony of the mind and death. And they themselves steadily deteriorated. And why? For what purpose? To point what lesson? It is all a darkness.' He condemns no one; in extremity he doesn't even condemn human nature, and I find one of the most moving understatements in literature his summing up of Leonora's attitude to her husband's temporary infatuation for the immature young woman, Maisie Maidan: 'I think she would really have welcomed it if he could have come across the love of his life. It would have given her a rest.'

I don't know how many times in nearly forty years I have come back to this novel of Ford's, every time to discover a new aspect to admire, but I think the impression which will be left strongly on the reader is the sense of Ford's involvement. A novelist is not a vegetable absorbing nourishment mechanically from soil and air: material is not easily or painlessly gained, and one cannot help wondering what agonies of frustration and error lay behind *The Saddest Story*.

3

It seems likely that, when time has ceased its dreary work of erosion, Ford Madox Ford will be remembered as the author of three great novels, a little scarred, stained here and there and chipped perhaps, but how massive and resistant compared

127

with most of the work of his successors: *The Fifth Queen, The Good Soldier*, and *Parade's End*, the title Ford himself gave to what is often known, after the name of the principal character, as the Tietjens tetralogy – the terrifying story of a good man tortured, pursued, driven into revolt, and ruined as far as the world is concerned by the clever devices of a jealous and lying wife.

Ford always wanted to see his novel printed as one book, but he wanted to see it as a trilogy, consisting only of *Some Do Not ...*, *No More Parades* and *A Man Could Stand Up* – the final book, *Last Post*, was an after-thought which he had not intended to write and which later he regretted having written. In a letter dealing with the possibility of an omnibus edition, which is quoted by Mr John A. Meixner in his critical study, *Ford Madox Ford's Novels*, Ford wrote: 'I strongly wish to omit *Last Post* from the edition. I do not like the book and have never liked it and always intended to end up with *A Man Could Stand Up.*'

I think it could be argued that *Last Post* was more than a mistake – it was a disaster, a disaster which has delayed a full critical appreciation of *Parade's End*. The sentimentality which sometimes lurks in the shadow of Christopher Tietjens, the last Tory (Ford sometimes seems to be writing about 'the last English gentleman'), emerged there unashamed. Everything was cleared up – all the valuable ambiguities concerning the parenthood of Christopher's son (the suggestion chosen by his wife Sylvia to torture him), his father's possible suicide, his father's possible relationship to Valentine, Christopher's mistress – all, all are brought into the idyllic sunshine of Christopher's successful escape into the life of a Kentish smallholder. Even Sylvia – surely the most possessed evil character in the modern novel – groped in *Last Post* towards goodness, granted Christopher his divorce, took back – however grudgingly – her lies. It is as though Lady Macbeth dropped her dagger beside the sleeping Duncan.

This is a better book, a thousand times, when it ends in the confusion of Armistice Night 1918 – the two lovers united, it is true, but with no absolute certainties about the past so deformed by Sylvia's lies (if they are lies) or about the future with that witch-wife still awaiting them there. Those of us who, even though we were children, remember Armistice Day (so different from that sober, reflective V.E. day of 1945) remember it as a day out of time – an explosion without a future. It was the Armistice only which counted, it was the Armistice too for the poor tortured lovers: perhaps there would never be a peace ...

They were prancing. The whole world round them was yelling and prancing round. They were the centre of unending roaring circles. The man with the eye-glass had stuck a half-crown in his other eye. He was well-meaning. A brother. She had a brother with the V.C. All in the family.

Tietjens was stretching out his two hands from the waist. It was incomprehensible. His right hand was behind her back, his left in her right hand. She was frightened. She was amazed. Did you ever! He was swaying slowly. The elephant! They were dancing! Aranjuez was hanging on to the tall woman like a kid on a telegraph pole. The officer who had said he had picked up a little bit of fluff. ... well, he had! He had run out and fetched it. It wore white cotton gloves and a flowered hat. It said: 'Ow! Now!' ... There was a fellow with a most beautiful voice. He led: better than a gramophone. Better ...

Les petites marionettes, font! font! font ...

On an elephant. A dear, meal-sack elephant. She was setting out on ...

This is the end of *A Man Could Stand Up,* and this – not the carefully arranged happy *finale* of *Last Post* – was the true conclusion of a story of unhappy marriage, of Sylvia's tortuous intrigues which had begun, before the so-called Great War had closed in, in a little resort among the pine woods of Lobscheid. 'They were sitting playing bridge in the large, shadowy dining-hall of the hotel: Mrs Satterthwaite, Father Consett, Mr Bayliss. A young blond sub-lieutenant of great obsequiousness who was there for a last chance for his right lung and his career, and the bearded Kur-doctor cut in.' Sylvia had not yet entered 'like a picture of Our Lady by Fra Angelico', but I have always been reminded of another wicked setting, in a poem written at about the same time:

In depraved May, dogwood and chestnut,
    flowering judas,
To be eaten, to be divided, to be drunk
Among whispers; by Mr Silvero
With caressing hands, at Limoges
Who walked all night in the next room;

By Hakagawa, bowing among the Titians;
By Madame de Tornquist, in the dark room
Shifting the candles; Fraulein von Kulp
Who turned in the hall, one hand on the door.

Parade's End is not a war-book in the ordinary sense of the term; true, it was produced from the experiences of 1914–18, but while a novel like *All Quiet on the Western Front* confined its horror to the physical, to the terrors of the trenches, so that it is even possible to think of such physical terrors as an escape for some from the burden of thought and mental pain, Ford turned the screw. Here there was no escape from the private life. Sylvia pursued her husband even to the head-quarters of his regiment. Unlikely? Read in *The Memoirs of Lord Chandos* how, just out of the heavily shelled Ginchy valley, he and his friend were greeted by the disquieting tele-grams from home. I remember a week-end reunion with wives and mistresses in the dug-outs of Dien-Bien-Phu, as the troops waited day by day for the assault. The private life cannot be escaped and death does not come when it is most required.

1939 and 1962

FREDERICK ROLFE: EDWARDIAN INFERNO

T H E obscurity and what we curiously believe to be the crudity and violence of the distant past make a suitable background to the Soul. Temptation, one feels, is seldom today so heroically resisted or so devastatingly succumbed to as in the days of Dante or of Milton; Satan, as well as sanctity, demands an apron stage. It is, therefore, with a shock of startled incredulity that we become aware on occasion even today of eternal issues, of the struggle between good and evil, between vice that really demands to be called satanic and virtue of a kind which can only be called heavenly.

How much less are we prepared for it in the Edwardian age, in the age of bicycles and German bands and gold chamber ware, of Norfolk jackets and deerstalker caps. How distressingly bizarre seems the whole angelic conflict which centred around Frederick Rolfe, self-styled Baron Corvo, the spoilt priest, who was expelled from the Scots College at Rome, the waster who lived on a multitude of generous friends, the writer of genius, author of *Hadrian the Seventh* and *Don Tarquinio* and *Chronicles of the House of Borgia*. When Rolfe's fictional self prayed in his Hampstead lodging:

God, if ever You loved me, hear me, hear me. *De Profundis ad Te, ad Te clamavi*. Don't I want to be good and clean and happy? What desire have I cherished since my boyhood save to serve in the number of Your mystics? What but that have I asked of You Who made me? Not a chance do You give me – ever – ever –

it is disquieting to remember how in the outside world Mr Wells was writing *Love on Wheels*, the Empire builders after tiffin at the club were reading 'The Song of the Banjo', and up the crowded stairway of Grosvenor House Henry James was bearing his massive brow; disquieting too to believe that Miss Marie Corelli was only palely limping after truth when she brought the devil to London. For if ever there was a case of demonic possession it was Rolfe's: the hopeless piety, the screams of malevolence, the sense of despair which to a man of his faith was the sin against the Holy Ghost. 'All men are too vile for words to tell.'

The greatest saints have been men with more than a normal capacity for evil, and the most vicious men have sometimes narrowly evaded sanctity. Frederick Rolfe in his novel *Hadrian the Seventh* expressed a sincere, if sinister, devotion to the Church that had very wisely rejected him; all the good of which he was capable went into that book, as all the evil went into the strange series of letters which Mr Symons has described for the first time,* written at the end of his life, when he was starving in Venice, to a rich acquaintance.

He had become a habitual corrupter of youth, a seducer of innocence, and he asked his wealthy accomplice for money, first that he might use it as a temptation, to buy bait for the boys whom he misled, and secondly, so that he might efficiently act as pander when his friend revisted Venice. Neither scruple nor remorse was expressed or implied in these long accounts of his sexual exploits or enjoyments, which were so definite in their descriptions that he was forced, in sending them by post, so to fold them that only blank paper showed through the thin foreign envelopes.

These were the astonishing bounds of Corvo: the starving pander on the Lido and the man of whom Mr Vincent O'Sullivan wrote to his biographer: 'He was born for the Church: that was his main interest.' Between these bounds, between the Paradise and the Inferno, lay the weary purgatorial years through which Mr Symons has been the first to track him with any closeness. Mr Symons's method, unchronological, following the story as he discovered it from witness to witness, lends Rolfe's vacillating footprints a painful drama. Continually, with the stamp of an obstinate courage, they turn back towards Paradise: from the rim of the Inferno they turn and go back: but on the threshold of Paradise they turn again because of the devilish pride which would not accept even Heaven, except on his own terms; this way and that, like the steps of a man pacing a room in agony of mind. It is odd to realize that all the time common-or-garden life is going on within hailing distance, publishers are making harsh bargains, readers are reporting adversely on his work, friends are forming hopeless plans of literary collaboration. Mr Grant Richards and Monsignor Benson and Mr Pirie-Gordon and the partners of Chatto and Windus beckon and speak like figures on the other side of a distorting glass pane. They have quite a different reality, much thinner reality, they are not concerned with eternal damnation. And their memories of Rolfe are puzzled, a little amused, a little exasperated, as if they cannot understand the eccentricity

* *The Quest for Corvo*, by A. J. A. Symons.

132

of a man who chooses to go about sheathed in flame in the heyday of the Entente Cordiale, of Sir Ernest Cassel, and Lily Langtry.

Mr O'Sullivan wrote of Rolfe to Mr Symons as a man 'who had only the vaguest sense of realities', but the phrase seems a little inaccurate. His realities were less material than spiritual. It would be easy to emphasize his shady financial transactions, his pose as the Kaiser's god-son, his complete inability to earn a living. It is terrible to think what a figure of cruel fun a less imaginative writer than Mr Symons might have made of Rolfe, turned out of an Aberdeen boarding house in his pyjamas, painting pictures with the help of magic-lantern slides, forced to find employment as a gondolier, begging from strangers, addressing to the Pope a long indictment of living Catholics. But against this material reality Mr Symons with admirable justice sets another: the reality of *Hadrian the Seventh*, a novel of genius, which stands in relation to the other novels of its day, much as *The Hound of Heaven* stands in relation to the verse. Rolfe's vice was spiritual more than it was carnal: it might be said that he was a pander and a swindler, because he cared for nothing but his faith. He would be a priest or nothing, so nothing it had to be and he was not ashamed to live on his friends; if he could not have Heaven, he would have Hell, and the last footprints seem to point unmistakably towards the Inferno.

1934

FREDERICK ROLFE: FROM THE DEVIL'S SIDE

'HE was his own worst enemy': the little trite memorial phrase which, in the case of so many English exiles, disposes discreetly and with a tasteful agnosticism of the long purgatories in foreign *pensions*, the counted coppers, the keeping up of appearances, sounds more than usually unconvincing when applied to Frederick Rolfe. It is the measure of the man's vividness that his life always seems to move on a religious plane: his violent hatreds, his extreme ingratitude, even his appearance as he described it himself, 'offensive, disdainful, slightly sardonic, utterly unapproachable', have about them the air of demonic possession. *The Desire and Pursuit of the Whole*, the long autobiographical novel of the last dreadful years in Venice, the manuscript of which was rediscovered by Mr A. J. A. Symons, has the quality of a medieval mystery play, but with this difference, that the play is written from the devil's side. The many excellent men and women, who did their best, sometimes an unimaginative best, to help Rolfe, here caper like demons beside the long Venetian water-fronts: the Rev. Bobugo Bonsen (known on the angels' side as Monsignor Benson), Harry Peary-Buthlaw, Professor Macpawkins, Lady Pash. It is instructive and entertaining to see the great and the good for once from the devil's point of view.

And the devil has been fair. Anyone who has read Mr Symons's biography of Corvo will recognize how very fair. The facts (the correspondence with Bonsen and Peary-Buthlaw, for example) appear to be quite truthfully stated; it is Rolfe's interpretation which is odd. Offer the starving man a dinner or the homeless man a bed and instantaneously the good deed is unrecognizably distorted. The strangest motives begin obscurely to be discerned. Is it that one is seeing good from the devil's side: 'The lovely, clever, good, ugly, silly wicked faces of this world, all anxious, all selfish, all mean, all unsatisfied and unsatisfying': or is it possibly only a horribly deep insight into human nature?

The difficulty always is to distinguish between possession by a devil and possession by a holy spirit. Saints have starved like Rolfe, and no saint had a more firm belief in his spiritual vocation. He loathed the flesh (making an unnecessary oath to remain twenty years unmarried that he might demonstrate to unbelieving ecclesiastics his vocation for the priesthood) and he loved the spirit. One says that he writes from the devil's side, because his shrill rage has the same lack of dignity as Marlowe's cracker-throwing demons, because he had no humility ('he came as one to whom Mystery has a meaning and a method, as one of the intimate, and fortunate, as one who belonged, as a son of the Father'), and because, of course, he had a Monsignor among his enemies. But the devil, too, is spiritual, and when Rolfe wrote of the spirit (without the silly rage against his enemies or the sillier decorated style in which he tried to make the best of a world he had not been allowed to renounce) he wrote like an angel; our appreciation is hardly concerned in the question whether or not it was a fallen angel:

He slowly paced along cypress-avenues, between the graves of little children with blue or white standards and the graves of adults marked by more sombre memorials. All around him were patricians bringing sheaves of painted candles and gorgeous garlands of orchids and everlastings, or plebeians on their knees grubbing up weeds and tracing pathetic designs with cheap chrysanthemums and farthing night-lights. Here, were a baker's boy and a telegraph-messenger, repainting their father's grave-post with a tin of black and a bottle of gold. There, were half a dozen ribald venal dishonest licentious young gondoliers; quiet and alone on their wicked knees round the grave of a comrade.

It was Saturday. The little triptych on the altar lay open – *Sedes Sapientiae ora pro nobis.* – How altogether lovely these byzantine eikons are! That is because they have Christian tradition – they alone, in religious art. Undoubtedly that council of the Church was inspired divinely which uttered the canon prohibiting painters from producing any ideals save those ecclesiastically dictated. Whoever dreams of praying (with expectation of response) for the prayer of a Tintoretto or a Titian, or a Bellini, or a Botticelli? But who can refrain from crying 'O Mother!' to these unruffleable wan dolls in indigo on gold?

Literature is deep in Mr Symons's debt, and in debt, too, to all the libelled philanthropists without whose permission this book could hardly have been published.

1934

FREDERICK ROLFE: A SPOILED PRIEST

HUBERT'S ARTHUR, the latest work of Frederick Rolfe to be brought into print by Mr Symons, is a laborious experiment in imaginary history. The assumption is that Arthur was not murdered by King John but escaped and, after recovering a treasure left him by Richard Lion-Heart, won the crown of Jerusalem and finally, with the help of Hubert de Burgh, the chronicler of his deeds, gained the throne of England. Originally Rolfe collaborated with Mr Pirie-Gordon, but after the inevitable quarrel he rewrote the story during the last months of his life. The style, we are told, 'was meant to be an enriched variant upon that of the *Itinerarium Regis Ricardi* and of William of Tyre, with an admixture of Maurice Hewlett'. Hewlett, alas, in this appallingly long and elaborate fantasy is too much in evidence, and perhaps only a knowledge of the circumstances in which it was written, to be gained from Mr Symons's biography, gives it interest.

For if Rolfe is to be believed (a very big assumption) he brought this book to its leisurely decorative close at the very time when he claimed to be starving in his gondola on the Venetian lagoons.

The moment I cease moving, I am invaded by swarms of swimming rats, who in the winter are so voracious that they attack even man who is motionless. I have tried it. And have been bitten. Oh my dear man you can't think how artful fearless ferocious they are. I rigged up two bits of chain, lying loose on my prow and poop with a string by which I could shake them when attacked. For two nights the dodge acted. The swarms came (up the anchor rope) and nuzzled me: I shook the chains: the beasts plopped overboard. Then they got used to the noise and sneered. Then they bit the strings. Then they bit my toes and woke me shrieking and shaking with fear.

The very same day that he was writing this letter (whether truth or fiction doesn't really matter: one cannot doubt the imaginative vividness of the experience) he was penning, as if he had the whole of a well-fed life before him, some such

slow decorative sentimental description as this of the dead St
Hugh singing before King Arthur:

> The pretty eyes were closed, the eyes of the innocent perfectly-
> satisfied happy face of the little red-gleaming head which reposed
> on the pillow of scarlet samite: but the smiling mouth was a little
> open, the rosy lips rhythmically moving, letting glimpses of little
> white teeth be seen ...

That to me is the real dramatic interest of *Hubert's Arthur*.

For on the whole it is a dull book of small literary merit,
though it will be of interest to those already interested in the
man, who can catch the moments when he drops the Hewlett
mask and reveals more indirectly than in *The Desire and
Pursuit of the Whole* his painfully divided personality. Reading
his description of St Hugh, 'the sweet and inerrable canorous
voice of the dead', one has to believe in the genuineness of his
nostalgia – for the Catholic Church, for innocence. But at the
same time one cannot fail to notice the homosexual, sadistic
element in the lushness and tenderness of his epithets.

When he writes in the person of Hubert de Burgh:

> They would not let me have my will (which was for the life of a
> quiet clergyman). ... So once every day since that time, I have
> cursed those monks out of a full heart,

one pities the spoiled priest; when he describes Arthur,

> the proud gait of the stainless pure secure in himself, wholly
> perfect in himself, severe with himself as with all, strong in disgust
> of ill, utterly careless save to keep high, clean, cold, armed, intact,
> apart, glistening with candid candour both of heart and of aspect,
> like a flower, like a maid, like a star.

one recognizes the potential sanctity of the man, just as one
recognizes the really devilish mind which gives the formula for
throat-cutting with the same relish as in his book on the
Borgias he had translated a recipe for cooking a goose alive.
He is an obvious example to illustrate Mr T. S. Eliot's remark
in his study of the demonic influence:

> Most people are only a very little alive; and to awaken them to

137

the spiritual is a very great responsibility: it is only when they are so awakened that they are capable of real Good, but that at the same time they become first capable of Evil.

1935

REMEMBERING MR JONES

THIS book* is as much a memorial to Edward Garnett as to Conrad: a memorial to the greatest of all publishers' readers, the man behind the scenes to whom we owe Conrad's works. A publisher's claim to the discovery of an author is suspect: it is the author who usually discovers the publisher, and the publisher's part is simply to pay a reliable man to recognize merit when it is brought to him by parcel-post. But we have Conrad's own testimony that had it not been for Edward Garnett's tactfully subdued encouragement he might never have written another book after *Almayer's Folly*, and one suspects it was Garnett who organized critical opinion so that Conrad had the support of his peers during the years of popular neglect. As for Garnett himself nothing could be more illuminating than his son's biographical note. Edward Garnett was brought up by parents who blended 'Victorian respectability with complete liberality of opinion. The children were undisciplined and completely untidy; only when they exhibited anything like worldliness or self-seeking were their parents surprised and shocked.'

Conrad's prefaces are not like James's, an elaborate reconstruction of technical aims. They are not prefaces to which novelists will turn so frequently as readers: they are about life as much as about art, about the words or the actions which for one reason or another were excluded from the novels – Almayer suddenly breaking out at breakfast on the subject of the ambiguous Willems, then on an expedition up-river with some Arabs, 'One thing's certain; if he finds anything worth having up there they will poison him like a dog'; about the prototype of Mr Jones of *Victory*:

---

* *Conrad's Prefaces to his Works*, with an essay by Edward Garnett.

Mr Jones (or whatever his name was) did not drift away from me. He turned his back on me and walked out of the room. It was in a little hotel in the Island of St Thomas in the West Indies (in the year '75) where we found him one hot afternoon extended on three chairs, all alone in the loud buzzing of flies to which his immobility and his cadaverous aspect gave a most gruesome significance. Our invasion must have displeased him because he got off the chairs brusquely and walked out, leaving with me an indelibly weird impression of his thin shanks. One of the men with me said that the fellow was the most desperate gambler he had ever come across. I said: 'A professional sharper?' and got for answer: 'He's a terror; but I must say that up to a certain point he will play fair . . .' I wonder what that point was. I never saw him again because I believe he went straight on board a mail-boat which left within the hour for other ports of call in the direction of Aspinall.

They make an amusing comparison, these germs of stories, anecdotes remarkable as a rule for their anarchy (an appalling Negro in Haiti) or ambiguity (as when Lord Jim passed across Conrad's vision – 'One sunny morning in the commonplace surroundings of an eastern roadstead, I saw his form pass by – appealing – significant – under a cloud – perfectly silent') – they make an amusing comparison with those neat little dinner-table stories which set James off constructing his more intricate and deeper fictions, holding up his hand in deprecation to prevent the whole story coming out ('clumsy Life again at her stupid work'), just as the settings are socially widely dissimilar: Conrad on a small and dirty schooner in the Gulf of Mexico listening to the ferocious Ricardo's low communings 'with his familiar devil', while the old Spanish gentleman to whom he served as confidant and retainer lay dying 'in the dark and unspeakable cudd'; and James on Christmas Eve, before the table 'that glowed safe and fair through the brown London night', listening to the anecdotes of his 'amiable friend'. It was a strange fate which brought these two to settle within a few miles of each other and produce from material gained at such odd extremes of life two of the great English novels of the last fifty years: *The Spoils of Poynton* and *Victory*.

The thought would have pleased Conrad. It would have satisfied what was left of his religious sense, and that was little more than a distant memory of the Sanctus bell and the incense. James spent his life working towards and round the Catholic Church, fascinated and repelled and absorbent; Conrad was born a Catholic and ended – formally – in consecrated ground, but all he retained of Catholicism was the ironic sense of an omniscience and of the final unimportance of human life under the watching eyes. Edward Garnett brings up again the old legend of Slavic influence which Conrad expressly denied. The Polish people are not Slavs and Conrad's similarity is to the French, once a Catholic nation, to the author for example of *La Condition Humaine*: the rhetoric of an abandoned faith. 'The mental degradation to which a man's intelligence is exposed on its way through life': 'the passions of men short-sighted in good and evil': in scattered phrases you get the memories of a creed working like poetry through the agnostic prose.

1937

THE DOMESTIC BACKGROUND

THE domestic background *is* of interest: to know how a writer with the peculiar sensitivity we call genius compromises with family life. There is usually some compromise; few writers have had the ruthless egotism of Joseph Conrad who, at the birth of his first child, delayed the doctor whom he had been sent to fetch by sitting down with him and eating a second breakfast. The trouble is that a writer's home, just as much as the world outside, is his raw material. His wife's or a child's sickness: Conrad couldn't help unconsciously regarding them, as Henry James regarded the germinal anecdote at the dinner table, as something to cut short when he had had enough human pain for his purpose. 'Something human', he put as epigraph to one of his novels, quoting Grimm, 'is dearer to me than the wealth of all the world.' But no quotation more misrepresented him in his home, if Mrs Conrad's memory is accurate.* Out of a long marriage she has remembered nothing

* *Joseph Conrad and his Circle*, by Jessie Conrad.

tender, nothing considerate. On her own part, yes; she is the heroine of every anecdote.

It makes rather repellent reading, this long record of slights, grievances, verbal brutalities. Is it a true portrait? We are dealing with a mind curiously naïve (on one occasion she refers to Edward Thomas in uniform, wearing his khaki 'without ostentation, but correct in every detail'), unable to realize imaginatively her husband's devotion to his art, a mind peculiarly retentive of injuries. The triviality of her attacks on Ford Madox Ford, for example, is astonishing. For how many years has the grievance over a laundry bill fermented in this not very generous brain? After a quarter of a century the fact that Henry James served Mrs Hueffer first at tea has not been forgotten.

She writes of Ford that he has reviled Conrad 'when he is beyond the power of defending himself'. The truth is that no one did more than Ford to preserve Conrad's fame, and no one has done more than Mrs Conrad to injure it in this portrait she has drawn of a man monstrously selfish, who grudged the money he gave his children, who avoided responsibilities by taking to his bed, who was unfaithful to her in his old age. Of this last story we should have known nothing if it were not for Mrs Conrad's dark hints and evasions here. 'I made no comment': this is the phrase with which the story of his slights so often ends. But I do not think she is conscious of its complacency any more than she is conscious that the phrase with which she describes herself at the end of her book, one who has 'the privilege and the immense satisfaction of being regarded as the guardian of his memory', must seem to her readers either heartless or hypocritical.

It would be easy to cast doubt upon these ungrammatical revelations (on one occasion her memory fails her completely in the course of a paragraph). But there is obviously no conscious dishonesty in the one-sided record; the writer does not realize how damaging it is. 'The dear form', 'the dear fellow', 'the beloved face', one need not believe that these are meaningless endearments; it is simply that her mind is of a kind which harbours slights more easily than acts of kindness. She suffered

– you cannot help believing that – suffered bitterly in this marriage, but it has never occurred to her that Conrad suffered too:

From the sound next door (we have three rooms) I know that the pain has aroused Borys from his feverish doze. I won't go to him. It's no use. Presently I shall give him his salicylate, take his temperature, and then go and elaborate a little more of the conversation of Mr Verloc with his wife. It is very important that the conversation of Mr Verloc and his wife should be elaborated – made more effective – more *true* to the character and the situation of these people.

By Jove! I've got to hold myself with both hands not to burst into a laugh which would scare wife, baby, and the other invalid – let alone the lady whose room is on the other side of the corridor. Today completes the round dozen years since I finished *Almayer's Folly*.

'His own picturesque language' is Mrs Conrad's phrase for this tortured irony.

1935

THE PUBLIC LIFE

THIS record * of amazing energy, of dinners and cruises and casinos and Blue Trains, of a life crammed with public appearances and yet a life which found time in the small hours before the first engagement for a literary production of enormous quantity, is curiously reminiscent of James's fantasy of *The Private Life*. James, it will be remembered, was fascinated by his vision of Robert Browning, the diner-out, with his 'loud, sound, normal, hearty presence, all bristling with prompt responses and expected opinions and usual views', and his other personality 'who sat at a table all alone, silent and unseen, and wote admirably deep and brave and intricate things'. And for comparison there was another figure in the London of his time:

* *Arnold Bennett's Letters to his Nephew Richard Bennett.*

that most accomplished of artists and most dazzling of men of the world whose effect on the mind repeatedly invited to appraise him was to beget in it an image of representation and figuration so exclusive of any possible inner self that, so far from there being here a question of an *alter ego*, a double personality, there seemed scarce a question of a real and single one, scarce foothold or margin for any private and domestic *ego* at all.

One must not press the comparison with Browning or Wilde too far, for Bennett was obviously a man of as much greater honesty and human kindliness than the one as he was a much smaller writer than the other. His engaging vanity about his clothes (the shoes which cost five guineas a pair) and the hotels he stayed in, his sometimes rather absurd self-assurance ('I may say that I disagree with Einstein's theory of curved space'), were only aspects of his honesty. He may have led as public a life as Wilde's, but he was not concerned, except in his superficial vanities, with the appearance he made; he spoke of what he thought whether it might damage him in the eyes of the unsympathetic or not.

And unlike Browning's his public life had become his work: the huge hotels, the yachts, the *wagons-lits*, the company of millionaires and Cabinet Ministers: these were his material. No writer has been more shaped by success: genuinely shaped, for the literary conscience which was nurtured on Flaubert never allowed him in his serious work to write for the sake of popularity. Popularity simply overtook him. For the public life was not his first material – at the time of *The Old Wives' Tale* – and he made one mysterious, because so unexpectedly successful, return, away from Lord Raingo, to the people for whom his sympathy had been deeper, who moved his creative brain, perhaps because they belonged to his earlier years, in a far more poetic manner, in *Riceyman Steps*.

In these letters, kindly, sympathetic, occasionally harsh when he felt his nephew's conduct needed improving *socially*, we read between the accounts of dinner parties and theatre parties of a few early morning visits to Clerkenwell: to 'get' the scene of *Riceyman Steps* took much less time than his exploration of the Savoy for *Imperial Palace*, perhaps because it connected, as that excellent piece of documentary reporting did not, directly with his imaginative experience.

Usually the documentary eye served him only too well. Vivid descriptive informative writing came to him easily. Again and again the character of places springs admirably alive in Bennett's letters but very seldom the character of people. The documentary eye was always vivid: at rehearsals – 'The theatre is very large, very fine, and very cold. A sort of Arctic hell'; driving home after the restrained riot of the Olympia Circus – 'we came home with the brougham full of hydrogen balloons, which occasionally swept out on their strings through the window into the infinite ether'; noting the quality of the lemonade at a dance hall; recording that Lord Rothermere's house had seventeen bathrooms. He had an unfailing interest for the scene, and the scene in these letters is crammed with properties, but one has a curious sense that this kindly, honest, lovable man was its only living inhabitant, as if popularity had robbed him of the only kind of people he really, deeply, knew. In 1930 he recorded with his usual innocent and candid pleasure that the publication of his *Journal* in the *Daily Mail* was making a 'great stir', but one cannot help wondering where that stir was to be noticed among the plane crashes and the unemployed suicides, a year's births and deaths, except perhaps at Lord Raingo's.

1936

GOATS AND INCENSE

M Y generation lived so long with the old Kipling that it is hard for us to capture the first excitement of his contemporaries, that feeling for the amazing boy who came from India and set the literary world aflame. It is one of the virtues of Mr Carrington's admirable biography that through the care and the sobriety of his narrative we catch the pulse of the legend.* After two hundred pages of close writing Kipling has

* *Rudyard Kipling. His Life and Work*, by Charles Carrington.

not yet in this biography reached the age of thirty. By thirty he had written *Plain Tales From the Hills*, *Soldiers Three*, *Wee Willie Winkie*, *The Light That Failed*, *Barrack Room Ballards*, *Many Inventions*, *The Jungle Books*: he had been accepted as an equal by Stevenson and James – no wonder that at sixty-one he seemed to Hugh Walpole already an old man on the brink of second childhood: 'A wonderful morning with old Kipling in the Athenaeum. He was sitting surrounded by the reviews of his new book, beaming like a baby.' He had been a 'leading writer' for more than the span of most men's literary lives.

There is no sensational surprise in Mr Carrington's Life. A full account of Kipling's extraordinary quarrel with Balestier, his American brother-in-law, and a fantastic story of how a homicidal lunatic pursued him from England to the Cape and back and finally ran Kipling to earth on the steps of the Athenaeum – these are the unexpected high lights. Those who anticipated intimate revelations, perhaps of the Anglo-Indian order, had mistaken Kipling's reporting talent for direct personal experience. His prose, unlike his poetry, has not lasted well and the tricks of the reporter are apparent even in the few stories that still have the power to excite or move – *The Man Who Would be King*, *Without Benefit of Clergy*.

Our memories are so much more satisfactory than the reality. Even *The Finest Story in the World* no longer seems quite true. One had remembered the description of a leaking ship in a still sea given by the man who had gone down in her, how the water-level paused for an instant 'ere' it fell on the deck. But now one notices how Kipling spoilt his effect with typical bravado. 'He had paid everything except the bare life for this little valueless piece of knowledge, and I had travelled ten thousand weary miles to meet him and take his knowledge at second-hand.'

Even *The Man Who Would Be King* seems marred today, after its magnificent opening, by the description of Freemasonry (that King Charles's head) in an Afghan tribe.

There is almost an inability to experience truly: observation is ruined time and again by the pretence of personal emotion.

The horror, the confusion, and the separation of the murderer from his comrades were all over before I came. There remained only on the barrack square the blood of a man calling from the ground. The hot sun had dried it to a dusky goldbeater's-skin film, cracked lozenge-wise by the heat; and as the wind rose each lozenge, rising a little, curled up at the edges as if it were a dumb tongue.

It is one of the most famous openings in Kipling, and how shoddy it is today, apart from the one brilliantly realized scrap of description. 'The blood of a man calling from the ground' apparently with 'a dumb tongue' – always in his prose he protests too much. He is determined to 'make his story stand up', like any *Express* reporter; he calls on emotions which are not really there.

Then who should come to tuck him up for the night but the mother? And she sat down on the bed, and they talked for a long hour, as mother and son should, if there is to be any future for our empire. With a simple woman's deep guile she asked questions and suggested answers that should have waked some sign in the face on the pillow, but there was neither quiver of eyelid nor quickening of breath, neither evasion nor delay in reply. So she blessed him and kissed him on the mouth, which is not always a mother's property ...

Surely Tinker Bell danced when Kipling was born. Of greatly gifted writers perhaps the two who have written with most falsity of human relations are Barrie and Kipling. We know more of Barrie's private failure: we only get a hint of Kipling's in that long drawn feud with his brother-in-law Balestier, the inability to realize another man's feelings. False poeticisms, the exaggerated use of technical phrases which make some of his later stories incomprehensible to the reader who has not picked the brains of a ship's designer or an engine-room hand, scraps of Biblical English, the overpowering shyness of the schoolboy intellectual who doesn't want to admit to the hearties of the prefect's room that he really takes literature seriously – as the years pass we see how the young man never grew up and how patchily in prose his promise was realized.

To me there is only one story, *The Miracle of Purun Bhagat*, in which Kipling does control his enormous capacity for play, play with images, phrases, the sound of vowels. The bravado, the knowingness, the caste-prejudices, the qualities which so often made him intrude a second-rate phrase to express a second-rate mood, are absent. In this story of an Indian hermit, once the Prime Minister of his State, there is a dignity of subject which compels him to write with the simple verbal music of the master he should always have been:

> Immediately below him the hillside fell away, clean and cleared for fifteen hundred feet, where a little village of stone-walled houses, with roofs of beaten earth, clung to the steep tilt. All round it the tiny terraced fields lay out like aprons of patchwork on the knees of the mountain, and cows no bigger than beetles grazed between the smooth stone circles of the threshing floors.

Oddly it was in poetry – and often in occasional poetry at that – that Kipling reached maturity. Even at his most popular, in such poems as 'The Song of the Banjo', we realize the extent of his mastery when we read his imitators. Here he has enlarged the scope of English poetry to include the outer, the un-English world. In so much of Canadian and Australian poetry of his time the exotic tree, the bird with the italicized name, the mugwump – if such exists – stuck out of the verse, less absorbed by the imagination than Carroll's slithy toves. In Kipling's poetry the exotic is naturalized: we only notice the stranger a long while after he has gone.

> In the desert where the dung-fed camp smoke curled.
> Day long the diamond weather,
> The high, unaltered blue,
> The smell of goats and incense . . .
>
> And the lisp of the split banana frond . . .

But perhaps Kipling never wrote better than when he wrote out of hate, and poetry is a better medium for hatred than prose. In his prose – in such a crude story for example as *The Village That Voted the Earth Was Flat* – his victims are unworthy of his obsession. For hatred is an obsession, hatred confines, hatred is monotonous – Dryden and Pope drove it as far and sometimes a little farther than it will go. Kipling was their worthy successor. Who cares now for the subject of 'MacFlecknoe'? We read it for the accurate statement of Dryden's own mood. So too we are no longer interested in the fact that a British Government some time in the first decade of our century contemplated a joint naval demonstration with Germany against Venezuela, but Kipling's poem is the picture of a mind in hate and we can read it still. The Marconi Scandal, because of the distinction of the accused, may still have an interest, but what was that Declaration of London on June 29, 1911, apparently just after the Coronation, which so roused Kipling's bitterness against Government and Parliament? It doesn't matter: the stupid bullish victim is secondary to the sword and the cape of the slayer.

> We were all one heart and one race
>> When the Abbey trumpets blew.
> For a moment's breathing space
>> We had forgotten you.
> Now you return to your honoured place
>> Panting to shame us anew.

It is the fate of a good biographer that the reviewer neglects him for random reflections on his subject. Mr Carrington's is a very good biography – we are not left, as we so often are when we have closed an official life, with the thought, 'At least here is a quarry where other men in the future may dig more profitably.' Mr Carrington has dug with effect: the quarry is exhausted, and, as Kipling would have wished, future writers need concern themselves only with the work.

1956

SOME NOTES ON SOMERSET MAUGHAM

1

'A WRITER', Somerset Maugham declared in these 'variations on some Spanish themes', 'is not made by one book, but by a body of work. It will not be of equal value; his books will be tentative while he is learning the technique and developing his powers; and if, as most writers do, for it is a healthy occupation, he lives too long, his later work will show the decline due to advancing years, but there will be a period during which he will bring forth what he had it in him to bring forth in the perfection of which he is capable.' To this last-mentioned period *Don Fernando* belongs; it is Maugham's best book.

It will be an unexpected book for those to whom Maugham still primarily means adultery in China, murder in Malaya, suicide in the South Seas, the coloured violent stories which have so appreciably raised the level of the popular magazine. But there is a more important Mr Maugham than that: the shrewd critical humane observer of *Cakes and Ale*, of the best Ashenden stories, of the preface to the collected tales. The characteristic most evident in these books and in *Don Fernando* is honesty. It has emerged slowly out of the cynical and romantic past; there are passages in *The Trembling of a Leaf* and *The Painted Veil* which Maugham must have found acutely embarrassing to remember, and it is interesting to learn in *Don Fernando* that Maugham's extensive knowledge of Spanish literature was accumulated when he was young, to provide him with material for a romantic Juanesque novel which he never wrote. Instead of Don Juan then we have Don Fernando, the innkeeper and curio dealer who forced Maugham unwillingly to buy an old life of Ignatius Loyola, and it is with this life that his study of old Spain starts.

The contrast is peculiarly piquant between the opulence of the material (the fierce asceticisms of Loyola and St Peter of Alcantara, the conceits of Lope de Vega, the ribaldry of the picaresque novelists, the food and the architecture and the painters of Spain, the grim bright goaty land) and Maugham's honest unenthusiastic mind. I do not mean pedantic or unimaginative. Honesty is a form of sensitivity, and you need a very sensitive ear to detect in the verbose plays of Calderon 'faintly audible, while this or the other is happening, the sinister drums of unseen powers'. One may smile at the idea of Maugham doing one of Loyola's 'Spiritual Exercises' and finding it extremely severe ('I thought I was going to be sick'), but it is that quality of honest experience which gives his style such vividness.

Tarragona has a cathedral that is grey and austere, very plain, with immense, severe pillars; it is like a fortress; a place of worship for headstrong and cruel men. The night falls early within its walls and then the columns in the aisles seem to squat down on themselves and darkness shrouds the Gothic arches. It terrifies you. It is like a dungeon. I was there last on a Monday in Holy Week, and from the pulpit a preacher was delivering a Lenten sermon. Two or three naked electric globes threw a cold light that cut the outline of the columns against the darkness as though with scissors. ... Each angry, florid phrase was like a blow and one blow followed another with vicious insistence. From the farthest end of the majestic church, winding about the columns and curling round the groining of the arches, down the great austere nave, and along the dungeon-like aisles, the rasping, shrewish voice pursued you.

Don Fernando may be superficially discursive; Maugham is in turns critic, tourist, biographer (to find short lives as shrewd and amusing we must go back to Anthony à Wood and Aubrey), but he is working steadily forward towards the statement of his main argument: 'It looks as though all the energy, all the originality, of this vigorous race had been disposed to one end and one end only, the creation of man. It is not in art that they excelled, they excelled in what is greater than art – in man.' To that man Maugham has rendered the highest kind of justice, whether he is the playwright of artificial situations or the unknown sailor who, when the Armenian bishop, Martyr, begged a passage, replied, 'I will take him in my ship; but tell him I go to range the universal sea.'

2

Somerset Maugham's short stories are so well-known that a reviewer may be forgiven for dwelling chiefly on the preface which Maugham contributed to the collected tales. It is a delightfully 'sensible' essay on the short story, and the more valuable because it represents a point of view not common to many English writers. English short-story writers of any merit of recent years have followed Chekov rather than Maupassant.

Maugham is a writer of great deliberation even when his style is most careless ('burning mouth', 'nakedness of soul', 'mouth like a scarlet wound'); he will never, one feels, lose his head; he has a steady point of view. The banality of the phrases I have noted do not indicate an emotional abandonment; they indicate a rather blasé attitude towards the details of his stories; narrative is something which has to be got through before the point of his anecdote appears, and Maugham is sometimes a little bored and off-hand in the process. The anecdote to Maugham is very nearly everything; the anecdote, and not the characters, not the 'atmosphere', not the style, is primarily responsible for conveying Maugham's attitude; and it is the anecdote as contrasted with spiritual analysis, Maupassant with Chekov, that he discusses in his preface with great justice to the opposite school.

I do not know that anyone but Chekov has so poignantly been able to represent spirit communing with spirit. It is this that makes one feel that Maupassant in comparison is obvious and vulgar. The strange, the terrible thing is that, looking at man in their different ways, these two great writers, Maupassant and Chekov, saw eye to eye. One was content to look upon flesh, while the other, more nobly and subtly, surveyed the spirit; but they agreed that life was tedious and insignificant and that men were base, unintelligent and pitiful.

This comes very generously from a disciple of Maupassant, and Maugham's praise of his master is never exaggerated. 'Maupassant's stories are good stories. The anecdote is interesting apart from the narration, so that it would secure attention if it were told over the dinner table; and that seems to me a very great merit indeed.' The best of Maugham's stories too are anecdotes, the best are worthy of Maupassant, and his failure really to reach Maupassant's rank is partly his failure to stick to the anecdote. Too many of his short stories sprawl into the proper region of the novel. Take for example *The Pool*, where the scene changes from the South Seas to Scotland and back to the South Seas, where the action covers years, and of which the subject is the marriage of white and half-caste. Nor did Maupassant's preference for the anecdote imply a method which Maugham finds only too necessary: the method of the 'yarn', of the first person singular. He defends the convention ably in his preface, but in a collected volume the monotony of the method becomes apparent. One has only to remember how this convention of the first person was transformed by Conrad, to realize a strange limitation to Maugham's interest in his craft.

This air of being at ease in a Sion which he so candidly and rightly despises is rather pronounced in his defence of the popular magazines. As he explains in his preface, he came to the short story late in his career, he was already known as a dramatist, and it is not surprising that his stories have always been welcomed by the magazines. His good fortune has blinded him to the demands which the popular magazine makes on less famous writers. When he remarks: 'It has never been known yet that a good writer was unable to write his best owing to the conditions under which alone he could gain a public for his work', he has been misled, I think, by his own success. Writers belonging to a less easily appreciated school than the anecdotal, who depend for their market on the intellectual magazine, are lucky if they can earn twenty pounds by a short story, while the writer who fits the taste of the popular magazine may well earn ten times that sum.* It is seldom that financial worry is a condition for the best work.

3

Kinglake once referred to 'that nearly immutable law which compels a man with a pen in his hand to be uttering every now and then some sentiment not his own', and compared an author with a French peasant under the old *régime*, bound to perform a certain amount of work upon the public highways. I doubt if any author has done – of recent years – less highway labour than Maugham. I say 'of recent years' because, as he himself admits in this summing-up of his life and work,† he passed like other writers through the stage of tutelage – and to the most unlikely people, the translators of the Bible and

* I was writing in 1934.
† *The Summing-Up.*

Jeremy Taylor. That stage lasted longer with Maugham than with most men of equal talent – there is at the heart of his work a humility and a self-distrust rather deadening in their effects, and his stories as late as *The Painted Veil* were a curious mixture of independent judgement, when he was dealing with action, and of clichés, when he was expressing emotion.

An author of talent is his own best critic – the ability to criticize his own work is inseparably bound up with his talent: it *is* his talent, and Maugham defines his limitations perfectly: 'I knew that I had no lyrical quality. I had a small vocabulary and no efforts that I could make to enlarge it much availed me. I had little gift of metaphor; the original and striking simile seldom occurred to me', and in a passage – which is an excellent example of his hard-won style at its best, clear, colloquial, honest – he relates his limitations to his character:

It did not seem enough merely to write. I wanted to make a pattern of my life, in which writing would be an essential element, but which would include all the other activities proper to man. ... I had many disabilities. I was small; I had endurance but little physical strength; I stammered; I was shy; I had poor health. I had no facility for games, which play so great a part in the normal life of Englishmen; and I had, whether for any of these reasons or from nature I do not know, an instinctive shrinking from my fellow-men that has made it difficult for me to enter into any familiarity with them. ... Though in the course of years I have learned to assume an air of heartiness when forced into contact with a stranger, I have never liked anyone at first sight. I do not think I have ever addressed someone I did not know in a railway carriage or spoken to a fellow-passenger on board ship unless he first spoke to me. ... These are grave disadvantages both to the writer and the man. I have had to make the best of them. I think it was the best I could hope for in the circumstances and with the very limited powers that were granted to me by nature.

'It did not seem enough to me merely to write', and even in this personal book the author is unwilling to communicate more than belongs to his authorship; he does not, like a professional autobiographer, take us with commercial promptitude into his confidence. His life has contained material for dramatization, and he has used it for fiction. There is the pattern in his writing and we are not encouraged to look for its reverse in life: the hospital career (the public pattern is in *Liza of Lambeth*); the secret agent in Geneva (we can turn to *Ashenden*); the traveller – there are many books. The sense of privacy, so rare and attractive a quality in an author, deepens in the bare references to secret service experiences in Russia, just before the Revolution, of which we find no direct trace in his stories.

The nearest Maugham comes to a confidence is in the description of his religious belief – if you can call agnosticism a belief, and the fact that on this subject he is ready to speak to strangers makes one pause. There are signs of muddle, contradictions . . . hints of an inhibition. Otherwise one might trace here the deepest source of his limitations, for creative art seems to remain a function of the religious mind. Maugham the agnostic is forced to minimize – pain, vice, the importance of his fellowmen. He cannot believe in a God who punishes and he cannot therefore believe in the importance of a human action. 'It is not difficult', he writes, 'to forgive people their sins' – it sounds like charity, but it may be only contempt. In another passage he refers with understandable scorn to writers who are 'grandiloquent to tell you whether or not a little trollop shall hop into bed with a commonplace young man'. That is a plot as old as *Troilus and Cressida*, but to the religious sixteenth-century mind there was no such thing as a commonplace young man or an unimportant sin; the creative writers of that time drew human characters with a clarity we have never regained (we had to go to Russia for it later) because they were lit with the glare and significance that war lends. Rob human beings of their heavenly and their infernal importance, and you rob your characters of their individuality. ('What should a Socialist woman do?') It has never been Maugham's characters that we have remembered so much as the narrator, with his contempt for human life, his unhappy honesty.

1935–8

THE financial expert's office was under a banyan tree: his office furniture an old tin box. From the first pages of Mr Narayan's novel *The Financial Expert* we are back in the town of Malgudi with which for nearly twenty years we have been as familiar as with our own birthplace. We know, like the streets of childhood, Market Road, the snuff stalls, the vendors of toothpaste, Lawley Extension with its superior villas, the Regal Haircutting Saloon, the river, the railway. We expect at any moment to see the Bachelor of Arts waving a long farewell to a friend from the platform, small Swami wrapped in his adventurous dreams coming down Market Road, Mr Sampath at the door of his dubious film studio. It is through their friendly offices that we have been able to meet these new – and rather doubtful – characters: Margayya, the financial expert himself, who graduates from the banyan tree to publishing, and back to more elaborate and more crooked banking (but how innocent is all his crookedness); Dr Pal, 'journalist, correspondent and author'; and Margayya's son Balu whose progress from charming childhood to spoilt frustrated manhood is perhaps the saddest episode Mr Narayan has written.

All Mr Narayan's comedies have had this undertone of sadness. Their gentle irony and absence of condemnation remind us how difficult comedy is in the West today – farce, savage, boisterous, satirical, is easy, but comedy needs a strong framework of social convention with which the author sympathizes but which he does not share. Miss Compton-Burnett is forced to place her stories in the Edwardian or Victorian past; Mr Henry Green substitutes elaborate conventions of his own for our social vacancies, so that his characters move in the kind of dance we learnt at kindergarten – 'one step forward, one step to the right, twirl on the right toe'. But the life of Malgudi – never ruffled by politics – proceeds in exactly the same way as it has done for centuries, and the juxtaposition of the age-old convention and the modern character provides much of the comedy. The astrologer is still called in to examine the horoscopes for a marriage, but now if you pay him enough he will fix them the way you want: the financial expert sits under his banyan tree opposite the new Central Co-operative Land Mortgage Bank. To push away a tumbler of milk is to insult a goddess; the caste of a great-grandfather is still of great importance, Margayya, astute about mortgages, consumed by the modern desire for wealth and motorcars, yet consults the priest of the Goddess Lakshmi and finds himself seeking a red lotus to pound up in the milk drawn from a smoke-coloured cow (the forty days of prayer have results: he becomes the owner of a pornographic manuscript called first *Bed Life or the Science of Marital Happiness* but afterwards, through the caution of the printer, *Domestic Harmony*).

Margayya – the sad ambitious absurd financial expert – is perhaps the most engaging of all Mr Narayan's characters. In his ambitions for his boy, his huge dreams, his unintended villainies and his small vanities, his domestic tenderness, he has the hidden poetry and the unrecognized pathos we so often find in Chekov's characters who on the last page vanish into life.

He knew that he had a scheme somewhere at the back of his mind, a scheme which would place him among the elect in society, which would make people flock to him and look to him for guidance, advice and management. He could not yet say what the scheme would be, but he sensed its presence . . . he felt he ought to wait on that inspiration with reverence and watchfulness.

Whom next shall I meet in Malgudi? That is the thought that comes to me when I close a novel of Mr Narayan's. I am not waiting for another novel. I am waiting to go out of my door into those loved and shabby streets and see with excitement and the certainty of pleasure a stranger approaching, past the bank, the cinema, the haircutting saloon, a stranger who will greet me, I know, with some unexpected and revealing phrase that will open a door on to yet another human existence.

1952

How seldom in the literary life do we pause to pay a debt of gratitude except to the great or the fashionable, who are like those friends that we feel do us credit. Conrad, Dostoevsky, James, yes, but we are too ready to forget such figures as A. E. W. Mason, Stanley Weyman, and Rider Haggard, perhaps the greatest of all who enchanted us when we were young. Enchantment is just what this writer exercised; he fixed pictures in our minds that thirty years have been unable to wear away: the witch Gagool screaming as the rock-door closed and crushed her; Eric Brighteyes fighting his doomed battle; the death of the tyrant Chaka; Umslopagaas holding the queen's stairway in Milosis. It is odd how many violent images remain like a prophecy of the future; the love passages were quickly read and discarded from the mind, though now they seem oddly moving (as when Queen Nyleptha declares her love to Sir Henry Curtis in the midnight hall), a little awkward and stilted perhaps, but free from ambiguities and doubts, and with the worn rhetoric of honesty.

I am glad that his daughter's vivid and well-written biography * leaves Rider Haggard where he was in the imagination: the tall bearded figure with the presence of Sir Henry Curtis and the straightforwardness of Quatermain. This life does not belong to the unhappy world of letters; there are no rivalries, jealousies, nerve storms, no toiling miserably against the grain, no ignoble ambivalent vision which finds a kind of copy even in personal grief. The loss of his only son in childhood nearly broke Haggard in middle life, but yet his grief had the common direct quality: he was not compelled to watch himself turn it into words. 'Jock was dead, so he mustn't be mentioned', Sir Godfrey Haggard writes.

To come on a book or a toy that once belonged to my young cousin (whom I never knew) was to strike a hush over the room such as might almost have been observed towards a relative who

* *The Cloak that I Left*, by Lilias Rider Haggard.

had been hanged for murder. There was a guilty silence. Jock haunted the house far more obtrusively because everyone there pretended they could not see him, and the poor schoolboy wraith seemed to be begging piteously for some notice, so that at last he might be laid to rest.

A few words from Allan Quatermain on how the joy of life had left him with his son's death – 'I have just buried my boy, my poor handsome boy of whom I was so proud, and my heart is broken. It is very hard having only one son to lose him thus; but God's will be done. Who am I that I should complain?' This is all Haggard allowed himself. He was a public author and the private life remained the private life in so far as he could control it.

The poetic element in Haggard's work breaks out where the control fails. Because the hidden man was so imprisoned, when he does emerge through the tomb, it is against enormous pressure, and the effect is often one of horror, a risen Lazarus – next time he must be buried deeper. Perhaps that is why some of his early readers found his work obscene (it seems incredible to us). An anonymous letter-writer wrote to him:

As regards *She*, it is a tissue of the most sickening trash that was ever printed, the only parts worth reading are borrowed – I could quote the books if I liked. None but a foul-minded liar could invent such sickening details. I trace a good deal of diabolical murders that have been lately committed to the ideas promulgated by your foul trash. Of course, it *pays* and you don't care a damn, nevertheless the opinion of the decent public is that you are a skunk and a very foul one.

Even of *King Solomon's Mines* another anonymous correspondent wrote: 'We approached this book with feelings of curiosity – we left with those of loathing and disgust.'

It is simple to trace the influence of the public life on his work, the public life of the boy as well as of the man. There is, for example, a neighbouring farmer, 'a long lank man in a smocked frock, called Quatermain'. In Zululand, where he went whilst still a boy on the staff of the Governor of Natal, he met Gagool in the body (we suspect he had met her in the spirit long before). Pagéte's warriors are performing a war dance.

Suddenly there stood before us a creature, a woman – tiny, withered, and bent nearly double by age, but in her activity passing comprehension. Clad in a strange jumble of snake skins, feathers, furs and bones, a forked wand in her outstretched hand, she rushed to and fro before the little group of white men, crying:

> Ou, Ou, Ai, Ai, Ai,
> Oh! ye warriors that shall dance before the great ones
>   of the earth, come!
> Oh! ye dyers of spears, ye plumed suckers of blood,
>   come!
> I, the witch finder;
> I, the wise woman;
> I, the seer of strange sights;
> I, the reader of dark thoughts; call ye!

Umslopagaas with the great hole in his head above the left temple, carrying his spiked axe Imkosi-kaas, came down one day from Swaziland and became Haggard's friend. All through his life we can find superficial material for his books, even for the dull adult books like *Mr Meeson's Will*. His life provides Zulu impis, war, flight, shipwreck, a treasure hunt in Mexico, even the City of London, but what we do not so easily detect is the very thing that makes these books live today with undiminished vitality – the emergence of the buried man.

There are some revealing passages in his friendship with Rudyard Kipling. Fishing together for trout at Bateman's, these two elderly men – in some ways the most successful writers of their time, linked together to their honour even by their enemies ('the prose that knows no reason, and the unmelodious verse', 'When the Rudyards cease from Kipling, and the Haggards ride no more'), suddenly let out the secret. 'I happened to remark', Haggard wrote, 'that I thought this world was one of the hells. He replied he did not think – he was certain of it. He went on to show that it had every attribute of hell; doubt, fear, pain, struggle, bereavement, almost irresistible temptations springing from the nature with which we are clothed, physical and mental suffering, etc., ending in the worst fate man can devise for man, Execution!'

Haggard's comment starts shockingly from the page in its very casualness, and then we begin to remember the passages we skated so lightly over in the adventure stories when we were young and the world held promise: there was, for example, Allan Quatermain dying and resigned:

Well, it is not a good world – nobody can say that it is, save those who wilfully blind themselves to the facts. How can a world be good in which Money is the moving power, and Self-Interest the guiding star? The wonder is not that it is so bad but that there should be any good left in it.

Quatermain remembers the good things of life, how he 'watched the wild game trek down to the water in the moonlight. But I should not wish to live again.' And we remember too the Brethren and the quite casual comment, not unlike Haggard's to Kipling, 'So they went, talking earnestly of all things, but, save in God, finding no hope at all.'

They seemed so straightforward to us once, those books we first encountered behind the steel grille of the school library, casting a glow over the dull neighbouring H's: Henty already abandoned and Hope not yet enjoyed: *The Wanderer's Necklace* (with the hero blinded by the queen to whom he remains faithful to the last), *Montezuma's Daughter* (and her suicide beside her lover), *Ayesha* (with the mad Khan's hunting), *Nada the Lily* (and the death of the beloved). We did not notice the melancholy end of every adventure or know that the battle scenes took their tension from the fear of death which so haunted Haggard from one night in his childhood when he woke in the moonlight:

He put out his hand ... how odd it looked in the moonlight, dead – dead. Then it happened. He realized that one day that hand would be limp also, that he could not lift it any more – it would be dead – he would be dead. The awful, inescapable certainty hung over him like a pall of misery. He felt it would be better if he died at once – he wished he were dead, rather than have to live with that in front of him.

Haggard's own melancholy end, with falling royalties and the alienation of the Norfolk lands he loved, departing from the doomed house with a flower in his buttonhole to the operation he guessed would be final, comes closer to adult literature perhaps than any of his books. It is not the sound of Umslopagaas's axe that we hear, cracking the marble monument in the moment of his death, so much as the sound of trees falling, the strokes of the axe far away in the cherry orchard. We think again of how much we loved him when we were young – the gleam of Captain Good's monocle, the last stand of the Greys, de Garcia tracked through the snows – and of how little we knew. 'Occasionally one sees the Light, one touches the pierced feet, one thinks that the peace which passes understanding is gained – then all is gone again.' Could we ever have believed that our hero wrote that, or have been interested if we had known?

1951

JOURNEY INTO SUCCESS

WHY is it, one asks about certain authors, in a kind of envy of their talent and in the belief that, if one had been given so much, one could have progressed a little further, they have stayed just there? Why didn't they grow, with such a technical start – well, a little more worthy of consideration?

A. E. W. Mason was an admirable writer of detective stories – the modern fairy tales – and of such period pieces as *Clementina* and *The Watchers* which excited us when we were young and still hold a nostalgic charm. The year 1719, the country Italy, a vagrant Irishman with a lame horse, an early autumn morning, and a beautiful young woman in need of a postilion – he could do all this as cleverly as Weyman and his dialogue was sharper and better timed. How could a boy's attention be more swiftly caught than by the opening of *The Watchers*?

It was a story of a youth that sat in the stocks of a Sunday morning and disappeared thereafter from the islands; of a girl named

161

Helen; of a Negro who slept, and of men watching a house with a great tangled garden that stood at the edge of the sea.

One is reminded of another writer who began in much the same way, but when he died in his early forties had reached the height of *Weir of Hermiston*. Mason lived till old age, and perhaps, if we had been young when it appeared, *Fire Over England* might have seemed to us as satisfying as *Clementina*. But readers grow up and it is sad when an author does not grow up with them. Literature has no room for Peter Pans.

In Mr Green's workaday biography * we seek an answer to the problem: why did he not progress like Stevenson? We read of a young Mason, the son of a chartered accountant in Camberwell, and his education at Dulwich – a long way from General Faversham's old house in Surrey with the portraits of the military ancestors on the walls, and a long way, too, from the courteous monocled member of the Garrick, a leading social figure who shot in North Africa and yachted in the Mediterranean and discussed his novels with the King. (At George the Fifth's request, Mason temporarily abandoned a novel on Koenigsmark and, perhaps as a reward for his loyalty, was offered a knighthood. This eminently suitable honour, which had been accepted by his friends Anthony Hope and James Barrie, he turned down for the rather confused reason that he was a childless man.) Between the not very happy Camberwell boy and the first-nighter cartooned by Tom Titt lay Oxford and the stage and failure as an actor. Trinity wiped out the middle-class stain, but perhaps the stage gave Mason a fear of failure: failure in a sense would have been a return to Camberwell.

So from the moment that he began writing we feel his great talent bent on success – not just ugly commercial success, but the success of esteem, the esteem of those he considered his peers. Unfortunately, he had the modesty of a good fellow rather than the pride of the artist and he rated himself too low. Yeats decided to 'dine at journey's end with Landor and with Donne': in the celestial club Mason would not have

* *A. E. W. Mason*, by Roger Lancelyn Green.

seated himself higher than the author of *The Dolly Dialogues* or Quiller-Couch. It is as if his journey into success, social and financial, had not allowed him time for thought, thought about the technique of his profession, thought even about its values. 'Hardy had dropped out of his Pantheon, but the greater understanding took in Victor Hugo now and a full appreciation of Trollope's Barchester novels, with Hugh Walpole's series as a pendant.' It will be seen that his biographer shares the uncertain 'understanding' of his subject. Mr Green refers to the 'immortal' *Beau Geste*, to 'that superannuated classic' (odd phrase) *Phra, the Egyptian*, to 'a first-class writer, Mr R. C. Sherriff', and to *Musk and Amber*, 'the uttermost pinnacle of (Mason's) every power ... the perfection of restraint ... the sheer poetry'. What words has Mr Green left if he comes to deal with literature? Mason is interesting enough to deserve criticism, and this is the language of advertising.

Financial success – and the applause of those he considered his peers – came to Mason very quickly, with his second novel. How deliberately he sought it can be read in his biography. 'Not feeling that the novel of contemporary manners and the psychological dissection of rather trivial characters demanded in such a work' (this is only one of Mr Green's critical *non sequiturs*) 'was quite in his line, Mason cast about for new ground – *and ground from which might spring a quick and widespread success*. He read the works of that day's most popular story-teller, Stanley Weyman. ... and decided that in the realms of historical fiction lay his most likely province.' (The italics are mine.)

Writing novels was not a career – it was an element in his career: an aid in leading his full bachelor life. One has the impression of a man who never surrendered himself. Life touched him only from across the footlights. We remember Conrad struggling with a novel in lodgings while his small son lay dangerously ill in the next room, the agony of his divided allegiances, but there were no allegiances to bring Mason painfully in touch with the ordinary emotions of his fellows. From the evidence provided by his biography (the

163

death of a young secretary seems to have been his worst pain) a succession of light flirtations took the place of a wife or mistress. Even his participation in the First World War had a touch of the old Lyceum about it: Major Mason of the Secret Service sailing around the Mediterranean, intercepting anthrax germs, in Mexico stealing the audion lamps (whatever they may be) from a German-operated wireless station. He must have been a happy man and we do not grudge him his happiness. He has given most of us a lot of happiness at one stage of our lives. But if only, with so much skill and invention, he had been involved; if only he had worked at his craft.

I have been re-reading his most popular book, *The Four Feathers*. It is a study of fear, the fear of cowardice. The illustration he has chosen, a general's son, heir to a long line of military ancestors, brought up for the Service, is an obvious and conventional one, but the story still holds us for a few lazy hours. Indeed, I think I liked it better than I did as a boy. Unlike the film adaptations most of the story takes place in England, off-stage, and I remember that when I was fifteen I wanted to skip all those pages of love and misunderstanding. The boy was bored by what the adult can't quite swallow. And yet the book has many merits: the military mind of the parent is critically regarded. There are – in so conventional a story – unexpected notes of harshness: the girl who presents her lover with the fourth white feather of cowardice hates his three comrades who started the cruel affair and rejoices when one is killed in the Sudan. These are the touches of reality which force us today to read on, and which make it, I think, a better book than its close kin, *The Light that Failed*. But the dialogue is hopelessly unreal: it is there to advance the story and not to express character. When the hero is delirious in the Omdurman prison, his feverish utterances are sufficiently lucid and chronological to explain to the man he has come to rescue all the events leading to his capture. It is as if the author had an urgent appointment to keep when the story was done, and he must take the easiest way to reach the end. His task finished (and his MS was like a clean copy) there was mountaineering in the Alps, during the autumn a 2,000-acre shoot, a trip to South Africa. One remembers Conrad writing: 'It's late. I am tired after a day of uphill toil. Now it is always up-hill with me. And the worst is one doesn't seem any nearer the top when the day is done.' One doubts whether Mason would have understood. They had set themselves different summits.

1952

ISIS IDOL

One break comes every year in my quiet life. Then I go to Dresden, and there I am met by my dear friend and companion, Fritz von Tarlenheim. Last time, his pretty wife Helga came and a lusty crowing baby with her. And for a week Fritz and I are together, and I hear all of what falls out in Strelsau; and in the evenings, as we walk and smoke together, we talk of Sapt, and of the King, and often of young Rupert; and, as the hours grow small, at last we speak of Flavia. For every year Fritz carries with him to Dresden a little box; in it lies a red rose, and round the stalk of the rose is a slip of paper with the words written: 'Rudolf – Flavia – always'.

So *The Prisoner of Zenda* ended. How one swallowed it all at the age of fourteen, the clever, brittle sentiment of a novel that has been made a schoolbook in Egypt, has been serialized in Japan, which has been filmed and staged time and again. Now it begins to fade out, like the ghost 'with a melodious twang'.

There is a true Edwardian air about *The Prisoner of Zenda*, *Phroso* and *The Dolly Dialogues*; and they may still survive awhile as period pieces. If one had tried without Sir Charles Mallet's help,* to imagine the author surely one would have hit on this frontispiece: the long well-bred nose, the pointed legal face, the top hat gleaming in the late summer sun, the silver-headed cane, and the chair beside the Row. Ladies with large picture-hats slant off under the trees towards Hyde Park Corner. The author is amused; he has just come up to town

* *Anthony Hope and His Books*, by Sir Charles Mallet.

from Lady Battersea's; he is composing a light whimsical letter on the latest political move and his own idleness to the Duchess of Sutherland, whom he knows affectionately as Griss. It is the atmosphere of Sargent, of Fabergé jewels, but one is not sorry that to this author, who enjoyed with such naïve relish the great houses, the little political crisis, the vulgarity was hidden.

> Rich Jews at Court, in London and at Baden;
> Italian slang and golden chamberware;
> Adultery and racing; for the garden
> Muslin and picture-hats and a blank stare.

He was a thoroughly Balliol best-seller: a double first, a President of the Union, he took his popularity (£70,000 earned in the first ten years of writing) with admirable suavity. He was never really a professional writer: it is mainly the respectable underworld of literature that is represented in the letters of which Sir Charles Mallet's book is more or less a *précis*: he turned his novels off in a couple of months. Sometimes there were as many as three manuscripts awaiting publication. He managed in his delicate dealings with tragic or even black-guardedly themes to retain the Union air of not being wholly serious. You could forgive his sentimentality because it struck so artificial an attitude. He was a Balliol man: he wasn't easily impressed by his great contemporaries. It seemed to him that Hardy was rather limited in his opinions, and when Henry James died, he wrote: 'a dear old fellow, a great gentleman ... The critics call him a "great novelist". I can't think that.' His own work was highly praised by Sir James Barrie and Sir Gilbert Parker, but he was not conceited. 'Have you read my *Phroso*? I wrote it in seven weeks laughing, and now I have to be solemnly judged as though it were the effort of a life. It's really like explaining a kiss in the Divorce Court. ...' An Isis Idol knows that next week he must inevitably be dethroned, and he was quite prepared to see himself superseded by another generation of popular writers who would appeal to a taste which was already beginning to reject the sentimental badinage of *The Dolly Dialogues*.

'I should describe you, Lady Mickleham,' I replied discreetly,
'as being a little lower than the angels.'

Dolly's smile was almost a laugh as she asked:

'How much lower, please, Mr Carter?'

'Just by the depth of your dimples,' I said thoughtlessly.

He always said that a run of about fifteen years would be
his limit, and he wrote towards the end of his time: 'If I live
to advanced age, I shall, I think, be dead while I yet live in
the body. I don't complain. It is just . . . I've had a pretty good
run.' It was sporting, the thoroughly Isis manner, and one is
rather sorry that he did live long enough to see his sales decline,
that he didn't die, like Mr Rassendyll, still king in Ruritania.
His heart ought to have given way in his own fragile, romantic,
rather bogus style at the highest leap – of his carefully recorded
statistics.

1935

THE LAST BUCHAN

MORE than a quarter of a century has passed since Richard
Hannay found the dead man in his flat and started that long
flight and pursuit – across the Yorkshire and the Scottish
moors, down Mayfair streets, along the passages of Government buildings, in and out of Cabinet rooms and country
houses, towards the cold Essex jetty with the thirty-nine steps,
that were to be a pattern for adventure-writers ever since.
John Buchan was the first to realize the enormous dramatic
value of adventure in familiar surroundings happening to un-
adventurous men, members of Parliament and members of the
Athenaeum, lawyers and barristers, business men and minor
peers: murder in 'the atmosphere of breeding and simplicity
and stability'. Richard Hannay, Sir Edward Leithen, Mr Blenkiron, Archie Roylance, and Lord Lamancha; these were his
adventurers, not Dr Nikola or the Master of Ballantrae, and
who will forget the first thrill in 1916 as the hunted Leithen –
the future Solicitor-General – ran 'like a thief in a London
thoroughfare on a June afternoon'?

Now I saw how thin is the protection of civilization. An accident and a bogus ambulance – a false charge and a bogus arrest – there were a dozen ways of spiriting one out of this gay and bustling world.

Now Leithen, who survived the perils of the Green Park and the mews near Belgrave Square, has died in what must seem to those who remember *The Power House* a rather humdrum way, doing good to depressed and starving Indians in Northern Canada, anticipating by only a few months his creator's death.*

What is remarkable about these adventure-stories is the completeness of the world they describe. The backgrounds to many of us may not be sympathetic, but they are elaborately worked in: each character carries round with him his school, his regiment, his religious beliefs, often touched with Calvinism: memories of grouse-shooting and deer-stalking, of sport at Eton, debates in the House. For men who live so dangerously they are oddly conventional – or perhaps, remembering men like Scott and Oates, we can regard that, too, as a realistic touch. They judge men by their war-record: even the priest in *Sick Heart River*, fighting in the desolate northern waste for the Indians' salvation, is accepted by Leithen because 'he had served in a French battalion which had been on the right of the Guards at Loos'. Toc H and the British Legion lurk in the background.

In the early books, fascinated by the new imaginative form, the hair-breadth escapes in a real world, participating wholeheartedly in the struggle between a member of the Athenaeum and the man who could hood his eyes like a hawk, we didn't notice the curious personal ideals, the vast importance Buchan attributed to success, the materialism ... *Sick Heart River*, the last adventure of the dying Leithen seeking – at Blenkiron's request – the missing business man, Francis Galliard, who had left his wife and returned to his ancestral North, has all the old admirable dry ease of style – it is the intellectual content which repels us now, the Scotch admiration of success. 'Harold has a hard life. He's head of the Fremont Banking

---

* *Sick Heart River*, by John Buchan, 1940.

Corporation and a St Sebastian for everyone to shoot arrows at.' Even a nation is judged by the same standard: 'They ought to have made a rather bigger show in the world than they have.' Individuals are of enormous importance. Just as the sinister Mr Andrew Lumley in *The Power House* was capable of crumbling the whole Western world into anarchy, so Francis Galliard – 'one of Simon Ravelston's partners' – must be found for the sake of America. 'He's too valuable a man to lose, and in our present state of precarious balance we just can't afford it.'

But though *Sick Heart River* appears at the moment least favourable to these ideas (for it is not, after all, the great men – the bankers and the divisional commanders and the Ambassadors, who have been holding our world together this winter, and if we survive, it is by 'the wandering, wavering grace of humble men' in Bow and Coventry, Bristol and Birmingham), let us gratefully admit that, in one way at any rate, Buchan prepared us in his thrillers better than he knew for the death that may come to any of us, as it nearly came to Leithen, by the railings of the Park or the doorway of the mews. For certainly we can all see now 'how thin is the protection of civilization'.

1941

EDGAR WALLACE

I ONLY saw Edgar Wallace once, but the moment has stayed in my memory like a 'conversation piece'. I was twenty-five years old, I had published a first novel, and I found myself a junior guest, very much 'a stranger and afraid' at a great publisher's do at the Savoy Hotel – a banquet (no lesser word will serve) given jointly by the English and American firms of Heinemann and Doubleday, who were then in uneasy partnership.

Dinner at the long tables, set at right angles, seemed a kind of frozen geometry, but for a young man it was worse when the geometrical figure was eventually broken and I found myself with my coffee seated beside Arnold Bennett who, when a waiter gave me a glass of 'something' (I was too frightened to refuse), remarked sternly, 'A serious writer does not drink liqueurs.' At that moment (which doomed me, so far as liqueurs were concerned, to a lifetime's abstinence) I looked away from him and saw Edgar Wallace at his first meeting with Hugh Walpole.

I feel quite certain it was the first time these two giants of the commercial novel had met: the giant of the circulating library and the giant of the cheap edition, the writer who wanted, vainly, to be distinguished and recognized and applauded as a literary figure, and the writer who wanted, vainly too, to have all the money he needed, not to bother about debts, to win the Derby every first Wednesday in June, and to escape – to escape from the knowledge of the world which perhaps the other would have given half his success to have shared.

I remember Walpole's patronizing gaze, his bald head inclined under the chandeliers like that of a bishop speaking with kindness to an unimportant member of his diocese. And the unimportant member? – he was so oblivious of the bishop's patronage that the other shrank into insignificance before the heavy confident body, the long challenging cigarette-holder, the sense that this man cared not so much as a flybutton for the other's world. They had nothing in common, not even an ambition. Even in those days I found myself on the side of Wallace.

From what environment Wallace escaped we learn from Margaret Lane's careful, sensitive and beautifully organized biography * (has there ever before been so literate a biography of a writer completely outside the world of serious letters?). There is a curious likeness between the early world of Wallace and the early world of Chaplin: East London and South London were not so far apart.

The mothers of both men were small figures in the theatrical world who never made good. Chaplin was abandoned for periods to the workhouse; Wallace was abandoned altogether to a friendly family in Billingsgate. Chaplin had brief know-

* *Edgar Wallace*, by Margaret Lane.

ledge of his father; Wallace, who was illegitimate, none at all. Of the two children Wallace was the more abandoned, though Chaplin had the crueller experience, and the long distance between love and hate separates the careers of these two men. Chaplin remained, even in his success, rooted to Kennington; Wallace seems to have been concerned only to forget, and there is one repulsive moment in Miss Lane's biography – otherwise the record of a very generous man – when his old mother, penniless and out of work, appeals to him for help and is sent away with the harsh word to expect nothing from him.

At about the same period Wallace wrote to his wife: 'I hate the British working man; I have no sympathy with him; whether he lives or dies, feeds or starves, is not of the slightest interest to me.' You can feel the flames of the burning boats flushing his face. One attitude to the hard childhood produced the immortal Charlie, the other at its best *The Four Just Men* bent on their mission of vengeance.

No one – the theologians and the psychologists agree – is responsible for his own character: he can make only small modifications for good or ill. Chaplin chose the route of the artist and assimilated the hard childhood which Wallace rejected. And Wallace? Instead of the artist we have a phenomenon which might have been invented by Balzac – the human book-factory. We cannot help wondering, reading of the 150 novels he wrote in twenty-seven years (twenty-eight of them written at £70 a time), whether he could not have found an easier road than words to – what? Not exactly financial success, for at his death he left £140,000 of debts, but at least to that state of life where there was money to burn.

Sometimes, looking in the windows of art-dealers south of Picadilly, I find myself wondering how it is that a painter has stopped just here. I could no more paint that sunset or that beetling cliff, that moorland with the clump of sheep, than I could draw a recognizable human face; but with that amount of enviable skill what has made the painter stop? Perhaps the answer is that if he had ever possessed the capacity to enlarge his skill he would never have begun on that sunset, that cliff, that moorland.

171

The parallel is not exact, for Wallace at the very beginning of his writing career had one great quality: he could create a legend. I read *The Four Just Men* for the first time when I was about ten years old, with enormous excitement, and when I re-read it the other day it was with almost the same emotion. The plain style sometimes falls into clichés, but not often; the melodrama grips in the same way as *The New Arabian Nights* (Stevenson, too, had a family history from which he tried to escape through fantasy); Wallace tells an almost incredible story with very precise realistic details. The Foreign Secretary pursued by the four anarchists doesn't dress up as an old Jew, like the detective in *The Flying Squad*, nor as a toothless Arab beggar, like the American diplomat in *The Man From Morocco*, and there is no, thank God, love interest at all. The story moves at a deeper level of invention than he ever tapped again.

Afterwards he invented so rapidly that sometimes he forgot the opening of a paragraph before he reached its end, as in this description of a rather unlikely Bond Street flat (the italics are mine):

The room in which he sat, with its high ceiling fantastically carved into scrolls and arabesques by the most cunning of Moorish workmen, was wide and long and singular. The walls were of marble, the floor an amazing mosaic covered with the silky rugs of Ispahan. ... With the exception of the desk, incongruously gaudy *in the severe and beautiful setting*, there was little furniture.

Grant the initial unlikelihood of four anarchists who terrorize London, the police force, the Government, and then every detail is authentic – so a legend is created. When the hour of doom for the Foreign Secretary pronounced by the Four Just Men approaches, he is locked in his room and detectives fill the passages. The whole city is in the hands of the police.

By order of the Commissioner, Westminster Bridge was closed to all traffic, vehicular or passenger. The section of the Embankment that runs between Westminster and Hungerford Bridge was next swept by the police and cleared of curious pedestrians; Northumberland Avenue was barred, and before three o'clock there was no space within five hundred yards of the official residence of Sir Philip Ramon that was not held by a representative of the law. Members of Parliament on their way to the House were escorted by mounted men, and taking on a reflected glory, were cheered by the crowd. All that afternoon a hundred thousand people waited patiently, seeing nothing, save, towering above the heads of a host of constabulary, the spires and towers of the Mother of Parliaments, or the blank faces of the buildings – in Trafalgar Square, along the Mall as far as the police would allow them, at the lower end of Victoria Street, eight deep along the Albert Embankment, growing in volume every hour. London waited, waited in patience, orderly, content to stare steadfastly at nothing, deriving no satisfaction for their weariness but a sense of being as near as it was humanly possible to be to the scene of a tragedy. A stranger arriving in London, bewildered by this gathering, asked for the cause. A man standing on the outskirts of the Embankment throng pointed across the river with the stem of his pipe.

'We're waiting for a man to be murdered,' he said simply, as one who describes a familiar function.

Surely at the start this man could write. If only he had cared enough. But the illegitimate child left with the Billingsgate family, the boy on the milk-run, had not dreamt of being a writer. He had dreamt of a fortune, a first-class suite in some great liner, of a racing stable; he had dreamt of escape, and the greatness of the debts when Wallace came to die represented fairly enough the greatness of the escape, for the bank manager in Tanner's Hill would surely not have allowed even Wallace's employer on the milk-run an overdraft exceeding ten pounds.

1964

BEATRIX POTTER

'I T is said that the effect of eating too much lettuce is soporific.' It is with some such precise informative sentence that one might have expected the great Potter saga to open, for the obvious characteristic of Beatrix Potter's style is a selective realism, which takes emotion for granted and puts aside love and death with a gentle detachment reminiscent of Mr E. M. Forster's. Her stories contain plenty of dramatic action, but it is described from the outside by an acute and unromantic observer, who never sacrifices truth for an effective gesture. As an example of Miss Potter's empiricism, her rigid adherence to what can be seen and heard, consider the climax of her masterpiece *The Roly-Poly Pudding*, Tom Kitten's capture by the rats in the attic:

'Anna Maria,' said the old man rat (whose name was Samuel Whiskers), 'Anna Maria, make me a kitten dumpling roly-poly pudding for my dinner.'
'It requires dough and a pat of butter, and a rolling pin,' said Anna Maria, considering Tom Kitten with her head on one side.
'No,' said Samuel Whiskers. 'Make it properly, Anna Maria, with breadcrumbs.'

But in 1908, when *The Roly-Poly Pudding* was published, Miss Potter was at the height of her power. She was not a born realist, and her first story was not only romantic, it was historical. *The Tailor of Gloucester* opens:

In the time of swords and periwigs, and full-skirted coats with flowered lappets–when gentlemen wore ruffles and gold-lace waistcoats of paduasoy and taffeta – there lived a tailor in Gloucester.

In the sharp details of this sentence, in the flowered lappets, there is a hint of the future Potter, but her first book is not only hampered by its period setting but by the presence of a human character. Miss Potter is seldom at her best with human beings (the only flaw in *The Roly-Poly Pudding* is the introduction in the final pages of the authoress in person), though with one human character she succeeded triumphantly. I refer, of course, to Mr MacGregor, who made an elusive appearance in 1904 in *The Tale of Benjamin Bunny*, ran his crabbed earthmould way through *Peter Rabbit*, and met his final ignominious defeat in *The Flopsy Bunnies* in 1909. But the tailor of Gloucester cannot be compared with Mr MacGregor. He is too ineffective and too virtuous, and the atmosphere of the story – snow and Christmas bells and poverty – is too Dickensian. Incidentally in Simpkin Miss Potter drew her only unsympathetic portrait of a cat. The ancestors of Tom Thumb and Hunca-Munca play a humanitarian part. Their kind hearts are a little oppressive.

In the same year Miss Potter published *Squirrel Nutkin*. It is an unsatisfactory book, less interesting than her first, which was a good example of a bad *genre*. But in 1904, with the publication of *Two Bad Mice*, Miss Potter opened the series of her great comedies. In this story of Tom Thumb and Hunca-Munca and their wanton havoc of a doll's house, the unmistakable Potter style first appears.

It is an elusive style, difficult to analyse. It owes something to alliteration:

Hunca Munca stood up in her chair and chopped at the ham with another lead knife.

'It's as hard as the hams at the Cheesemonger's,' said Hunca-Munca.

Something too it owes to the short paragraphs, which are fashioned with a delicate irony, not to complete a movement, but mutely to criticize the action by arresting it. The imperceptive pause allows the mind to take in the picture: the mice are stilled in their enraged attitudes for a moment, before the action sweeps forward.

Then there was no end to the rage and disappointment of Tom Thumb and Hunca-Munca. They broke up the pudding, the lobsters, the pears, and the oranges.

As the fish would not come off the plate, they put it into the redhot crinkly paper fire in the kitchen; but it would not burn either.

It is curious that Beatrix Potter's method of paragraphing has never been imitated.

The last quotation shows another element of her later style, her love of a precise catalogue, her creation of atmosphere with still-life. One remembers Mr MacGregor's rubbish heap:

There were jam pots and paper bags and mountains of chopped grass from the mowing machine (which always tasted oily), and some rotten vegetable marrows and an old boot or two.

The only indication in *Two Bad Mice* of a prentice hand is the sparsity of dialogue; her characters had not yet begun to utter those brief pregnant sentences, which have slipped, like proverbs, into common speech. Nothing in the early book equals Mr Jackson's 'No teeth. No teeth. No teeth.'

In 1904 too *The Tale of Peter Rabbit*, the second of the great comedies, was published, closely followed by its sequel, *Benjamin Bunny*. In Peter and his cousin Benjamin Miss Potter created two epic personalities. The great characters of fiction are often paired: Quixote and Sancho, Pantagruel and Panurge, Pickwick and Weller, Benjamin and Peter. Peter was a neurotic, Benjamin wordly and imperturbable. Peter was warned by his mother, 'Don't go into Mr MacGregor's garden; your father had an accident there; he was put in a pie by Mrs MacGregor.' But Peter went from stupidity rather than for adventure. He escaped from Mr MacGregor by leaving his clothes behind, and the sequel, the story of how his clothes were recovered, introduces Benjamin, whose coolness and practicality are a foil to the nerves and clumsiness of his cousin. It was Benjamin who knew the way to enter a garden: 'It spoils people's clothes to squeeze under a gate; the proper way to get in is to climb down a pear tree.' It was Peter who fell down head first.

From 1904 to 1908 were the vintage years in comedy; to these years belong *The Pie and the Patty Pan*, *The Tale of Tom Kitten*, *The Tale of Mrs Tiggy Winkle*, and only one failure, *Mr Jeremy Fisher*. Miss Potter had found her right vein and her right scene. The novels were now set in Cumberland; the farms, the village shops, the stone walls, the green slope of Catbells became the background of her pictures and her prose. She was peopling a countryside. Her dialogue had become memorable because aphoristic:

'I disapprove of tin articles in puddings and pies. It is most undesirable – (especially when people swallow in lumps).'

She could draw a portrait in a sentence:

'My name is Mrs Tiggy Winkle; oh yes if you please'm, I'm an excellent clear-starcher.'

And with what beautiful economy she sketched the first smiling villain of her gallery. Tom Kitten had dropped his clothes off the garden wall as the Puddle-Duck family passed:

'Come! Mr Drake Puddle-Duck,' said Moppet, 'Come and help us to dress him! Come and button up Tom!'

Mr Drake Puddle-Duck advanced in a slow sideways manner, and picked up the various articles.

But he put them on himself. They fitted him even worse than Tom Kitten.

'It's a very fine morning,' said Mr Drake Puddle-Duck.

Looking backward over the thirty years of Miss Potter's literary career, we see that the creation of Mr Puddle-Duck marked the beginning of a new period. At some time between 1907 and 1909 Miss Potter must have passed through an emotional ordeal which changed the character of her genius. It would be impertinent to inquire into the nature of the ordeal. Her case is curiously similar to that of Henry James. Something happened which shook their faith in appearance. From *The Portrait of a Lady* onwards, innocence deceived, the treachery of friends, became the theme of James's greatest stories. Mme Merle, Kate Croy, Mme de Vionnet, Charlotte Stant, these tortuous treacherous women are paralleled through the dark period of Miss Potter's art. 'A man can smile and smile and be a villain,' that, a little altered, was her recurrent message, expressed by her gallery of scoundrels: Mr Drake Puddle-Duck, the first and slightest, Mr Jackson, the least harmful with his passion for honey and his reiterated, 'No teeth. No teeth. No teeth', Samuel Whiskers, gross and brutal, and the 'gentleman with sandy whiskers' who may be identified with Mr Tod. With the publication of *Mr Tod* in 1912, Miss Potter's pessimism reached its climax. But for the nature of her audience *Mr Tod* would certainly have ended tragically. In *Jemima Puddle-Duck* the gentleman with sandy whiskers had at least a debonair impudence when he addressed his victim:

'Before you commence your tedious sitting, I intend to give you a treat. Let us have a dinner party all to ourselves!

177

'May I ask you to bring up some herbs from the farm garden to make a savoury omelette? Sage and thyme, and mint and two onions, and some parsley. I will provide lard for the stuff – lard for the omelette,' said the hospitable gentleman with sandy whiskers.

But no charm softens the brutality of Mr Tod and his enemy, the repulsive Tommy Brock. In her comedies Miss Potter had gracefully eliminated the emotions of love and death; it is the measure of her genius that when, in *The Tale of Mr Tod*, they broke the barrier, the form of her book, her ironic style, remained unshattered. When she could not keep death out she stretched her technique to include it. Benjamin and Peter had grown up and married, and Benjamin's babies were stolen by Brock; the immortal pair, one still neurotic, the other knowing and imperturbable, set off to the rescue, but the rescue, conducted in darkness, from a house, 'something between a cave, a prison, and a tumbledown pig-sty', compares grimly with an earlier rescue from Mr MacGregor's sunny vegetable garden:

The sun had set; an owl began to hoot in the wood. There were many unpleasant things lying about, that had much better have been buried; rabbit bones and skulls and chicken's legs and other horrors. It was a shocking place and very dark.

But *Mr Tod*, for all the horror of its atmosphere, is indispensable. There are few fights in literature which can compare in excitement with the duel between Mr Tod and Tommy Brock (it was echoed by H. G. Wells in *Mr Polly*):

Everything was upset except the kitchen table.
And everything was broken, except the mantelpiece and the kitchen fender. The crockery was smashed to atoms.
The chairs were broken, and the window, and the clock fell with a crash, and there were handfuls of Mr Tod's sandy whiskers.
The vases fell off the mantelpiece, the canisters fell off the shelf; the kettle fell off the hob. Tommy Brock put his foot in a jar of raspberry jam.'

Mr Tod marked the distance which Miss Potter had travelled since the ingenuous romanticism of *The Tailor of Gloucester*.

The next year with *The Tale of Pigling Bland*, the period of the great near-tragedies came to an end. There was something of the same squalor, and the villain, Mr Thomas Piperson, was not less terrible than Mr Tod, but the book ended on a lyric note, as Pigling Bland escaped with Pig-Wig:

They ran, and they ran, and they ran down the hill, and across a short cut on level green turf at the bottom, between pebble-beds and rushes. They came to the river, they came to the bridge – they crossed it hand in hand –

It was the nearest Miss Potter had approached to a conventional love story. The last sentence seemed a promise that the cloud had lifted, that there was to be a return to the style of the earlier comedies. But *Pigling Bland* was published in 1913. Through the years of war the author was silent, and for many years after it was over, only a few books of rhyme appeared. These showed that Miss Potter had lost none of her skill as an artist, but left the great question of whither her genius was tending unanswered. Then, after seventeen years, at the end of 1930, *Little Pig Robinson* was published.

The scene was no longer Cumberland but Devonshire and the sea. The story, more than twice as long as *Mr Tod*, was diffuse and undramatic. The smooth smiling villain had disappeared and taken with him the pungent dialogue, the sharp detail, the light of common day. Miss Potter had not returned to the great comedies. She had gone on beyond the great near-tragedies to her *Tempest*. No tortured Lear nor strutting Antony could live on Prospero's island, among the sounds and sweet airs and cloudcapt towers. Miss Potter too had reached her island, the escape from tragedy, the final surrender of imagination to safe serene fancy:

A stream of boiling water flowed down the silvery strand. The shore was covered with oysters. Acid-drops and sweets grew upon the trees. Yams, which are a sort of sweet potato, abounded ready cooked. The breadfruit tree grew iced cakes and muffins ready baked.

It was all very satisfying for a pig Robinson, but in that

rarefied air no bawdy Tommy Brock could creep to burrow, no Benjamin pursue his feud between the vegetable-frames, no Puddle-Duck could search in wide-eyed innocence for a 'convenient dry nesting-place'.

Note. On the publication of this essay I received a somewhat acid letter from Miss Potter correcting certain details. *Little Pig Robinson*, although the last published of her books, was in fact the first written. She denied that there had been any emotional disturbance at the time she was writing *Mr Tod*: she was suffering however from the after-effects of flu. In conclusion she deprecated sharply 'the Freudian school' of criticism.

1933

HARKAWAY'S OXFORD

M Y father used to have hanging on his bathroom wall a photographic group of young men in evening dress with bright blue waistcoats. They were, I think, the officials of an Oxford undergraduate wining club, but with their side-whiskers and heavy moustaches they had more the appearance of Liberal Ministers. Earnest and well-informed, they hardly seemed to be members of the same world as Jack Harkaway, whose adventures at Oxford were published in twopenny numbers – or bound together in two volumes at 6*d*. apiece – by the 'Boys of England' office some time in the early eighties. They seemed, sitting there on dining-room chairs, squarely facing the camera to hark back more naturally to that much earlier Oxford described by Newman, when *Letters on the Church by an Episcopalian* was a book to make the blood boil – 'One of our common friends told me, that, after reading it, he could not keep still, but went on walking up and down in his room.' But unless we are to disbelieve the literary evidence of *Jack Harkaway at Oxford*, the earnest moustache is deceptive: it is the bright blue waistcoat which is the operative image, and I like to imagine that my father's photograph contained the whole galaxy – Tom Carden, Sir Sydney Dawson, Fabian Hall, Harvey, and the Duke of Woodstock – of what must have been known universally as a Harkaway year, for in 188— Harkaway

succeeded in the then unprecedented feat of winning his Blue
for rowing, cricket, and football and ending the academic
year with a double-first. All this too in spite of the many
attempts upon his life and honour engineered by Davis of
Singapore whom he had baffled while still a schoolboy in the
East. Their reunion at Sir Sydney Dawson's 'wine' is an impressive scene – impressive too in its setting:

A variety of wines were upon the table with all sorts of biscuits
and preserved fruits. Olives, however, seemed to be the most
popular. A box of cigars, which cost four guineas, invited the
attention of smokers. ... Jack walked over to a tall, effeminate
looking young man, with a pale complexion, and having his hair
parted in the middle.
'How do, Kemp?' he said.
'Ah, how do?' replied Kemp, with a peculiar smile. 'Allow me
to introduce you to my friend, Mr Frank Davis of Singapore.'
Jack stared in amazement. Before him was his sworn and determined enemy. Davis had told him that he was going to England
to complete his education at a University. He had added that
wherever Jack was, he would still hate him, and seek for his
revenge. ... That it was Davis of Singapore he had no doubt. He
had lost one ear.
Making a cold and distant bow, Davis replied – 'Mr Harkaway
and I have met before.'
'Really?' exclaimed Kemp. 'I'm glad of that. It's such a nuisance
helping fellows to talk. Davis is not in our college. He's a Merton
man.'

It was unwise of Harkaway towards the end of this same
'wine' to transfix Kemp's hand to the table with a fork when
he detected him cheating at cards. The incident led directly to
the corruption of Sir Sydney with drink so that he could not
ride in the steeplechase against the Duke of Woodstock's horse,
Kemp up; to Jack's imprisonment for debt on the eve of
the Boat Race (but the Jew's beautiful daughter Hilda, whom
he had saved from drowning in the Cher, foiled *that* plot);
to the kidnapping of Hilda and Emily, Jack's betrothed, by
Davis and the Duke of Woodstock ('"Let's have – aw – one
kiss before we part," said the Duke, with an amorous glance

in Hilda's direction. "Dash my – aw – buttons, but one kiss." ');
to the foul attempt on Jack's life in a railway train, and to
Kemp setting Emily alight – a rather bizarre episode:

> He approached Emily, who was standing with her back to him
> in her muslin ball dress, looking very gauzy and fairylike.
> Drawing a wax match from his pocket, he struck it gently, and
> held it under her skirt lighting the inflammable material in three
> places.
> Then he retired with the same snakelike, gliding manner.

The story is, of course, a sensational one (it isn't often that
an undergraduate arrives in Oxford with so teeming a past,
and with a private tutor – Mr Mole – who had been secretly
married to a black woman in the east), but its chief value, I
think, lies in its incidentals: the still-life of an Oxford breakfast – 'At ten o'clock a very decent breakfast stood on the
table, consisting of cold game, hot fish, Strasbourg patties,
honey in the comb, tea and coffee, with other trifles'; in the
delightful turns of phrase:

> 'Do you dine in Hall?'
> 'No, we have ordered our mutton at the Mitre,'

and the local manners:

> 'What shall we do?'
> 'Go and screw Scraper up,' said an undergraduate in his second
> year.
> 'Splendid!' replied Sir Sydney Dawson. 'Get a hammer and
> gimlet and some screws.'
> Mr Scraper was an unpopular tutor, and they did not care for
> consequences. ... The Dean heard the noise, and summoning two
> tutors, went with the porter carrying a lantern to the scene of the
> disturbance.
> 'What is the matter, Mr Scraper?' said the Dean.
> 'I am screwed up, sir,' said Mr Scraper.

One notices in this wild scene outside Mr Scraper's window
an odd change in the character of one college: 'A friend of
Dawson's who was a Brasenose man sank on his knees overcome by wine, and began to recite a portion of Demosthenes'
oration on the crown.'

But above all I value the book for its picture of Sir Sydney Dawson, imprudent, good-hearted, arrogant, the apotheosis of the wining club. With his aristocratic brutality and his spend-thrift kindliness, he must have been every inch a blue waistcoat. Take, for example, the incident of the explosive cigars in Sir Sydney's room: ' "I keep them for my tradesmen. The fellows come here worrying for orders and I give them a cigar, which soon starts them," replied the baronet laughing', but when he had blown up Mr Mole, scorched his face, and tumbled him in a bowl of goldfish, he feels for the tutor – ' "By Jove, this is not right. I must write a letter of apology." ' In the theatre 'as if to show his contempt for Oxford society, Sir Sydney Dawson took out his handsome cigar-case, and lighted up, though he knew it was against the rules', but his treatment of Franklin who does lines for commoners in return for a consideration (' "I am one of the servitors of the college. Perhaps you do not know what that is," he added with a sad smile') shows he has a kind heart. ' "I wonder what a poor man at Oxford is like. I should like to see him. Perhaps an hour or two with a poor man would do me good, always supposing he's a gentleman. I can't stand a cad." '

It may be argued, of course, that, because the author, Edwin J. Brett, had never been to Oxford, this whole setting is imaginary, an Oxford of the heart, but I do not see why the well-known argument in favour of immortality should not apply here too – that 'an instinct does not exist unless there is a possibility of its being satisfied', and certainly the instinct exists in this confused uncertain age – a will to return to Sir Sydney's reckless self-assurance and his breakfasts, to 'mutton at the Mitre', a dogcart 'spanking along the Iffley Road', to screwing Scraper up.

1938

PART III

Some Characters

POETRY FROM LIMBO

MISS GUINEY began this magnificently thorough anthology in 1913.* Her work was nearly finished when she died in 1920, and it was completed by her friend, Mr Edward O'Brien, who brought up to date the biographical and bibliographical notes. Miss Guiney in her introduction makes the modest claim that the value of the collection is as much historical as literary; the scholar must decide on that, but the general reader will be astounded by its wealth of little-known poetry.

The term recusant has been given the widest possible meaning – to include any Catholic who suffered from the civil power for his faith, but the contributions have been wisely confined to those which have some bearing on Catholic doctrine or ideals. Many of the poets, of course, are familiar: More himself, Constable, Lodge, Southwell, Surrey; some have been known only to specialists, and a few make their appearance for the first time in print. It is by no means a purely heroic company, and far from a saintly one – here is the turncoat Alabaster and cowardly, light-headed Copley, who, when he was a student in Rome – so Father Parsons reported – went up to the pulpit to preach with a rose in his mouth. It is a pleasant irony that this Bye Plot conspirator, who made a confession implicating his friends, should have been the author of the fine stoic lines:

> Give me the man that with undaunted spirit
> Dares give occasion of a Tragedie.

Here, too, are the merely unattractive or the grotesque – Myles Hogarde, of Pudding Lane, with his eye for other men's errors, and Pickering, the too-careful Dominican of the Pilgrimage of Grace, who tried to rewrite the popular songs of that wild and hopeful year in a seemly and pedantic way:

* *Recusant Poets*, by Louise Imogen Guiney. With a selection from their work: Sir Thomas More to Ben Jonson.

It is wrytyn in the machabies – Loke well the storie –
Accingemini potentes que estote filii.

It is interesting to watch how, among these unprofessional poets, the heroic and the uncertain, the rash and the too politic, the main themes change. At first the theme is social – the decay of charity and hospitality: the greed for wealth. Men who were born in the pre-capitalist age describe with indignation the new capitalist spirit – which they still hope to see pass:

Such bribyng for the purse, which ever gapes for more,
Such hordyng up of worldly wealth, such keeping much in store ...
Such falshed undercraft, and such unstedfast wayes,
Was never sene within men's hartes, as is found nowadayes.

This is the theme, too, of the magnificent and anonymous marching song of the Pilgrims of Grace: it is astonishingly explicit in a poem by William Forrest, who inventories in minute detail the old just wages for a winter or a summer day, and such post-Reformation abuses as paying a woman less than a man for the same work. As time goes on, this theme vanishes: people can no longer remember the old social system; if the subject re-emerges, as in one of Lodge's poems, it is in the form of nostalgia for something which will never return:

> Then, then did flourish that renowned time,
> When earth and ashes thrusted not to clime.

This was the swan-song of the social conscience among Roman Catholic poets.

The subject of martyrdom next began to take the principal place as the Douai victims accumulated: the peril of informers, the activities of Topcliffe, the warder knocking at the cell-door; and the anonymous author of *Calvary Mount* recounts the whole routine of martyrdom, from the stretching of the joints to the last horrible ride. Again we notice the concreteness of the expression, which became yet barer with the years, until in a poem, not printed here as it dates from 1646, we read:

> But quick and live they cut him down
> And butcher him full soon:
> Behead, tear and dismember straight,
> And laugh when all is done.

A practised poet, of course, dealt very differently and most exquisitely with the same material:

> Rue not my death rejoyce at my repose
> It was no death to mee but to my woe
> The bud was opened to let out the rose
> The cheynes unloosed to let the captive goe;

but we can be glad that those others – who were only poets by accident – stuck to the bare fact.

It is not till the second half of this period that the third subject emerges – the doctrinal. The social changes had been obvious from the start and martyrdoms did not take place in a corner: it needed time for men to feel the weight of the sacramental loss. It was not really oppressive until they had reached that state described by Constable in a sonnet outside the scheme of this book: 'Hope, like the hyena coming to be old.' An anonymous poet writes on 'the new learning'; William Blundell of Crosby carefully notes the changes one by one and concludes in a tone which reminds us of his cavalier descendant:

> The time is now as all men see
> new faiths have kild ould honestie.

And Constable in a sonnet describes the Blessed Sacrament with the exactness of a theologian – again we note the admirable, almost prosaic precision of these poets, which seems more alive to us today than the rich imagery of Spenser.

Only occasionally do I feel inclined to quarrel with the editor – for the suggestion that the lovely singable lament over Walsingham may have been written by Southwell (surely it lacks altogether the heavy intellectual ground-swell of his poetry?) and for the inclusion of so much of Surrey's beautiful and inapposite verse. This is to draw the net too wide – the mainspring of his poetry was mainly aristocratic. It wasn't the faith he missed in prison so much as the 'palme play' at Windsor, the cry of hounds, 'the wanton talk, the divers change of play', the favour of a Court. He seems more out of place in the company of the martyrs than the coward Copley or poor uncertain Alabaster: dying a patrician death on Tower Hill, unacquainted with that dingy cell in Newgate which was known to more base-born recusants as Limbo.

1939

AN UNHEROIC DRAMATIST

R OGER B OYLE, Earl of Orrery, is one of the great bores of literature, and it can hardly have been a labour of love for Mr Clark to edit for the first time eight ponderous heroic plays, hardly lightened by two attempts at comedy. Yet all admirers of the period will be grateful: there is a peculiar satisfaction in seeing one more gap in Restoration scholarship filled with such immense efficiency: no crack between the bricks. Not for them the rather hollow excuse that Orrery was the pioneer of heroic drama in England. They will read with gorged satisfaction that one of these plays, *The Tragedy of Zoroastes*, has never before been printed and that Orrery's first play (Mr Clark leaves us in no doubt of this), *The Generall*, has been previously printed only in a private edition of eighty copies. Another great booming bogus piece, *The Tragedy of King Saul*, is added to the Orrery canon for the first time. All this, with the really magnificent notes on Restoration stage-craft, is a not unworthy harvest of eight years' labour.*

Roger Boyle (let us extend praise as far as it will go) was not always a worse poet than was Lee in his earliest plays: there are a few charming lines to be unearthed in *The Generall* (Mr Clark curiously prefers the maturer, emptier *Henry the Fifth*):

The Dramatic Works of Roger Boyle, Earl of Orrery, edited by William Smith Clark.

Death which mankind in such high awe does keep
Can only hold us in eternal sleep,
And if a life after this life remains,
Sure to our loves belong those happier plains,
There in blest fields I'll pass the endless hours,
And him I crown with love, I'll crown with flowers.

It is very minor poetry, of course, but it does shine out among the heroic sentiments. Otherwise the chief pleasure in this his best play is in the period note. Surfeited with action on the screen, one finds a curious charm in the passivity and irrelevance of a scene which opens: 'Filadin: Lett us then of our mistresses discourse.'

Roger Boyle was not the man for heroic drama. Dryden with his inalterable belief in authority which took him logically by way of Cromwell to the Catholic Church, yes: Lee with the turbulent generous mind that brought him to Bedlam, yes: but we are aware of too great a gap between the man and his poetry when we get as low as Settle, and Boyle presents us with the same incongruity. Mr Clark has written his life in greater detail, though with infinitely less charm, than Eustace Budgell (to whose eighteenth-century biography he might surely have paid the tribute of a footnote), and the portrait he rather stiffly draws is that of a very polite man, a man who lived on the dubious borderline between patronage and treachery. He played no part in the Civil War in England, being fortunate enough to be occupied in Ireland against the Catholic rebels: on the King's death he began to correspond with Charles II, but Cromwell got possession of the letters and in a remarkable scene, which Mr Clark should have given in detail, presented him with the choice between the Tower and a command in Ireland. Boyle, of course, took the command, and on Cromwell's death began again his political moves. But he was forestalled by Monck: the patriot always moves faster than the politic. Nevertheless he became a friend of the King, wrote plays at the Royal command and, when he had the gout, served in Ireland, intrigued against Ormonde, and died unlamented by Burnet at the age of fifty-nine.

A man quite remarkably free from the impediments of friendship, how can he do else but write a little hollowly on that favourite heroic theme?

> But that I may be better understood
> Knowe friendshipp is a greater tye than blood.
> A sister is a name must not contend
> With the more high and sacred name of friend.

Burnet, if not his chaplain Morrice, saw through his pretence to religion, and there is one moment in *The Generall* when a somewhat similar dramatic situation allows a direct comparison with Dryden. It will be remembered how Don Sebastiano dealt with the theme of suicide:

> Brutus and Cato might discharge their Souls,
> And give them furlo's for another world:
> But we like Centries are oblig'd to stand
> In starless nights, and wait th' appointed hour.

But hear the politic accents of Burnet's 'very fickle and false man' in the character of Altemara:

> When I am forc'd of two ills one to choose,
> 'Tis virtue then the greatest to refuse.
> When in this straight I by the Gods am plac'd,
> I'll rather cease to Live than live unchaste.

Without religion and without friendship, Orrery tried to write heroic dramas: the succession of plays, one imitated from the other, soon palled, even on Pepys, and he tried his hand at comedy. *Guzman* is quite unreadable buffoonery, but of *Mr Anthony* it is just possible to say that it is as good as the worst of D'Urfey. He was, if that is in his favour, a clean writer, but then he seems to have had as little passion as he had religion.

1937

DOCTOR OATES OF SALAMANCA

MISS LANE is to be congratulated on her courage in undertaking so grim and unrelieved a work as a biography of Titus Oates (a work that has deterred biographers for nearly two hundred and fifty years) as well as on her skill and scholarship. No biographer can ever have been able to claim with more likelihood of truth that his work is definitive.*

It is interesting sometimes to speculate on how our ideas of a period would be modified if one character or one episode were removed. A man like Titus Oates occurs like a slip of the tongue, disclosing the unconscious forces, the night-side of an age we might otherwise have thought of in terms of Dryden discussing the art of dramatic poesy, while his Thames boatmen rested on their oars and the thunder of an indeterminate sea battle came up from the Medway no louder than the noise of swallows in a chimney. The reach of human nature in his day, if Oates had not enlightened us, would not have extended much lower than the amiable vices of the Court: Rochester acting Dr Bendo, Sedley prancing naked on the Epsom balcony, sin fluttering with the unimportance of a fan through the delicate cadences of Etherege's prose, that played so charmingly with the same counters, the Park, the Mulberry Gardens, the game of ombre, and as night falls ' 'tis now but high Mall, Madam, the most entertaining time of all the evening'. And reaching the other way, would our hand have extended, without the martyrs of the Plot, much further than the piety of Bunyan? Until Oates came on the scene, it seemed hardly a period for courage any more than for evil. The career of Oates ploughed up the age and exposed the awful unchanging potentialities of human nature.

If we wished to present a portrait of evil in human terms it would be hard to find a more absolute example than the Salamanca doctor. At no point in his career does he seem to have been touched by any form of idealism. At no point is it possible to say that he was led on by a false fanaticism, or that

* *Titus Oates*, by Jane Lane.

he did wrong with any idea that right might come. His career was one of unexampled squalor, from his snotty-nosed childhood. 'I thought that he would have been a natural,' his mother is said to have reported, 'for his Nose always run and he slabbered at the mouth, and his Father could not endure him; and when he came home at night the Boy would use to be in the Chimney corner, and my Husband would cry take away this snotty Fool, and jumble him about, which made me often weep, because you know he was my child.' Yet the early years are the lighter side of Oates's life. So long as he was unsuccessful we can be entertained by the grotesqueness of his career: expelled from school, sent down from Cambridge, turned out of his living, wanted for his first perjury (he had coveted a schoolmaster's post at Hastings and therefore brought against the poor man an accusation of committing an unnatural offence in the church porch), a chaplain in the Navy and expelled again. The shadows fall with his success – his 'conversion' to Catholicism, his stay at St Omer's College, and last the Plot itself.

Miss Lane is careful to give only such details of the Plot and the trials as come directly within the scope of her subject. She does not concern herself, for example, in any detail with the unsolved murder of Sir Edmund Berry Godfrey, a wise austerity perhaps in a book so long and necessarily so unrelieved in its horror. Her judgement of Charles II is admirably balanced and her condemnation brief and pointed. Of Oates's final trial she writes: 'King James left Oates to the Law, which was precisely what King Charles had done in the case of Oates's victims; but whereas Charles knew those victims to be innocent, James was convinced that Oates was guilty.' We prefer this final sentence on the King to the sentimental championship of Mr Arthur Bryant: 'Alone, vilified, driven on every side, Charles remained calm and patient, etc.' The King, it is true, was fighting for the survival of the House of Stuart, but those innocent men, cut down from the gallows while still alive to be drawn and quartered, may well have wondered whether the price the King paid was not too vicarious. 'Let the blood lie on them that condemned them,'

Charles is reported to have said, 'for God knows I sign with tears in my eyes', but even if an appeal is made to God, responsibility cannot be so easily shifted and tears are more becoming after a crime than at the moment of commission. Perhaps this was the chief horror in the career of Oates, the corruption he exercised through fear. If he had had one redeeming quality, physical or mental, if he had charmed as some dictators have done with *bonhomie* or inspired confidence with false oratory, the corruption would have seemed less extreme, but fear was his only weapon, and Charles II joins the poor ex-schoolmaster William Smith as one of those on whose cowardice Oates found he could rely.

1949

ANTHONY À WOOD

WHEN Anthony à Wood, the Oxford antiquarian, died in 1695 and left his books, manuscripts and pamphlets to the Ashmolean Museum, a colleague wrote: 'This benefaction will not perhaps be so much valued by the University as it ought to be because it comes from Anthony Wood.' He was the best-hated man in the University; he was malicious, he was dangerous because he had a power over words; he noted everything. They burnt his great book, *Athenae Oxoniensis*, and he recorded the event in his diary with a venomous certainty of posterity's judgement. In five volumes, published forty years ago by Dr Andrew Clark, the Oxford of his day stands pricked in acid.

There is Mr Smith, of University College, whose lecture in the Theatre was attended by two thousand people. 'Mr Smith was very baudy among the women: he had a grand auditory, while some lecturers had none – so you may see what governs the world'; he hears certain 'bachelors' and masters (he never fails to give names) 'uttering fluently romantick nonsense, unintelligible gibberish, flourishing lyes and nonsense'; he dines with his brother Kit – 'cold meat, cold entertainment, cold

reception, cold clownish woman': he writes of poor John
Aubrey, and Aubrey's most passionate defenders cannot deny
the truth in the caricature: 'a shiftless person, roving and
magotie-headed, and sometimes little better than crased'; the
Court comes and goes again: 'rude, rough, whoremongers;
vaine, empty, carelesse'. Mr Peter Allan, of Christ Church,
'with his pupill Lord Shandoes and Mr Jeanson (who the
Sunday before preached at St Giles) with Sir Willoughby
D'ews' are eternalized in his diary in the act of entering a
bawdy house in Mew Inn Lane. The great Doctor Fell does
not escape the pen which notes also 'a calf with a face like a
man' exhibited at the 'Golden Lion', the rotting bones on a
gibbet on Shotover, a brass here, a natural phenomenon
there.

The Oxford scholars tried to turn the tables. They pretended
he had a bastard at Headington, they made him angry by
accusing him of keeping drunken company; in the days of the
Popish Plot they spread the rumour that he was a papist: 'a
man that is studious and reserved is popishly affected'; but
not one of them left a record to supersede his. William
Prideaux's letters to John Ellis confirm Wood's picture of
seventeenth-century Oxford; there is nothing quainter in Wood
than Prideaux's description of Doctor Fell making a surprise
visit to the Clarendon Press and finding it secretly employed in
printing an edition of Aretine for 'the gentlemen of All Souls';
of Bodley's Librarian nearly beaten to death by his wife, 'an
old whore'; of the Vice-Chancellor's undergraduates 'bubbe-
ing' at the 'Split Crow' with his approval.

Anthony Wood is not concerned only with local history. The
Oxford of the Great Western Railway is more remote from
political life than the Oxford which could just be reached in a
day by a fast coach from London. It was the birth-place of
several of Charles's bastards, the scene of the most dramatic
Parliamentary dissolution of his reign; and James II, too,
presented himself as closely as Doctor Fell to Wood's careful,
malicious eyes: 'Afterwards the King, with a scarlet coat on,
his blew ribbon and Georg, and a star on his left papp, with
an old French course hat on edged with a little seem of lace

(all not worth a groat as some of the people shouted).' But a certain distance from London had its advantages, and during the terror of the Popish Plot Wood's study of character and familiarity with slander kept him from running with the crowd. In 1679 he confided to his diary – he would not have been rash enough to have told it abroad – a story of Oates and Bedlow which ended with the words, 'So the King's worthy evidence sneaked away.'

1932

JOHN EVELYN

IF it were necessary to play at the Shakespeare–Bacon game with the seventeenth century, and having lost the sources of all its lyrics arbitrarily to choose the authors from those men whose careers are still remembered, *The Garden* might easily be assigned to John Evelyn, the author of *Sylva*, rather than to Marvell, the rough satirist, the bishop baiter, the M.P. for Hull. For Evelyn lived very much the life to which Marvell's poetry is an escape.

> The Nectaren, and curious Peach,
> Into my hands themselves do reach

well described his life at Sayes Court; and Lord Ponsonby,* with his unerring eye for the interesting detail, speaks of Evelyn's long list in *Kalendarium Hortense* of apples unknown today, of peaches and nectarines. But a wider gulf than ambition separated the two men. Evelyn, the scholar of gardens, a man so modest that, while he had the entry to the King's presence and walked Whitehall familiarly with Charles, he petitioned for no office more important than the care of the trees in the Royal forests (and that he was not granted), differed from the poet above all in this: the garden was not his escape from life (an escape which very faintly tinges Marvell's poetry with sentimentality), but life itself.

* *John Evelyn*, by Arthur Ponsonby.

Fair quiet, have I found thee here,
And Innocence thy Sister dear,

Marvell wrote, but to the owner of Sayes Court his garden meant a great deal more, or a great deal less, than quiet and innocence. It meant study (he was the translator of *The French Gardener* in his youth, of *The Complete Gardener* in his age). It meant labour:

The hithermost Grove I planted about 1656; the other beyond it, 1660; the lower Grove 1662; the holly hedge even with the Mount hedge below 1670. I planted every hedge and tree not only in the gardens, groves, &c., but about all the fields and house since 1653, except those large, old and hollow elms in the stable court and next the sewer, for it was before, all one pasture field to the very garden of the house, which was but small.

It meant the arid grief of work wasted when Admiral Benbow, to whom Evelyn had let Sayes Court, relet it to Peter the Great, who spoilt the bowling green, demolished fruit trees, and had himself driven daily in a wheelbarrow through the great holly hedge that Evelyn loved. It seems to have been the image by which he could visualize immortality: at his birthplace, at Wotton, to which he returned to live in his old age, he began to labour again: 'I am planting an evergreen grove here to an old house ready to drop.' It was certainly his most enduring passion. 'The late elegant and accomplished Sir W. Temple, tho' he laid not his whole body in this garden, deposited the better part of it (the heart) there; and if my executors will gratify me in what I have desired, I wish my corpse may be interred as I have bespoke them.' But this man of few wants seldom had them gratified, and he was buried within the church. Lord Ponsonby speaks of 'the darkness, the locked door, and the iron railings'.

Evelyn had not Pepys's power of transmitting himself to posterity. He is himself the least character in his own diary; and his knowledge of other men was no more penetrating than his knowledge of himself. He worked hard on a multiplicity of committees, but these were to him as much an escape from real life as the garden was to Marvell. One imagines him selfless, innocent, taken advantage of. He had no instinctive know-lege of psychology; he believed implicitly in the high moral worth of Lady Sunderland, because she kept her garden in good order; he was puzzled by her husband's inconsistencies, rather than distressed by his treacheries. Though he was not deceived in the goodness of Margaret Godolphin, his life of her shows no perception of character. She is Virtue as the Court is Sin, she is Alabaster as it is Clay.

No man, indeed, could be less judged by his friendships, but in that strange company, which included Jeremy Taylor, as well as Lady Sunderland, I wish that Lord Ponsonby had found room for William Oughtred, the mathematician, who, according to Aubrey, came very near to discovering the philo-sopher's stone, and who died with joy at the Restoration. For Evelyn, who had successfully avoided the slaughterings of civil war, came near to killing his friend, when a grotto in the gardens he had designed at Albury collapsed.

His lack of psychological penetration prevented Evelyn from being a good diarist. His merits as a writer showed themselves when he wrote as a specialist, and he was a specialist not only on gardens, but on salads, on coins, on sculpture, on Spinoza, on navigation. I confess that I have to take Lord Ponsonby's word for the value of his great work, *Sylva*. But the same meticulous detail ('Whenever you sow, if you prevent not the little field mouse, he will be sure to have the better share'), can be seen in *Fumifugium* with its plan for a green belt round London planted with sweet smelling flowers and herbs. His style is peppered with pedantries, but there is a kind of Baconian beauty in the accumulation of detail, and a touch all Evelyn's own in the sudden lyrical quickening, the sudden widening of his horizon, as a memory of his early travels comes back on him.

I propose ... That these *Palisads* be elegantly planted, diligently kept and supply'd with such *Shrubs*, as yield the most fragrant and odoriferous *Flowers*, and are aptest to tinge the *Aer* upon every gentle emission at a great distance: Such as are (for instance amongst many others) the *Sweet-brier*, all the *Periclymenas* and *Woodbinds*; the Common *white* and *yellow Jessamine*, both the

Syringas or *Pipe trees*; the *Guelder-rose*, the *Musk* and all other *Roses*; *Genista Hispanica*: To these may be added the *Rubus odoratus, Bayes, Juniper, Lignum-vitae, Lavender*: but above all, *Rosemary*, the *Flowers* whereof are credibly reported to give their scent above thirty Leagues off at Sea, upon the coasts of Spain: and at some distance towards the meadow side, *Vines, yea, Hops*.

The seventeenth century has been lucky lately in its biographers; Lord Ponsonby's *Evelyn* has followed hard on the heels of Mr Bryant's *Pepys*; it is not Lord Ponsonby's fault that he cannot lay claim to finality in his study. Mr Bryant had at his disposal the complete diary, and all the papers collected by Tanner and Wheatley. But Evelyn's diary remains to-day in great part unpublished, and Lord Ponsonby was denied access to the manuscripts at Wotton, and was even refused permission to see the house and grounds. All the more praise is due to him for a biography which certainly ranks as high as Mr Bryant's. There is no nonsense about Lord Ponsonby's work, no trying flowers of fancy, and the character of Evelyn emerges, the more clearly for his biographer's restraint, in its slight conceit, its rather silly pedantry ('You will consult,' Evelyn wrote to Pepys, when the latter was contemplating his history of the navy, 'Fulvius Ursinus, Goltzius, Monsieur St Amant, Otto, Dr Spon, Vaillant, Dr Patin and the most learned Spankemius'), in its essential goodness.

1934

BACKGROUND FOR HEROES

'HE drank a little tea and some sherry. He wound up his watch, and said, now he had done with time and was going to eternity.' So Burnet on Lord William Russell's last hour. History may no longer consist of the biographies of great men, but perhaps our deepest pleasure in Miss Thomson's analysis* of the account books belonging to the Bedford household at Woburn remains in our awareness that this is the way of life of a

* *Life in a Noble Household, 1641–1700*, by Gladys Scott Thomson.

familiar hero, the life he set a period to with the winding of his watch. William, the fifth earl, with whose domestic economy this book chiefly deals, was happy in having no history, but there is an extra-special interest in the fact that his heir, William Russell, was brought up among these surroundings, the huge house of ninety rooms, including the little artificial grotto with the gilt chairs and the Bedford arms among the shells and stalagmites; that he read in this library so ponderously stocked with the works of Baxter (not one play, not a single volume of even sacred poetry), took his impress even from the gardens designed and stocked (the details are here) by the beloved John Field, was fed and clothed out of the family bank, the great chest in Bedford House made in the Netherlands 'painted in the characteristic Dutch fashion, squares showing prim landscapes and flowers, roses and tulips'.

Miss Thomson in a book of great fascination – with little but account books to draw on she has composed a picture of a family as complete as that contained in the Verney Memoirs – analyses the duties and expenditure of the various officials belonging to a household more than regal in its wealth: the receiver-general dealing with the money chest in Bedford Street, the steward of the west looking after the estates in Devon and the neighbouring counties, the steward of the household, the gentleman of the horse, the clerk of the kitchen, the tutor buying books for the library, the gardener plants for the Woburn gardens. The household leaps into life in the small details: the maid Rose lending her master five shillings at a moment of sudden need, sixpence given to a scolding woman who wasn't satisfied with the bargain struck for the hire of a horse, a 'hawk called Tomson'.

Historically the chief interest is in the financial change towards the technique of modern banking from the early cumbrous method by which all the money for the household was kept in the great chest (the income from the western estates being paid by bills of exchange drawn on a London goldsmith, the money fetched by porters, a thousand pounds at a time, in sacks from Lombard Street to Bedford Street). For the first time in the middle '60s the money for the chest was laid out first on deposit and then on credit account with the goldsmith, and modern banking methods may be said really to have started in 1687, when the rents were paid directly into the account with Child and Rogers and the great chest lay almost empty. We watch other changes: the first appearance in the wine cellars of glass bottles instead of stone (1658), in 1664 the purchase of 'Shably', the first mention of the wine in any account book known to M. André Simon, in 1665 the first purchase of 'Shampaigne', and in 1684 of port. It is like the gradual development of a family photograph. William Russell may still in his studied scaffold gestures belong to the obscure heroic age, but the details of a life we share are springing up all round him.

I have only one complaint to make of this ingenious book, and that is that Miss Thomson does not print, in an appendix, the complete catalogue of the 152 books in the Duke's library at Woburn and the 247 in Bedford House. A great many Baxters and other divines (curiously enough Miss Thomson mentions nothing by Burnet, that popular death-bed vulture who was with William Russell at the end), a few books of ceremony, a little travel, the usual crop of anti-Catholic works published at the time of the Plot, and for light relief a few 'twopenny dreadfuls', *Murder in Gloucestershire*, *The Murder in Essex*, *The Prentice that Murdered his Mistress*: it is a sombre collection and compares oddly with another contemporary library known to us, with its Juvenal and Homer, Dryden and Burton, Milton, Donne, Denham and Montaigne and 'the Matchless Orinda'. A family library is a breeding-place of character, and the great Puritan family would have felt justified in their aversion to poetry and the humanities if they had been able to contrast the library in which the political martyr studied with that of 'Apollo's Viceroy', Sir Charles Sedley, 'a very necessary man among us women'.

1937

A HOAX ON MR HULTON

No one, I suppose, will ever discover the authors of the odd elaborate hoax played on Mr Hulton, the elderly printseller of Pall Mall, in 1744; the story itself has been hidden all these years in an old vellum manuscript book I bought the other day from a London bookseller. With its vivid unimportance it brings alive the geography of eighteenth-century tradesman's London, the wine-merchants at Wapping, the clockmakers in Fleet Street, the carriers and printers and bust-makers, all the aggrieved respectable victims of an anarchic imagination, and in the background memories of Layer's conspiracy and the word 'Jacobite' and a vague uneasiness.

The story is told in letters and occasional passages of dialogue with notes in the margin on the behaviour of the characters. It might be fiction if these people did not all belong to fact. Who copied it out? It is hard to believe that any innocent person could have known so much. Mr Hulton suspected his apprentices, and the whole world; there was a young man called Mr Poet Rowzel, who knew more than he should have done; and an auctioneer, for some reason of his own, spoke of an upholsterer.

It began quite childishly on 21 January 1744, with a letter which purported to come from Mr Scott, a carpenter of Swallow Street, who wrote that he had many frames to make for the Prussian Ambassador, that he was ill of the gout and his men were overworked, and would Mr Hulton call on him. Mr Hulton had the gout himself, but he limped to Mr Scott's house, when 'finding the whole was an imposition upon him and Scott, he hobbled back again muttering horrible imprecations against the letter-writer all the way'. Two days later the hoax really got under way. A stream of unwanted people arrived at Mr Hulton's shop: Mr Hazard, a cabinet maker of the 'Hen and Chickens' in London's Inn, with a quantity of Indian paper; Mr Dard, a toy maker from the King's Arms in the Strand, who had received a letter from the pseudo-Hulton offering to sell him a curious frame; a surgeon to bleed him, and a doctor from Bedlam. It would take too long to describe the events of these crowded days, how a Mr Boyd brought snuffboxes and Mrs Hulton had to buy one to quiet him before her husband returned, how Mr Scarlett, an optician, arrived loaded with optic glasses, and was so ill-used by Mr Hulton that he threatened proceedings, how Mr Rutter, a dentist of Fleet Street, came to operate on an impostume, and was turned away by Mrs Hulton, who pretended her husband had died of it. Three pounds of anchovies arrived, and the printer of the *Harlaeian Miscellany,* who was pushed roughly out of doors, and Mr Cock, an auctioneer in the Great Piazza, who 'muttered something of an Irish upholsterer', and a female optician called Deane – Mrs Hulton bolted the door against her, and spoke to her through the pane, which Mrs Deane broke. 'Mr Hulton at the noise of breaking glass came forth from his little parlour into the shop, and was saluted by a porter with a dozen of port wine.' By this time he was losing control, and when Mr Rogers, a shoemaker of Maiden Lane, wanted to measure him, 'Mr Hulton lost all temper ... and cursing, stamping and swearing, in an outrageous manner, he so frightened Mr Rogers that the poor man, who is a Presbyterian, ran home to Covent Garden without once looking behind him.' After that Mr Hulton shut up his shop, and went to bed for three days, so the man who had been told he had a perukemaker's shop to dispose of failed to get him. Even when the shop reopened, Mr Hulton thought it safer to stay upstairs and leave things to his son. His son too was choleric and what he did to a young oculist who thought his father needed spectacles is unprintable here.

On 2 February there is a break in the record, twenty-seven pages missing; but when the story begins again on 4 September Mr Hulton is still on the run. Three dozen bottles of pale ale arrived that day; Mr Hulton was obliged to pay for them, and 'Mrs Hulton and her maid were fuddled while it lasted'. We must pass over the incident of the silversmith's wife, who pulled off Mrs Hulton's nightcap, and the venison-pasty man who saw through the deceit, and enclosed the pseudo-Hulton's letter in piecrust and sent it to Mr Hulton (the crust was given to the dog Cobb as they suspected poison). A more subtle form of hoax was in train. It began with an illiterate letter to Mr Pinchbeck (son of Edward Pinchbeck, inventor of the alloy), accusing Hulton of having abused him 'in a monstrous manner' at a tavern, but this plot misfired; the two victims got together over a four-shilling bowl of punch.

It was then that the Reverend Aaron Thompson, of Salisbury, came on the scene (he who had baptized the conspirator Layer's child and allowed the Pretender to be a godparent by proxy). Somebody using his name ordered a number of articles which he said his agent Hulton would pay for – four canes with pinchbeck heads, a bust of Mr Pope, a set of *The Gentleman's Magazine*, 'the books (of which you know the titles) against Bishop Berkley's Tar-Water', a complete set of Brindley's Classics, and even a chariot. This persecution caused Mr Hulton to write to Mr Thompson accusing him of being a Papist and a Jacobite and threatening him with the pillory, and the amazed Mr Thompson 'receiving this letter kept himself three weeks in a dark room lest he should see a letter of any kind: by the persuasion of his wife, he at length came forth; but wore a thin handkerchief over his eyes for about a month'. A lot of people's nerves were getting jumpy as the hoax enlarged its scope, taking in Bath and such worthy local characters as Mr Jeremy Peirce, author of an interesting little book about a tumour, and Mr Archibald Cleland, the surgeon who, it may be remembered, was concerned with Smollett in a controversy over the Bath waters. They all received letters from the pseudo-Hulton, Cleland being told that Thompson had libelled him and Peirce that Thompson had ordered him a set of *The Rake's Progress*. The real Aaron Thompson was by now convinced that he was the victim of a mad printseller, just as Hulton believed he was the victim of a mad clergyman, and they both – egged on by their pseudoselves – appealed to a Mr Pitt of Salisbury, who assumed they both were mad. The story becomes inextricably confused with counter-accusations, the pseudo-Hulton writing to the real Aaron Thompson:

You write, you read, you muzz or muse as you call it, till you are fitter for Bedlam than the Pulpit: poor man! poor Aaron Thompson. I remember you in Piccadilly knocking at the great Gates and returning bow for bow to the bowing Dean, your lean face, your awkward bow, your supercilious nod of the head are still in my mind ...

and the pseudo-Thompson would send the accusation flying back, regretting to hear that Hulton and all his family had gone mad, and recalling his strange way of walking about his shop 'and turning his thumbs one over another, a sure sign of madness'. And all the while goods continued to pour in, particularly drink – three gallons of the best Jamaica rum from Wapping New-Stairs, which Mrs Hulton drank and paid for, a gallon of canary, a gallon of sherry, and a pint of Madeira.

We shall never know the end – the last pages are torn out with any clue they might have contained to the hoaxer. It was an age of practical jokes, and he may have been one of those who baited Pinchbeck because he was a 'King's friend', mocking at his nocturnal remembrancers and writing odes about his patent snuffer. Perhaps Hulton, by his careful prosperity, had aroused the same balked malice of men who sympathize with the defeated and despise the conqueror and dare do nothing but trivial mischief to assert their independence – as next year proved when Charles Stuart turned back from Derby.

1939

A JACOBITE POET

In 1679 the Duchess of York, Mary of Modena, visited Cambridge University. She was a little over twenty, very graceful and witty and cunning. Even Burnet found it hard to speak ill of her at that time: 'all her diversion was innocent cheerfulness, with a little mixture of satirical wit'. George Granville, a thirteen-year-old Master of Arts and already a poet, read her an address in couplets in the library of Trinity College. The couplets were more formal and sedate than the poems 'to

Myra' which followed, for these later poems were the fruit of
his eyes, and if we remember his age and the rank and beauty
of the girl, it is not hard to recapture the emotion of that
moment when he dedicated himself, like a troubadour, to her
service:

> No warning of th' approaching flame;
> Swiftly, like sudden death, it came,

he wrote in a poem which I wish Miss Handasyde* had quoted
for she has been a little less than just to her subject. Her biography is a brilliant example of by-way scholarship, comparable to Miss Waddell's *The Wandering Scholars* and Miss
Tomkins's *The Popular Novel in England* for its grace and
erudition; she writes with insight of Granville's verse:

The general impression made by his songs is of something sweet
and sad and infinitely faint, like the tinklings of the musical boxes
whose glassy roulades come slightly muffled from the dust of last
century. He was old-fashioned even in his own day; for his poems,
published in the cold dawn of the Age of Reason, belong by sentiment and even by date to the warm uncritical twilight of the
Restoration.

But she has, I think missed that touch of fatality which raises
Lansdowne's life to the level of tragedy; minor tragedy, for
everything he touched from a play to a conspiracy was doomed
to be a minor.

Mary of Modena ruined him as she ruined many more important men. If she had not visited Cambridge that year
Granville would have found a safer inspiration; he might
have lived and died quite happily a minor poet and dramatist.
During the reign of William he passed a pleasant exile from
court, writing poetry and improving Shakespeare. He had admirers and flatterers; Pope immortalized him in *Windsor
Forest*: 'What Muse for Granville can refuse to sing?';
Dryden in beautifully-weighted verse resigned him his laurels
– a gesture a little spoilt by the actor Powell's comment (one

* *Granville the Polite: The Life of George Granville Lord Lansdowne*,
by Elizabeth Handasyde.

remembers Colley Cibber's study of 'giddy' Powell, how 'he naturally lov'd to set other people wrong'): 'this great Wit, with his Treacherous Memory, forgets, that he had given away his Laurells upon record, no less than twice before, *viz.*, once to Mr Congreve, and another time to Mr Southerne'. But during that swift moment in Trinity Library Granville had mortaged his future. Inevitably when William died he was drawn into politics, trying to hold a balance between the brilliant and erratic Bolingbroke and cautious, trimming Harley. He married, too, unluckily, to become later, through his hopeless idealism, a complaisant husband, shutting his eyes with miserable fidelity to his wife's affairs. With that instinct for doing the right thing, which sometimes conflicted with the still deeper instinct for being on the wrong side, he inscribed these lines on a glass in which her toast was drunk:

> If I not love you, Villiers, more
> Than ever Mortal loved before,
> With such a passion fixt and sure,
> As ev'n Possession could not cure,
> Never to cease but with my Breath;
> May then this Bumper be my Death.

He was not unfaithful to Myra: all his loves were platonic (in spite of children).

After Queen Anne's death he soon became involved in the same chain of circumstances as drew the fiery Atterbury from the see of Rochester to a peevish senility in Rome. It began with secret letters, proceeded inevitably through house searchings (manuscripts of unpublished poems were burned by his servants, who mistook them for dangerous documents), imprisonment, financial ruin and exile on the Continent. Walpole's government was hardly more corrupt than the Jacobite court. Miss Handasyde describes in detail the libels and bickerings and jealousies of Paris. It was not an air which suited the foolish idealism but unselfish fidelity of Lansdowne; he was happy for a while, raised to the dizzy height of a shadow dukedom, but the bubble eventually burst. He had heard plenty of other men falsely accused of treachery, and his own turn came.

He was called a traitor by James's sister-in-law, the Princess of Turenne, at the Hôtel de Bouillon, 'where all France assembles'. He wrote a letter of pathetic literary dignity to James III, he paraphrased Shakespeare and declared: 'God knows, sir, I have had no occasion to betray you; if I had consider'd my fortune I needed but to have forsaken you.' The son of Mary of Modena did not reply and Lansdowne made his peace with Hanover.

He had ten more years of life, spent much of it in literary controversy (characteristically his feud was against the dead and on behalf of the dead), revised an old play and called it (again characteristically) *Once a Lover; and always a Lover*. It brought, Miss Handasyde writes, 'a pale reflection of the glitter and polish of Congreve on to the dull and respectable stage of George Lillo and Moore'. His niece was a little shocked by it; her uncle was old-fashioned. He died a fortnight after his wife, who had buzzed busily from infidelity to infidelity till the end. His life had not been a very happy one. Fortune had consistently frowned on him, fobbing him off with occasional fictitious successes, like his shadow dukedom. He had written with some wit:

> Fickle and false to others she may be,
> I can complain but of her constancy.

1933

CHARLES CHURCHILL

WHEN Charles Churchill died in Boulogne in 1764, all the English ships in the harbour struck their colours. Fifty years later Byron found his grave neglected, among 'the thick deaths of half a century', and the gardener quite ignorant of Churchill's fame. The very quality in his work which gave him immediate popularity (he profited nearly one thousand pounds, Mr Laver states,* by his two first poems) made his name short-lived. Like other minor satirists, Rochester and Oldham, he was

* *The Poems of Charles Churchill*, edited by James Laver.

down in the dust of the every-day battle; his satires are less often of the great than of those small tiresome provocative men as teasing as horse-flies whom history forgets. Dryden's satires belonged from the first to history; Churchill's to the newspapers; and his poems have the fascination of an old news-sheet still stained from the coffee-house, the charm of something evanescent which has survived against all odds.

Here are the echoes of queer cases and queer people: Mary Tofts of Godalming who bore, according to her own account, a litter of fifteen rabbits; Betty Canning, who claimed that she had been kidnapped by a procuress; the Cock Lane Ghost, as fraudulent as either; the Chaplain of the Lock Hospital, who wrote a book in favour of polygamy; the Rev. John Browne, the dramatist who committed suicide because his doctors forbade him to go to St Petersburg to organize Russian education for the Empress; and all the horde of actors who in their beginnings were everything in the world but men of the theatre: sadler, wigmaker, tallow chandler, apothecary, old Etonian, bar-tender, silversmith, wine merchant.

Mr Laver's notes on these people are invaluable, but he seems uncertain in what educational strata he will find his readers. This beautiful edition can hardly be intended for an ignorant public, and its purchasers might be spared some of the notes – on Clive, David Garrick, and Sir Isaac Newton for example. Otherwise if the notes err at all, it is that they are too businesslike. With the horrid example before him of Tooke, Churchill's former editor, Mr. Laver has been afraid of digressions. Something is lost. One misses in the note on Woodward, the comic actor, this revealing touch: 'The moment he opened his mouth on the stage, every muscle of his face ranged itself on the side of levity. The very tones of his voice inspired comic ideas, and though he often wished to act tragedy, he could never speak one serious line with propriety.' A note like this is more valuable than the date of a birth and a death.

The comparison of Churchill to Rochester is inevitable. Both satirists died worn out in the early thirties; both were men without moral fastidiousness, the frequenters of brothels, who, retiring at intervals to be cured from the same diseases, damned the world for the vices they did not share (one remembers Gleeson White's remark quoted by Mr Yeats: 'Wilde will never lift his head again, for he has against him all men of infamous life'). Both remained loyal to one friend, Rochester to Savile, Churchill to Wilkes, and to one mistress (Elizabeth Barry joins hands across the years with Elizabeth Carr). The comparison must not be drawn too closely. Churchill was a far finer satirist. Rochester's lines were too rough and angry; he had not the coolness of temper to find, as Churchill did, the final damning epithet. These lines on Webberburn are beyond the accomplishment of uncontrolled hate:

> To mischief train'd, e'en from his mother's womb,
> Grown old in fraud, though yet in manhood's bloom,
> Adopting arts by which gay villains rise,
> And reach the heights which honest men despise;
> Mute at the bar, and in the senate loud,
> Dull 'mongst the dullest, proudest of the proud,
> A pert, prim, prater of the northern race,
> Guilt in his heart, and famine in his face,
> Stood forth; and thrice he waved his lily hand,
> And thrice he twirl'd his tye, thrice stroked his band.

There are moments when Churchill stands almost level with Dryden and Pope; it is only because his lyrical talents were so inferior to his satirical that in the final estimate he cannot be ranked with Rochester, perhaps not even with Oldham. Mr Laver picks out of *Gotham*, his rather tedious essay in Utopian politics, a few charming lines on flowers as formal as a Dutch parterre. They are hardly enough to justify even Mr Laver's modest claim that 'in his rural retreat he had time to look about him, the sights and sounds of the country steal imperceptibly into his verse'. He was urban through and through. If he had not given all his genius to satire, he might possibly have made a reputation as a lyric poet, but he would have belonged to the school of Prior. The lines which conclude the first book of *The Ghost* (a poem Mr Laver rather underestimates) have all Prior's prettiness, saved by all his sophistication:

Give us an entertaining sprite,
Gentle, familiar, and polite,
One who appears in such a form
As might an holy hermit warm,
Or who on former schemes refines,
And only talks by sounds and signs,
Who will not to the eye appear,
But pays her visits to the ear,
And knocks so gently, 'twould not fright
A lady in the darkest night.
Such is our Fanny, whose good will,
Which cannot in the grave lie still,
Brings her on earth to entertain
Her friends and lovers in Cock Lane.

1933

THE LOVER OF LEEDS

RALPH THORESBY, the topographer of Leeds, traced – rather dubiously – his family back to the reign of Canute; and certainly he could not have picked a better origin for a topographer than the reign of a king who tried to turn back the tide. That is the hopeless task on which they are all engaged, beating time back from a gravestone, a piece of pottery, a grassy mound. One finds them on their knees in little country churches rubbing brasses: they push ungainly bicycles up steep country lanes towards a Roman *vallum*: they publish at their own expense the churchwardens' accounts of Little Bilbury. Vestry books and Enclosure Acts ruin their eyesight. It is one of the most innocent – and altruistic – of human activities, for a topographer never becomes a rich man through his researches: no Kidd's treasure has ever been discovered under a hawk-stone, at best a piece of Roman piping; and fame in their lifetime is severely limited to men of their own kind and after death to historians' footnotes, unless like Aubrey or Anthony à Wood some eccentricity, some untopographical malice, catches the attention of posterity. Often they are clergymen – they have so much to do with churches, some-times they are civil engineers (the profession somehow goes with the bicycle), and sometimes, as in the case of Thoresby, merchants.

Thoresby, the unsuccessful cloth merchant, will never be a popular figure like Aubrey and Wood, although he kept a diary – the town he chose is perhaps against him, for who today will trouble to hunt through the streets of that black city for the sites of his mills and bridges? But none the less in honesty, disinterestedness, piety, and precision he may be taken as the pattern of a topographer. I don't know what the dictionary distinction may be between a topographer and an antiquarian, but I think of an antiquarian as a man who dwells permanently among the hawk-stones and *vallums*, never coming nearer to his own day than a *wapentake*, one with little interest in human beings – in So-and-So who must pay to the Church use 'at Wytsentyd next a stryk of mawllte' and somebody else who was a 'defrauder' and owes 2d. The topographer takes a small familiar patch of ground and repopulates it: he experiments with time as much as Mr Dunne, so that it is not Leeds – or your own country parish – as you know it that he presents, so much as a timeless God's-eye Leeds with all the houses that ever stood there re-erected, interpenetrating. Is the result some-thing nearer Leeds than a guide book, a collection of photo-graphs, a map? One doesn't know, but certainly men like Thoresby, and earlier men like Plot and Aubrey, thought so, and even if we do not share their religious belief (I have yet to come across an atheistic topographer), their work attracts by its very inutility. Out of wars and the decay of civilizations the historian may spin theories which whether true or not can affect human lives, but this – this is beautifully useless, this precise painstaking record of superseded stone.

A little above this is the *Moot-Hall* in the Front of the *Middle-Row*, on one side of which is one of the best-furnished *Flesh-Shambles* in the North of England; on the other the *Wool-Market* for *Broad-Cloth* which is the All in All.

There speaks the lover, the lover of what you see in the plate called 'The Prospect of Leeds' – two churches, a town hall like a German toy, a little river with a few sailing ships and a bridge, and perhaps two hundred houses trailing gently off into the fields where an artist sits on the grass.

What sort of life do topographers lead? We know the bicycle and the back bent by brasses, but if we want to know more we cannot do better than read Thoresby's diary. For the times, with topographers hardly change. Born just before the Restoration, Thoresby's period included the Popish Plot, the Revolution, the wars with France. The wars *did* affect him – they made the price of paper dear and delayed a little the publication of *Ducatus Leodiensis,* and at the time of the Revolution the rumour that the Irish were ravaging the country, spread by God knows what Orange agents, struck home in Leeds with a night alarm – 'Horse and arms! Horse and arms! Beeston is burnt, and only some escaped to bring the doleful tidings!' – a fine topographical lament. Yet Thoresby admits himself that he was 'more immediately concerned' that year with a little fire in his house which burnt his children's coats hanging on a line. No, he had little interest in great events, in his trade or even the government of his local town. He paid a fine of £20 rather than be an alderman and his eventual 'conversion' from nonconformity was partly, one feels, due to the presence of good antiquarians on the bench of bishops, partly his desire simply to avoid trouble – for the sake of his studies. There is a charming passage in which he refers to a friend's 'little Paradise, his library', but Thoresby himself was no bookworm. He would ride miles to hear a story, to copy an epitaph, to preserve from time. ... Topographers are not selective – everyone who ever lived, any building which ever existed, contributes to the ideal city, so that the habit of collecting grows and Thoresby's museum included such various things as a toothbrush from Mecca, the Crown of an Indian King, a large Prussian Boot, the hand and arm of quartered Montrose, just as his successors collected postage stamps, cigarette cards, even tram tickets. Pedigrees of all the leading families, 'strange accidents' like the 'Stones that came out of the Hands and Feet of the Rev. and pious Mr Blackbeard, once Lecturer at *Leedes*'

– all were part of this city in the mind. Sometimes he arrived too late: we watch him peer in vain at an inscription: 'Alexander Foster, who departed this life the 27th June, 167 ... aetat 61:

> Once to our liking growing daily fast,
> But by Death's ... at the last.

The rest not legible.'

But one is glad he was in time to preserve from weather and lichen:

> Under this Stone doe lye six children small
> Of John Willington of the North-hall,

and this sad conceit:

> Here near God's Temple lies at rest
> A Martyn in his Earthly Nest.

Alas! a topographer needs a topographer in turn to preserve what he has preserved. Thoresby's book, of course, is there, but his collection left to a clerical son was sold, scattered, destroyed. Montrose's arm found a temporary home with a Dr Burton, but against other items in the auctioneer's catalogue there are grim notes. 'Eggs – All broken', 'Serpents – Thrown away', 'Plants – all rotten and thrown on the dunghill'. And as for Leeds itself – well, we may question whether the dunghill, too, was not its proper destination, though Thoresby would not have thought so, glad of a chance to record another century of sooty life. He would have said, perhaps, with his plainness and simplicity and the smirk of satisfaction you see on his portrait, that one can fare further and fare worse, and it is true that his own family came to an abrupt end in far away Calcutta, in a worse Black Hole than his ideal city was ever to become.

1938

THE place lies there below you roughly in the shape of a cross – or a man pegged out on a table for examination. His legs lie up the Banbury and the Woodstock roads among the don's wives and Ruskin villas; one arm goes out by the High and the other extends past the stations towards Botley which the Devil visited a few years ago; a thin neck stretches by Christ Church and Pembroke, and the poor head – that, I'm afraid, must lie – not unsuitably – in St Aldates among a jumble of old houses, mean streets and shops selling confectionery, second-hand boots and fishing tackle. Now for the operation. Make an incision: lay back a flap of the flesh and see what's there – in the region of the breast – in a timeless Dunnelike eternity. There goes Professor Freeman, the man who made the Victorians Anglo-Saxon-conscious so that they called their dogs Wulfric and their sons Ethelbert (I have an old faded letter of his in which the ruling passion rather quaintly expresses itself: 'The wives of priests and bishops are spoken of civilly in Domesday: that is to say they are entered without remark'); there he goes 'repeating poetry to himself as he walked in the streets, and occasionally leaping into the air when the poem moved him to any enthusiasm'. Another flap is raised, and there is the austere face of the late Dr Farnell, as he tries 'to stiffen our standard of living', objecting to the café habit, 'undergraduates of both sexes sitting there together indulging themselves with pleasant conversation and unnecessary and unmanly food'.

The compilers of this fascinating and very funny anthology* have divided it into four parts – the Place, the Seniors, the Juniors, and Etcetera, with interludes of witty and often wise discussion, and the subdivisions which include such subjects as Visiting Oxford (Verlaine reading his poems in a room behind Blackwell's shop watched by an anxious Fellow: Thackeray insulted by several bland illiterate dons), Crimes

* *Anatomy of Oxford*, an Anthology compiled by C. Day Lewis and Charles Fenby.

and Punishments ('It is startling to realize that if, while passing through Oxford, or even Reading [*Ginnett* v. *Wittingham*, 16 Q.B.D. 761] for the first time, a citizen of York is knocked down by the negligent conduct of a member of the University, the former is deprived of all remedy and relief in the High Court of Justice'), Scandals, Famous Men, and Strange and Original Characters. In that rich section my own favourite is Dr Kettel, the seventeenth-century President of Trinity – 'He did not care for the country revells because they tended to debauchery. Sayd he, at Garsington revell, Here is, Hey for Garsington! and Hey for Cuddesdon! and Hey Hockley! but here's nobody cries, Hey for God Almighty!' Trinity has a wealth of such characters, for Dr Kettel is followed by Dr Bathurst who was detected throwing stones at Balliol windows, and it is an encouraging thought that the Trinity tradition is admirably maintained to this day.

A review of so delightful a collection cannot fail to degenerate into an anthology of an anthology. As we would expect, Anthony Wood and Hearne are strongly represented, and I am grateful to the compilers for introducing me to the *Reminiscences* of the Rev. W. Tuckwell and to the anonymous contributor to the *Oxford Mail* (can it be one of the compilers?) who acts as our contemporary Aubrey. I am less grateful for the frequent quotations from George Cox's dull poem *Red Coats and Black Gowns*, especially when no room is found for *Merton Walks*. May one hope that this collection may prove popular enough to justify many editions and additions, a section say for Ghosts – the Pembroke ghost (whom men cannot recognize as a ghost, but after seeing him – in the shape of a scout, a tutor, who knows? – they commit suicide), the Merton and the Balliol ghosts and the unknown inhabitants of 10 Holywell. Among Curiosities I miss the Devil's signature at Queen's, and there are more or less contemporary scandals and hoaxes which deserve to be collected as soon as they are safe from the law of libel: one may now record the bogus Prime Minister's telephone call to the late Sir Herbert Warren at Magdalen offering him the Poet Laureateship, an appointment he immediately announced to his guests at dinner. And to the Strange and Original Characters I hope it may be possible to add that distinguished necromancer always to be seen in the company of his familiar who sometimes takes the shape of an undergraduate and sometimes that of a small black dog.*

From the distant past a few characters neglected by the compilers still clamour for recognition: the servant of Trinity (Trinity again) who kept a brothel, the Swiss barber called Le Maître who burgled the Ashmolean and got away – temporarily – with a gold coin of the Emperor Otto, and Captain Nathaniel Ogle, R.N., who drove the first steam carriage through Oxford in 1832 accompanied by his Negro servant Xurary.

1938

* One may safely now record his name—the questionably Reverend Montague Summers.

[2]

GEORGE DARLEY

A BOOK yet remains to be written on the tragedy of those rare poets who have been ruined by their own lack of conceit. It is a curious psychological fact that men with interests almost entirely intellectual will suffer a sense of inferiority and shame from a purely physical defect, which will sometimes cancel their whole work. There are cases, naturally, where that shame has not been disastrous, but none the less it has been present. Byron was driven by his lame leg to a bitter isolation and to satire: from the calm, but somewhat too facile loveliness of 'She walks in beauty like the night' to the tortured medley of buffoonery and grandeur which he called *Don Juan*. Byron's shame was our gain. Stevenson, however much he might sound the brazen trumpet of his heroics, was ashamed of his consumptive body. 'Shall we never shed blood?' he asked, only half-humorously, and he hoped that in the swords' clash of *Kidnapped*, his readers would forget that one man, by no stretch of imagination, could ever put himself in the round house with Alan Breck. And yet, because he too was forced like Byron, though by more material circumstances, into isolation, we have gained a level controlled prosé as likely to endure as that of Addison, and at least one great novel *Weir of Hermiston*.

George Darley's defect compared with that of Byron and that of Stevenson seems small and very ludicrous. He had a stutter, and perhaps its lack of any possibility of a romantic pose made it the harder to bear. He was a poet of infinite potentiality, and he spent his poetic life almost entirely on the writing of pretty songs and unactable plays. Now, more than a hundred years since his death, his work, and among most even his name, is forgotten. He is to be found occasionally in anthologies – Robert Bridges included a large number of extracts from his *Nepenthe* in *The Spirit of Man* – and to the general public he is known, if he is known at all, as the author of a charming song, a favourite of the Victorian drawing-rooms.

> I've been roaming! I've been roaming!
> Where the meadow dew is sweet,
> And like a queen I'm coming
> With its pearls upon my feet.

Darley was born in 1795 in Dublin of Irish parents, the eldest of a family of four sons and three daughters. His parents went from Ireland to the United States, when he was still a child, and left him at Springfield, Co. Dublin, in the care of his grandfather, with whom he remained until he was about ten years of age. The impediment in his speech was already with him and probably already exaggerated in a morbid and nervous mind. But past misery is easily transmuted into happiness, and later, looking back, he was very ready to find in those years, in what is known as the Garden of Ireland, joys which at the time he had not recognized.

> When a child [he wrote] I thought myself miserable, but now see that by comparison I was happy, at least all the 'sunshine of the breast' I now enjoy seems a reflection of that in the dawn of life. I have been to *La belle France* and to *bella Italia*, yet the brightest sun which ever shone upon me broke over Balleybetagh mountains.

Little of Darley's early youth is known to us. On his parents' return from America he joined them in Dublin, entered Trinity College there in 1815 and graduated in 1820. Science and mathematics had been his studies, and in his studies he had lived. Human intercourse then, as later, was less shut out from him by his stutter than by the morbid introspection into which it plunged him. It made him first shy and then bold with the exaggerated self-importance which is so often to be found in dwarfs. He recoiled and sprang. He was determined in those first days, when nothing had been tried and therefore nothing had yet failed, to make the world take notice of him and forget the stutter. And the world, in the person of passing acquaintances, would never have noticed the stutter without his own self-conscious underlining. He was beautiful in a delicate, somewhat Shellyan fashion, 'tall and slight with the stoop of the student; delicate features slightly aquiline; eyes not large but very earnest, with often a far away expression; hair dark brown and waving'. There were times in those days when he completely forgot his impediment in excited conversation.

He had not been pre-eminently successful at Trinity College. Although he had a great talent for mathematics, his stutter had impeded him in at least one examination. No high academical post was open to him, and in any case a career of teaching was impossible. It was therefore with some sense, as well as some courage, that he flung himself in 1822 upon literary London, with his first volume of verse *The Errors of Ecstasie*. He was twenty-seven years old, but the majority of the poems must have been written years before, for they are completely devoid of merit. The lyrics are full of the conceits of roses and bees from which the future poet never freed himself. They are tuneful but seldom musical. The title poem is a long and very wearisome blank verse dialogue between a poet contemplating suicide and the moon. It is of interest for a few clearly autobiographical lines:

> Didst thou not barter Science for a song?
> Thy gown of learning for a sorry mantle?

and for a very occasional line where Darley is caught in a youthful pride and defiance which he lost too soon:

> I would not change the temper of my blood
> For that which stagnates in an idiot's veins,
> To gain the sad salvation of a fool.

When he wrote that, poor and halting though the blank verse might be, there was hope for Darley. Vitality and pride, two most necessary sources for poetry, were his 'and at the rainbow's foot lay surely gold'.

Literary London was not unkind to the new poet. A critic wrote of his book that it was

> a work as well of intellect as of temperament, although his fancy
> has been inadequately controlled. ... His poetry is to be blamed
> for the wildness of imagination, not the weakness of sensuality.

and the next year found him a regular contributor to the
London Magazine. It was the time of the proprietorship of
Taylor and Hessey, when the contributors were invited to meet
one another at dinner once a month at the offices of the firm in
Waterloo Place. Here he met De Quincey, Proctor, Talfourd,
Clare, Hazlitt, Hood, whose finest poems, the *Ode to Autumn*
and the sonnets on *Silence* and *Death*, appeared this very year
in the magazine, Henry Cary, the translator of Dante, and
Lamb. The two latter he was soon able to number among his
few friends. There are occasional references to him in Lamb's
letters, and he seems to have been a regular visitor at Enfield,
sometimes in the company of Cary, sometimes in that of Allan
Cunningham.

But the shyness induced by the stutter stood in the way of
his friendships. In a volume of tales, *The Labours of Idleness*,
which he published in 1826 under the name of Guy Penseval,
he gave a clear picture of his own self-consciousness. We can
see him at Waterloo Place sitting in the background of the
conversation, feeling himself neglected with a growing and unjust resentment, suddenly plunging into the conversation with
the same asperity as characterized the dramatic criticism
which he was now writing for the *London Magazine* under the
pseudonym of John Lacy:

> I always found myself so embarrassed in the presence of others,
> and everyone so embarrassed in mine – I was so perpetually in-
> fringing the rule of politeness, saying or doing awkward things,
> telling unpalatable truths, or giving heterodox opinions on matters
> long since established as proper, agreeable, becoming, and the
> contrary, by the common creed of the world; there was so much to
> offend and so little to conciliate in my manners, arrogant at one
> time, puling at another; dull when I should have been entertaining;
> loquacious when I should have been silent ... that I quickly per-
> ceived obscurity was the sphere in which Nature had destined me
> to shine. ... At first indeed there were several persons who liked, or
> seemed to like me, from a certain novelty of freshness in my

manner, but as soon as that wore off they liked me no longer. I was 'an odd being' or 'a young man of some genius but very singular': something to fill up the gaps of tea-time conversation when the fineness of the evening and the beauty of the prospect had already been discussed by the party.

This feeling of inferiority, the idea that people only 'seemed' to like him, was no doubt enhanced by the London dinners, where Lamb and Hood set the key to a conversation which chiefly consisted in a quick succession of bad puns. And yet Darley had met with undeserved good fortune. He had established himself in literary London with one book of very mediocre verse and a volume of short stories, interspersed with lyrics. And *Sylvia* was growing in his head, *Sylvia* which was to set him upon the pinnacle of fame. The idea that he was carrying a masterpiece in his mind must have made the alternatively shy and aggressive poet almost insupportable. Beddoes wrote to Kelsall in 1824, after a visit to Mrs Shelley's:

Darley is a tallish, slender, pale, light-eyebrowed, gentle-looking bald pate, in a brown suit and with a duo-decimo under his arm – stammering to a most provoking degree, so much so as to be almost inconversible – he is supposed to be writing a comedy or tragedy, or perhaps both in one.

The filibustering medical poet from the sea coast of Bohemia was not likely to find Darley attractive, and in 1826 he wrote to Proctor from Hanover a little impatiently: 'Is Darley delivered yet? I hope he's not a mountain.'

The next year *Sylvia* appeared, a pretty fairy comedy – as Miss Mitford said – 'something between *A Midsummer Night's Dream* and *The Faithful Shepherdess*'. Miss Mitford was charmed by it. So was the future Mrs Browning, who found it 'a beautiful pastoral'. Lamb thought it 'a very poetical poem' and was pleased with the stage directions in verse. Beddoes, if he ever read it, remained discreetly silent, as silent as the public. Yet the play is very readable, and at one point shows a little of the swing and power which Darley was later to display in *Nepenthe*. In the penultimate scene, the stage directions, which have been growing looser and looser in texture, are suddenly abandoned for a vivid comparison between Byron and Milton:

> One gloomy Thing indeed, who now
> Lays in the dust his lordly brow,
> Had might, a deep indignant sense,
> Proud thoughts, and moving eloquence;
> But oh! that high poetic strain
> Which makes the heart shriek out again
> With pleasure half mistook for pain;
> That clayless spirit that doth soar
> To some far empyrean shore
> Beyond the chartered flight of mind,
> Reckless, repressless, unconfined,
> Springing from off the roofed sky
> Into unceiled Infinity ...
> That strain, this spirit was not thine.

But the ears of the public were as firmly closed to the occasional beauty as to the rather imitative prettiness of the whole. The mountain had brought forth its mouse.

Darley was not a man with the courage to stand against silence. Attack might have made him aggressive, silence only made him question his own powers, the most fatal act an artist can commit. He published no other poetry for public circulation until 1840, when his long and tedious play *Thomas à Becket*, showing the influence of Sir Henry Taylor, appeared, followed the next year by a still duller play, *Ethelstan*. In writing to Proctor about the former play, he gave rein to the doubt which had been haunting him:

I am indeed suspicious, not of you but myself; most sceptical about my right to be called 'poet', and therefore it is I desire confirmation of it from others. Why have a score of years not established my title with the world? Why did not *Sylvia*, with all its faults, ten years since? It ranked me among the small poets. I had as soon be ranked among the piping bullfinches.

Sylvia's failure drove him back to science. In the next few years he published a series of volumes on elementary mathematics, *A System of Popular Geometry, A System of Popular*

Trigonometry, Familiar Astronomy, and *The Geometrical Companion,* several of which became popular. Indeed from this time on he was linked finally with mathematics. Carlyle spoke of him as:

> Darley (George) from Dublin, mathematician, considerable actually, and also poet; an amiable, modest, veracious, and intelligent man – much loved here though he stammered dreadfully.

Sir F. H. Doyle wrote of him as 'a man of true genius, and not of poetical genius alone, for he distinguished himself also as a mathematician and a man of science', and Allan Cunningham in *The Athenaeum* called him 'a true poet and excellent mathematician'. Darley himself, in a letter to Cary, wrote:

> I did not mean Mathematics inspired poetry but only that the Science was absolutely necessary for such an extravagates as I am. Only for this cooling study I should be out of my reason probably – like poor Lee's hero 'knock out all the start' and die like a mad dog foaming.

But the lyrics that Darley was writing, and occasionally publishing in the *London* and the *Athenaeum* to which he began to contribute a series of letters from abroad on foreign art, and his usual truculent dramatic criticism, show little of the fevered turmoil of mind at which the letter to Cary hints. That turmoil was to burst out once, and once only, unforgettably in *Nepenthe.* Now, as though his grip upon himself grew, as he became more and more conscious of the repressed, thwarted instincts within himself, the best of his lyrics show a calm, though sometimes complaining, restraint:

> Oh nymph! release me from this rich attire,
>   Take off this crown thy artful fingers wove;
> And let the wild-rose linger on the brier
>   Its last sweet days, my love!
>
> For me shalt thou, with thy nice-handed care,
>   Nought but the simplest wreath of myrtle twine,
> Such too, high-pouring Hebe's self must wear,
>   Serving my bower with wine.

When his grip relaxed, it was not yet into ungoverned imagination, but into pretty and cloying fancies, which sometimes break into a faint beauty of metaphor, as in the opening to his conventional and uninspired sonnet to Gloriana:

> To thee, bright lady! whom all hearts confess
> Their queen, as thou dost highly pace along,
> Like the Night's pale and lovely sultaness
> Walking the wonder-silent stars among.

But though it was his loneliness which caused his failure, it was loneliness that inspired some of his best lyrics. No one can contend that these short poems approach very close to greatness, but they are at their best extremely charming minor poetry. *The Dove's Loneliness* masters a music and rhythm which seem to lie just outside analysis, and its dying close might have been written by Mr de la Mare:

> Smile thou and say farewell! The bird of Peace,
> Hope, Innocence and Love and Loveliness,
> Thy sweet Egeria's bird of birds doth pray
> By the name best-belov'd thou'lt wend thy way
> In pity of her pain. Though I know well
> Thou woulds't not harm me, I must tremble still;
> My heart's the home of fear; ah! turn thee then,
> And leave me to my loneliness again.

Here are many of Mr de la Mare's technical artifices, the half rhymes – Peace and Loveliness, well and still – the fondness for the letter 'l' in conveying the sense of uncertain and undefined longing, the alliteration of words, as well as letters – Love and Loveliness. Mr de la Mare has been compared with Keats and Blake and Christina Rossetti. It is strange that no one has noted the affinity with Darley. The resemblance does not lie in one solitary poem, but is continually recurring:

> O was it fair:
> Fair, kind or pitiful to one
> Quite heart-subdued – all bravery done,
> Coyness to deep devotion turned,
> Yet pure the flame with which she burned, –
> O was it fair that thou shoulds't come,

226

Strong in this weakness, to my home,
And at my most defenceless hour,
Midnight, shoulds't steal into my bower,
In thy triumphant beauty more
Fatal that night than e'er before?

But it is with the extraordinary *Nepenthe* that George Darley will live or die. A few copies of the poem were printed for private circulation in 1835, as Miss Mitford wrote,

with the most imperfect and broken types, upon a coarse, discoloured paper, like that in which a country shop-keeper puts up his tea, with two dusky leaves of a still dingier hue, at least a size too small, for cover, and garnished at top and bottom with a running margin in his own writing.

It was not reprinted until 1897.

Nepenthe is one of the most remarkable poems that the nineteenth century produced. It was no wonder that Miss Mitford, before this wild medley of Shelley, Milton, and Keats, made a single whole by the feverish personality of Darley himself, wrote that 'there is an intoxication about it that turns one's brain'. Darley himself in a letter to Chorley gives a much needed explanation of its theme:

to show the folly of discontent with the natural tone of human life. Canto I attempts to paint the ill-effects of over-joy; Canto II those of excessive melancholy. Part of the latter object remains to be worked out in Canto III, which would otherwise show – if I could ever find confidence, and health and leisure to finish it – that contentment with the mingled cup of humanity is the true 'Nepenthe'.

But Darley, perhaps because he never found that Nepenthe, left the poem a fragment.

The poem opens with the same speed, the same magical rush of wings, on which it takes its whole course of 1600 odd lines:

Over a bloomier land, untrod
By heavier foot than bird or bee
Lays on the grassy-bosomed sod,
I passed one day in reverie:

> High on his unpavilioned throne
> The heaven's hot tyrant sat alone,
> And like the fabled king of old
> Was turning all he touched to gold.

The poem cannot be followed as a detailed plot. It remains in the mind as a succession of vivid images:

> Sudden above my head I heard
> The cliff-scream of the thunder-bird,
> The rushing of his forest wings,
> A hurricane when he swoops or springs,
> And saw upon the darkening glade
> Cloud-broad his sun-eclipsing shade.

of beautiful episodes – the death of the phoenix, with its lovely lyric *O Blest Unfabled Incense Tree*, which has found a place in many anthologies, and the less known but no less lovely:

> O fast her amber blood doth flow
>   From the heart wounded Incense Tree
> Fast as earth's deep embosomed woe
>   In silent rivulets to the sea!

> Beauty may weep her fair first-born,
>   Perchance in as resplendent tears,
> Such golden dewdrops bow the corn
>   When the stern sickleman appears.

> But oh! such perfume to a bower
>   Never allured sweet-seeking bee,
> As to sip fast that nectarous shower
>   A thirstier minstrel drew in me.

Then follow episodes drawn too closely from Keats, bands of bacchantes and nymphs, who dance with too self-conscious a flow of drapery. But soon the reader is whirled again over a changing panorama of sea and land, India, Petra, Palmyra, Lebanon, Ionia, the Dardanelles, sees from above the broken body of Icarus tossed backwards and forwards upon the reefs, sees Orpheus torn by the Furies and in a last moment of frenzy the two deaths are mingled and made his own, in the sound of the waves that beat upon Icarus, the sound of the Furies' voices calling to the hunt.

> In the caves of the deep – Hollo! Hollo! –
> Lost Youth! – o'er and o'er fleeting billows!
> Hollo! Hollo! – without all ruth! –
> In the foam's cold shroud! – Hollo! Hollo!
> To his everlasting sleep! – Lost Youth!

The second canto is less varied in note and less varied in sense. Darley falters a little on his long flight, but there is still much to admire:

> From Ind to Egypt thou art one,
> Pyramidal Memphis to Tanjore,
> From Ipsambul to Babylon
> Reddening the waste suburban o'er;
> From sandlocked Thebes to old Ellore,
> Her caverned roof on columns high
> Pitched, like a Giant Breed that bore
> Headlong the mountain to the sky.

When it is remembered that this poem was written after Shelley's death, when the most noted poets, with the exception of Wordsworth and Coleridge, were Hood, 'Barry Cornwall', Joanna Baillie, and Laetitia Elizabeth Landon, it is easy to realize something of the consternation with which it was greeted by Miss Mitford. None of Darley's friends, to whom the poem was sent, seems to have suggested a public printing. They were bewildered, a little stunned, perhaps inclined to laugh. Even Miss Mitford, who gave the hungry poet some measured praise, failed to read his poem to the end. Perhaps Darley himself was bewildered by this one flash of genius, this loud and boisterous changeling of his loneliness. The last lines of the poem express a wish to leave 'this busy broil' for his own accustomed clime:

> There to lay me down at peace
> In my own first nothingness.

Certainly his genius seems to have died at the moment of its first complete expression. The body of the poet lived on for another ten years, produced the two monumental plays, wandered about the Continent, wrote charming and growingly despondent letters, as the 'pains, aches, and petty tortures' of his ill health increased, to some pretty cousins in Ireland, and died at last from an unromantic decline in London on 23 November 1846, still uncertain and doubting of his own powers.

Am I really a poet? was the question which always haunted him.

You may ask could I not sustain myself on the strength of my own approbation? But it might be only my vanity, not my genius, that was strong. ... Have not I too, had some, however few, approvers? Why yes, but their chorus in my praise was as small as the voice of my conscience, and, like it, served for little else than to keep me uneasy.

'Seven long years,' he had written to Miss Mitford, in a letter, 'startling to receive ... and terrible to answer', 'have I lived on a saying of Coleridge's that he sometimes liked to take up *Sylvia*.'

1929

THE APOSTLES INTERVENE

THE Victorians were sometimes less high-minded than ourselves. The publication of a little booklet on the Spanish Civil War called *Authors Take Sides* has reminded me of an earlier group of English writers who intervened in Spain a hundred years ago. They were – questionably,– more romantic; they were certainly less melodramatic: they were a good deal wiser. 'With all my anger and love, I am for the People of Republican Spain' – that is not the kind of remark that anyone with a sense of the ludicrous should make on this side of the Channel. Alfred Tennyson did at least cross the Pyrenees, though his motives, to hysterical partisans like these, may appear suspect: there is every reason to suppose that he went for the fun of the thing – fun which nearly brought Hallam and himself before a firing squad as it did the unfortunate and quite unserious-minded Boyd. He doesn't in later years seem to have wished to recall the adventure, and only a few lines in the official life of Tennyson connect him and his Cambridge club, the Apostles, with the conspiracy of General Torrijos and the Spanish exiles.

It was the fashion among the Apostles to be Radical, a fashion less political than literary and metaphysical, connected in some recondite way with the reading of Charles and Arthur Tennyson's poetry, with long talks in Highgate between Coleridge and John Sterling, when the old poet did most of the talking, starting, according to Hazlitt, from no premises and coming to no conclusions, crossing and recrossing the garden path, snuffling softly of Kant and infinitudes, embroiling poor Sterling for ever in the fog of theology. When politics were touched on by the Apostles it was in an amused and rather patronizing way. ' 'Twas a very pretty little revolution in Saxony,' wrote Hallam in 1830, 'and a respectable one at Brunswick' (the dilettante tone has charm after the sweeping statements, the safe marble gestures, the self-importance of our own 'thirties – 'I stand with the People and Government of Spain'). Only in the rash Torrijos adventure did the Apostles come within measurable distance of civil war.

London in 1830 contained a small group of refugees who had been driven from Spain by the restored Bourbon, Ferdinand. Ferdinand after his long captivity in Bayonne had sworn to observe the Constitution. He broke his oath, dissolved the Cortes, and restored the Inquisition. After three years of civil war the French bayonets of the Duc d'Angoulême established him as absolute king. Foreign intervention again: it is difficult for the historian to feel moral indignation.

So in London the Spanish liberals gathered. 'Daily in the cold spring air,' wrote Carlyle, 'under skies so unlike their own, you could see a group of fifty or a hundred stately tragic figures, in proud threadbare cloaks; perambulating, mostly with closed lips' – a grotesque vision obtrudes of those other tragic figures who perambulated with open mouths – 'the broad pavements of Euston Square and the regions about St Pancras

new church.' Their leader was Torrijos, a soldier and diplomat, the friend of Sterling's parents, and soon therefore the
friend of the literary and metaphysical Apostles. In Sterling's
rooms in Regent Street and radicals met Torrijos and talked.
Sterling was twenty-four and Tennyson twenty-one.

The Apostles would probably have played no active part if
it had not been for Sterling's Irish cousin, Robert Boyd, a
young man of a hasty and adventurous temper, who had
thrown up his commission in the Army because of a fancied
insult and now, with five thousand pounds in his pocket,
planned to go privateering in the East. Torrijos needed capital
and promised Boyd the command of a Spanish cavalry regiment on Ferdinand's defeat. Even without the promise the
idea of conquering a kingdom would have been enough for
Boyd, whose ambition it was to live, like Conrad's Captain
Blunt, 'by his sword'. A boat was bought in the Thames and
secretly armed. Boyd and the Apostles were to sail it down
the river at night to Deal and there take on board Torrijos
and fifty picked Spaniards. The excitement, perhaps the sudden
intrusion of reality when the arms came on board, proved too
much for Sterling. 'Things are going on very well, but are very,
even frightfully near', he wrote in February 1830, and soon his
health gave way and furnished him with an excuse to stay behind, saved him for a Bayswater curacy, for the essays on
Revelation and Sin, for death at Ventnor. But he did not avoid
all danger; the Spanish Ambassador got wind of the prepara-
tions, the river police were informed, and one night they appeared over the side and seized the ship in the King's name.
Sterling dropped into a wherry, while a policeman brandished
a pistol and threatened to shoot, escaped to Deal and warned
Torrijos. The Spaniards crossed to France, and still accompanied by Boyd and a few of the Apostles, made their way in
small parties to Gibraltar.

Tennyson and Hallam were not with them – a Cambridge
term intervened. But for the long vacation they had a part to
play, not altogether without danger. While Torrijos waited at
Gibraltar, money and dispatches had to be carried to other
insurgents in the north of Spain. So Tennyson and Hallam

travelled across the Pyrenees by diligence, passing Cauteretz on the way, which Tennyson remembered thirty-two years later in a gentle poem to the memory of his friend, and reached the rebels' camp.

'A wild bustling time we had of it,' Hallam declared later. 'I played my part as conspirator in a small way and made friends with two or three gallant men who have since been trying their luck with Valdes.' One of these was the commander, Ojeda, who spoke to Tennyson of his wish *'couper la gorge à tous les curés'* but added with his hand on his heart, *'mais vous connaissez mon coeur.'* The two came back from the 'ferment of minds and stir of events' in the steamer *Leeds* from Bordeaux, and a young girl, who was travelling with her father and sister, paid particular attention to Hallam, 'a very interesting delicate looking young man'. He read her one of Scott's novels, and Tennyson listened in the background, wearing a large conspirator's cape and a tall hat. They did not confide their story to her.

Soon after they reached England a report came to Somersby Rectory that John Kemble – another of the Apostles – had been caught in the south and was to be tried for his life, and Tennyson in the early morning posted to Lincoln to try to find someone acquainted with the Consul at Cadiz, who might help to save his friend. But the rumour was false. It anticipated a more tragic story, for Torrijos and his band, commanded to leave Gibraltar in November 1831, sailed in two small vessels for Malaga, were chased by guardships and ran ashore. They barricaded themselves into a farmhouse, called curiously enough Ingles, and were surrounded. It was useless to resist and they surrendered, hoping for mercy. But they received none. They were shot on the esplanade at Malaga, after being shrived by a priest. Boyd received one favour: his body was delivered to the British Consul for burial.

He was the only Englishman to die, for the Apostles, tired of the long wait at Gibraltar, had already scattered through Spain with guidebooks, examining churches and Moorish remains. Sterling, who had his cousin's death on his conscience, never quite recovered from the blow. 'I hear the sound of that musketry,' he wrote in a letter; 'it is as if the bullets were tearing my own brain.' Hallam took the adventure lightly: 'After revolutionizing kingdoms, one is still less inclined than before to trouble one's head about scholarships, degrees, and such gear.' Tennyson's silence was unbroken. He may have reflected that only a Cambridge term had stood between him and the firing party on Malaga esplanade.

1937

MR COOK'S CENTURY

ALREADY they seem to belong to history – those tourists of the 1830s; they have the dignity and the pathos of a period, as they gather, the older ones in extraordinary hats and veils, the younger a little awkward and coltish, on the Continental platform at Victoria. Their baggage is all labelled for the Swiss *pensions*, the Italian lakes: in their handbags they carry sea-sick remedies and some of them tiny bottles of brandy; their tickets are probably in the hands of the courier, who now kindly and dexterously, with an old-world manner, shepherds them towards the second-class (first on boat), towards adventure – the first view of Mont Blanc, the fancy-dress dance at Grindelwald, the falls of Schaffhausen (seen through stained glass for a few francs extra). How sad it is that war prevents the one-hundredth anniversary of the first Cook's excursion being celebrated in a suitable atmosphere – with lots of eau-de-Cologne and steam and shiny picture-papers, and afterwards the smell of oil and sea-gulls and a sense of suppressed lady-like excitement, and the scramble along the corridor with the right coupons towards the first meal on the Basle express – everything paid for in advance, even the tips.

Of course there was so much more to Cook's than that: that little daily gathering on the Continental platform was rather like the unimportant flower a big business executive may wear in his button-hole for the sake of some early association. Thomas Cook and Son, who, in 1938, could have arranged you an independent tour to Central Africa as easily as to Ostend, had become a world-power which dealt with Prime Ministers: they transported Gordon up the Nile, and afterwards the relief expedition – 18,000 troops, 130,000 tons of stores, and 65,000 tons of coal; they reformed the pilgrim traffic to Mecca, deported 'undesirables' from South Africa during the Boer War, bought the railway up Vesuvius, and knocked a gap in the walls of Jerusalem to let the Kaiser in; before the end of the nineteenth century, under the son, they had far outstripped the dream of the first Thomas Cook, the young wood-turner and teetotaller and Bible-reader of Market Harborough, who on 5 July 1841, chartered a special train to carry his local temperance association from Leicester to Loughborough, where a meeting was to be held in Mr Paget's park. (The distance was twelve miles, and the return fare 1s.: it could hardly be less today.) The words of Mr John Fox Bell, secretary to the Midland Counties Railway, have the right historic ring: 'I know nothing of you or your society, but you shall have the train', and Mr Thomas Cook was quite aware that he was making history. 'The whole thing came to me', he said, 'by intuition and my spirit recoiled at the idea of imitation.' (This refers to the shameful attempt of the Mechanics Institute of Birmingham, who had run an excursion on 29 June to Cheltenham and Gloucester, to question the originality of his inspiration.) The cheers that greeted the thirsty teetotallers as they scrambled from their open scorching trucks, the music of the Loughborough band, the congratulatory speeches in Mr Paget's park bore Mr Cook on a great wave of local pride, inspecting hotels as he went, interviewing railroad secretaries, noting points of interest – the fourteenth-century cathedral, the abbey ruin, the majestical waterfall, on out of England into Wales – 'From the heights of Snowdon my thoughts took flight to Ben Lomond, and I determined to try to get to Scotland.' And get to Scotland he did with 350 men and women – we don't know whether they were teetotallers, and at Glasgow the guns were fired in their honour.

But Europe was another matter: Europe, to the Bible-reader and teetotaller, must have presented a knotty ethical problem, and it was not until 1860, after a personal look-round, that Mr Cook brought his excursions to the Continent. It is easy to mock nowadays at the carefully conducted tour, but there have been times and places when a guide was of great comfort. 'In 1865, through many difficulties, I got my first party to Rome and Naples, and for several years our way was through brigand-infested districts, where military escorts protected us.'

By the end of the century – under the rule of the second Cook – the firm had become the Cook's we know today. I have before me a copy of a paper called *Cook's Excursionist*, for 18 March 1899; already there were few places in the world to which an excursion had not been arranged – from the Tea and Coffee Rooms of Bora Bimki to the Deansgate Temperance Hotel in Manchester. The link with Mr Paget's park is still there, not only in the careful choice of hotel but in the advertisements – for Dr E. D. Moore's Cocoa and Milk, and the Compactum Tea Baskets. I like to feel that this – the spring of 1899 – marks the serene height of Mr Cook's tours, for brigands have ceased to trouble, and there is no suspicion that they may one day come again. Keating's Powder has taken the place of the military escort; Mrs Welsley Wigg is keeping 'an excellent table' in Euston Square, and a young lady, 'who last year found them perfectly efficacious', is cautiously recommending Roach's Sea-Sickness Draughts – perhaps this year won't be so lucky? At John Piggott's in Cheapside you can buy all the clothes you need for a conducted tour: the long black Chesterfield coat, the Norfolk suit, suitable for Switzerland, and the cap with a little button on top, the Prince Albert, the Leinster overcoat with velvet lapels, and with them, of course, the Gladstone bag strapped and double-strapped, secure against the dubious chambermaid and the foreign porter. What would they have thought – those serene men with black moustaches, and deer-stalkers for the crossing, if they could have seen in a vision the great familiar station-yard, dead and deserted as it was a few months back, without a cab, a porter or a policeman, just a notice, 'Unexploded Bomb', casually explaining what would have seemed to them the end of every-

thing: no trains for France, no trains for Switzerland, none for
Italy, and even the clock stopped? It is, when you come to
think of it, a rather sad centenary year.

1941

THE EXPLORERS

THE imagination has its own geography which alters with the
centuries. Each continent in turn looms up on the horizon like
a great rock carved with unintelligible hieroglyphics and symbols catching at the unconscious: in Shakespeare's youth it was
India, Arabia, the East, and a little later, in the days of Raleigh,
Central America and Eldorado: in the eighteenth century,
Australia and the South Seas: the nineteenth century, Africa –
in particular, West Africa and the Niger. Men have always tried
to rationalize their irrational acts, but the explanations given in
prospectuses like those of the South Sea Bubble and the African
Association are as unconvincing as last night's supper as the
cause of our fantastic dreams.

Little in history is more fantastic than the beginning of
West African exploration. There had been occasional travellers, but the exploration of this unknown territory six times the
size of Europe, the biggest white space on the contemporary
map, began at a meeting of the very select Saturday Club at
the St Alban's Tavern on 9 June 1788. We know the company
who were present, Lord Galloway, Lord Rawdon, General
Conway, Sir Adam Fergusson, Sir Joseph Banks, Sir William
Fordyce, Mr Pultney, Mr Beaufoy, and Mr Stuart, and even the
names of those who were absent – the Bishop of Llandaff,
Lord Carysfort, and Sir John Sinclair. The nine members (at
what stage of dinner is not recorded) decided to form themselves into an Association for Promoting the Discovery of the
Interior Parts of Africa and each agreed to subscribe five
guineas a year for five years. Before the Association had been
in existence for eight weeks two explorers had been chosen
and their routes assigned, but the subscription had already
proved inadequate.

The first main object was to discover the course of the Niger; and the motive? 'In 1783', Mr Plumb writes in his admirable introduction to Mr Howard's anthology,*

America had left the Empire. For some years merchants and financiers had confidently predicted her economic collapse, but no collapse came. And as yet no one realized that the political separation of Britain and America did not entail disastrous economic consequences, so that in mercantile circles the discovery of new markets seemed an urgent problem.

But the dream was more compelling than the motive can explain. Think of the German who

intended to travel as a Moslem trader. With great, perhaps excessive, thoroughness he trained on a diet of spiders, grasshoppers, and roots, and before sailing, in order to leave nothing to chance, had himself circumcised. These tribulations were suffered without reward, for the moment he set foot in Africa he caught fever and died.

Think too of the slender chances of survival. The phrase 'the White Man's Grave' has become a music-hall cliché to those who have never seen the little crumbling cemeteries of the West Coast like that on Bunce Island in Sierra Leone river. Mungo Park in the course of his second expedition reported: 'I am sorry to say that of forty-five Europeans who left the Gambia in perfect health, five only are at present alive, viz. three soldiers (one deranged in his mind), Lieutenant Martyn, and myself.' Forty years later the chances were hardly better. 'On the 18th' (Macgregor Laird reported)

Mr Andrew Clark, a fine young gentleman about eighteen years of age died. ... Poor fellow! He expired with the utmost calmness, drinking a cup of coffee; and his amiable and obliging disposition having endeared him to the crew, his death threw an additional gloom of despondency over these ill-fated men. In the afternoon James Dunbar, one of the firemen, died. On the 19th, my chief mate, Mr Goldie, and my sailmaker, John Brien, followed; and on the morning of the 20th, our super-cargo, Mr Jordan, expired. I thought at the time that Doctor Briggs had died also; as, while he

* *West African Explorers*, edited by C. Howard.

was endeavouring to revive Mr Jordan, he swooned and remained insensible for a long time. In the evening of the 20th, Mr Swinton also died ...

No other part of Africa has cast so deep a spell on Englishmen as the Coast, with the damp mists, the mangrove swamps, the malaria, the blackwater and the yellow fever (the only coast in the world dignified by a capital letter and needing no qualification). Is it that the explorer has the same creative sickness as the writer or the artist and that to fill in the map, as to fill in the character or features of a human being, requires the urge to surrender and self-destruction? – you cannot even surrender yourself so completely to a book or a picture as you can to the chances of death. Mary Kingsley was well aware of this suicidal streak that drove her to the Coast. In a letter to a friend she wrote quite frankly, 'Dead tired and feeling no one had need of me any more, when my father and mother died within six weeks of each other in '92, and my brother went off to the East, I went down to West Africa to die'; and in the sedate poetic prose of Mungo Park – the greatest of all writers on Africa – one can detect the same desire to lose himself for ever. The almost incredible privations and dangers of his first journey among the 'fanatic Moors' left him with life still on his hands and he had to return to Africa, giving up his quiet practice as a doctor in Peebles, to lose it – no one knows exactly where. (A Chief near Busa is said to wear his ring to this day.) 'When the human mind', he had written, 'has for some time been fluctuating between hope and despair, tortured with anxiety, and hurried from one extreme to another, it affords a sort of gloomy relief to know the worst that can possibly happen. ...' Again and again in Park's narrative the prose quickens with that gloomy relief as his fingers touched the rock bottom of experience.

It is right that Mungo Park should be the best represented of all the explorers in Mr Howard's excellent anthology. He w   born writer – the others, with the exception of B   ame good writers only because of the interest and oddity of their material. Burton here is very much the Burton of the *Arabian Nights* with his range of intricate experience: his eye for the bizarre concrete detail, like the golden crucifix dangling from the neck of a Dahomey official, 'but the crucifix is strangely altered, the crucified being a chameleon, the venerable emblem of the rainbow God': his wicked common sense about the Amazons of Dahomey – 'wherever a she-soldiery is, celibacy must be one of its rules, or the troops will be in a state of chronic functional disorder between the ages of fifteen and thirty-five': his malevolent tolerance – 'Human sacrifice in Dahomey is founded upon a purely religious basis, which not only strengthens but perpetuates the custom. It is a touching instance of the King's filial piety.' What a strange encounter it would have been in those days for a chance voyager to South Africa to call in passing on Her Majesty's Consul in Fernando Po.

There has been one deplorable change as the years passed – the growth of British superiority. To Mungo Park an African king deserved the same respect as his own. 'The king graciously replied', 'The good old king', such phrases are scattered through his work, and because he respected African sovereignty he respected the African, king or slave. There is a sense all the time of Christian equality. The Moors are cruel – they are not savages.

It is with the not very likeable – and I feel not very reliable – Major Dixon Denham in the 1820s that the white sneer can be observed for the first time. 'Nothing', he wrote, 'could be more absurd and grotesque than some, nay, all, of the figures who formed this court', though one believes that the sight of Major Denham naked and begging for a pair of trousers makes a higher claim to absurdity if we really believe in the episode. (I write *if*, for Major Denham's story frequently seems to echo hollowly not only the mood but the incidents of Mungo Park's narrative.)

Even the more likeable Macgregor Laird displays the white pride – 'Among other annoyances, they thrust a disgusting Albino close to me, and asked if he was my brother'; and with Captain Trotter's expedition up the Niger in the 1840s the tone has dismally darkened. 'Captain Trotter, Senior Commissioner, explained that Her Majesty the Queen of Great Britain ...

repugnant to the laws of God ... Her benevolent intentions for the benefit of Africa ...', and so on and so on.

We are not very far now from filibustering Stanley: the hundred lashes to a carrier, the chained and padlocked chiefs, the strong body of men armed with Remingtons, 'the withering fire', 'the Winchesters were worked handsomely'. The dream has vanished. The stores are landed, the trade posts established; civilization is on the way, the Anglican missionaries will build their fake Norman churches of laterite blocks, and as malaria and yellow fever are defeated, the wives will follow their Rugbeian husbands to hill stations and help them to administer the equal justice of a good public school. Even the savagery of Stanley had something of Africa still about it, more than the playing fields of Bo or the art classes of Achimota. We have much to be proud of in West Africa, of the indirect rule established by Lugard, of our protection – unknown to the same extent in East Africa – of the native, but the Christian equality which enabled Park to accept with humility the rebuke of a slave has vanished for ever.

1952

'SORE BONES: MUCH HEADACHE'

It is a sad thing about small nationalities that like a possessive woman they trap their great men: Walter Scott, Stevenson, Burns, Livingstone – all have to some extent been made over by their countrymen, they have not been allowed to grow or to diminish with time. How can they even shift in the grave under the weight of their national memorials? a whole industry of trinkets and souvenirs and statuettes depends on the conformity of the dead. A Civil Service of curators, secretaries, and guides takes charge of the memory. (65,000 people pass annually through the turnstiles of the Livingstone Memorial House at Blantyre with its coloured statuary and its Ancestry Room, Youth Room, Adventure Room.) An explorer can suffer from his legend as much as a writer – the explorer, too, has a passion to create, and just as a body carried to its grave at the summit of a Samoan hill obscures the writer struggling with the character of Hermiston, so the last trek of Livingstone's faithful carriers to the coast, with the obvious drama and the missionary moral, has intruded between us and the patience, the monotony, and the weariness incurred in adding a new line to a map, surveying an uncharted range, correcting an erroneous reading, above all it has obscured Livingstone's failure – you will not find photographs of the Lari massacre at Blantyre. (Dr Macnair does not help us to escape the legend by writing always in capital letters of the Explorer, the Traveller, the Missionary. I prefer the admirably clear and sensible geographical notes by Dr Ronald Miller.*)

The virtue of this selection from Livingstone's travel books and journals is its dullness – the reader must dig himself for the vivid fact or the revealing sentence. Livingstone was not primarily concerned with the beauty of the scenery or the drama of his journeys: he was concerned, at the beginning, with the location of healthy mission stations, later with discovering trade routes (which he considered might help towards the extinction of slavery) – the discoveries of Lake Shira and Lake Nyasa had no drama for him: they were incidental.

We discovered Lake Nyasa a little before noon on September 16, 1859. Its southern end is 14° minutes 25′ South lat., 35° 30′ E. long. At this point the valley is about 12 miles wide. There are hills on both sides of the lake.

The plot of the novel catches the attention, but the subject lies deeper. 'The Nile sources are valuable only to me as a means of opening my mouth with power.'

Literary expression was not Livingstone's object – a compass reading was more important for his mission. ('It seems a pity that the important facts about two healthy ridges should not be known to Christendom.') But in the early years when he wrote for publication, *Missionary Travels and Researches*, *The Zambesi and Its Tributaries*, he thought it necessary to take as his model the work of other Victorian travel books.

* *Livingstone's Travels*, edited by Dr James I. Macnair.

We proceeded rapidly up-river. The magnificent stream is often more than a mile broad and is adorned by many islands from three to five miles in length. The beauty of the scenery on some of these islands is greatly increased by the date-palm with its gracefully curved fronds and refreshing light-green colour, while the lofty palmyra towers above and casts its feathery foliage against a cloudless sky. The banks of the river are equally covered by forest and most of the trees on the brink of the water send down roots from their branches, like the banian. The adjacent country is rocky and undulating, abounding in elephants and all other large game, except leches and nakongs, which seem generally to avoid stony ground.

The airs and graces were to be shed when he was no longer concerned in advancing the sales of his books at home and increasing his opportunities for work. In the final journals we get the hard truthful writing of which he was capable. Written for no one but himself during that terrible seven-year journey, they present a picture quite different to those bas-reliefs of a missionary in a peaked consular cap, Bible in hand, surrounded by his native followers. Tired out, disillusioned (for now he was dependent upon the very slave traders whom he wished to put out of business for ever), uncertain of everything (even of the Zambesi whose navigability had been his obstinate dream) except of his simple evangelical faith, so free from the complex dogmas of a theologian – just God the Father, God the Son and God the Holy Ghost. (The Apostles' Creed was nearer to him than the Athanasian.)

How little experience is needed in a reader to make him realize the appalling nature of the seven-year journey. This writer has experienced only four weeks of African travel on foot, one strike of carriers, one bad Chief, a single night of high fever, only a few days when provisions grew short – but multiplying that small experience nearly a hundred times in days and how many hundred times in privation, it seems almost incredible that Livingstone could have gone on for so long without returning to civilization. Dr Miller admirably describes the condition of all African travel – the spider-web if tracks that may lead somewhere or nowhere:

One of the amazing features of Africa is the close network of footpaths that exists everywhere – and leads everywhere – highly convenient for movement within a limited neighbourhood, but most confusing for the stranger wishing to make a long cross-country traverse; and placing him at the mercy of guides who may mislead him, deliberately or accidentally, or simply immobilise him by withdrawing their services. ... Thus we find Livingstone, like many other African travellers, subjected to expensive and infuriating delays by the refusal of chiefs to supply guides. He navigated and fixed the framework of his maps by means of sextant observations, of course, but these could not tell him which fork of the path led merely to an outfield, and which to the next village on his route; which to a swamp and which to the ford on the river.

Here are a few jottings of his journey.

Christmas Day 1866. 'A little indigestible porridge, of hardly any taste, is now my fare and it makes me dream of better.'

January 1867 (the great journey was not yet a year old). Deserting carriers stole:

all the dishes, a large box of powder, the flour we had purchased dearly to help us as far as the Chambesi, the tools, two guns and a cartridge pouch; but the medicine chest was the sorest loss of all. I felt as if I had received a sentence of death, like poor Bishop Mackenzie.

October 1867. 'Sore bones; much headache; no appetite; much thirst.'

December 1867. 'I am so tired of exploration ...'

July 1868. 'Here we cooked a little porridge, and then I lay down on one side, and the canoe men and my attendants at the fire in the middle. I was soon asleep and dreamt I had apartments in Mivart's hotel.'

5 July 1872. (Stanley by this time had come and gone.) 'Weary! Weary!' – but there were still ten months to go.

All the last months of the seven years' trek were spent in a flat prairie waste of water; the earth, what there was of it, was like adhesive plaster. In one night six inches of rain fell. Canoes sank and stuck; tents became rotten, clothes were never dry. There are moments when the reader feels as though Livingstone had forgotten his true purpose, which was not to explore the limit of human endurance but to reach the Lualaba river and sail down it in the hope that it might lead him to the Nile and its sources (even that was only a means to the great white trade routes, the blessings as he believed of commerce, the end of slavery). He was in Childe Roland's territory now – 'a lion wandered into this world of water and anthills and roared night and morning'. What a long way he had come from the gracefully curved fronds, the magnificent streams, the lofty palmyra towers. Like Stevenson struggling with *Weir* he had reached rock at the moment of death.

The comparison between these two Scotsmen is oddly close. Under the literary polish of the Vailima Prayers was a simplicity of faith very similar to Livingstone's. Does it come from a Scottish upbringing – this ability to feel regret without remorse, to pardon oneself and accept one's weakness, the ability to leave oneself to God? 'For our sins forgiven or prevented, for our shame unpublished, we bless and thank Thee, O God.' Thus Stevenson, and thus Livingstone:

We now end 1866. It has not been so fruitful or useful as I intended. Will try to do better in 1867, and be better – more gentle and loving. And may the Almighty, to whom I commit my way, bring my desires to pass, and prosper me. Let all the sins of '66 be blotted out for Jesus' sake.

At the end they shared the same sense of failure. Who suffered more? Stevenson two months before his death writing, 'I am a fictitious article and have long known it. I am read by journalists, by my fellow novelists, and by boys', or Livingstone finding himself embroiled in the slave trade he hated: 'I am heart sore and sick of human blood. .... I doubt whether the divine favour and will is on my side.'

For the end their wish was the same. It is impossible not to recall the grave on Mount Vaea and the over-familiar verses, 'Here he lies where he longed to be', when we read in Livingstone's journal on 25 June 1868:

> We came to a grave in the forest. It was a little rounded mound, as if the occupant sat in it. It was strewn over with flour, and a number of large beads had been put on it. A little path showed that it had visitors. That is the sort of grave I should prefer. To lie in the still, still forest, with no hand ever to disturb my bones. Graves at home seem to me miserable and without elbow room, especially those in cold, damp clay.

Stevenson's wishes were the more respected, for Livingstone's embalmed body was brought home to the damp clay and the lack of elbow room in the nave of Westminster Abbey.

Less than a hundred years have gone by since Livingstone's death and we can see the measure of his failure in East Africa today. The trade routes have been opened up, the slave trade abolished, but the true lesson of Livingstone's life was completely forgotten. 'In attempting their moral elevation', Livingstone wrote of the Africans, 'it is always more conductive to the end desired that the teacher should come unaccompanied by any power to cause either jealousy or fear.' In the same book he wrote, 'Good manners are as necessary among barbarians as among the civilized', but during those weeks in Stanley's company he had failed to influence his companion except superficially. It was to Stanley and his Maxim guns and rawhide whips that the future in East Africa belonged, and it was Stanley's methods that left a legacy of hatred and distrust throughout Africa.

1954

FRANCIS PARKMAN

'My 23rd Birthday. Nooned at a mud puddle.' So Parkman noted in his journal * in 1846, and we shall look far for any comparable passage in the diaries of a creative artist. Certainly the wind has never played quite so freely at a historian's birth.

* *The Journals of Francis Parkman*, edited by Mason Wade.

The smell of documents, the hard feel of the desk-chair, are singularly absent. Parkman had already ridden for three weeks on the arduous and dangerous Oregon trail, and in an earlier passage, a week or two back, he had let his imagination dwell on the vast range of experience already crossed between the ages of eighteen and twenty-two.

> Shaw and Henry went off for buffaloes. H. Killed two bulls. The Capt. very nervous and old-womanish at nooning – he did not like the look of the hills, which were at least half a mile off – there might be Inds. there, ready to pounce on the horses. In the afternoon, rode among the hills – plenty of antelope – lay on the barren ridge of one of them, and contrasted my present situation with my situation in the convent at Rome.

Surely no other historian has planned his life work so young nor learned to write so hard a way. At the age of eighteen the whole scheme of his great work *France and England in North America* had captured his consciousness; there remained only to gather his material and to begin. One remembers the immense importance that Gibbon's biographers have attributed to his gentlemanly service in the Hampshire Militia, but what are we to think of a young historian who, before starting to write his first volume, *The Conspiracy of Pontiac*, finds it necessary to make the long journey to Europe and Rome, there to stay in a Passionist monastery so that he may attain some imaginative sympathy with the Catholic missionaries who are the heroes of his second volume (published twenty-four years later) and after that to undertake his journey along the Oregon trail in quest of Indian lore, thus ruining his health for a lifetime in the mere gathering of background material?

Parkman was an uncertain stylist (as the admirable editor of these journals writes: 'There seems to have been a natural instinct for the phrase that is just a shade too high, just as his ear was naturally faulty'), but his errors of taste are carried away by the great drive of his narrative, much as they are in the case of Motley and in our own day Mr Churchill. He had ridden off through the dangerous wilderness with a single companion, like one of the heroes of his epic or a character in

Fenimore Cooper, who had woken his genius, he had eaten dog
with the Indians and stayed in their moving villages, he had
watched the tribes gather for war and heard the news of traders'
deaths brought in. He had listened to Big Crow's own account
of his savagery – 'he has killed 14 men; and dwells with great
satisfaction on the capture of a Utah, whom he took personally; and, with the other Sioux, scalped alive, cut the tendons
of his wrist, and flung, still alive, into a great fire.' Since the
seventeenth century no historian had so lived and suffered for
his art. Like Prescott he all but lost his sight, so that he was
forced to use a wire grid to guide his pencil, he suffered from
misanthropy and a melancholia that snaps out like a dog even
from his early journals ('the little contemptible faces – the thin,
weak tottering figures – that one meets here on Broadway, are
disgusting. One feels savage with human nature'). The work
planned at eighteen, begun at twenty-eight, was only finished at
fifty-nine, in the year before his death, by working against time
and his own health. This was a poet's vocation, followed with
a desperate intensity careless of consequences, and the journals
are as important in tracing the course of the creative impulse
as the journals of Henry James. And how closely we are reminded of the James family and their strange melancholia
when we read in one of Parkman's letters:

Between 1852 and 1860 this cerebral rebellion passed through
great and seemingly capricious fluctuation. It had its ebbs and
floods. Slight and sometimes imperceptible causes would produce
an access which sometimes lasted with little respite for months.
When it was in its milder moods, I used the opportunity to collect
material and prepare ground for the future work, should work ever
become practicable. When it was at its worst, the condition was not
enviable. I could neither listen to reading nor engage in conversation even of the lightest. Sleep was difficult, and was often banished
entirely for one or two nights during which the brain was apt to be
in a state of abnormal activity which had to be repressed at any
cost, since thought produced the intensest torture. The effort
required to keep the irritated organ quiet was so fatiguing that I
occasionally rose and spent hours in the open air, where I found
distraction and relief watching the policemen and the tramps on the
Malls of Boston Common, at the risk of passing for a tramp my-

self. Towards the end of the night this cerebral excitation would seem to tire itself out, and give place to a condition of weight and oppression much easier to bear.

Mr Mason Wade is an impeccable editor, sensitive to the qualities of Parkman's style, its merits as well as its demerits, learned in his subject, passionately industrious in tracing the most transient character. His notes are often as fascinating as the text – on 'Old Dick' for example, an odd job man on Lake George, who collected rattlesnakes and exhibited them in a box inscribed: 'In this box a Rattel Snaick Hoo was Kecht on Black mountaing. He is seven years old last July. Admittance sixpence site. Children half price, or notten,' or on that strange character, Joseph Brant, alias Thayendanegea, Mohawk chief and freemason, who on one occasion saved from the stake a fellow mason who gave him the right sign. Brant was entertained by Boswell and painted by Romney. What a long way such a character seems from the murderers of the Jesuit Brébeuf (they baptized him with boiling water, cut strips of flesh from his living body and ate them, and opened his breast and drank his blood before he died).

Mr Wade himself discovered these journals, with the romantic and paradoxical simplicity of a Chesterton detective story, in Parkman's old Boston home on Chestnut Street.

Parkman's Indian trophies still hung on the walls; the bookcases still held the well-worn editions of Byron, Cooper, and Scott which were his life-long favourites; and in the centre of the room, covered with a dust sheet, stood the desk on which the great histories had been written. This desk was two-sided; the drawers on one side had obviously been inspected and emptied of most of their contents ... the drawers on the other side had been overlooked; they contained the missing journals and a great mass of correspondence, including some of the most important letters Parkman wrote and received.

For the general reader the most interesting of Mr Wade's discoveries is Parkman's journal of the Oregon Trail which Mr Wade rightly prefers to the work based on it – Parkman's first and most popular book, popular because of the way in which it

was adulterated to suit the fashion of the time by his friend
Charles Eliot Norton, 'carefully bowdlerized of much anthro-
pological data and many insights into Western life which
seemed too crude to his delicate taste'. Mr Wade quotes several
examples of these changes from the vivid fluid journal to the
stilted literary tones – the false Cooperisms – of the book.
These Cooperisms, still evident in *The Conspiracy of Pontiac*,
Parkman gradually shed. Life and literature at the beginning
lay uneasily with a sword between them, so that nothing in the
early books has the same sense of individual speech and
character that we find in the journals. Here from the journals is
a certain Mr Smith of Palermo:

'Don't tell me about your Tarpeian rock. I've seen it, and what's
more, the feller wanted I should give him half a dollar for taking
me there. "Now look here!" says I, "do you s'pose I'm going to
pay you for showing me this old pile of stones? I can see better
rocks than this any day, for nothing; so clear out!" I'll tell you the
way I do,' continued Mr Smith, 'I don't go and *look* and *stare* as
some people do when I get inside of a church, but I pace off the
length and breadth, and then set it down on paper. Then, you see,
I've got something that will keep.'

And here is an old soldier near the Canadian Border:

On entering the bar-room, an old man with a sunburnt wrinkled
face and no teeth, a little straw hat set on one side of his grey
head – and who was sitting on a chair leaning his elbows on his
knees and straddling his legs apart – thus addressed me: 'Hullo!
hullo! What's agoin' on, now? Ye ain't off to the wars already, be
ye? Ther' ain't no war now as I knows on, though there's agoin' to
be one afore long, as damned bloody as ever was fit this side o'
hell!' ... He then began to speak of some of his neighbours, one
of whom he mentioned as 'that G—d damnedest, sneakingest,
nastiest puppy that ever went this side of hell!' Another he likened
to a 'sheep's cod dried'; another was 'not fit to carry guts to a
bear'.

Only with his third book – *The Jesuits in North America* –
did the marriage satisfactorily take place. In the deeply moving
Relations of the Jesuits that form the greater part of his

material he found again the power of characteristic speech: like that of the tortured priest Bressani who wrote with bitter humour to his Superior, 'I could not have believed that a man was so hard to kill', and in another letter of ironic apology to the Jesuit General in safe Rome: 'I don't know if your Paternity will recognize the handwriting of one whom you once knew very well. The letter is soiled and ill-written; because the writer had only one finger of his right hand left entire, and cannot prevent the blood from his wounds, which are still open, from staining the paper. His ink is gunpowder mixed with water and his table is the earth.'

By this time, too, Parkman had learned the value of bald narrative:

Noel Chabanel came later to the mission; for he did not reach the Huron country until 1643. He detested the Indian life – the smoke, the vermin, the filthy food, the impossibility of privacy. He could not study by the smoky lodge-fire, among the noisy crowd of men and squaws, with their dogs, and their restless, screeching children. He had a natural inaptitude to learning the language, and laboured at it for five years with scarcely a sign of progress. The Devil whispered a suggestion into his ear: Let him procure his release from these barren and revolting toils, and return to France, where congenial and useful employments awaited him. Chabanel refused to listen; and when the temptation still beset him he bound himself by a solemn vow to remain in Canada to the day of his death.

And to complete the marriage Parkman had learned to control on occasion his poetic prose with fine effect as in this picture of Indian immortality:

In the general belief, however, there was but one land of shades for all alike. The spirits, in form and feature as they had been in life, wended their way through dark forests to the villages of the dead, subsisting on bark and rotten wood. On arriving they sat all day in the crouching posture of the sick, and when night came, hunted the shades of animals, with the shades of bows and arrows, among the shades of trees and rocks; for all things, animate and inanimate, were alike immortal, and all passed together to the gloomy country of the dead.

The last notebook Parkman kept contains an account of his desperate final battle against insomnia – the amount of sleeping draught, the hours of sleep gained. One column, *A Half-Century of Conflict*, had to be finished and raised in its place to complete the great architectural scheme. The hours of sleeping dropped as low as three and a half and only once in the three-year record rose above eight. In that bare mathematical catalogue there is something of the spirit of Chabanel. The historian had made his vow forty years before and it was kept.

1949

DON IN MEXICO

THIS is an account by a Cambridge professor of two trips to the tourist resorts of Mexico,* but it pretends to be rather more. The professor is a Spanish scholar – and that should have been an advantage; but he was handicapped by the unenterprising nature of his journey (the usual round-trip by way of Mexico City, Taxco, Cuernavaca, Puebla, Vera Cruz, Merida, Chichen-Itza), by his friendships with Spanish Republicans as strange to the country as himself, by his ignorance of and antipathy to the religion of the country, and by a whimsical prose style less successful in conveying the atmosphere of Mexico than that of Cambridge-jokes on the Trumpington Road, charades with undergraduates in red-brick villas, bicycles in the hall. His book is self-illustrated with little dark holiday snaps called 'Puebla: Tiled House', or 'Mexico: Aztec Calendar Stone', and like letters home his account is either very personal or else very guide-book at second-hand: 'The remains at Chichen-Itza lie in three groups. Those so far described belong to North Chichen; the others are referred to as Middle Chichen and Old Chichen. Following the trail from North Chichen to Middle Chichen, the first building one comes to ...' and so on. But one can go to more accurate and comprehensive guide-books, and it is for the portrait of the Cam-

* *Mexico: A New Spain With Old Friends*, by Professor J. B. Trend.

bridge don abroad that this book will be read by the irreverent: the self-portrait of a middle-aged professor, one of 'the cultured and civilized', with a liking for weak tea and 'amusing conversation' on 'the plane of ripe but frivolous scholarship' – the authorship of *The Young Visiters*, for example.

In spite of the unconscious humour of many of the scenes, the book would not be worth attention if it were not symptomatic – symptomatic of the inhumanity of the academic brain, and its unreliability. Professor Trend, touring round the beauty spots, saw no sign of religious persecution. He noticed, it is true, a few religious colleges turned into libraries, but that to the nineteenth-century progressive mind was all to the good; apparently he did not notice in Mexico City the garages and cinemas that had once been churches. Anyway, there were plenty without these – 'Mexico, like Spain, somewhat overbuilt itself in the way of churches.' A church to the professor was an 'interior', a style of architecture: he was appalled in Puebla at 'the religiosity of the place'; 'tracts thrust into your hands, individuals standing at the church doors to take a collection even before you could look in to see whether the interior was worth looking at'. (One is reminded of the Mr Smith whom Parkman encountered at Palermo.)

It would be funny – the whimsicality, the self-importance, the ignorance – if it were not so heartless. However strong the detestation of the Cambridge don for the Roman Catholic Faith, he might have remembered that those who held it were human. Shoot them and they bleed as copiously as a Republican. Starve them ... He may have observed in Mexico City the number of priests exercising their religious duties; he made no inquiries, or he would have learnt that in Mexico City, as in other tourist centres, the law is winked at, so that priests who are forbidden to say Mass in their own States and are, therefore, without means, flock to the capital to escape starvation. The professor visited Orizaba in 1939: the churches were certainly open. He did not ask the reason or he would have learnt how only two years before a child had been murdered by police officers on her way from a Mass house, and how the peasants in retaliation had broken the churches open throughout the State of Vera Cruz. He was in Mexico in 1938, too, and flew over Tabasco on his way to Yucatan. He did not alight from his plane at Villa Hermosa, or he might by some lucky chance have been present when the police fired on a crowd of peasants, men, women and children, who were setting up an altar in the ruins of a church. But, of course, no one interested in ecclesiastical architecture would have visited Tabasco, for there were no churches left in the State.

Blithely, whimsically, from his Cambridge study the professor writes: 'As to religious persecution, it is (so far as my experience goes, and as far as I have been able to find out by inquiry mostly imaginary.' His inquiries must have been as limited as his experience, and any writer who describes conditions of which the professor prefers to remain in ignorance he styles a 'propagandist'. He has all the suspicion of a provincial holiday-maker afraid of being 'had', and I shall probably be suspected of all sorts of dishonest motives if I assure him that in the very year he was in Mexico he had only to travel a little farther afield to discover States where the churches were either destroyed or locked, where priests were forbidden to say Mass, and where the sacraments of their Faith could be taken by the people only in secret. Propaganda? But I have attended these secret Masses myself in Chiapas. I doubt if my assurance will carry conviction, for as the professor writes, 'My Mexico is not like that', and on another page, 'I have always had a preference for legends rather than for more sober history.'

1940

[3]

SAMUEL BUTLER

ONE knows the man well in his suit of scrubby black, his stained greenish felt hat, with his umbrella, his boots, the odour of tobacco on his clothes: he leans over the bookstall fingering the ugly cheap reprints of the Rationalist Press or remains for a long while absorbed by the Kensit literature in a small dingy shop near St Paul's. Greeting him one is embarrassed by his inability to tell polite untruths. 'Good morning.' 'The morning is nothing of the kind.' He will not stoop to the medieval superstition of 'Good-bye'. He is an Honest Man and rather conscious of the fact, but he has gained little stature from his emancipation. One is instinctively aware in his past of an ugly, crippling childhood, attics and blackbeetles, and some grim grammar school, and sadistic masters, His favourite author is Samuel Butler, and one remembers Butler's idea of immortality, the desiccated sentiment of:

> Yet meet we shall, and part, and meet again,
> Where dead men meet, on lips of living men.

Here, in the dry deformed aggressive spirit, is Samuel Butler's life everlasting. Few others will be found to swallow whole *The Fair Haven* and *Life and Habit, Evolution Old and New* and *God the Known and God the Unknown*, or even the notebooks, of which this second selection has just appeared.* Out of the nineteen volumes of the collected works most people pick and choose, read *The Way of All Flesh* for the savour of hatred, *Erewhon* for the brilliant reporting of the opening chapters. But this would never have satisfied Butler who wanted to stuff himself neck and crop between the teeth of time.

These notebooks witness it. He never overtly made clear quite why he copied and re-copied these random jottings into the carefully bound, dismally designed volumes 'in half black

* *Further Extracts from the Note-Books of Samuel Butler*, chosen and edited by A. T. Bartholomew.

roan, with dark green pin-head cloth sides and shiny marbled end-papers'; it was not primarily as material for his books – 'I greatly question the use of making the notes at all. I find I next to never refer to them or use them'; if we are to believe him, 'they are not meant for publication', though a few lines later he writes, 'Many a one of those who look over this book – for that it will be looked over by not a few I doubt not – will think me to have been a greater fool than I probably was', but the motive is really obvious enough. These notes were to present to posterity the whole man in his wisdom, his wit, his hate, and even his triviality. There is something rather tryingly 'rough diamond' about the approach – 'You must take me just as you find me' – but alas, one finds him in these notes deep buried under the late Victorian rational dust. One digs and digs and is occasionally rewarded by the genuine gold glitter of a cuff-link.

The trouble is, he was not an artist. He remarks in one of the notes, 'I never knew a writer yet who took the smallest pains with his style and was at the same time readable.' To have thought twice about the words he used, to have tried to refine his language in order to express his meaning with greater exactitude, this would have been, in his view, to blaspheme against the essential Samuel ('You must take me just as you find me'). Better far to stick down everything as it came to mind, even when the note was as trivial as:

THE RIDICULOUS AND THE SUBLIME

As there is but one step from the sublime to the ridiculous, so also there is but one from the ridiculous to the sublime;

as cheaply smart as:

CHRIST

Jesus! with all thy faults I love thee still;

as meaningless as:

EVERYTHING

should be taken seriously, and nothing should be taken seriously.

There is a great deal of this kind of thing in the second selection from the notebooks: a great many exhibitions of rather cocky conceit in his own smartness – 'So and so said to me ... I said to him,' the smartness which makes *Erewhon* so insignificant beside *Gulliver*, many superficial half-truths in the form of paradoxes which have become aggravatingly familiar in the plays of his disciple; and always, on whatever subject he treats, the soreness of the unhealing wound. The perpetual need to generalize from a peculiar personal experience maimed his imagination. Even Christianity he could not consider dispassionately because it was the history of a Father and Son. In *The Way of All Flesh* he avenged a little of his childhood's suffering, but he was not freed from the dead hand. His most serious criticism has the pettiness of personal hate, and how will posterity be able to take with respect attacks on Authority (whether it be the authority of God, Trinity College, or Darwin) when the mask it wears is always the cruel, smug, unimportant features of Theobald Pontifex?

1934

THE UGLY ACT

THE wide and indiscriminating territory of literature, with all its range of human authorship, surely contains few figures less agreeable than W. E. Henley. His reputation would hardly have survived into a centenary year on the strength of such poems as *Out of the Night* with its bombast and muddled thought (although Mr Connell * finds them in all 'respectable anthologies' – odd epithet), and the fame of an editor must always be short lived. Only a biographer has time to look through the files of a dead review, listing the faded names of contributors that once, vivid with promise, seemed to cast a lustre over their leader – David Hannay, G. S. Street, Katherine Tynan, Marriott Watson, T. E. Brown, and the like. And yet, in some strange way, this ill-tempered cripple does still

* *W. E. Henley*, by John Connell.

live in literary history: we cannot quite forget him; he glares out at us from the shadows of the last century, breathing heavily through his big beard, his fist ready like Long John Silver with his crutch, arousing our attention by the venom of his quarrels, by his ignobility and violence and the long-drawn-out malignity of his character, that elephantine quality which ensured his never forgetting what he considered an injury, although he was always ready to extend the warm hearty palm of forgiveness to a victim when the injury had been inflicted by himself.

The most famous of his quarrels was, of course, that with Stevenson, and the most long lived, for Henley nursed his memory of it nearly twenty years, before at last he had his say about his dead friend in the famous *Pall Mall Magazine* review of Graham Balfour's biography. Of that review Henry James wrote, in a letter that Mr Connell might have quoted if he had taken a more impartial view of Henley:

It's really a rather striking and lurid – and so far interesting case – of long discomfortable jealousy and ranklement turned at last to post-humous (as it were!) malignity, and making the man do, *coram publico*, his ugly act, risking the dishonour for the assuagement ... the whole business illustrates how life takes upon itself to give us more true and consistent examples of human unpleasantness than expectation could suggest – makes a given man, I mean, live up to his ugliness.

Mr Connell, however, one must admit, is impartial enough for us to see Henley living up to his ugliness in a yet more extreme form. Wilde, unaffected by the attacks on *Dorian Gray* that had appeared under Henley's editorship, had written to him on the death of his daughter a letter of gentle and perceptive sympathy.

I am very sorry indeed to hear of your great loss – I hope you will let me come down quietly to you one evening and over our cigarettes we will talk of the bitter ways of fortune, and the hard ways of life. But, my dear Henley, to work – to work – that is your duty – that is what remains for natures like ours. Work never seems to me a reality, but as a way of getting rid of reality.

It is hard to uncover the source of Henley's rage against Wilde. Perhaps Wilde's very generosity – a quality in which Henley was deficient – called it out, in the same way that the money Henley regularly received from Stevenson, even after their friendship had ceased, made it all the more necessary for him to assert, however viciously, his independence. Perhaps it was simply the jealousy of a bad writer for his superior who had replied with such impervious wit and good humour to his critics in the *National Observer*. Wilde was not vulnerable to journalistic attack, and Henley seems to have felt a shabby delight at the thought that at least he was vulnerable to the law. And so again we have the sight of Henley exposing himself far more drastically than he exposed his victim in those ugly letters in which he kept Whibley in Paris posted on the news of the two trials.

Oscar at Bay was on the whole a pleasing sight ... Holloway and Bow Street have taken his hair out of curl in more senses than one. And I am pretty sure that he is having a dam bad time ...

As for Hosker, the news is that he lives with his brother, and is all day steeping, steeping himself in liquor, and moaning for Boasy! I am summoned to play the juryman next Monday (*je m'en fiche pas mal*), and it isn't impossible that I should have at least the occasion of sitting upon him. For, they say, he has lost all nerve, all pose, all everything; and is just now so much the Ordinary Drunkard that he has not even the energy to kill himself.

The depressing nature of the hero is emphasized by a certain drabness in his biographer. This is never at its best a well-written book, and Mr Connell show little power of discrimination in his choice of material. The letters to Whibley are, for the most part, incredibly tedious – repeated complaints of overdue articles, news of his own books, bluff out-dated slang. Here is one typical paragraph to stand for hundreds: 'The book seems to be thriving no end. Nutt had ordered all the edition from the binder: and therewith the remainder of Ed. Sec. of *A.B. of V*. So the oofbird may presently begin to flutter.'

1949

ERIC GILL

ROMAN CATHOLICISM in this country has been a great breeder of eccentrics – one cannot picture a man like Charles Waterton belonging to any other faith, and most of us treasure the memory of some strong individuality who combined a strict private integrity with a carefully arranged disregard of conformity to national ways of thought and behaviour. Eric Gill, with his beard and his biretta, his enormous outspokenness, his amorous gusto, trailing his family across the breadth of England with his chickens, cats, dogs, goats, ducks, and geese, belonged only distantly to this untraditional tradition; he was an intruder – a disturbing intruder among the eccentrics. He had not behind him the baroque internationalism of a great Catholic school, or the little primnesses of a convent childhood, to separate him from his fellow-countrymen along well-prepared lines, with the help of scraps of bizarre worldliness or the tag-end of peasant beliefs picked up in saints' lives.

Gill's father was a curate in the Countess of Huntingdon's Connexion in Brighton, who later conformed to the Anglican Church and became a different sort of curate in Chichester, doomed to bring up eleven children on £150 a year. 'He was from a "highbrow", intellectual, agnostic point of view, a complete nonentity; but he loved the Lord His God with all his sentimental mind and all his sentimental soul.' What Gill gained from his parents was a sense of vocation; money was never the standard by which values were gauged. 'They never complained about poverty as though it was an injustice. And they never put the pursuit of riches before us as an occupation worthy of good people.' There were tradesmen in the family, and missionaries in the South Seas. There was even in a sense art, for Gill's mother had been a singer in an opera company and his father read Kingsley and Carlyle and Tennyson's poems, and called his son after Dean Farrar's hero. It was all kindling-wood waiting for a fire – the grim Brighton railway viaduct with the huddled mean houses of Preston Park inserted between the railway lines, the small boy drawing engines and the father writing sermons, and the advertising sign of a machine-made bread against the sky, and a Mrs Hart whispering dreadfully, 'There was a black-beetle in it' – and yet a sense of infinite possibility. 'My favourite author at that time was G. A. Henty, and the only prize I ever got at school was *Through the Sikh War*. I remember walking home in the moonlight with my father and mother after the prize-giving and school concert in a daze of exaltation and pride.' The kindling-wood is always there if only a flame be found. In Gill's case Catholicism supplied the flame.

What followed in one sense is anti-climax, the progress of an artist not of the first rank – the railway engines giving place to architectural plans and those to letter-cutting and monumental masonry: the artist impressing himself on the face of London in W. H. Smith signs, in self-conscious Stations of the Cross. Is it for this – and the little albums of dimly daring nudes – that the father painfully taught the love of God? As an artist Gill gained nothing from his faith, but the flame had been lit none the less; and perhaps it was the inability to express his vision that drove him into eccentricity – to the community life at Ditchling, from which again he fled when it became advertised by his Dominican friends – the disciplined Catholic private life advertised like the machine-made bread. His beard and his biretta were the expressions of fury against his environment. He hated commercial civilization, and everything he did was touched by it – a new kind of repository art grew up under his influence; above all, he hated his fellow-Catholics because he felt that they had betrayed their Catholicism, and of them he hated the priesthood most. It seemed to him that they had compromised too easily with capitalism, like that Bishop of San Luis Potosi, who hid the Papal Encyclical, *De Rerum Novarum*, in the cellars of the Palace because he believed it would encourage Communism.

The clergy seem to regard it as their job to support a social order which as far as possible forces us to commit all the sins they denounce. ... A man can be a very good Catholic in a factory, our parish priest used to be fond of saying. And he was very annoyed and called us bolshevists when we retorted: yes, but it requires heroic virtue and you have no right to demand heroic virtue from anyone, and certainly not from men and women in thousands and millions.

And again he wrote: 'Persons whom you would have thought could hardly exist, Catholic bank clerks and stock-brokers for instance, are the choice flower of our great Catholic schools.'

There, of course, he went wrong; Waterton is a much more likely product of Stonyhurst than a bank clerk, but he was right on the main issue – that in this country Catholicism which should produce revolutionaries produces only eccentrics (eccentricity thrives on an unequal social system), and that Conservatism and Catholicism should be as impossible bed-fellows as Catholicism and National Socialism. Out of his gritty childhood and his discovered faith a rebel should have been born; he wrote like a rebel with a magnificent disregard for grammar, but something went wrong. Perhaps he made too much money, perhaps he was half-tamed by his Dominican friends; whatever the reason his rebellion never amounted to much – an article in a quarterly suppressed by the episcopate, addresses to a working men's college, fervent little articles on sex. That overpowering tradition of eccentricity simply absorbed him until even his most outrageous anti-clerical utterances caused only a knowing smile on the face of the faithful. The beard and the biretta won – he was an eccentric too.

1941

HERBERT READ

S O M E years ago Mr Read published an account of his child-hood under the title *The Innocent Eye*. It must have come as a surprise to many of his readers that the critic of *Art Now* was brought up on a Yorkshire farm: a whole world of the imagina-tion seems to separate the vale, the orchard, the foldgarth, the mill, and the stockyard – the fine simple stony architecture of his childhood – from what was to come, which one is tempted unfairly to picture as a long empty glossy gallery with one abstraction by Mr Ben Nicholson on the farther wall, perhaps two Ideas and a Navel in clay by Mr Hans Arp on a pedestal on the parquet, and a Calder decoration of wires with little balls attached dangling from the ceiling.

The basin at times was very wide, especially in the clearness of a summer's day; but as dusk fell it would suddenly contract, the misty hills would draw near, and with night they had clasped us close: the centre of the world had become a candle shining from the kitchen window. Inside, in the sitting-room where we spent most of our life, a lamp was lit, with a ground glass shade like a full yellow moon. There we were bathed before the fire, said our prayers kneeling on the hearthrug, and then disappeared up the steep stairs lighted by a candle to bed.

Now Mr Read has written a sequel to *The Innocent Eye*,* taking the account of his own life on out of the Yorkshire vale: a grim Spartan orphan's school with a strong religious tone and the young Read absorbed in Rider Haggard; a clerkship in a Leeds Savings Bank at £20 a year, and the slightly older Read becoming a Tory and reading Disraeli and Burke; then Leeds University and loss of faith, religious and political, and so the war, and after it the literary career – and the settled literary personality, the agnostic, the anarchist, and the romantic, bearing rather heavily the load of new knowledge and new art, the theories of Freud blurring the clear innocent eye. The first book was one of the finest evocations of childhood in our language: the second – finely written as it often is – records a rather dusty pilgrimage towards a dubious and uninteresting conclusion: 'This book will attempt to show how I have come to believe that the highest manifestation of the immanent will of the universe is the work of art' – sight giving place to thought: to abstractions which have not been abstracted but found ready-made – and in an odd way it doesn't quite ring true. There's an absence of humility, and no one can adequately write of his own life without humility. When Mr

* *Annals of Innocence and Experience.*

Read, writing of his youth, remarks that 'in a few years there was scarcely any poem of any worth in my own language which I had not read;' when he writes of religion in a few dogmatic sentences as the phantasy of an afterlife conceived in the fear of death, we have travelled a long way with him – too far – from the objective light of childhood and the first 'kill'. 'I do not remember the blood, nor the joking huntsmen; only the plumed breath of the horses, the jingle of their harness, the beads of dew and the white gossamer on the tangled hedge beside us.'

We have travelled too far, but we should never have known without *The Innocent Eye* quite how far we had travelled. That is the astounding thing – Mr Read was able to go back, back from the intellectual atmosphere personified in Freud, Bergson, Croce, Dewey, Vivante, Scheller. ... And if we examine his work there have always been phases when he has returned: the creative spirit has been more than usually separated in his case from the critical mind. (He admits himself in one essay that submitting to the creative impulse he has written poetry which owes nothing to his critical theories.) The critic, one feels, has sometimes been at pains to adopt the latest psychological theories before they have proved their validity – rather as certain Anglican churchmen leap for confirmation of their faith on the newest statement of an astronomer. But the creative spirit has remained tied to innocence. 'The only real experiences in life', writes Mr Read, 'being those lived with a virgin sensibility – so that we only hear a tone once, only see a colour once, see, hear, touch, taste, and smell everything but once, the first time.' One of the differences between writers is this stock of innocence: the virgin sensibility in some cases lasts into middle age: in Mr Read's case, we feel, as in so many of his generation, it died of the shock of war and personal loss. When the Armistice came: 'There were misty fields around us, and perhaps a pealing bell to celebrate our victory. But my heart was numb and my mind dismayed: I turned to the fields and walked away from all human contacts.' In future there was to be no future: as a critic he was to be sometimes pantingly contemporary, and when he was most an artist he was to be farthest removed from his time.

'When most an artist': we are not permanently interested in any other aspect of Mr Read's work. Anarchism means more to him than it will ever mean to his readers (in spite of that vigorous and sometimes deeply moving book, *Poetry and Anarchism*) – sometimes we suspect that it means little more to him than an attempt to show his Marxist critics that he too is a political animal, to give a kind of practical everyday expression to the 'sense of glory' which has served him ever since youth in place of a religious faith; and I cannot share his belief that criticism with the help of Freud will become a science, and a critical opinion have the universality of a scientific law. As an artist he will be assessed, it seems to me, by *The Innocent Eye*, by his only novel, *The Green Child*, by a few poems – notably *The End of a War*, by his study of Wordsworth, informed as it is by so personal a passion that it is lifted out of the category of criticism ('we both spring from the same yeoman stock of the Yorkshire dales, and I think I have a certain "emphatic" understanding of his personality which gives a sense of betrayal to anything I write about him'), and some scattered essays in which, too, the note of 'betrayal' is evident – the essays on Froissart, Malory, and Vauvenargues in particular.

It is that author with whom we wish to dwell – however much lip service we may pay to books like *Art and Society*, *Art Now*, *Art and Industry* and the rest – the author who describes himself: 'In spite of my intellectual pretensions, I am by birth and tradition a peasant.' Even his political thought at its most appealing comes back to that sense of soil, is tethered to the Yorkshire farm – 'real politics are local politics'. The result of separating Mr Read's creative from his critical work has an odd effect – there is colour, warmth, glow, the passion which surrounds the 'sense of glory', and we seem far removed from the rather dry critic with his eyes fixed on the distinctions between the ego and the id. The mill where the hero of *The Green Child* rescues Siloën from the sullen bullying passion of Kneeshaw is his uncle's mill – just as the stream which had reversed its course is 'the mysterious water' which dived underground and re-emerged in his uncle's field. And it may not be too imaginative to trace the dreadful sight that met Olivero's eyes through the mill window as Kneeshaw tried to force the Green Child to drink the blood of a newly-killed lamb to that occasion in the foldgarth when the child crushed his finger in the machine for crushing oil-cake. 'I fainted with the pain, and the horror of that dim milk-white panic is as ineffaceable as the scar which my flesh still bears.'

'Milk-white panic': like the Green Child himself Mr Read has a horror of violence – a horror which preceded the war and did not follow it. The conflict always present in his work is between the fear and the glory – between the 'milk-white panic' and the vision which was felt by 'the solitary little alien in the streets of Leeds', the uncontrollable ambition which 'threw into the cloudy future an infinite ray in which there could always be seen, like a silver knight on a white steed, this unreal figure which was myself, riding to quixotic combats, attaining a blinding and indefinable glory'. If art is the resolution of a combat, here surely is the source of Mr Read's finest work. Very far back – farther than the author can take us – the conflict originated: it was already established when the machine closed, when the small boy felt the excitement of *King Solomon's Mines* and *Montezuma's Daughter*. Both sides of the conflict are personified and expressed in his poem *The End of a War*, in which the sense of glory is put first into the mouth of a dying German officer and then into the dialogue between the soul and body of the girl whom the Germans had raped and murdered – the glory of surrender to nationality and to faith, and last the revulsion in the mouth of an English officer waking on the morning of peace and addressing his dead enemy – the revulsion of an ordinary man crushed by the machine who has no sense of glory in martial action or in positive faith, caught up in violence and patiently carrying out of the conflict only the empirical knowledge that he has at least survived.

> The bells of hell ring ting-a-ling-a-ling
> for you but not for me – for you

whose gentian eyes stared from the cold
impassive alp of death. You betrayed us
at the last hour of the last day
playing the game to the end,
your smile the only comment
on the well-done deed. What mind
have you carried over the confines?
Your fair face was noble of its kind,
some visionary purpose cut the lines
clearly on that countenance.
But you are defeated : once again
the meek inherit the kingdom of God.
No might can win against this wandering
wavering grace of humble men.
You die, in all your power and pride:
I live, in my meekness justified.

Because we have detected a conflict between the sense of glory and the fear of violence it mustn't be thought that we have mistaken the meaning Mr Read has attached to glory: glory, he has written many times, is not merely martial glory, or ambition.

Glory is the radiance in which virtues flourish. The love of glory is the sanction of great deeds; all greatness and magnanimity proceed not from calculation but from an instinctive desire for the quality of glory. Glory is distinguished from fortune, because fortune exacts care; you must connive with your fellows and compromise yourself in a thousand ways to make sure of its fickle favours. Glory is gained directly, if one has the genius to deserve it: glory is sudden.

In that sense glory is always surrender – the English officer also experienced glory in the completeness of his surrender to the machine: the 'wavering grace' too is glory. But just as the meaning of glory extends far beyond great deeds, so the fear of violence extends to the same borders. Surrender of any kind seems a betrayal: the milk-white panic is felt at the idea of any self-revelation. The intellect strives to be impersonal, and the conflict becomes as extensive as life – life as the artist describes it today, 'empty of grace, of faith, of fervour, and magnanimity'.

Glory in that sense cannot be attained by the artist, for glory is the cessation of conflict: it is private like death. The mystic, the soldier, even the politician can attain glory – the artist can only express his distant sense of it. In his novel, *The Green Child*, Mr Read conveyed as he had never done before, even in *The End of a War*, that private sense of glory. We see it working inwards from political glory – from the ideal state which Olivero found in South America back to the source of inspiration, the home of the 'innocent eye', back through fantasy to the dream of complete glory – the absolute surrender. Alone in his crystalline grotto, somewhere below the earth's surface, to which the Green Child led him, sinking through the water at the mill-stream's source, Olivero awaits death and petrifaction – the sense of sin which came between Wordsworth and his glory has been smoothed out, passion, the fear of death, all the motives of conflict have been eliminated as they had been from the dying German. Desire is limited to the desire of the final surrender, of becoming first rock, then crystal, of reaching permanency – ambition could hardly go farther.

When the hated breath at last left the human body, that body was carried to special caves, and then laid out in troughs filled with petrous water that dripped from roof and walls. There it remained until the body turned white and hard, until the eyes were glazed under the vitreous lids, and the hair of the head became like crisp snail-shells, the beard like a few jagged icicles ...

It is the same sense of glory that impelled Christian writers to picture the City of God – both are fantasies, both are only expressions of a sense unattained by the author, both, therefore, are escapes: the solution of conflict can come no other way. The difference, of course, is that the Christian artist believes that his fantasy is somewhere attainable: the agnostic knows that no Green Child will ever really show him the way to absolute glory.

The difference – though for the living suffering man it represents all the difference between hell and purgatory – is not to us important. Christian faith might have borne poorer fruits than this sense of unattainable glory lodged in the child's brain on a Yorkshire farm forty years ago. Mr Read's creative production has been small, but I doubt whether any novel, poem, or work of criticism, is more likely to survive the present anarchy than *The Green Child*, *The End of a War*, and *Wordsworth*. The critic who has hailed so many new fashions in painting and literature has himself supplied the standards of permanence by which these fashions will be condemned.

1941

THE CONSERVATIVE

ALL along the wide stony high street of Chipping Campden one is aware of stopped clocks. Time has been strenuously and persistently defied – almost successfully. Even the public telephone box – after a short struggle with the Post Office – has been allowed to wear the protective colouring of Cotswold stone. At one time a lady did rebel, painting her seventeenth-century door scarlet, but the slow pressure of well-directed public opinion won in the end. Everything here is preserved – even the smells. So remarkable an attempt to halt the passage of time is of more than local interest: its success can be judged in the late F. L. Griggs's drawings now published, together with an introduction by Mr Russell Alexander.* As drawings they are not of wide interest, but to anyone who knows Campden they will recall very vividly the geography of this strange experiment in escape – with its stone continuity of building from the fourteenth to the eighteenth century, as if the mind of man here had always taken as his main motto: 'Conserve.'

No one conserved more passionately than the late F. L. Griggs: he built his own house of solid stone with little medieval rooms, no telephone and no electric light. New bungalows and workmen's cottages were pushed under his leadership beyond the imaginary walls of what was in effect a dream town – they littered the road to the station and the road to Broadway, which was always to Campden an example of a town that

Campden: xxxiv Engravings after Pen Drawings, by F. L. Griggs, R.A.

had not sufficiently conserved. Griggs was a Roman Catholic,
and so were most of the inhabitants of Campden. He believed
in guilds and the love of craftsmanship: he had a mind's eye
picture – which he sometimes engraved – of what an English
town had been like before the Reformation, and to this he
wanted Campden to conform.

But when you begin to conserve, you conserve more than
you ever intend. Griggs had not meant to conserve the puritan
spirit, and he certainly had no intention of conserving the slum
cottages where women had to sleep in wet weather with a basin
on the bed to catch the rain, or the one pump which served a
whole hamlet. Some of Griggs's impressions are given in his
friend's introduction – the qualities of the stillness and the
light, the sound of bells and the smoke of jam-making; he
tells us of the old names still left: Poppetts Alley and Calf
Lane and the Live and Let Live Inn. There are anecdotes of
old almspeople – Mrs Beales saying of her husband, Noah,
' 'Twere a bit thoughtless of him to die just as the currants
wanted picking', and Mrs Nobbs avoiding an aristocratic
festivity in a local park, 'I didn't go, for I shouldn't a knowed
nobody, and what with the junketing and the music I should
ha'bin fair moictered. So I spended the day in the Churchyard
amongst the folks as I knowed, areading of their stwuns.'
It is tempting to believe that by conserving the architecture
you conserve such simple, wise, patient people as this – but is
it true? In any case you conserve, too, the imprisoning conditions which led, as I can remember, one young married
woman to leave home early of a winter morning, walk the
three miles to Batsford Park, and break her way through the
ice of an artificial lake until she had reached a depth where
she could drown.

The ghost of the dancing bear that haunts the pump at the
bottom of Mud Lane, the ghost of the great hound on Aston
Hill, out of superstitions like these it is easy to construct a
dream town where unhappiness has the faded air of history.
But to live there you must build the walls, not round the town,
but round yourself, excluding any knowledge that the eye
doesn't take in – the strange incestuous relationships of

the very poor, the wife starved to death according to country gossip, the agricultural labourers who lived on credit all the winter through.

1941

NORMAN DOUGLAS

IN those last years you would always find him between six and dinner-time in the Café Vittoria, unfashionably tucked away behind the Piazza. Through the shabby windows one stared across at Naples – one could go only a few steps further without tumbling off the island altogether. Crouched over an aperitif (too often in the last years almost unalcoholic), his fingers knotted with rheumatism, squawking his 'Giorgio, Giorgio' to summon the devoted waiter who could hear that voice immediately above all the noises of Capri, snow-white hair stained here and there a kind of butterfly-yellow with nicotine, Norman Douglas sat on the borders of the kingdom he had built house by house, character by character, legend by legend.

One remembers him a few months before he died, handling the typescript of this book,* re-sorting the loose carbon pages: there wasn't enough room on the café table what with the drinks, the old blue beret, the snuff-box, the fair copy; the wind would keep on picking up a flimsy carbon leaf and shifting it out of place, but the old ruler was back at the old game of ruling. He wouldn't have given even the menial task of assembly to another. With a certain fuss of pleasure and a great tacit pride he was handling a new book of his own again. There hadn't been a new book for – how many years? Sometimes something seemed to be wrong with the typescript: a monologue of exaggerated grumbles marked the misprints – not one of those earlier misprints carefully preserved in proof, to be corrected later in manuscript gratis for a friend and at a price for collectors – 'Cost him a tenner, my dear' – and that

* *Venus in the Kitchen.*

271

sudden laugh would break like an explosion in a quarry, over before the noise has reached you.

My generation was brought up on *South Wind*, although I suppose the book was already five years old before we opened it and read the first sentence, 'The bishop was feeling rather sea-sick', which seemed to liberate us from all the serious dreary immediate wartime past. Count Caloveglia, Don Francesco, Cornelius van Koppen, Miss Wilberforce, Mme Steynlin, Mr Eames, Saint Dodekanus, the Alpha and Omega Club: Nepenthe had not been Capri, but Capri over half a century has striven with occasional success to be Nepenthe. *South Wind* appeared in 1917, superbly aloof from the catastrophes of the time: it was the age of Galsworthy, Wells, Bennett, Conrad: of a sometimes inflated, of a sometimes rough-and-ready prose. Novelists were dealing with 'big' subjects – family panoramas, conflicts of loyalty. How reluctantly we came to the last sentence: 'For it was obvious to the meanest intelligence that Mr Keith was considerably drunk.' This wasn't the world of Lord Jim or the Forsytes or the dreary Old Wives.

South Wind was to have many inferior successors: a whole Capri school. Douglas was able to convey to others some of his tolerance for human foibles: characters like Mr Parker and Mr Keith were taken up like popular children and spoiled. It became rather easy to write a novel, as the reviewers would say, 'in the manner of *South Wind*'. None of Douglas's disciples had learnt to write as he had. Nearly a quarter of a century of clean, scholarly, exact writing, beginning so unrewardingly with a Foreign Office report on the Pumice Stone Industry of the Lipari Islands by the Third Secretary of Her Majesty's Embassy in St Petersburg, published by the Stationery Office at a halfpenny, went to the creation of Perelli's Antiquities and 'the unpublished chronicle of Father Capocchio, a Dominican friar of licorous and even licentious disposition, a hater of Nepenthe ...'

Douglas died in the middle eighties after a life consistently open, tolerant, unashamed. 'Ill spent' it has been called by the kind of judges whose condemnation is the highest form of praise. In a sense he had created Capri: there have been sui-

cides, embezzlements, rapes, thefts, bizarre funerals and odd
processions which we feel would not have happened exactly
in that way if Douglas had not existed, and some of his tolerance perhaps touched even the authorities when they came to
deal with those events.

It is fitting, I think, that his last book should be as unserious
and shameless as this collection of aphrodisiac recipes, to
close a life in which he had enjoyed varied forms of love, left
a dozen or so living tokens here and there, and been more loved
himself than most men. (One remembers the old gypsy family
from northern Italy who travelled all the way to Capri to
spend an afternoon with Douglas and proudly exhibit to him
another grandchild.) With its air of scholarship, its blend of
the practical – the almond soup – the wildly impracticable –
Rôti sans Pareil, the crispness of the comments (we only have
to add his customary endearments to hear the ghost speak):
'Very stimulating, my dear', 'Much ado about nothing', 'Not
very useful for people of cold temperament', with a certain
dry mercilessness in the introduction, this book will be one of
my favourite Douglases: it joins *Old Calabria, Fountains in the
Sand, They Went, Looking Back, London Street Games*, the
forbidden anthology of limericks.

He will be delighted in the shades at any success we may
have with his recipes and bark with laughter at our ignominious failures, and how pleased he will be at any annotations
and additions, so long as they are exact, scholarly, uninflated,
and do not carpingly rise from a cold temperament. For even
his enormous tolerance had certain limits. He loved life too
well to have much patience with puritans or fanatics. He was
a gentleman and he disliked a boor. One of the finest passages
of invective written in our time is his pamphlet against D. H.
Lawrence in defence of Maurice Magnus, and an echo of
that old controversy can be found in these pages.

Not many years ago I met in the South of France a Mr D. H.
Lawrence, an English painter, whom I interested in this subject
and who certainly looked as if his own health would have been
improved by a course of such recipes as I had gathered together.

There are said to be certain Jewish rabbis who perform the operation of circumcision with their thumbnail so rapidly and painlessly that the child never cries. So without warning Douglas operates, and the victim has no time to realize in what purgatorio of lopped limbs he is about to awake, among the miserly, the bogus, the boring, and the ungenerous.

1952

INVINCIBLE IGNORANCE

IN a book * which is at times crude and conceited, at others perceptive and tender, Havelock Ellis tells the story of an 'advanced' marriage. That is really the whole subject – there are chapters on his family and his childhood, on his experiences in Australia as a young school-teacher buried in a bush station and first conceiving his career in sexology, but these are only introductory to his meeting with Edith Lees, the secretary of the New Fellowship, and their long unhappy theoretical marriage. The background is already period: an odd charm hangs around the Fabian Society, around anarchists, feminism, what Ellis himself calls in an admirable phrase, 'that high-strung ethical tension': it is necessary to be reminded that encased in those years were real people, muddled and earnest and tortured.

This is an extraordinarily intimate autobiography, far too intimate to be suitable for general reading.

What can it matter when we are both dead? Who can be hurt if she and I, who might have been hurt, are now only a few handfuls of ashes flung over the grass and flowers? To do what I have done here has been an act of prolonged precision in cold blood, beyond anything else that I have ever written. For I know that, to a large extent, the world is inhabited by people to whom one does too much honour by calling them fools. ... All mankind may now, if they will, conspire together to hurt us. We shall not feel it.

But it was really they who conspired together to hurt each

* *My Life*, by Havelock Ellis.

other, talking it all out beforehand – economics, heredity, birth-control – strolling along a Cornish beach, an odd, earnest pathetic pair of lovers, who had left out of account all natural uneugenic feelings of jealousy or possession. Members of the New Fellowship presented them with a complete set of Emerson's Works.

But even under those auspices the marriage went wrong. There was never much passionate love between them, and Ellis soon considered himself at a liberty to take a mistress. Writing forty years later he remained convinced that his wife had no ground for objection. Objection in any case was swept away by theory: the wife had to be friends with the mistress, and Ellis could see no reason for her pain when she pleaded against a meeting between the lovers in the Cornish village where she and Ellis had first loved. So it went on – the woman always more natural than the man and struggling to be reasonable in his way. The pain stabs out from letter after letter, but Ellis never saw it, chiding her tenderly for failure in sympathy or understanding.

After a time they ceased to live as man and wife, though a kind of passionate tenderness always remained like a buoy to mark the position of a wreck. In London, Ellis had a flat of his own, and in the country they lived in two adjoining cottages (the middle-aged man, when his wife was ill, lay with one ear glued to the intervening wall). All the while Mrs Ellis was being driven to the last breakdown of health and sanity by the remorseless Moloch theories that love was free, jealousy ignoble, possession an indignity. She couldn't always keep it up. 'Oh: Havelock, don't you feel you don't want me. I let myself drift into thinking you only want Amy and not me. ... All I feel I want in the world is to get into your arms and be told you want me to live.' This towards the end of her life, for the miracle was that their love was never killed by the theory – it was only tortured. On his side he never relented: he would write coolly, tenderly back about the spring flowers, and his work was never interrupted: the sexology studies continued to appear, full of case histories and invincible ignorance. And yet, between this ageing man with his fake prophet's air

– rather like a Santa Claus at Selfridge's – and the woman haunted by extending loneliness and suspicion, so much love remained that one mourns at the thought of what was lost to them because they had not been born into the Christian tradition. Years after her death he writes with a kind of exalted passion and a buried religious feeling:

Whenever nowadays I go about London on my business or my recreation, I constantly come upon them [places where they had met]: here she stood; here we met; here we once sat together; just as even in places where she never went, I come upon some object, however trifling, which leads, by a tenuous thread of suggestion, to her. So that it sometimes seems to me that at every step of my feet and at every movement of my thought I see before me something which speaks of her, and my heart grows suddenly tender and my lips murmur involuntarily: 'My darling!'

1940

THE VICTOR AND THE VICTIM

ONCE when I was spending some weeks in a *léproserie* in the Belgian Congo, across the border from Dr Schweitzer's famous hospital at Lambaréné, the doctor spoke to me of 'sentimental' and 'scientific' leper colonies. He did not use the word sentimental in any pejorative sense – the sentimental hospital offers something to the human mind in pain or despair which the scientific may not be able to do, and the scientific sometimes fails by reason of its own dogmas. (In Brazil, in the wonderfully organized leper colonies there, the babies are separated at birth from the mother, so that for the sake of statistics – no leper children – there is a thirty per cent rate of infantile mortality.)

Nobody could fail, after reading Dr Franck's fascinating account * of his stay at Lambaréné where he organized a dental clinic, to put this hospital and the adjoining leper village in the category of sentimental, and his admirable drawings,

* *Days with Albert Schweitzer*, by Frederick Franck.

which remind one sometimes of a Segonzac transported to Central Africa, bring the reader closer than any photographs to the heroism and squalor and the unexpected laissez-faire of this strange settlement on the Ogowe river.

Here is the Doctor, myopic in his thick glasses, bent close over his writing desk while the ants, whom he feeds daily with raw fish, swarm across his papers: here is the makeshift room which has yet lasted a long lifetime with the old-fashioned iron bedstead, the mosquito net, the ewer and basin, the oil lamp, the books stacked on the floor with the wooden crates, and the palm trees with their piano-key leaves blocking the view outside. So much here is makeshift: the bed on pulleys for the paralysed patient made out of packing cases, the bed-ridden man hatching eggs, Dr Franck's own cubby-hole of a clinic, only partially separated from an emergency operating room on one side and a delivery room on the other. And as for the laissez-faire, here are the animals which roam Lambaréné, the cats, dogs, monkeys, pigs, antelopes, and the Nubian goats, a present from the States – they proved to be milkless and yet linger on, producing a few anaemic kids:

You feed the animals when ever you feel like it, you can even pet them within limits but always with the back of your hand, because all these goats and dogs and cats visit sick wards teaming with microbial life of the most horrifying varieties, walk through grass through which lepers just waded, and are (if someone wanted to establish records) perhaps the greatest microbe carriers per square inch of body surface anywhere on earth.

It is easy to notice the debit side of a 'sentimental' African hospital. I have visited one myself in the bush near the river Ruki, a *léproserie* of mud huts without a doctor, served by two African dispensers and one European nun who bicycles through the forest every morning from her convent by the river, and sometimes in depression I am haunted by the memory of the woman who, hearing me enter the darkness of her hut, crawled out of a pitch black inner room like a dog from a kennel, unable even to raise her head, making sounds which even my African companion could not interpret into human words.

277

But certainly in the case of leprosy there is a credit side to the sentimental. Now that leprosy is curable more and more attention must be paid to the psychological problem of the patient. The careful can never be quite carefree, and in a squalor shared by those who serve perhaps a relationship grows. 'The hospital without the animals', Dr Franck writes, 'would perhaps be wiser but certainly much sadder.'

Dr Schweitzer has become a victim of his own legend, a legend which would not have grown up around a more scientific hospital. Other men – Dr Harley, of Ganta in Liberia, is only one example – have given up their lives as completely to the Africans, but because of Dr Schweitzer's prowess on the organ, his life of Bach, his books of philosophy, the Nobel Prize, the camera-eye of the popular Press has picked out Lambaréné, a camera-eye which more often than not distorts the image. And in the wake of publicity, however unsought, inevitably comes denigration. (Envy is one of the distinguishing marks of man.)

Journalists writing emotionally and inaccurately of Schweitzer, lying in little ways for the sake of the newspaper story, have conveyed to the world a false Schweitzer whom it is easy to attack. Some of us who have at best one talent to develop become jealous and critical of a man who has developed, as Dr Franck writes, 'every one of his potentialities to its utmost limits'. The man who sometimes seems hidden in limelight more than in forest may not be a great musician or a great philosopher or a great doctor, but his achievement, at this moment of history, is more important than his music, his writing, or his medical skill: 'The *Grand Docteur* will live on as the man in whom the Western conscience became incarnate long before it was exploited in order to adorn a political holding-action in black Africa.'

1959

SIMONE WEIL

SIMONE WEIL was a young Jewish teacher of philosophy who died in exile from her native France in 1943 at the age of thirty-four. Since that time knowledge of her has spread by word of mouth, like the knowledge of some underground leader in wartime. This is her first book * to be published in English, the first message to reach us, though we had known that she had been acclaimed by both Catholics and Protestants in France. We read with excitement as the signals are handed in: contact at last has been made: and with a growing doubt. Here is a moment of vision: this we understand; but this? – surely the message must have been mutilated, for it seems to contradict what went before; and this? – the phrases seem jumbled, they mean little to us.

The most important part of the book, apart from the essay 'Forms of the Implicit Love of God', does literally consist of messages, letters written to a Father Perrin, a Dominican in Marseilles, the first three explaining why she is hesitating to be baptized, the last three giving her spiritual autobiography, an account of her intellectual vocation, and her thoughts before leaving North Africa for England and being finally separated from her spiritual adviser (if one can so call one whose advice was never taken, and who was more often than not the victim of her preaching). It is a great pity that we cannot read Father Perrin's replies. From her references to them we can imagine their careful sympathetic approach to her problems, the vain attempt to guide the wide wash of her mystical thought into a channel where it could increase in depth.

Her abiding concern was her relationship to God and the Church. She had come to believe in the Christian God, in the Incarnation, and the dogmas of the Roman Catholic Church (of its social functions, perhaps naturally, as one who had experienced for some weeks the hardships of the Catalonian front, she remained suspicious), but she had no will to take the next step. She expected God to intervene, to push her

* *Waiting on God*, by Simone Weil.

279

into the Church if he so desired. She would not act except under orders. 'If it is God's will that I should enter the Church, He will impose this will upon me at the exact moment when I shall have come to deserve that He should so impose it.' But how can one deserve without some action, if only of the mind? She pays lip-service occasionally to free-will, but we cannot help feeling that she unduly restricted its scope. There are traces of Gnosticism in her postponement of baptism until she could be certain of perfection.

I think that only those who are above a certain level of spirituality can participate in the sacraments as such. For as long as those who are below this level have not reached it, whatever they may do, they cannot be strictly said to belong to the Church.

It was a strange attitude for a woman who wished ardently to share the labours of the poor, working with broken health in the Renault works, and who in safe England confined herself to the rations of those she had left in France. The Church was for the perfect. She could not see it as a being like herself, anxious to share the sufferings not only of the poor but of the imperfect, even of the vicious. She speaks to us in terms of 'abandonment', but her abandonment always stops short of surrender, like a histrionic marble figure caught in a gesture not far removed from pride.

Her claims on our submission to her thought, and on our credulity, too, are vast. She tells us how once when she was reciting George Herbert's poem 'Love', 'Christ Himself came down and took possession of me', and again, referring to the Our Father, 'sometimes also, during this recitation or at other moments, Christ is present with me in person, but His presence is infinitely more real, more moving, more clear than on that first occasion'. We cannot help comparing this blunt claim with the long painful journey towards the Beatific Vision described by St John of the Cross and St Teresa of Avila. But perhaps the greatest claim she makes is to a kind of universal inclusiveness:

The degree of intellectual honesty which is obligatory for me, by reason of my particular vocation, demands that my thought should be indifferent to all ideas without exception, including for instance materialism and atheism; it must be equally welcoming and equally reserved with regard to every one of them.

One cannot deny, however, that these claims are sometimes supported by moments of vision: passages of great power and insight capable of drawing many enthusiasts to her side. The essay on Friendship is the most sustained of these passages, but again and again they flash through the contradictions and the muddled thought:

The outward results of true affliction are nearly always bad. We lie when we try to disguise this. It is in affliction itself that the splendour of God's mercy shines; from its very depths, in the heart of its inconsolable bitterness. If, still persevering in our love, we fall to the point where the soul cannot keep back the cry, 'My God, why hast thou forsaken me?', if we remain at this point without ceasing to love, we end by touching something which is not affliction, which is not joy; something which is the central essence, necessary and pure; something not of the senses, common to joy and sorrow; something which is the very love of God.

What makes us in the end unwilling to accept her claims? What is it that more often than not distorts her genuine love and truth? Is it that confusion arises first from her pride, and secondly – because she was a woman of great nobility – from the tension and pain in her own mind caused by that possessive demon? She claims too much (St Joan heard rightly when she was told to tell no one of her visions), and sometimes too stridently. She talks of suffering 'atrocious pain' for others, 'those who are indifferent or unknown to me ... including those of the most remote ages of antiquity', and it is almost as if a comic character from Dickens were speaking. We want to say, 'Don't go so far so quickly. Suffer first for someone you know and love', but love in these pages is only a universal love. She strikes out blindly in her personal pain, contradicting herself, allowing herself to believe that an 'infinite' mercy can be shown in its entirety in a 'finite' world. She no sooner seizes a truth than she lets it go in the pride of a too startling image. We leave her at the end on the edge of the abyss, digging her feet in, refusing to leap like the common herd (whom she loved in her collective way), demanding that she alone be singled out by a divine hand on her shoulder forcing her to yield.

1951

THREE PRIESTS

1. The Oxford Chaplain

A PRIEST presents even more difficulties to his biographer than a writer. As with an iceberg, little shows compared with what lies beneath: we have to dive for depth, but if we so dive we have the sense of breaking into a life more private and exclusive than a bedroom. We need not hesitate much over a man's love affairs; they are in a sense public, for they are shared with another human being, if not with waiters, chambermaids, that intimate friend; but when a man prays he is quite alone. His biographer – except when controversy, persecution, sanctity, or disgrace lend to the story a spurious drama – must write a life of his hero which excludes the hero's chief activity.

This Mr Waugh does with a sense of style which would have delighted his subject and an exquisite tact which Father Knox had obviously foreseen in asking him to be his biographer.* It is no fault of Mr Waugh that the story lags a little in the middle, during the years of the Oxford chaplaincy, the years of the satirical essayist and the detective writer, the years of popularity, the years of 'Ronnie'. Every Catholic, I suppose, has his favourite type of priest. The Knox of Oxford, the Knox of the rather precious style and of the Latin verses, the chaplain and the translator, had his apostolate in a region which I have always found uninteresting and even at moments repellent. Writing an obituary of Father John Talbot, of the Oratory, Knox describes this world with a, to me, terrible precision. He knew it to the last drain of the glass of dry sherry:

* *The Life of Ronald Knox*, by Evelyn Waugh.

He was always there if you wanted him; and perhaps from long acquaintance you marked yourself as the sort of young man one meets in John Talbot's room. ... If the comparison may still be used, the simplest thing to say of him is that he was the opposite number, in London, of Sligger at Oxford; his rooms had their characteristic clientèle, on Sunday mornings especially, which irresistibly carried your mind back to a don's rooms in the garden quad at Balliol: and indeed there were many there who drifted on, as if predestined, from one salon to the other. ... He had indisputably St Philip's own knack of making people come to see him by always being at home when they came; and his clients, like those of the Santo, were in great measure the young men of fashion who are commonly reproached with shunning clerical society.

These priests are as necessary to the Church as the apostles of the darker, poorer, more violent world – the priests I have encountered on the borders of a battlefield in Vietnam, in the region of the Mau Mau or in the dying white world of the Congo, but it is Mr Waugh's very great achievement that he holds the interest even of the unsympathetic. He is no blind hero-worshipper and long friendship has not made him indifferent to the tiny warts. He quotes Knox's extraordinary entry in the list of pros and cons which he drew up before his conversion: 'You'll be a more important person – but in a less important show', and Mr Waugh adds:

He was complacently insular, and in many respects remained so all his life. His travels were meagre and superficial; he had a gently humorous distrust of everything foreign; he had been brought up in an age when 'Land of Hope and Glory' had no undertone of irony, and the stability and expansion of the British Empire and with it the Church of England, seemed to follow a law of nature. Even so, when all these limitations are considered, the two propositions still seem preposterous.

To me the beginning and the end of Mr Waugh's biography are outstanding: the end where Mr Waugh had his 'villain' and can show Knox meeting the meanness, jealousies, and misunderstandings of the hierarchy without complaint, and the early pages which include, besides the troubled years of the conversion, a hero of extraordinary interest, Knox's grandfather, the Anglican Bishop of Lahore. This old man, after his retirement, set out 'unpaid and alone' for the Muslim strongholds of North Africa and Muscat and died in solitude attended at the last by a family of Goanese Catholics whom he had never consciously known. Only a writer like Mr Waugh, who has himself travelled in a hard poor fashion, could have picked out so accurately the illuminating details, 'the waxing incandescent wind of summer' and ' the dirty upper room of a Goanese grog shop', which is so distant from the Old Palace at Oxford.

I must be forgiven if I prefer as a character the Bishop of Lahore. He may have been no more a mystic than his grandson, but would he have wished to substitute for the passage of St John translated at Douai: 'He was in the world and the world was made by him and the world knew him not', that smooth and ambiguous version: 'He, through whom the world was made, was in the world and the world treated him as a stranger', which seems to echo the Oxford common-room rather than the hut of wattle and thatched leaves where the grandfather began his last agony?

1959

2. The Paradox of a Pope

IT is strange to come on a monument to a living man,* for even the greatest usually appear only on tablets and tombstones after death, but if we suppose a close observer wandering through the yellow squares, the churches and the *trattorie*, among the fountains and flower-stalls and broken columns of Rome, he would notice here and there about the city the memorials to a man still living, Eugenio Pacelli: in an obscure side street, on the wall of a house that has come down in the world – 'In this house was born ...': in the hall of a school – 'Student of this Lyceum during the years ...': at the entrance of a church – 'Here he meditated upon the choice

* Written in 1951.

of his vocation ...': Pope Pius XII mummified in marble before his death.

Our imaginary observer might well wonder at this great harvest of tablets. For it is not enough to say that Pacelli is the Pope. There have been so many Popes. They stretch away like a column of ants, busy about affairs that have often seemed to the world of small importance. An odd anonymity shrouds the greater number of them – we don't remember them as we remember Kings, or even as we remember Presidents. Their titles, stiff and unoriginal, have a kind of text-book air. Pacelli becomes Pius XII and already he seems fixed on a page of history (rather dull history) with all the other Piuses (who were they?), fixed like a butterfly on cork, pinned out for dusty preservation.

A few Popes, even to such a Protestant schoolboy as I was, broke through their anonymity, generally because they clashed with Kings or Emperors who were the more interesting characters since they wore armour and swore great blinding oaths and made wars and memorable sayings. The only memorable saying of a Pope that we learnt at school was far too smug – Gregory the Great, remarking, *Non angli sed angeli* at the sight of the young blond British slaves. One remembered too Innocent III fulminating against King John, though his victory over the King seemed a bit underhand; corpses lying unburied because of the interdict did not seem to compare in chivalry with burning lead. The Emperor Henry knelt in the snow at Canossa and our sympathy was always with the Emperor (already I have forgotten which was the Pope he knelt to). Pius V (was it?) excommunicated Queen Elizabeth, Pio Nono fled from Rome, conquered by Garibaldi and his romantic Red Shirts. And of course there were the wicked Popes – Alexander VI (the Borgia) and John XXII (I was taught for some reason that it was very wicked to celebrate Mass in a stable, though in our day Masses have been celebrated in places quite as strange, in garages, peasant huts, at Russian breakfast tables).

One knew very little about the living Pope in England in those days just after the First World War. He was associated rather disagreeably with a peace offer the Allies had rejected. We were the victorious powers, or so we then thought, so there was a somewhat disreputable air about premature peace offers, and in any case to the young, peace has small appeal. Our history books dealt mainly with wars, and as for any peace that passes understanding, it was not in the school or university curriculum.

I don't think it ever occurred to us that the Pope was a priest, or that he could be a saint. A priest was a small sour man in black who had a tin-roofed church in a back street of the country town where one lived: his congregation consisted mainly, so one was told, of Irish servant girls, and he was never invited to dinner as the vicar was. But still, he was a human being and had no connexion with the out-dated tiaraed ruler in Rome. I remember the shock of surprise at seeing a box inside a Roman Catholic church marked Peter's Pence – I thought that all that had been stopped some time in the Middle Ages, probably by King John.

But even later when I became a Catholic the Pope remained a distant hierarchic figure, and one imagines he remained so for many Catholics until contemporary history began to break into our homes with the sound of explosives and the sight of refugees and the sudden uncertainty – where shall we be next year? The Pope became a man when we grew aware that he suffered from the same anxieties and tensions as ourselves, only infinitely extended by his responsibility and his solitude. When Pius XI was elected on the fourteenth ballot, the Cardinal Mercier said, 'We have dragged Ratti through the fourteen Stations of the Cross: now that he has arrived on Golgotha we leave him alone.' For nearly twenty years now we have become aware of the Papacy as the point of suffering, the needle of pain, and a certain love always arises for the man who suffers. Pain makes an individual, whether it is a Chinese woman weeping for her dead child or a patient figure in a hospital bed or this man in the Vatican.

We have worked slowly towards the one particular Pope – this priest, not so far removed from our parish priest, forced against his will into a position of responsibility without material power, but we cannot see him fully as an individual man unless we see him in relation to his immediate predecessors. They have all had the same aim – to be the servants of God, to serve the world, to temper the winds of hate, corruption, injustice, to give us such peace as it is possible to get here. Pacelli becomes individual when we see how he differs from the others in trying to attain this aim.

Since the days of Pius X that word 'Peace' seems to chime through all the encyclicals and papal letters and speeches, just as it chimes through the Mass so that we become accustomed to it in its every declension, *pax, pacis, pacem*. Pius X was Pope when the First World War broke out. When he was asked to bless some armaments, he replied, 'War! I don't want war, I don't bless war, I bless only peace. Gladly I would sacrifice my life to obtain peace.' A fortnight after war was declared he was dead.

Benedict XV, his successor, whose peace proposals in 1917 were rejected, who was called Papa Bosch by the French and 'The French Pope' by the Germans, said, 'They want to silence me, but they shall not succeed in sealing my lips; nobody shall prevent me from calling to my own children, peace, peace, peace.' And his successor, to whom he said these words, Pius XI remarked to an English archbishop as the alignment for the new Hitlerian war became evident, 'Peace is such a precious good that one should not fear to buy it even at the price of silence and concessions, although never at the price of weakness.'

The world has darkened progressively since those days. Pius X was an old man ready to give his life, but a prayer is not always answered as we want it answered. Benedict believed in reasoned diplomacy and failed. Pius XI believed in a mixture of shrewdness and pugnacity, and he failed too. Now a new note sounds from the man who was his Secretary of State and who from that inner position saw the shrewdness and pugnacity outwitted, and observed the limits of diplomacy. Isn't there a hint of despair, so far as this world is concerned, in Pacelli when he speaks of 'Golgotha – that hill of long awaited peace between Heaven and earth'? Sometimes we

almost feel he is abandoning those vast hordes of people we
call nations, the dealings with the War Lords and Dictators,
and like a parish priest in the confessional, a curé d'Ars, he is
concentrating on each individual, teaching the individual that
peace can be found on Golgotha, that pain doesn't matter,
teaching the difficult lesson of love, dwelling on the liturgy
of the Church while the storm rages – the storm will pass. In
1943, the year of the North African campaign and the final
disaster to the Italian armies, he issued two encyclicals –
on 'The Mystical Body of Jesus Christ' and on 'Biblical
Studies'. They must have seemed to the Italian people very far
removed from their immediate worries, but those worries
pass, and the subject of the encyclicals goes on as long as
human life.

And yet, one cannot help exclaiming in parentheses, if only
they were more readable: less staid, tight, pedantic in style. I
doubt whether many of the laity read these encyclicals and
yet they are addressed by form 'to all the clergy and faithful of the Catholic world'. The abstract words, the sense
of distance, the lack of fire make them rather like a leading
article in a newspaper: the words have been current too long.
There are no surprises. 'As it is by faith that on this earth we
adhere to God as the source of truth, so it is by virtue of Christian hope that we seek Him as the source of beatitude.' The
words have no bite, no sting, no concrete image: we feel that
a man is dictating to a dictaphone. Compare the encyclicals
with such writing as St Francis de Sales, using his chaste elephant or his bees as metaphors, arousing our attention with a
startling image: 'My tongue, while I speak of my neighbour,
is in my mouth like a lancet in the hand of the surgeon, who
wishes to make an incision between the nerves and sinews:
the incision that I make with my tongue must be so exact that
I say neither more nor less than the truth.' In the encyclicals
the incision has not been made: the words clothe the thought
as stiffly as a plaster cast on an injured limb.

Not all the Popes have been quite so dry or cautious in
their encyclicals – Leo XIII in his *Rerum Novarum* wrote with
a kind of holy savagery on the abuse of property (didn't the

Bishop of San Luis Potosi in Mexico preserve the copies in his cellar till the revolution for fear of offending the rich?) and Pius XI, attacking the Hitlerian State in *Mit Brennender Sorge,* allowed the personal tone of voice to be heard.

But a Pope – or a saint or a parish priest – is not necessarily a writer, and in any case many – if not most – of Pacelli's encyclicals are not personally written by himself, only very carefully revised and approved. (The comparison with a newspaper article is reasonably apt. One can always tell for example which leader in the London *Times* is written by the Editor: there is a masterfulness, a lack of caution – not the same as lack of prudence – which appears also in the encyclicals of Pius XI who was usually his own author.) I express, of course, a private opinion based on translations. One distinguished writer has compared the Pope's style to the Roman fountains, formal even in their ornateness, the Latin words, colourless as water but pure and exact, falling with certainty into the ageless basins – Roman? Renaissance? Is his formality closer perhaps to music than literature? Bossuet, Dante, St Augustine – these are among the very few literary references that occur in his writing, but he speaks with real understanding of music. Again one is reminded of many parish priests whose worldly interests seem narrowed by the love of God to a few books and the enjoyment of classical music.

This is the essential paradox in a Pope who many believe will rank among the greatest. By the gossipers of Rome he is often described as a priest first and a diplomat afterwards. But how was it with his background that he did not become a diplomat first and foremost? He belongs to an aristocratic Roman family. Although his own inclinations seem to have been to ordinary parish work and to the confessional, he was steered by those who may have known his talents better, from a very early period in his life as a priest, towards an official career, first the Congregation of Extraordinary Ecclesiastical Affairs, which is the papal Secretariat of State, under Monsignor Gaspari who was to assist Pius XI in framing the Vatican Treaty. The paradox persisted: Pacelli combined his official work with pastoral work, just as during his public audiences he has been known to go into a corner of the audience hall at a peasant's request and hear his confession.

The steady ecclesiastical career drove on: Papal Nuncio in Munich in 1917 so that he could act as intermediary for the Pope in his efforts to attain peace (here he saw violent revolution for the first time when the Communists broke into his palace); in 1920 with the formation of the German Republic he became Nuncio in Berlin and later when Hitler began his campaign for power he maintained close ties with the Centre Party. The leader of the Centre Party, now Monsignor Kaass, has remained the Pope's friend, is administrator of St Peter's and is responsible for the excavations under the Vatican which have disclosed the old Roman cemetery where St Peter was buried. He has built the Pope a private staircase, so that he can make his way alone into these caverns and talk to the workmen. Walking with me among his tombs the Monsignor referred with affection to his friend, pointing a finger upwards, 'him up there'.

In 1929 when Pacelli left Germany the inevitable Cardinalate followed: the parish priest was doomed, you would have said, and yet he obstinately stayed alive. We can hear him speaking in the words of Pacelli's farewell so different from the formal encyclicals that were to follow. 'I go the way in which God, by the mouth of the Pontiff, commands me to go. I go this way fully conscious of my weakness, believing in Him who uses the weak to put the strong to shame. What I was, is nothing; what I am is little; but what I shall become is eternal.' 'What I shall become.' As the Pope placed the Red Hat on his head he spoke the traditional words that in our day have taken a real significance: 'Accept the red hat, a special sign of the Cardinal's dignity. This means that you should be ready to shed your blood and to die, if need be, in the fearless defence of our Holy Faith, for the preservation of quiet and peace among the Christian people. . . .'

Only a month later he was appointed Secretary of State to Pius XI, perhaps the most politically active Pope since the Middle Ages, the man who revived the Vatican State, who fought Mussolini so firmly that Mussolini rejoiced in public at his death, who began the struggle against Hitler not only by his encyclicals but by personal affront – he left Rome when Hitler came there and closed the Vatican Museum which Hitler had intended to visit. On his death bed in February 1939 he finished his last encyclical – the final words written on the night he died, his last blow, it was to have been, so they say, at the Totalitarian State. His successor never issued it.

Yet the new Pope as Secretary of State had been closely associated with his predecessor's policy, and his attitude to affairs in Germany was well known. At a party which he gave in Rome after his return from Germany, an old Conservative friend of his, the Marchese Patrizi, was overheard by him to remark that it was a good thing Germany had a strong man now who would deal with the Communists. Cardinal Pacelli turned on him. 'For goodness' sake, Joseph,' he said, 'don't talk such nonsense. The Nazis are infinitely worse.' We can assume therefore that neither Hitler nor Mussolini were gratified when the Conclave, breaking a tradition of nearly 300 years, elected the Secretary of State Pope in March 1939 at the age of sixty-three. Perhaps the foreign Cardinals turned the balance in Pacelli's favour. He was almost the only Cardinal they could have met personally.

For this is another paradox of the Pope – that this priest, whom I have heard described as a Franciscan by one who knows him well, is regarded as a very travelled, very modern man. There are the new gadgets of the Vatican, from the white typewriter and the white telephone and the electric razor to the short-wave wireless station and the latest television equipment provided by an American company. But the television transmitter is apparently not working very well and the service is starved for money, while the programmes of the Vatican radio are astonishingly uninspired – relays of leaders from the *Osservatore Romano*, local pieces of Catholic news.

As for travel it is true that Pacelli moved about a good deal of the earth's surface before he became Pope, but it is a reasonable guess that the only two countries that made any deep impression on him were Germany and America. For both countries he has retained great affection. The administrator of

St Peter's is German and only recently Cardinal Faulhaber was invited to consecrate the new altar of the restored basilica of Constantine under St Peter's. As for America his personal feeling of friendship for Cardinal Spellman seems certain, though somewhat surprising considering the marked divergency of their characters (the cynical sometimes point out that the United States is the only country of importance left that is able to transmit Peter's Pence to Rome: the Catholics of other nations are bound by their currency laws).

As for his other travels they have been widespread but brief and filled with the official duties of the Pope's representative: to the Eucharistic Congress at Buenos Aires in 1934; to Lourdes in 1935 on the nineteenth centenary of the Redemption; to Lisieux during the Eucharistic Congress in 1937; and to the Congress in 1938 at Budapest. How much during such journeys does the Pope's representative see? There is a passage in Tolstoy's *War and Peace* that describes the travels of an army.

A soldier on the march is hemmed in and borne along by his regiment as much as a sailor is by his ship. However far he has walked, whatever strange, unknown and dangerous places he reaches, just as a sailor is always surrounded by the same decks, masts and rigging of his ship, so the soldier always has around him the same comrades, the same sergeant-major, the same Company dog, and the same commanders.

The Papal Secretary of State moving from country to country, Eucharistic Congress to Eucharistic Congress, is hemmed in by the pack wagons of the Church, the dignitaries in skull caps, the distant crowds that hide by their pious bulk even the shape of the buildings.

One cannot believe that the journeys of Pacelli have influenced him much except in so far as they have driven him to learn many languages. One must not exaggerate his knowledge, however. We hear the gentle precise voice speaking to us in English, and we forget the strict limits of his vocabulary. He sends his blessings to our families 'with deep affection' – that is a favourite phrase often repeated and emphasized – but inevitably he has to address the pilgrim in certain set formulas.

For the priest this is a smaller handicap than for the diplomat. A priest in the confessional too is apt to speak in formulas, but into the straitjacket of a limited vocabulary some priests are able to introduce an extraordinary intimacy, gentleness, a sense of love. That is Pius XII's achievement, if we can call the grace of great charity an achievement. We become aware that he loves the world as another man may love his only son. The enemies whom Pius XI pursued with such vigour, he fights with the weapon of charity. In his presence one feels that here is a priest who is waiting patiently for the moment of martyrdom, and his patience includes even the long drawn conversations of the nuns who visit him. From another room one hears the stream of aged feminine talk while the Monsignors move restlessly in their purple robes, looking at their watches or making that movement of the hand to the chin forming an imaginary beard, that is the Latin way of exclaiming at a bore. Out comes the last nun, strutting away with the happy contented smile of a woman who has said her say and out from his inner room comes the Pope with his precise vigorous step ready to greet the next unimportant stranger 'with deep affection'.

How endless these audiences must seem to him – private audiences to diplomats, authors, civil servants, the people 'with a pull', public audiences to Italian cyclists, to actors, Boy Scouts, aircraft engineers, directors of American companies, Fiat workers, bankers, tram conductors. We seem to hear a village priest speaking, rather than the ex-Nuncio to Berlin, the ex-Secretary of State, when he speaks to the tram conductors and describes their own troubles to them. 'He has to warn some passengers, to give advice to others, and in selling the tickets he usually has to give the change – a duty which complicates things still more. He must see to it that people enter by the rear door and leave by the front door and that they observe the smoking regulations.' How long is it since the Pope travelled in a tram? The description is so simple that we smile. 'A duty which complicates things still more.' We had not thought of the complication of change-giving, but the conductors had and so had the Pope.

One is reminded sometimes in these addresses of the controversy between Henry James and the popular Victorian novelist, Walter Besant. Besant had made fun at the notion of a woman writing a novel about men's affairs, and James replied that any girl with sufficient talent could write a novel about the Brigade of Guards after once looking through the window of a Mess. It was a question of talent, not of knowledge. What is true of the writer is true of the priest, who from a hint in the confessional has to build his knowledge of a whole world outside his experience, and one finds in these private addresses of the Pope – what one seldom finds in the encyclicals – an intuitive genius. For example here is this celibate, this hermit buried in the Vatican cave, addressing a special audience of newly married couples on the heroic energy required in everyday life, the boredoms and frustrations and torn nerves of two people living under one roof. 'When one should remember during a chilly dispute that it is better to keep quiet, to keep in check a complaint, or to use a milder word instead of a stronger, because one knows that the stronger word, once it is out, will relieve, it is true, the tension of the irritated nerves, but will also leave its darkening shadow behind.'

Many soldiers, Allied and German, Protestants, atheists, Jews, had their audiences with the Pope during the war. The Neutrality of the Vatican was rigidly guarded: Rome was protected from the Allies as from the Germans to the best of the Pope's ability, but soldiers of all sides were welcome as pilgrims. Many stories have been told of these wartime audiences. Here is one more.

While a London priest was making his rounds in his parish a year or two ago, a working man shouted to him from across the road that 'his bloody Pope' was the greatest man alive. The priest, who supposed the man was drunk, stopped and spoke to him since the view he had expressed was hardly common in that area. The man told him that he had lost his only son in the war and that they had been very attached to one another. The thought that he would never see his son again was driving him crazy, for he had no religious faith to help him. He was in the army and went to the Vatican with a military party to see the Pope. As the Pope moved amongst them, chatting to this man and that, the father shouted after him. The Pope asked him what he wanted and he said that he wanted to know if there was any hope of his seeing his son again. The Pope replied that that was one of those short questions which required a long answer. He told one of the attendants to bring the man after the audience to his private room. There he sat down and for an hour explained the reasons for believing in the immortality of the soul. The man left the Pope convinced that he would see his son again and happy in the knowledge.

This is the Pope whom most of us before the war regarded as a diplomat. Even his photographs, where the eyes have lost expression behind deep glasses, where the lips keep their thinness and lose their sensitivity, add to the impression of an ex-Secretary of State. It is true he keeps that office still in his own hands, assisted by Monsignor Montini,* but one who has had close dealings with the Pope, denied to me that diplomacy was important in his eyes. This is not a world where diplomatic action counts for much. In the last thirty years the Pope has seen the consistent failure of diplomacy, but it is a world he once knew well – the world of ambassadors and visiting Ministers – and he retains these contacts in his own hands much as a man keeps the trophies on his wall of a sport long abandoned. The world cannot be saved by diplomacy.

What can save it?

So much time for audiences public and private, so much time for work (the light in his study over St Peter's burns till one in the morning), so much time like any other priest for his breviary, and in the background one is aware of the huge threatening world, the conferences in Moscow, the speeches at Lake Success, the troops pouring down in Korea, big business bulling and bearing in the skyscrapers of Wall Street. He presses into one more visitor's hand a little green envelope with the Papal arms containing a small nickel holy medal. Can this Thing – so defenceless it seems – survive?

Every morning at breakfast the Pope lets loose his two

* Now Pope Paul VI.

295

canaries and his favourite bird – a small bird with a green breast, I don't know its name. They walk over the table pecking at his butter, and his favourite takes crumbs from between his fingers and perches on the white shoulder. 'He talks to children', my informant said, 'as though they were his birds and to his birds, as though they were children . . .' That was why he called the Pope Franciscan, and the Franciscans next to the Jesuits are his favourite Order. Even in this short period of relaxation he seems to be making a hieratic gesture symbolizing charity. If a man loves enough, every act will represent his love.

I have said he gives the impression of a man patiently waiting for martyrdom. He has already barely escaped it. At his coronation, the German ambassador was heard to remark, 'Very moving and beautiful, but it will be the last', and a moment came during the war, under the German Occupation, when the end was expected. Hitler was said to have uttered the threat that he would raze the Vatican to the ground, and it is certainly true that the administrator received orders one day from 'him up there' to produce a plan for summoning the ambassadors of the powers at a moment's notice to St Peter's so that the Pope if necessary might make an announcement of grave importance. But the threat of exile or death passed: the order was revoked. Now again the danger threatens. The Church's borders are widespread, in Poland and Korea, but war travels fast these days. Hitler was handicapped by the presence of the Church in Germany: in Russia the Church is represented only by a few priests in hiding.

Sometimes a Pope can be known by the saints he canonizes. Pius XI, the pugnacious priest, canonized Thomas More and John Fisher, over-ruling the requirements of miracles: they were men who fought the totalitarian state of their day. Pacelli has canonized the child Maria Goretti, who died forgiving her murderer.

It is a long time since a Pope has awoken, even in those of other faiths, such a sense of closeness. One remembers Henry James's description of Pius IX among his guards coming up the Via Condotti in his great rumbling black-horsed coach 'so capacious that the august personage within – a hand of automatic benediction, a large, handsome, pale old face, a pair of celebrated eyes which one took, on trust, for sinister – could show from it as enshrined in the dim depths of a chapel'.

Pius XII gives no automatic benediction, though there are still dim depths, one feels, in the Vatican, in spite of the Roman sunshine glinting on the orders and the swords, as one is sieved from one audience chamber to another by scarlet flunkeys, who will later grab the guileless visitor and extort the money for drinks. The huge civil service has to go on functioning, and sometimes in our irritation at its slowness, its caution, or its pedantry, we may feel that it is obscuring the white-clothed figure at the centre. But a feeling like this comes and goes: it is not the impression that remains.

One visitor replying to a polite formal enquiry of the Pope said that there were two Masses he would always remember: one was at 5.30 in the morning at a side altar, in a small Franciscan monastery in Apulia, the Host raised in Padre Pio's hands marked with the black ugly dried patches of the stigmata: the other was the Pope's Jubilee Mass in Rome, the enormous crowd pressed into St Peter's, and men and women cheering and weeping as the Pope passed up the nave, boys flinging their Scout hats into the air: the fine transparent features like those on a coin going by, the hand raised in a resolute blessing, the smile of 'deep affection', and later the Pope alone at the altar, when the Cardinals who served him had stepped aside, moving with grace and precision through the motions of the Mass, doing what every priest does every day, the servant of the servants of God, and not impossibly, one feels, a saint.

But how much more difficult sanctity must be under the Michelangelo frescoes, among the applauding crowds, through the daily audiences with the bicyclists and the tram conductors, the nuns and the ambassadors, than in the stony fields of Apulia where Pio is confined. It is the strength of the Church in Italy that it can produce such extremes, and exactly the same thought came to one kneeling among a dozen women one early morning in the Franciscan monastery, and pressed among

the cheering crowds in St Peter's. It was not after all the
question, can this Thing survive? it was, how can this Thing
ever be defeated?

1951

3. Eighty years on the Barrack Square

THIS book is hardly more for general reading than is a
Manual of Infantry Training: the comparison is not too
loosely made.* Here and there, as I hope to show, flashes of
illumination occur, phrases typical of the old man we learned
to love, but the greater part of the book, begun when Angelo
Roncalli was fourteen years old at the minor seminary of
Bergamo and concluded in 1962, a year before the Pope's
death, is a record of retreats, spiritual exercises, meditations.

It begins with a section called 'Rules of Life to be observed
by young men who wish to make progress in the life of piety
and study' and it ends in old age with a section 'Summary of
great graces bestowed on a man who thinks poorly of himself'.
Open the book at random anywhere and you may be discouraged: 'I will observe the greatest caution and reserve in
my conversation, especially when speaking of others. Free
and open-hearted, yes! but always with prudence' (age twenty-
two, a seminarist in Rome); 'Know how to preserve silence,
how to speak with moderation, how to refrain from judging
people and their attitudes, except when this is an obligation
imposed by Superiors, or for grave reasons' (age sixty-four,
Papal Nuncio in France).

How dull it often seems, this long discipline on the barrack-
square from boyhood to old age, and then suddenly a phrase
occurs, not couched in the terms of the King's Regulations,
and we are in the presence of the saint we knew, with his
genius for simplicity – 'I really need a good box on the ears',
'I have always been a bit crazy, a bit of a numskull, and more
than ever so in recent days. This is all my virtue amounts to!'
He was still the raw recruit aged eighteen, when he wrote that,
but surely there has seldom been so unchanging a character

* *Journal of a Soul: Diary of Pope John XXIII.*

from youth to age. He describes, at a much later period, his imagination as 'the crazy inmate of the house', and he seems always to have been aware of a kind of divine folly. He is Patriarch of Venice when he writes: 'I would not mind being thought a fool if this could help people to understand what I firmly believe.'

I found it a great aid in reading the Journal to concentrate on certain threads which run throughout: one thread was the sense of time passing. When Roncalli was elected Pope at the age of seventy-seven he had no illusion about the motive of the Conclave ('everyone was convinced that I would be a provisional and transitional Pope'), but the sense of so much to do and so little time frightened him not at all, for that sense had always been there – 'the crazy inmate' had seen to that. 'Time is running out. Today at twenty-one I must start at the beginning again', and in his fiftieth year, 'Everything to be done at once, speedily and well; no waiting about, no putting lesser things before the more important.'

No wonder that there is an exultant note in his eightieth year – the exercises have borne fruit, the barrack square had been no wasted ordeal, he was prepared. 'Here I am, already on the eve of the fourth year of my pontificate, with an immense programme of work in front of me to be carried out before the eyes of the whole world, which is watching and waiting.'

Another thread I found it fascinating to pursue through the retreats and the formal conventional meditations is the presentation of his own faults. In what he considered his faults we see so often indications of the man we loved. 'I am really very greedy about fruit. I must beware, I must watch myself.' 'I tend to linger too long in the kitchen after supper, talking things over with my family.' 'The longing to read newspapers.' 'Excessive mirth' (all these at the age of seventeen); and at nineteen 'all the words, the witticisms prompted only by a secret desire to show off how much I have studied, all my castles in the air, my castles of straw and castles in Spain'. (How many are praying now that the Vatican Council will not prove to be one of these?)

299

A little later, 'As regards purity ... I do not feel any strong temptations contrary to this virtue – yet I must confess that I have two eyes in my head which want to look at more than they should.' (He had a certain fear of women only possible for a man of normal passions, and he noted with relief in 1940, 'Advancing years, when one is in the sixties like me, wither the evil impulses to some extent, and it is a real pleasure to observe the silence and tranquillity of the flesh.') As for some of his other young faults, they amuse us and sometimes surprise us: 'the rather mischievous expression' (that surely he never lost), 'the affected gesture, the furtive glance, that strutting about like a professor, that carefully-studied composure of manner, with the well-fitting cassock, the fashionable shoes ...'

There are a few pages in this book which, I think, all readers of any creed will find profoundly moving. They describe the day of Roncalli's ordination as a priest in Rome. The ceremony is over, he has written to his family, and now in his joy he cannot stay indoors.

I went out. Utterly absorbed in my Lord, as if there were no one else in Rome. I visited the churches to which I was most devoted, the altars of my most familiar saints, the images of Our Lady. They were very short visits. It seemed that evening as if I had something to say to all those holy ones and as if every one of them had something to say to me. And indeed it was so.

Someone else, too, had spoken to him that day, and history contains few more touching scenes than this encounter between a young priest of twenty-three, who was to become the great Pope John, and Pius X, who was to become Saint Pius.

The Pope then, still bending down, placed his hand on my head, and speaking almost into my ear said: 'Well done, well done, my boy ... this is what I like to hear, and I will ask the good Lord to grant a special blessing on these good intentions of yours, so that you may really be a priest after his own heart. I bless all your other intentions too, and all the people who are rejoicing at this time for your sake.' He blessed me and gave me his hand to kiss. He passed on and spoke to someone else, a Pole, I believe: but all at once, as if following his own train of thought, he turned back to me and asked when I should be back at my home. I told him: 'For the feast of Assumption.' 'Ah, what a feast that will be,' he said, 'up there in your little hamlet (he had earlier asked me where I came from), and how those fine Bergamasque bells will peal out on that day!' and he continued his round smiling.

The illustrations are many and satisfying, one in particular. Pope John is caught by the camera talking to a little girl sick with leukemia – he speaks with extreme gravity and she listens with the same deep seriousness. It is impossible to say which of them is the elder, which will be the first dead. He speaks to her as to an equal.

1965

THREE REVOLUTIONARIES

1. The Man as Pure as Lucifer

THROUGHOUT the French war there was a school of thought which believed Ho Chi Minh to be dead, so unwilling were those who had encountered him in 1945 and 1946 to believe that he was a genuine Communist. One of Ho Chi Minh's strongest opponents in the south had described him to me with unwilling admiration. *Un homme pur comme Lucifer.*

When I met him* (I had guaranteed that I would not publish the details of our conversation) it was in a small room in Bao Dai's former palace, over a cup of tea, and I could not believe him to be a figurehead. Another Minister was present, but a Minister known to be *effacé*. He was there only because I had asked to see him, and he sat silent like a small boy so long as Ho Chi Minh was with us.

Dressed in khaki drill, with thick dark woollen socks falling over his ankles, Ho Chi Minh gave an impression of simplicity and candour, but overwhelmingly of leadership. There was nothing evasive about him: this was a man who gave orders

* Written in 1955.

and expected obedience and also love. The kind, remorseless face had no fanaticism about it. A man is a fanatic about a mystery – tablets of stone, a voice from a burning bush – but this was a man who had patiently solved an equation. So much love had to be given and received, so many sacrifices demanded and suffered. Everything had contributed to the solution: a merchant ship, the kitchens of the Carlton Grill, a photographer's studio in Paris, a British prison in Hongkong, as well as Moscow in the hopeful spring days of the Revolution, the company of Borodin in China.

'Let us speak as though we are at home,' he said, and I wondered whether it was in the Carlton Grill that he had learnt his easy colloquial English (only once did he fumble for a word). I am on my guard against hero-worship, but he appealed directly to that buried relic of the schoolboy. When he put on his glasses to read a paper, bending a little down and sideways, shifting his English cigarette in long, bony, graceful fingers, the eyes twinkling at some memory I had stirred, I was reminded of a Mr Chips, wise, kind, just (if one could accept the school rules as just), prepared to inflict sharp punishment without undue remorse (and punishment in this adult school has lasting effect), capable of inspiring love. I regretted I was too old to accept the rules or believe what the school taught.

He was working fourteen hours a day, but there was no sign of fatigue. He got up to return to work (the National Assembly was meeting the next day), and his socks flapped as he waved back at me from the doorway, telling me not to hurry, to stay as long as I liked, to have another cup of tea. I could imagine them flapping all across the school quad, and I could understand the loyalty of his pupils.

There was sadness and decay, of course, in Hanoi, as there couldn't help being in a city emptied of all the well-to-do. For such as I there was sadness in the mere lack of relaxation: nothing in the cinemas but propaganda films, the only restaurants prohibitive in price, no café in which to while away the hours watching people pass. But the peasant doesn't miss the café, the restaurant, the French or the American film – he's never had them. Perhaps even the endless compulsory lectures and political meetings, the hours of physical training, are better entertainment than he has ever known.

We talk so glibly of the threat to the individual, but the anonymous peasant has never been treated so like an individual before. Unless a priest, no one before the Commissar has approached him, has troubled to ask him questions, or spent time in teaching him. There is something in Communism besides the politics.

I thought with more sympathy now of the southern President Diem, for in Saigon where there is nothing else but politics he represents at least an idea of patriotism. He has some words in common with Ho Chi Minh, as Catholicism has some words in common with Communism, but he is separated from the people by cardinals and police cars with wailing sirens and foreign advisers droning of global strategy, when he should be walking in the rice-fields unprotected, learning the hard way how to be loved and obeyed – the two cannot be separated.

One pictured him there in the Norodom Palace, sitting with his blank, brown gaze, incorruptible, obstinate, ill-advised, going to his weekly confession, bolstered up by his belief that God is always on the Catholic side, waiting for a miracle. The name I would write under his portrait is the Patriot Ruined by the West.

1955

2. *The Marxist Heretic*

> They seek him here,
> They seek him there . . .
> Those Yanquis seek him everywhere.
> Is he in heaven or is he in hell . . . ?

No one since the Scarlet Pimpernel has been so 'demned' elusive as Fidel (whom no Cuban except an enemy calls by the name of Castro). He will see you, if that is his wish, in his own good time and in his chosen place, but there will never – that is certain – be a rendezvous appointed for eleven-thirty on a Tuesday morning in an office on such and such a floor in Havana. For one thing he is seldom in Havana. Cuba is a country now and not merely a pleasure-capital as it was in Batista's day. The new apartment prepared for Fidel in the palace of the revolution holds small attraction for him, with the exception of the big toy installed there, a map of Cuba as big as a billiard table with a great switch-board enabling him to illuminate the grazing areas, the areas of sugar, coffee, tobacco. This agricultural landscape is his home.*

Once we nearly stumbled on him on the Isla Turiguano, the state farm in Las Villas surrounded on three sides by marshes – an island of prize cattle, prize horses, and prize pigs. We had arrived at the cowboys' motel in the evening, but we were a day late by our schedule (cars have a way of shedding parts after seven years' hard use), and Fidel had left that morning. At Moron we arrived at mid-day to find that he had passed the night there and moved on somewhere else. In Camaguey they knew nothing of his movements at the Party headquarters, but the secretary significantly was absent 'somewhere', and Fidel appeared in Camaguey soon after we left. He was always ahead of us or behind us as we drove East to Santiago and Guantenamo.

On the second night of my arrival in Cuba, I watched him as he made one of his marathon speeches (four hours without a note) to the Congress of the Trade Unions. Knowing little Spanish I observed his physical performance rather than listened to his speech. I could have divided it like a play into acts: in the first act he was a grave formidable figure, almost motionless at the podium, the word *conciencia* chimed in his sentences. Then suddenly all changed to comedy and farce, as he imitated the ignorant member of a political *cadre*, 'No sé. No sé.' He began to play with his six microphones, touching, shifting, aligning them as though they were flowers; he knew exactly which one of them, if he bent above it, would emphasize best a purr, a laugh, an angry sneer, a humorous imitation. The arms moved all the time now, as he mimicked, play-acted, plucked laughter out of his audience. 'There is no people more

* Written in 1966.

sensitive to ridicule than here.' He savaged Señor Frei of Chile: you could almost see the poor man's corpse slung over his shoulder.

After this speech he vanished into the countryside as effectively as he had vanished ten years ago from Batista's troops and planes into the forests of the Sierra Maestre. But not till ten days later would reports and photographs of his travels appear in *Granma* – the daily paper with what seems to be an odd nursery title until you remember that *Granma* was the boat which brought him and his eighty-three revolutionaries from Mexico to Cuba – seventy-one were dead or captured in the first week – to overthrow Batista's dictatorship.

This elusiveness is, of course, partly a matter of security. A gunman would find it difficult to choose the right spot at the right time, and in one of the last plots against his life, betrayed by a double agent in the C.I.A., the would-be assassins made a ruthless plan to ensure his presence at a given place at a given time. They began to shadow the car of Haydée Santamaria on her way home from work in the Casa America where she is in charge of relations with the Communist parties of Latin America. Her death, they believed, would lead them to Fidel.

There are three principal heroines of the revolution: Celia Sanchez, who in 1956 awaited Fidel in the Sierra Maestre, Vilma Espin, who fought with Raul Castro in Oriente and later married him, and Haydée Santamaria. Haydée (her surname is no more used than Fidel's) fought in the unsuccessful attack on Moncada Barracks in Santiago in 1953. Her brother was killed there and his eyes torn out, her fiancé was killed and his testicles cut off, and the bodies were shown her in the prison. Four years later, married to Armando Hart, she fought in the Sierra. (I met her first in 1957 when she and her husband were hiding in a safe-house in Santiago on their way to the mountains.) If the assassins had succeeded in killing her, she would inevitably have been buried in the heroes' pantheon, and her funeral would have been a rendezvous they could be certain Fidel would keep. But she noticed the lights of the following car and took evasive action.

So there is reason enough for Fidel to make few appointments for fixed hours and to be notoriously unpunctual at his public appearances (on August 29 the curtain rose on the C.T.C. Congress an hour late). But his enemies come only from outside. He has no cause to fear an unpremeditated attack. The nation is a nation in arms, and no tyrant could long survive his constant journeys through the countryside. But the paramount motive for his travels is not personal safety; he is discovering his own country for the first time, with a sense of excitement over the smallest details. In his speech to the Trade Union delegates he said: 'I have never learnt as much as I have when talking with workers, students, and peasants. I have passed through two universities in my life: one where I learnt nothing, one where I have learnt all that I know.' He is a Chestertonian man who travels towards home as though it were to a foreign land.

I was more fortunate than many my last night in Cuba, for a messenger came to fetch me from dinner and I was able to spend the early hours with him in a house on the outskirts of Havana. As soon as we sat down, Fidel began to describe to me, compulsively as though he needed a stranger in order to taste the pleasure of recounting his story again, how on his last journey he had entered a small pueblo after dark and noticed there were no lights in the streets – only in the house of the Party. In a bar two men sat playing dominoes and he sat down with them and joined the game. The rumour of his presence spread and the villagers gathered. They demanded a speech. (I was reminded how an intellectual had told me that in 1965, the bad year of drought and political uncertainty, Fidel had not spoken once between July 26, the National Day, and October, and how people had become nervous and unsettled by his silence.) In this pueblo he told them he would return another day to speak: now he wanted to ask questions ... the shrewd humorous Socratic eyes looked me quickly over ... he discovered why there were no lights in the street, how far a man had to walk to get his shoes repaired, how deeply dependent they were upon a town some fifteen kilometres away ... they were small details, probably familiar to any country dweller, but most of his adult years have been spent in war, prison or exile. Now at forty he is really beginning to live. I had sometimes wondered how he would fare with the heroic days in the Sierra Maestre over, but perhaps the heroic days for him are only just beginning.

He spoke about that pueblo for more than half an hour: I would interrupt with a question and he would stop in mid-sentence, replying quickly and without hesitation, then pick up the unfinished phrase exactly where it had been left. He would change in a flash from the sly humorous observer to the enthusiast. If I had not missed him in the Isla Turiguano, if I had been with him in the country, I would have seen what he saw, I would have been present at the birth of his idea. It had come to him suddenly there, over the dominoes ...

He intended to make an experiment in this remote pueblo. The inhabitants would be removed from their dependence on the town. Everything they needed would be provided free of charge. Their houses would be free (already in his speech of August 29 he had foreseen the universal abolition of rents in 1970), they already had a primary school – a secondary school would be built, they would have their own generator of electricity, there would be a nursery for the children and a communal restaurant free of charge which would relieve the women of most work in the home ('In my opinion this will help many marriages to last'), there would be a free cinema twice a week, a cobbler cobbling free. Money would not be abolished, but the need of money would practically disappear. Socialism in one country had been tried elsewhere. This would be Communism in one pueblo. Sociologists and psychologists would watch the experiment. How would the people use their greater leisure? Would productivity rise or fall? And if the experiment didn't work? If productivity didn't rise? 'We shall have to think again.' How seldom have Communist leaders allowed that degree of doubt in any plan?

Fidel is a Marxist, but an empirical Marxist, who plays Communism by ear and not by book. Speculation to him is more important than dogma, and he rejoices in the name of heretic. 'We belong to no sect, we belong to no international freemasonry, to no church. We are heretics, yes, heretics – fine, let them call us heretics.' And again in the same speech: 'If there exists a Marxist-Leninist party which knows by heart all the "Dialectic of History" and everything written by Marx, Engels, and Lenin, and still does not do a damned thing about it, are others obliged to wait and not make revolution?' He sees Communism elsewhere becoming conservative and bureaucratic – revolution dying on an office desk within tightly drawn national frontiers. (I suggested to him that Russia was now nearer to a managerial revolution than a Communist one. He had not read James Burnham's book, but a note was made to buy it.)

In his turn he listened, with sympathy, while I argued for the possibility, not of a mere chilly co-existence, but of cooperation between Catholicism and Communism. On both sides the philosophy of Marx forms a wide area of disagreement, but this man will never allow a nineteenth-century philosophy to stand between him and any action to advance the economic aims of Communism. Of the Papal Nuncio in Cuba he spoke in terms of warm friendship and respect. Just across the water lie the great impoverished areas of South America – poverty and riches in revolutionary juxtaposition – vast opportunities for Communist expansion denied to Russia in Europe. Catholicism in Cuba has always been a religion of the bourgeoisie and so without deep roots: the religion of the peasant is Afro-Christian – Ogoune and Erzulie and Legba share their altars as in Haiti with a Christian god. But in South America, with the possible exception of Brazil, the Catholic Church is the natural religion of the peasant, and if Communism is to be imported from Cuba, Fidel will not appear in South America as the persecutor of the Church. Nor would it be his wish. The enemies of the Church in Cuba are not the Communist leaders: they are Cardinal Spellman and Bishop Fulton Sheen, those doughty champions of cold war and counter-revolution, churchmen for whom Pope John XXIII seems to have lived in vain.

As Russia drifts towards state capitalism and China towards some fantastic variant of her own (*Granma* has been mercilessly funny about the cult of Mao Tse Tung), Cuba may well become the real testing ground of Communism. There is something of the Athenian forum here – the island is small enough for the people to be consulted, informed, confided in: they can see their leaders day by day in the streets of their towns and villages. Those four-hour speeches of Fidel are not made up of evasions and oratorical tricks and big abstract words – they are full of information, down to earth, filled with detail; from them we learn the worst, more than from any enemy, because he trusts his people – the 'appalling' situation in Moa, the lack of sewerage in Nueva Geron. His speeches are nearer to Cobbett than Churchill and in my opinion the greater for that. The enormous will to educate is there, as in the new schools and technical colleges which are transforming the countryside. Nor does Fidel lay down decisions already taken: he announces mistakes, he describes dreams which may later prove to be mistakes: he is the revolutionary brain visibly in action, like one of those glass-sided clocks in which you can see the wheels in motion. A girl said to me with excited anticipation as Fidel began to speak on August 29; 'We never know *what* he may say.' The same is hardly true of our politicians.

This man, so Pauline in his labours and in his escapes from suffering and death, has a quality of generosity which calls for loyalty. (Of the original twelve followers who reached the Sierra Maestre two have died but none has defected.) A young minister, at the time in charge of agriculture, made a bad administrative blunder which deprived Havana temporarily of milk. Fidel told him that if he respected himself he would go into voluntary exile to the Isle of Pines. He went for six months and worked there on a farm. 'What would have happened,' I asked, 'if you had not gone?' 'Nothing,' he said, 'but I would have felt outside the revolution.'

'All nerves are strung for the future, and prepared to enjoy the present', Sir Walter Scott wrote of a very different revolution. 'All?' no, not all. Two American planes a day coming from Miami arrive at Veradero, the holiday resort outside Havana, and are filled with refugees who are brought to the airport in Leyland buses. Twice a week the Iberian airlines, which have arrived in Havana almost empty, depart with every seat filled, both first class and tourist. Anyone not of military age (else young Cubans might be called up for the army in Vietnam) is free to leave with one bundle or suitcase. A sympathetic visitor like myself lives, of course, in the bright sunlight of the revolution; these Cubans who have chosen exile must have seen the shadows, some of them perhaps imaginary, some of them real enough.

1966

3. *The Spy*

ESPIONAGE today is really a branch of psychological warfare. The main objective is to sow mistrust between allies in the enemy's camp. Fuchs and Nunn May may have enabled Russia to advance their manufacture of atomic bombs by a few years, but sooner or later in any case the Soviet would have reached sufficient parity in the ability to destroy the world and the interval, whether short or long, contained no real danger. The West, after the traumatic shock of Hiroshima, was not prepared to make another unilateral atomic attack.

The real value of the two scientists to the Soviet was not the benefit they received from their scientific information but from their capture, and the breakdown in Anglo-American relations which followed. A spy allowed to continue his work without interference is far less dangerous than the spy who is caught. How right SIS was to defend Philby and how wrong MI5 to force him into the open. The West suffered more from his flight than from his espionage.

I sometimes like to imagine what would have occurred if Kim Philby had in fact, as many foretold, become C, the Chief of the Secret Service. The kind of information he would have had at his disposal as C could hardly have increased greatly in interest, and it might even have diminished: no nuts and bolts, only the minutes of great vacuous high-level conferences. The moment would certainly have arrived sooner or later when the KGB thought it time to arrange a tip-off to MI5, followed by C's successful flight and the world's laughter.

Since espionage has taken to psychological warfare, it has taken, too, to literature, so that it is just as well to examine carefully any spy memoirs. All the same *My Silent War* is not the book which Kim Philby's enemies anticipated. His autobiography is an honest one, well written, often amusing, and the story he has to tell, after the flight of Burgess and Maclean, is more gripping than any novel of espionage I can remember. We were told to expect a lot of propaganda, but it contains none, unless a dignified statement of his beliefs and motives can be called propaganda. The end, of course, in his eyes is held to justify the means, but this is a view taken, perhaps less openly, by most men involved in politics, if we are to judge them by their actions, whether the politician be a Disraeli or a Wilson. 'He betrayed his country' – yes, perhaps he did, but who among us has not committed treason to something or someone more important than a country? In Philby's own eyes he was working for a shape of things to come from which his country would benefit. Anyway moral judgements are singularly out of place in espionage. 'He sent men to their death' is the kind of stock phrase which has been used against Philby and Blake. So does any military commander, but at least the cannon fodder of the espionage war are all volunteers. One cannot reasonably weep at the fate of the defecting spy Volkov, who was betraying his country for motives perhaps less idealist than Philby's.

Like many Catholics who, in the reign of Elizabeth, worked for the victory of Spain, Philby has a chilling certainty in the correctness of his judgement, the logical fanaticism of a man who, having once found a faith, is not going to lose it because of the injustices or cruelties inflicted by erring human instruments. How many a kindly Catholic must have endured the long bad days of the Inquisition with this hope of the future as a riding anchor. Mistakes of policy would have had no effect on his faith, nor the evil done by some of his leaders. If there was a Torquemada now, he would have known in his heart that one day there would be a John XXIII. 'It cannot be very surprising that I adopted a Communist view point in the thirties; so many of my contemporaries made the same choice.

But many of those who made their choice in those days changed sides when some of the worst features of Stalinism became apparent. I stayed the course', Philby writes, and he demands fairly enough what alternative there could possibly be in the bad Baldwin-Chamberlain era. 'I saw the road leading me into the political position of the querulous outcast, of the Koestler-Crankshaw-Muggeridge variety, railing at the movement that had let *me* down, at the God that had failed *me*. This seemed a ghastly fate, however lucrative it might have been.'

His account of the British Secret Service is devastatingly true. 'The ease of entry surprised me. It appeared later that the only inquiry made into my past was the routine reference to MI5, who passed my name through their records and came back with the laconic statement: "Nothing recorded Against".' (He was luckier than I was. I had a police record, for in a libel action brought against me by Miss Shirley Temple the papers had been referred to the Director of Public Prosecutions, and the trace had therefore to be submitted to C himself.) There was even a moment when Philby wondered whether it really was the Secret Service which he had entered. His first factual reports inclined his Soviet contact to the view that he had gone into the wrong organization.

His character studies are admirable if unkind. Don't talk to me of ghost writers: only Philby could have been responsible for these. Anyone who was in Section V will agree with his estimate of its head, Felix Cowgill, whom he was to displace. 'Cowgill revelled in his isolation. He was one of those pure souls who denounce all opponents as "politicians".' The Deputy Chief of the Secret Service is immediately recognizable. 'Vivian was long past his best – if, indeed, he had ever had one. He had a reedy figure, carefully dressed crinkles in his hair, and wet eyes.' To C himself, Brigadier Menzies, Philby is unexpectedly kind, though perhaps the strict limitations of his praise and a certain note of high patronage would not have endeared the portrait to the subject. For Skardon, the MI5 interrogator who broke Fuchs down, he has a true craftsman's respect.

312

If this book required a sub-title I would suggest: The Spy as Craftsman. No one could have a better chief than Kim Philby when he was in charge of the Iberian section of V. He worked harder than anyone and never gave the impression of labour. He was always relaxed, completely unflappable. He was in those days, of course, fighting the same war as his colleagues: the extreme strain must have come later, when he was organizing a new section to counter Russian espionage, but though then he was fighting quite a different war, he maintained his craftsman's pride. He was determined that his new section should be organized better than any other part of the ramshackle SIS. 'By the time our final bulky report was ready for presentation to the Chief, we felt we had produced the design of something like a service, with enough serious inducements to tempt able young men to regard it as a career for life.' He set about recruiting with care and enthusiasm. 'The important thing was to get hold of the good people while they were still available. With peacetime economies already in sight, it would be much easier to discard surplus staff than to find people later to fill in any gaps that might appear.' No Soviet contact this time would be able to wonder whether he had penetrated the right outfit. A craftsman's pride, yes, and of course something else. Only an efficient section could thoroughly test the security of the Russian service. It was a fascinating manoeuvre though only one side knew that it was a mock war.

The story of how, to attain his position, he eliminated Cowgill makes, as he admits, for 'sour reading, just as it makes sour writing' – one feels for a moment the sharp touch of the icicle in the heart. I saw the beginning of this affair – indeed I resigned rather than accept the promotion which was one tiny cog in the machinery of his intrigue. I attributed it then to a personal drive for power, the only characteristic in Philby which I thought disagreeable. I am glad now that I was wrong. He was serving a cause and not himself, and so my old liking for him comes back, as I remember with pleasure those long Sunday lunches at St Albans when the whole sub-section relaxed under his leadership for a few hours of heavy drinking, and later the meetings over a pint on fire-watching nights at the pub behind St James's Street. If one made an error of judgement he was sure to minimize it and cover it up, without criticism, with a halting stammered witticism. He had all the small loyalties to his colleagues, and of course his big loyalty was unknown to us. I find it not the least admirable of Philby's human qualities that for all those dangerous years he put up with Burgess, without nerve or humour failing him, or his affection.

Some years later, after his clearance by Macmillan in the House of Commons, I and another old friend of Kim were together in Crowborough and we thought to look him up. There was no sign of any tending in the overgrown garden and no answer to the bell when we rang. We looked through the windows of the ugly sprawling Edwardian house, on the borders of Ashdown forest, in this poor man's Surrey. The post hadn't been collected for a long time – the floor under the door was littered with advertising brochures. In the kitchen there were some empty milk bottles, and a single dirty cup and saucer in the sink. It was more like an abandoned gypsy encampment than the dwelling of a man with wife and children. We didn't know it, but he had already left for Beirut – the last stage of his journey to Moscow, the home which he had never seen. After thirty years in the underground surely he had earned his right to a rest.

1968

PORTRAIT OF A MAIDEN LADY

READING *No Place Like Home* by Beverley Nichols I found myself thinking of Guy Walsingham, the author of *Obsessions*, in Henry James's *The Death of a Lion*. It will be remembered how Mr Morrow, of *The Tatler,* interviewed her, for Guy Walsingham was a woman, just as Dora Forbes, author of *The Other Way Round*, was a man. 'A mere pseudonym' – that was how Mr Morrow put it – 'convenient you know, for a lady who goes in for the larger latitude.'

A confusing literary habit, which led me to wonder a little about the author of *No Place Like Home*. For all I know Mr Nichols may be another Mr Walsingham. A middle-aged and maiden lady, so I picture the author, connected in some way with the Church: I would hazard a guess that she housekeeps for her brother, who may be a canon or perhaps a rural dean. In that connexion she may have met the distinguished ecclesiastics who have noticed a previous book so kindly. ('The chapter on Sex', writes a dean, 'is the best sermon on the subject I have ever read.') She is not married, that I am sure, for she finds the sight of men's sleeping apparel oddly disturbing: 'It was almost indecent, the way he took out pyjamas and shook them', and on her foreign holiday, described in this book, she hints – quite innocently – at a Man. 'His knowledge was encyclopaedic. His name was Paul. He was about forty-five. We had better leave it at that.'

It is impossible not to grow a little fond of this sentimental, whimsical, and poetic lady. She conforms so beautifully to type (I picture her in rather old-fashioned mauve with a whalebone collar): Christian, but only in the broadest sense, emotional, uninstructed, and a little absurd, as when she writes of the Garden of Gethsemane: 'Here I had the greatest shock of all. *For the Garden was not even weeded!*' She is serious about Art ('Try a little experiment. Hold up your hand in front of your eyes so that you bisect a picture horizontally') a little playful ('Dürers so great that you felt you must walk up to them on tip-toe'). She loves dumb animals, and hates to see even a field mouse killed ('One mustn't let oneself wonder if perhaps the mice were building a house, which has now been wrecked, if perhaps Mrs Field Mouse was going to have babies, which will be fatherless') and in *their* cause she shows considerable courage. ('On more than one occasion I have created useless and undignified scenes at theatres in a vain protest against the cruelty of dragging terrified and bewildered animals to the footlights for the delectation of the crowd.') This almost masculine aggressiveness is quite admirable when you consider the author's timidity, how nervous she is in aeroplanes. ('It is with the greatest difficulty that I refrain from asking the pilot if he is sure about the tail. Is it on? Is it on *straight*? What will happen if it falls off?') and how on one occasion, climbing a pyramid, she very nearly had what she calls a 'swooning sickness'.

But what engaging company on these foreign cruises and excursions a maiden a lady of her kind must have been, exhilarated as she was by her freedom from parish activities. ('All that matters is that we are alone and free, *free*. Nobody can telephone to us. Nobody can ask us to lecture on the Victorian novelists. It is beyond the realms of possibility that anybody, for at least twenty-four hours, will ask us to open a chrysanthemum exhibition'), and hilarious with the unaccustomed wine ('We are, beyond a shadow of doubt, Abroad. And not only Abroad. At Large. And not only at Large but in a delirious haze of irresponsibility, and white wine'). Her emotions are so revealing: she weeps, literally weeps, over Athens. She disapproves of women who don't grow old gracefully ('I also thought how very much nicer and younger the average woman of forty-five would look, in this simple uniform, than in the stolen garments of her daughter'), she feels tenderly towards young people ('The silvery treble of youth that is sweeter because it is sexless'), her literary preferences are quite beautifully commonplace: 'What a grand play Galsworthy would have written round the theme of Naboth's Vineyard.' Excitable, sound at heart, genuinely attached to her brother and the vicarage. 'The old dear,' one exclaims with real affection, and I was overjoyed that she got safely home to her own garden before – but I mustn't spoil her closing paragraphs:

There they were, dancing under the elm, exactly as I had planned them.
I was in time for the daffodils.

1936

FILM LUNCH

'I F ever there was a Christ-like man in human form it was Marcus Lowe.'

Under the huge Union Jack, the Stars and Stripes, the massed chandeliers of the Savoy, the little level voice softly intones. It is Mr Louis B. Mayer, head of Metro-Goldwyn-Mayer, and the lunch is being held to celebrate the American Company's decision to produce films in this country. Money, one can't help seeing it written on the literary faces, money for jam; but Mr Mayer's words fall on the mercenary gathering with apostolic seriousness.

At the high table Sir Hugh Walpole leans back, a great bald forehead, a rather softened and popular Henry James, like a bishop before the laying-on of hands – but oddly with a long cigar. Miss Maureen O'Sullivan waits under her halo hat ... and Mr Robert Taylor – is there, one wonders, a woman underneath the table? Certainly there are few sitting anywhere else; not many, at any rate, whom you would recognize as women among the tough massed faces of the film-reviewers. As the voice drones remorsely on, these escape at intervals to catch early editions, bulging with shorthand (Mr Mayer's voice lifts: 'I must be honest to myself if I'm to be honest to you ... a 200,000,000-dollar corporation like the Rock of Gibraltar ... untimely death ... tragedy'); they stoop low, slipping between the tables, like soldiers making their way down the communication trenches to the rest-billets in the rear, while a voice mourns for Thalberg, untimely slain. The bright Very lights of Mr Mayer's eloquence soar up: 'Thank God, I say to you, that it's the greatest year of net results and that's because I have men like Eddy Sankatz' (can that have been the name? It sounded like it after the Chablis Supérieur, 1929, the Château Pontet Canet (Pauillac), 1933, G. H. Mumm, Cordon Rouge, 1928, and the Gautier Frères Fine Champagne 20 *ans*).

'No one falls in the service of M.G.M. but I hope and pray that someone else will take his place and carry on the battle. Man proposes and God in his time disposes. ...' All the speakers have been confined to five minutes – Mr Alexander Korda, Lord Sempill, Lord Lee of Fareham, and the rest, but of course that doesn't apply to the big shot. The rather small eyes of Mr Frank Swinnerton seem to be watching something on his beard, Mr Ivor Novello has his hand laid across his stomach – or is it his heart?

One can't help missing things, and when the mind comes back to the small dapper men under the massed banners Mr Mayer is talking about his family, and God again. 'I've got another daughter and I hope to God . . .' But the hope fumes out of sight in the cigar smoke of the key-men. 'She thought she'd like a poet or a painter, but I held on until I landed Selznick. "No, Ireen," I'd say, "I'm watching and waiting." So David Selznick, he's performing independent now.'

The waiters stand at attention by the great glass doors. The air is full of aphorisms. 'I love to give flowers to the living before they pass on. ... We must have entertainment like the flowers need sunshine. ... A Boston bulldog hangs on till death. Like Jimmy Squires.' (Jimmy Squires means something to these tough men. They applaud wildly. The magic name is repeated – 'Jimmy Squires'.) 'I understand Britishers,' Mr Mayer continues, 'I understand what's required of a man they respect and get under their hearts.'

There is more than a religious element in this odd, smoky, and spirituous gathering; at moments it is rather like a boxing match. 'Miss O'Sullivan' – and Miss O'Sullivan bobs up to her feet and down again: a brown hat: a flower: one misses the rest. 'Robert Taylor' – and the world's darling is on his feet, not far from Sir Hugh Walpole, beyond the brandy glasses and Ivor Novello, a black triangle of hair, a modest smile.

'He comes of a lovely family,' Mr Mayer says. 'If ever there was an American young man who could logically by culture and breeding be called a Britisher it's Robert Taylor.'

But already we are off and away, Robert Taylor abandoned to the flashlight men. It's exactly 3.30 and Mr Mayer is working up for his peroration: 'It's midday. It's getting late. I shall pray silently that I shall be guided in the right channels. ... I want to say what's in my heart. ... In all these years of production, callous of adulation and praise ... I hope the Lord will be kind to you. We are sending over a lovely cast.'

He has spoken for forty minutes: for forty minutes we have listened with fascination to the voice of American capital itself: a touch of religion, a touch of the family, the mixture goes smoothly down. Let the literary men sneer ... the whip cracks ... past the glass doors and the sentries, past the ashen-blonde sitting in the lounge out of earshot (only the word 'God' reached her ears three times), the great muted chromium studios wait ... the novelist's Irish sweep: money for no thought, for the banal situation and the inhuman romance: money for forgetting how people live: money for 'Siddown, won't yer' and 'I love, I love, I love' endlessly repeated. Inside the voice goes on – 'God ... I pray ...' and the writers, a little stuffed and a little boozed, lean back and dream of the hundred pounds a week – and all that's asked in return the dried imagination and the dead pen.

1937

THE UNKNOWN WAR

THERE are legendary figures in this war* of whom most of us know nothing. Secretly, week by week, they fight against the evil things: against Vultz, the mad German inventor, against Poyner, preparing to unleash plague-stricken rats on India, and the sneering sarcastic Group-Captain Jarvis, who

* Written in 1940.

319

was really Agent 17 at Air Base B. Billy the Penman; Nick Ward, heroic son of a heroic father; Steelfinger Stark, the greatest lock expert in the world, who broke open the headquarters of the German Command in Norway; Worrals of the WAAFs; Flight-lieutenant Falconer, with a price of 20,000 marks on his head, 'framed' as a spy; Captain Zoom, the Bird Man of the RAF – these are the heroes (and heroines) of the unknown war. This can never at any time have been a 'phoney' war: from the word go, these famous individuals were on the job.

It is not surprising in some of these cases that we know little or nothing about it: even his fellow schoolboys are still unaware of the identity of Billy Baker. His biography records one occasion when he was rebuked in class for an untidy piece of dictation. 'The Headmaster would have got a shock if he had known he was scolding the boy who was known as "Billy the Penman", the hand-writing genius of the British Secret Service. That was a secret shared by few people indeed.' (It was a fine piece of work which enabled Billy the Penman to substitute 500 'lines' – 'I must do my best handwriting' – for the details of a new anti-aircraft gun before the Nazi plane swooped down to hook the package from a clothes-line.)

On the other hand only the extreme discretion of his schoolfellows can have prevented news of Nick Ward's activities reaching the general ear. Nick Ward, because of a certain birthmark on his body, is considered sacred by Indian hillmen, and periodically he visits the Temple of Snakes in the Himalayas to gather information of Nazi intrigues. (To Ward we owe it that a plot to enable German bombers to cut off Northern India failed.) Unfortunately on one of these journeys he was spotted by enemy agents. 'It was because he had been recognized and because the Headmaster wished to protect him that all the boys at Sohan College had been ordered to wear hoods over their heads. It had thus become impossible for the Nazi agents to pick out Nick from the others. Later, Nick discovered that the local Nazi leader was Dr Poyner, the school medical officer.' Only a school medical officer was capable of conceiving the dastardly stratagem that nearly betrayed Ward into enemy hands. Hillmen crept up to the dormitory with pegs on their noses and blew sneezing powder into the room, so that the boys were forced to take off their hoods. (The pegs on their noses prevented the Indians being affected.)

Perhaps the spirit of these heroes is best exemplified by a heroine – Worrals, who shot down the mysterious 'twin-engined high-wing monoplane with tapered wings, painted grey, with no markings' in area 21-C-2. Her real name is Pilot-Officer Joan Worralson, WAAF, and we hear of her first as she sat moody and bored on an empty oil drum, complaining of the monotony of life. 'The fact is, Frecks, there is a limit to the number of times one can take up a light plane and fly it to the same place without getting bored. . . .' Boredom is never allowed to become a serious danger to these lone wolves: one cannot picture any of them ensconced in a Maginot line.

But the man who inspires one with the greatest admiration is Captain Zoom the lone flyer who beats away on his individualistic flights borne up on long black condor wings, with a small dynamo ticking on his breast. Even his mad enemy Vultz could not withhold admiration. 'For a pig-dog of a Briton, he must have brains! This is a good invention. By the time I have improved it, it will be fit to use. Ja!' Vultz, it should be explained, was engaged in building a tunnel from Guernsey to Britain. 'The Nazis, since their occupation of the Channel Islands, had thought out a a new scheme for invading Britain. They were tunnelling from Guernsey to Cornwall using an entirely new type of boring-machine invented by a brilliant engineer named Vultz. This machine made tunnelling almost as quick as walking. Vultz, a fiend in human form, had a fixed hatred of RAF men, and for this reason employed them as slaves in the tunnel.' No wonder Nick Ward on another occasion exclaimed that 'the Nazis stopped at nothing. They did not mind how foul were the tricks they tried or how helpless victims died.' Listen to Vultz himself:

'It is here we must finish our tunnel,' he croaked. 'Portland Bill is the place. I don't care what the High Command says. If they want me to help them they must listen to me. It is the shortest distance across the Channel from here.'

'*Ja*, that is right, Herr Vultz, but they say –' began a red-faced colonel.

'Bah, I will hear no more of it,' screeched the greatest engineer in Germany. 'I don't care what they say. You can tell them I will build my tunnel to Portland Bill or nowhere. It will be finished one week from today – if only they send me some more prisoners of war to work for me.'

The second man spoke up.

'We have hundreds of thousands of prisoners of all kinds, British, French, and Polish. We send you thousands of them, but you demand RAF men. Not enough RAF men are being captured to supply you, Herr Vultz. Why will you not use someone else?'

The face of the mad engineer became twisted like that of a demon. He thumped the table.

'Because my boring-maching kills those who work in it. It shakes them to pieces. I have reason to hate them. I will have RAF men or none. If they cannot capture enough, they must do so in some other way. I want five hundred RAF men.'

In fact, Vultz lost even the men he had: they were rescued by Zoom, and the Guernsey tunnelling camp was pounded to pieces by the RAF. 'The Birdman had succeeded in his biggest job, the saving of Britain.'

But Vultz, one assumes, escaped. None of the leaders in this war ever dies, on either side. There are impossible escapes, impossible rescues, but one impossibility never happens – neither good nor evil is ever finally beaten. The war goes on; Vultz changes his ground – perhaps in happier days he may become again only a Pirate sniggering as his lesser victims walk the plank: Falconer, the air ace, is condemned to the firing squad, but the bullets have not been moulded that will finish his career. We are all of us seeing a bit of death these days, but we shall not see their deaths. They will go on living week after week in the pages of the *Rover*, the *Skipper,* the *Hotspur*, the *B.O.P.,* and the *Girl's Own Paper*; in the brain of the boy who brings the parcels, of the evacuee child scowling from the railway compartment on his way to ignominious safety, of the shelter nuisance of whom we say: 'How can

anyone live with a child like that?' The answer, of course, is
that he doesn't, except at meal-times, live with *us*. He has other
companions: he is part of a war that will never come to an
end.

1940

GREAT DOG OF WEIMAR

M Y title is not, I must explain at once, a disrespectful reference
to the great German poet, but to another inhabitant of
Weimar, equally interesting but less well known. Perhaps I
should have heard long ago of the unbearable Kurwenal, the
companion (it would be inaccurate and flippant to call him the
pet) of Mathilde, Baroness von Freytag-Loringhoven, but if
I had not opened by chance a little book called *When Your
Animal Dies*, written by Miss Sylvia Barbanell and recently
published by the Psychic Press, I should have remained in
ignorance that dogs had ever spoken – not only Kurwenal, the
dachshund of Weimar, but Lola Kindermann, the airedale, and
her father Rolph Meokel, of Mannheim. I have always suspected dogs: solid, well-meaning, reliable, they seem to possess
all the least attractive human virtues. What bores, I have
sometimes thought, if they could speak, and now my most
appalling conjectures have been confirmed.

Miss Barbanell's is – let me emphasize it – a serious book:
the unbearable Kurwenal could have no place in a humorous
one. He is here a minor character: Miss Barbanell is mainly
concerned with the after-life of animals towards which she
gently leads us by her stories of animal intelligence – an after-
life not only for the unbearable Kurwenal and his kind but
also for cats, pet pigs, and goats. We hear of two pet frogs
materializing, and of Red Indian 'guides' who answer evasively
– in language oddly unlike Fenimore Cooper's – embarrassing
questions about bugs. (The lesser – undomesticated – creatures, it appears, join a group soul: there is a group soul for
every species and sub-species, but nobody seems worried at the
thought of how the group bug grows every time a Mexican

crushes one with his toe: as for roast chicken, in future it will seem to me like eating a theosophist.)

But to return to the unbearable Kurwenal. Nobody can question *his* claim to immortality, with his strong moral sense, his rectitude, and his little clean clerical jokes. Perhaps I should have explained that the Baroness von Freytag-Loringhoven (with a name like that she must have been a friend of Rilke) taught him to speak a language of barks, and the appalling dog was only too ready to learn. Five hundred investigators investigated him, including Professor Max Müller, but he seems on the whole to have endured them with exemplary patience. Only once did he rebel, and that momentarily, against a young neurologist of Berne University, exclaiming, 'I answer no doubters. Bother the asses.' It is the only recorded instance when this vile dog behaved other than well; there is no suggestion that he ever buried a bone, and the imagination boggles with embarrassment at the thought of the intimate scenes that must have taken place between Kurwenal and the Baroness when he was being house-trained. He would have done nothing to make the situation easier. 'To me', he was in the habit of saying with priggish self-approval, 'learning is a great happiness', and to a young scientist who visited him, he said, 'I like to have you here. You are more sincere than most people.' He was that kind of dog: one pictures the earnest melting brown gaze between the ears like ringlets.

Dachshunds, of course, are always serious and usually sentimental, but occasionally one has seen them shocked into abandon by a fleshy bone, a good smell, or an amiable tree. Not so the unbearable Kurwenal. Miss Barbanell writes that he had an 'attractive personality and grand sense of humour', but those words one uses of a dean who does – sometimes – unbend.

Kurwenal had a roguish sense of fun. The Baroness was given a very fine Roman rug for him on his birthday. Kurwenal said, 'I find rug nice, will tear.' Then he paused before he added with a sly look in his eye, 'Not'.

If you accompanied Kurwenal on his walks you were more likely to be edified than amused. He was fond of discussing religion in a rather evangelical way. 'On one of these occasions he said to the Baroness, "I often pray". She asked, "What do you pray for?" Kurwenal answered, "For you." ' Once, during tea, Professor Max Müller discussed with his hostess the slaughter of dogs for food. 'He thought that the topic must be of particular interest to Kurwenal and asked the dog whether he had followed the conversation. "Yes," replied Kurwenal. "Do you wish to say something about it?" "Yes," answered the dog, and barked out the following: "The Christian religion prohibits killing." ' Sometimes when I remember that all this was spoken in the German language I feel sorry even for the unbearable Kurwenal: to think of those constructions – that awful drift of guttural words – expressed with a sort of slow pedantry in barks. For Conversations with Kurwenal were quite as protracted as Conversations with Eckermann. With the same neurologist from Berne who was the victim of Kurwenal's only breach of good manners the dachshund carried on a conversation lasting nearly an hour. One pictures him on a hard ornate chair facing the scientist across a salon table: I doubt if even the Baroness ever held Kurwenal on her knees (it would hardly have been proper and it certainly would not have been suitable). 'When the scientist was about to leave, he turned to the dachshund and said, "I nearly forgot to ask you what you think about a dog's soul." "It is eternal like the soul of a man," replied Kurwenal.'

Earnest, thoughtful, full of familiar quotations (he knew his *Hamlet*), his manner lightened very rarely by a touch of diocesan humour, this dachshund possessed as well the awful faculty of always saying – and doing – the right thing. There was the message he sent with his photograph to the Animal Defence Society in London: there was the emotional scene with the military widower.

The Baroness tells how she was visited by a friend, an army officer, who was very sad because his wife had recently passed on. Kurwenal said to his owner, 'We must cheer him up.' The dog approached the downcast man. 'Do you want to say something to him?' asked the Baroness. 'Yes,' replied Kurwenal.

'You can make up such nice little poems now,' she said. 'Make one for him.'

Without much delay Kurwenal recited:

> I love no one as much as you.
>   Love me too.
> I should like you with me every day.
>   Of happiness a ray.

Touched by the intelligent dog's sympathy, the depressed man's spirits brightened considerably.

Kurwenal, I am heartlessly glad to say, has 'passed on'. Otherwise he would probably have become a refugee, for his Christian principles would never have allowed him to support the Nazi party; around Bloomsbury therefore we should have heard continually his admonitory barks, barks about the great Teutonic abstractions – eternity, the soul, barks of advice, reproof, consolation. Strangely enough there is no record in a book crammed with séances, apparitions, invisible pawings, of the great dog's return. Silence has taken him at last, but I for one feel no doubt at all that somewhere he awaits his mistress – no, that is not a word one can use in connexion with Kurwenal and the Baroness – his former companion, ready to lead the Baroness von Freytag-Loringhoven firmly among the group souls and the Red Indian 'guides', among the odd frequenters of the Kluski séances – the buzzard, the Eastern sage and his weasel, the Afghan with his maneless lion – into the heart of the vague theosophic eternity.

1940

THE BRITISH PIG

THE pig in our literature has always been credited with qualities peculiarly British. Honest, a little stupid, commercially-minded perhaps, but with a trace of idealism in his love affairs, the pig's best nature is shown in domestic surroundings at a period of peace and material comfort. 'They led pros-

perous uneventful lives, and their end was bacon', Miss Potter
has written of Miss Dorcas and Miss Porcas, but the sentence
might stand as the epitaph of the whole race. In the latest
variant on the tale of the *Three Little Pigs*, published by the
Walt Disney Studios, one notices that same serenity in the
portraits of the older generation hanging in the house of the
provident pig: 'Mother', an old-fashioned parent drawn tenderly in the act of suckling eight children; 'Uncle Otto',
changed to a Rugby football, but a football at rest, unprofaned
as yet by the clamorous, vulgar game; 'Father', uncarved,
sporting his paper frill with the heavy dignity of a Victorian
parent in a Gladstone collar. It is impossible to doubt this
strong domestic affection when we find it noticed by an earlier
and less sympathetic observer than Miss Potter. The Rev. W.
Bingley, using the very terms in which foreign historians have
so often described Englishmen, wrote, 'Selfish, indocile and
rapacious, as many think him, no animal has greater sympathy
for those of his own kind than the hog.'

But perhaps the British quality of the pig has never been
more thoroughly expressed than in the early poem: 'This
little pig went to market (one remembers the pride with which
Englishmen have always repeated Napoleon's jeer); This little
pig stayed at home ('O sweet content! O sweet, O sweet content!'; 'Sweet Stay-at-Home, sweet Well-Content'; 'I love thee
for a heart that's kind – Not for the knowledge in thy mind'
– it is sometimes hard to remember that Dekker and Mr Davies
are writing of men and not of pigs); This little pig had roast
beef (no need to emphasize the parallel); This little pig had
none; This little pig cried wee wee wee all the way home.' Perhaps no pig was more British than this last; a literary pig,
for the mother-fixation, the longing for the womb has been the
peculiar peril of our minor poets. 'O mother quiet, breasts of
peace': Rupert Brooke is the obvious modern example, but all
through the Georgian period one is aware of the patter of little
hoofs along the dark road that leads back to the country sty,
the roses round the door, the Mothering Sunday that goes on
and on.

Sexual references, it will be noticed, are quite absent from this early poem, as they are from the rather cruel, politically-conscious story of the *Three Little Pigs*. It really seems that at this period of pig literature the bigger the litter the greater the inhibition, a situation closely paralleled in Victorian England. Miss Potter, I think, was the first to throw any real light on the Love Life of the Pig, and this she did with a delicacy and a psychological insight that recall Miss Austen. She drew for the first time in literature the feminine pig. Hitherto a pig had been just a pig; one usually assumed the sex to be masculine. But in Pig-Wig, whom Pigling Bland, it will be remembered, rescued from the cottage of the fatal Mr Peter Thomas Piperson, the female pig was revealed to be as completely British as the male: inquisitive, unromantic, demanding to be amused, fond of confectionery and admirably unselfconscious:

She asked so many questions that it became embarrassing to Pigling Bland.
He was obliged to shut his eyes and pretend to sleep. She became quiet, and there was a smell of peppermint.
'I thought you had eaten them?' said Pigling, waking suddenly.
'Only the corners,' replied Pig-Wig, studying the sentiments (they were conversation peppermints) by the firelight.
'I wish you wouldn't; he might smell them through the ceiling,' said the alarmed Pigling.
Pig-Wig put back the sticky peppermints into her pocket. 'Sing something,' she demanded.
'I am sorry ... I have toothache,' said Pigling much dismayed.
'Then I will sing,' replied Pig-Wig. 'You will not mind if I say iddy tiddity? I have forgotten some of the words.'

It is impossible to deny that this is a peculiarly English love scene; no other nation, except perhaps the Russian, would have behaved or written quite like this, and the sentiment of the ending, the luxurious indulgence in wistfulness and idealism: 'They ran, and they ran, and they ran down the hill, and across a short cut on level green turf at the bottom, between pebble beds and rushes. They came to the river, they came to the bridge – they crossed it hand in hand' would be inconceivable to a race of pigs whose prosperity had been more precarious, to whom the struggle for existence had been more crudely presented. American pigs, for example, who meet their end, like so many other Americans, abruptly in Chicago, would have been at the same time more brutal and more soft-hearted.

Both these rather contradictory qualities appear in the Walt Disney Studios' brilliant adaptation of *Three Little Pigs* (and I should like, before I forget in the fascination of the story, warmly to congratulate all those concerned in the production of this book: the chief electrician, the cameraman, the fashion designer, the art editor, the scenario writer, the director and assistant director, the producer, the author and the composer of the theme song). These pigs are no longer quite so British, which is to say that they are no longer quite so piggish. The curled tails, the improvident flutings, the house of straw and the house of twigs and the house of brick have never been more tenderly portrayed, but the wolf never more brutally. This is the wolf of experience, not of dream; Wall Street smashes, financiers' suicides, the machine guns of the gangster are behind this wolf. Watch him outside the house of twigs, sitting in a basket, a sheepskin falling on either side of his ferocious muzzle like the wig of a Jeffreys: this is Justice conniving at unjust executions and letting the gangster free. And watch him again outside the house of bricks in a rusty hat, in an overcoat, in a false yellow beard: 'I'm the Kleen-e-ze Brush man, I'm giving away free samples': he is every share pusher personified, the man who knows of a new gold mine, a swell oil field.

But just because the whole story is more realistic than the English version, the American mind shrinks from the ruthless logical *dénouement*. The two improvident pigs are not swallowed by the wolf, they escape and take refuge with their brother in the brick house, and even the wolf escapes with a scalding. The wolf's escape, indeed, is the most American aspect of this transplanted tale. How often one has watched the methods of justice satirized upon the screen with a realism that would be impossible in England; yet nothing is done about it, the wolf escapes. The English story is the better one, to sacrifice two pigs that the third may live in safety, to sacrifice the improvident pigs that the provident pig may be remembered for ever in his famous aphorism: 'The price of liberty is eternal vigilance.'

1934

GEORGE MOORE AND OTHERS

A SUNK railway track and a gin distillery flank the gritty street. There is something Victorian about the whole place – an air of ugly commercial endeavour mixed with odd idealisms and philanthropies. It isn't only the jumble of unattractive titles on the dusty spines, the huge weight of morality at sixpence a time; even the setting has an earnestness. . . . The public-houses are like a lesson in temperance.

It isn't all books by any means in the book market: a dumb man presides over the first stall given up to paint-brushes and dividers; we pass wireless parts, rubber heels, old stony collections of nuts and bolts, gramophone records, cycle tyres, spectacles (hospital prescriptions made up on the spot under the shadow of the gin distillery), a case of broken (I was going to say motheaten) butterflies – privet-hawks and orange-tips and red admirals losing their antennae and powder, shabby like second-hand clothes. One stall doesn't display its wares at all: only labels advertising Smell Bombs, Itching Powder, Cigarette Bangs – Victorian, too, the painful physical humour reminding us of Cruickshank on the poor and Gilbert on old age.

And then at last the books. It is a mistake to look for bargains here, or even to hope to find any books you really want – unless you happen to want Thackeray, Froude, or Macaulay on the cheap. Those authors are ubiquitous. No, the book market is the place for picking up odd useless information. Here, for instance, is Dibdin's *Purification of Sewage and Water*, published by the Sanitary Publishing Company, next to *Spiritual Counsel for District Visitors*, *Submarine Cables*, and *Chicago Police Problems*, published – it seems broadminded – by the Chicago University Press. Of course, there are lots of folios called *View of the Lakes* or of Italy, Switzerland, the Tyrol, as the case may be; and one can buy, in pale-blue paper parts, Bessemer on *Working Blast Furnaces*. *Doll Caudel in Paris* seems to be part of a series and looks a little coarse.

Somebody had left a book open on a stall, and I read with some amazement: 'George Moore had a great idea of duty. "If I have one thing," he says in his diary, "it is an imperative sense of duty." He was always possessed with the full sense of 'doing his duty.' He wished to do it; and he prayed to God to help him do it. But what duty?' What, indeed? Of course, one remembers the scene in *Salve*, when Moore said a prayer with Mr Mahaffy and was presented with a prayer-book, but this emphasis on duty seemed a little odd until I found the title-page and the author – Samuel Smiles, LL.D. This George Moore was not a writer, but a wholesale merchant and a philanthropist, and here, perhaps, is the real delight of the book market – nowhere else would one be likely to find the life of a Victorian draper. And it is rewarding. Smiles deserved his popularity; there is a bold impressionist vitality about his style; he roughs in very well the atmosphere of commercial travelling: the astute offer of a favourite snuff, the calculated jest, the encounters in hotel rooms – the Union Hotel, Birmingham, and the Star at Manchester, the seedy atmosphere of benevolence, what he calls 'Mr Moore's labours of love': the hospital for incurables, the penny bank, the London Porters' Benevolent Association, the Kensington Auxiliary Bible Society, the Pure Literature Society (Mr Moore's favourite book, unlike his namesake's, was *The Memoirs and Remains of Dr M'Cheyne*). His oddest philanthopy perhaps was 'in marrying people who were not, but who ought to have been, married' – or else his attempt to introduce copies of the Bible into the best Paris hotels. But Dr Smiles had more than vigour; he had a macabre if ungrammatical imagination, as when he describes the end of the first Mrs Moore. 'Her remains were conveyed to Cumberland. On arrival at Carlisle, Mr Moore slept in the Station Hotel. It seemed strange to him that while in his comfortable bed, his dead wife should be laying cold in the railway truck outside, within sight of the hotel windows.'

331

Macabre – but not quite so macabre as this other book which had lost half its title-page, but seems to be called *The Uncertainty of the Signs of Death*. Published in 1746, and illustrated with some grim little copper-plates, it contains 'a great variety of amusing and well-attested Instances of Persons who have return'd to Life in their Coffins, in their Graves, under the Hands of the Surgeons, and after they had remain'd apparently dead for a considerable Time in the Water'. A scholarly little work, which throws some doubts upon the story that Duns Scotus 'bit his own Hands in his Grave', it carries in the musty pages some of the atmosphere of an M. R. James story – there is an anecdote from Basingstoke too horrible to set down here which might have pleased the author of *O Whistle and I'll Come to You*. I was pleased to find a few more details of Ann Green, who was executed at Oxford in 1650 and was revived by her friends – about whose resurrection, it may be remembered, Anthony à Wood wrote some rather bad verses – and before laying the book back beside the battered brown tin trunk which carried the salesman's stock, I noted this recipe for reviving the apparently dead: 'We ought to irritate his Nostrils by introducing into them the Juice of Onions, Garlick, and Horse-radish, or the feather'd End of a Quill, or the Point of a Pencil: stimulate his Organs of Touch with Whips and Nettles; and if possible shock his Ears by hideous Shrieks and excessive Noises.'

Poor human body which must be clung to at all costs. There is very little light relief in the book market – an old copy of *Three Men on the Bummel*, that boisterous work, all sobs and horseplay, and a promising folio out of my reach called simply *The Imperial Russian Dinner Service*. The smell of mortality, morality, and thrown-out book go together – and the smell of the antiquated Metropolitan Line. Here is another moralist. In *Posthuma Christiana* (1712, price 6d.) William Crouch, the Quaker, laments the Restoration – 'The Roaring, Swearing, Drinking, Revelling, Debauchery, and Extravagancy of that Time I cannot forget,' and a few lines, as I turned the pages, caught the imagination as Blind Pew once did at the Benbow Inn. He is quoting an account of the Quakers, thirty-seven men and eighteen women, who were banished to Jamaica. 'The Ship was called *The Black Eagle*, and lay at anchor in *Bugby's Hole*, the Master's name was *Fudge,* by some called *Lying Fudge*.' They lay in the Thames seven weeks, and half of them died and were buried in the marshes below Gravesend. 'Twenty-seven survived, and remained on board the Ship; and there was one other Person of whom no certain Account could be given.'

That is the kind of unexpected mystery left on one's hands by a morning in the book market. A storm was coming up behind the gin distillery, and the man with the Itching Powder was packing up his labels – trade isn't good these days for his kind of bomb. It was time to emerge again out of the macabre past into the atrocious present.

1939

AT HOME

ONE gets used to anything: that is what one hears on many lips these days,* though everybody, I suppose, remembers the sense of shock he felt at the first bombed house he saw. I think of one in Woburn Square neatly sliced in half. With its sideways exposure it looked like a Swiss chalet: there were a pair of skiing sticks hanging in the attic, and in another room a grand piano cocked one leg over the abyss. The combination of music and skiing made one think of the Sanger family and Constant Nymphs dying pathetically of private sorrow to popular applause. In the bathroom the geyser looked odd and twisted seen from the wrong side, and the kitchen impossibly crowded with furniture until one realized one had been given a kind of mouse-eye view from behind the stove and the dresser – all the space where people used to move about with toast and tea-pots was out of sight. But after quite a short time one ceased to look twice at the intimate exposure of interior furnishings, and waking on a cement floor among strangers, one no

* October 1940.

longer thinks what an odd life this is. 'One gets used to anything.'

But that, I think is not really the explanation. There are things one never gets used to because they don't connect: sanctity and fidelity and the courage of human beings abandoned to free will: virtues like these belong with old college buildings and cathedrals, relics of a world with faith. Violence comes to us more easily because it was so long expected – not only by the political sense but by the moral sense. The world we lived in could not have ended any other way. The curious waste lands one sometimes saw from trains – the cratered ground round Wolverhampton under a cindery sky with a few cottages grouped like stones among the rubbish: those acres of abandoned cars round Slough: the dingy fortune-teller's on the first-floor above the cheap permanent waves in a Brighton back street; they all demanded violence, like the rooms in a dream where one knows that something will presently happen – a door fly open or a window-catch give and let the end in.

I think it was a sense of impatience because the violence was delayed – rather than a masochistic enjoyment of discomfort – that made many writers of recent years go abroad to try to meet it half-way: some went to Spain and others to China. Less ideological, perhaps less courageous, writers chose corners where the violence was more moderate; but the hint of it had to be there to satisfy that moral craving for the just and reasonable expression of human nature left without belief. The craving wasn't quite satisfied because we all bought two-way tickets. Like Henry James hearing a good story at a dinnertable, we could say, 'Stop. That's enough for our purpose', and take a train or a boat home. The moral sense was tickled: that was all. One came home and wrote a book, leaving the condemned behind in the back rooms of hotels where the heating was permanently off or eking out a miserable living in little tropical towns. We were sometimes – God forgive us – amusing at their expense, even though we guessed all the time that we should be joining them soon for ever.

All the same – egotistical to the last – we can regard those journeys as a useful rehearsal. Scraps of experience remain with one under the pavement. Lying on one's stomach while a bomb whines across, one is aware of how they join this life to the other, in the same way that a favourite toy may help a child, by its secret appeal, to adapt himself to a strange home. There are figures in our lives which strike us as legendary even when they are with us, seem to be preparing us like parents for the sort of life ahead. I find myself remembering in my basement black Colonel Davis, the dictator of Grand Bassa, whose men, according to a British Consul's report, had burned women alive in native huts and skewered children on their bayonets. He was a Scoutmaster and he talked emotionally about his old mother and got rather drunk on my whisky. He was bizarre and gullible and unaccountable: his atmosphere was that of deep forest, extreme poverty, and an injustice as wayward as generosity. He connected like a poem with ordinary life (he was other people's ordinary life): but it was ordinary life expressed with vividness. Then there was General Cedillo, the dictator of San Luis Potosi (all my dictators, unlike Sir Nevile Henderson's, have been little ones). I remember the bull-browed Indian rebel driving round his farm in the hills followed by his chief gunmen in another car, making plans for crops which he never saw grow because the federal troops hunted him down and finished him. He was loved by his peasants, who served him without pay and stole everything he owned, and hated by the townspeople whom he robbed of water for his land (so that you couldn't even get a bath). His atmosphere was stupidity and courage and kindliness and violence. Neither of these men were of vintage growth, but they belonged to the same diseased erratic world as the dictators and the millionaires. They started things in a small way while the world waited for the big event. I think of them sometimes under the pavement almost with a feeling of tenderness. They helped one to wait, and now they help one to feel at home. Everybody else in the shelter, I imagine, has memories of this kind, too: or why should they accept violence so happily, with so little surprise, impatience, or resentment? Perhaps a savage schoolmaster or the kind of female guardian the young Kipling suffered from or some beast in himself has prepared each man for this life.

That, I think, is why one feels at home in London – or in Liverpool or Bristol, or any of the bombed cities – because life there is what it ought to be. If a cracked cup is put in boiling water it breaks, and an old dog-toothed civilization is breaking now. The nightly routine of sirens, barrage, the probing raider, the unmistakable engine ('Where are you? Where are you? Where are you?'), the bomb-bursts moving nearer and then moving away, hold one like a love-charm. We are not quite happy when we take a few days off. There is something just a little unsavoury about a safe area – as if a corpse were to keep alive in some of its members, the fingers fumbling or the tongue seeking to taste. So we go hurrying back to our shelter, to the nightly uneasiness and then the 'All Clear' sounding happily like New Year's bells and the first dawn look at the world to see what has gone: green glass strewn on the pavement (all broken glass seems green) and sometimes flames like a sticky coloured plate from the *Boy's Own Paper* lapping at the early sky. As for the victims, if they have suffered pain it will be nearly over by this time. Life has become just and poetic, and if we believe this is the right end to the muddled thought, the sentimentality and selfishness of generations, we can also believe that justice doesn't end there. The innocent will be given their peace, and the unhappy will know more happiness than they have ever dreamt about, and poor muddled people will be given an answer they have to accept. We needn't feel pity for any of the innocent, and as for the guilty we know in our hearts that they will live just as long as we do and no longer.

1940

PART IV

Personal Postscript

THE SOUPSWEET LAND

A GHOST – a *revenant* – does not expect to be recognized when he returns to the scenes of his past; if he communicates to you a sense of fear, perhaps it is really his own fear, not yours. Places have so changed since he was alive that he has to find his way through a jungle of new houses and altered rooms (concrete and steel can proliferate like vegetation). Because *he* hasn't changed, because his memories are unaltered, the *revenant* believes that he is invisible. Coming back to Freetown and Sierra Leone last Christmas, I thought I belonged to a bizarre past which no one else shared. It was a shock to be addressed by my first name on my first night, to feel a hand squeeze my arm and a voice say, 'Scobie, eh, who's Scobie?' and 'Pujehun, don't you remember we met in Pujehun? I was in PWD. Let's have a drink at the City.'

I came to Sierra Leone to work more than a quarter of a century ago, landing in Freetown from a slow convoy four weeks out of Liverpool. I felt a strong sense of unreality: how had this happened? A kitchen orchestra of forks and frying-pans played me off the Elder Dempster cargo ship into a motor launch where my temporary host, the Secretary of Agriculture, awaited me, expecting something less flippant. The red Anglican cathedral looked down on my landing as it had done in 1935 when I first visited Freetown. Nothing in the exhausted shabby enchanted town of bougainvillaea and balconies, tin roofs and funeral parlours, had changed, but I never imagined on my first visit that one day I would arrive like this to work, to be one of those tired men drinking pink gin at the City bar as the sun set on the laterite.

The sense of unreality great stronger every hour. A passage by air had been arranged to Lagos where I was to work for three months before returning, and I thought it best to warn my host that he would be seeing me again. 'What exactly are you going to do here?' he asked, and I was studiously vague, for no one had yet told me what my 'cover' in this far from James Bond world was to be. I knew my number, and that was all (it was not 007). I was glad when a major with a large moustache looked in, with an air of stern premeditation, for drinks, and the subject could be changed. 'Come for a walk?' he suddenly asked. It seemed an odd thing to do at that hour of the day, but I agreed. We set out down the road in the haze of the harmattan.

'Find it hot, I suppose?' he said.

'Yes.'

'Humidity is 95 per cent.'

'Really?'

He swerved sideways into a garden. 'This house is empty,' he said. 'Fellow's gone on leave.' I followed him obediently. He sat down on a large rock and said, 'Got a message for you.' I sat gingerly down beside him, remembering the childhood warning that sitting on a stone in the heat gives you piles.

'Signal came in last Friday. You're an inspector of the DOT. Got it?'

'What's DOT?'

'Department of Overseas Trade,' he said sharply. Ignorance in this new intelligence world was like incompetence.

All the same I felt relieved to know and at lunch gently led the conversation back to my future in Freetown. 'As a matter of fact,' I said to my host, 'I can tell *you*, though it's not been officially announced yet, that I am to be an Inspector of the DOT.'

'DOT?'

'Department of Overseas Trade.'

He looked a little sceptical. He had every right to be, for by the time I returned I had become something quite different. The DOT, I learnt too late in Lagos, had refused to give cover to a phoney inspector, and an equally unsuccessful attempt had been made on the virginity of the British Council. After that I was threatened in turn with a naval rank and an air force rank, until it was found that unless I was given the rank of commander or group-captain I could not have a private office and a safe for my code-books. When I flew up to Freetown again it was with a vague attachment to the police force which was a little difficult to explain to those who awaited an inspector of Overseas Trade.

The whole of my life in Freetown had the same unreality; for the secretariat I did not exist, for I was not on the Colonial Office list where everyone's salary and position were set down, and for the Sierra Leonians I was another unapproachable Government servant. I lived alone in a small house on the edge of what in the rains became a marsh, with a Nigerian transport camp opposite me which helped to collect the vultures and behind the scrub which collected flies, for it was used as a public lavatory. Over this I had one successful brush with the administration. When I wrote to the Colonial Secretary demanding a lavatory for the Africans he replied that my request should go through the proper channels by way of the Commissioner of Police; I quoted in reply what Churchill had said of 'proper channels' in wartime, and the shed was built. I wrote back that in the annals of Freetown my name like Keats's would be writ in water. My isolation for a while was increased when I quarrelled with my boss 1,200 miles away in Lagos and he ceased to send me any money to live on (or to pay my almost non-existent agents.)

During that long silence I had plenty of time to wonder again why I was here. Our lives are formed in the years of childhood, and when a while ago I began writing an account of my first twenty-five years, I was curious to discover any hints of what had led a middle-aged man to sit there in a humid solitude, far from his family and his friends and his real profession. Out of my experience was to come my first popular success *The Heart of the Matter*, but I did not begin to write that book for another four years, after the absurdities had already faded from my mind. I had been instructed not to keep a diary for security reasons, just as I was taught the use of secret inks that I never employed and of bird-droppings if these were exhausted. (Vultures were the most common bird – there were usually three or four on my tin roof – but I doubt whether their droppings had been contemplated.)

The start of my life as 59200 was not propitious. I announced my safe arrival by means of a book code (I had chosen a novel of T. F. Powys from which I could detach sufficiently lubricious phrases for my own amusement), and a large safe came in the next convoy with a leaflet of instructions and my codes. The code-books were a constant source of interest, for the most unexpected words occurred in their necessarily limited vocabulary. I wondered how often use had been made of the symbol for 'eunuch', and I was not content until I had found an opportunity to use it myself in a message to my colleague in Gambia: 'As the chief eunuch said I cannot repeat cannot come.' (Strange the amusements one finds in solitude. I can remember standing for half an hour on the staircase to my bedroom watching two flies make love.)

The safe was another matter. I am utterly incapable of reading instructions of a technical nature. I chose my combination and set it as I believed correctly, put away my newly acquired code-books, shut the safe and tried in vain to reopen it. Very soon I realized the fault I had made: my eye had passed over one line in the instructions and the combination was set now to some completely unknown figure. Telegrams were waiting to be decoded and telegrams to be sent. Laboriously with the help of T. F. Powys I lied to London that the safe had been damaged in transit; they must send another by the next convoy. The code-books were rescued with a blow flame and lodged temporarily in Government House.

I used to look forward to the evenings when I would take a walk along the abandoned railway track on the slopes below Hill Station, returning at sunset to get my bath before the rats came in (at night they would swing on my bedroom curtains). Then – free from telegrams – I would sit down to write *The Ministry of Fear*. Whisky, gin and beer were severely rationed, but some friendly naval officers supplied me with demi-johns of wine which had come from Portuguese Guinea without passing the customs. On nights of full moon the starving pi-dogs kept me awake with their howling, and I would rise, pull boots over my pyjamas, and get rid of my rage by cursing and throwing stones in the lane behind my house where the very poor lived. My boy told me I was known there as 'the bad man', so before I went away from Freetown as I believed for ever, I sent some bottles of wine to a wedding in one of the hovels, hoping to leave a better memory behind.

It was not very often I went to the City Hotel, where *The Heart of the Matter* began. There one escaped the protocol-conscious members of the secretariat. It was a home from home for men who had not encountered success at any turn of the long road and who no longer expected it. They were not beach-combers, for they had jobs, but their jobs had no prestige value. They were failures, but they knew more of Africa than the successes who were waiting to get transferred to a smarter colony and were careful to take no risks with their personal file. In the City bar were the men who had stayed put into the beginnings of old age, and yet they were immeasurably younger than the new assistant secretaries. The dream which had brought them to Africa was still alive: it didn't depend on carefully mounting the ladder of a career. I suppose I felt at home at the City because, after six months or more, I was beginning to feel a failure too.

All my brighter schemes had been firmly turned down: the rescue by bogus Communist agents of a left-wing agitator who was under house-arrest (I intended to have him planted in Vichy-held Conakry believing himself to be an informant for Russia): a brothel to be opened in Bissau for visitors from Senegal. The Portuguese liners came in and out carrying their smuggled industrial diamonds, and not one search – from the rice in the holds to the cosmetics in the cabins – had ever turned up a single stone. In the City bar I could occasionally forget the insistent question what am I doing here? because the answer was probably much the same as my companions might have given: an escape from school? a recurring dream of adolescence? a book read in childhood?

The City Hotel I found on my return last Christmas had not altered at all. A white man looked down from the balcony where my character Wilson sat watching Scobie pass in the street below, and he waved to me as if it was but yesterday that I looked in last for a coaster. Only the turbaned Sikh was absent who used to tell fortunes – in the communal douche for the sake of privacy. A Sierra Leonian played sad Christmas calypsos in a corner of the balcony and a tart in a scarlet dress danced to attract attention (tarts were not allowed inside). Even the kindly sad Swiss landlord was still the same; he hadn't left Freetown in more than thirty years. He had survived, and to that extent he was successful, but perhaps it was the very meagreness of the success which made his shabby bar the 'home from home'.

Next day I went to look for my old house. A quarter of a century ago it had been condemned by the health authorities, so it might well have disappeared, and I thought at first it had. A brand-new Italian garage stood on the site of the Nigerian transport camp, the bush where the lavatory had been built had disappeared under a housing-estate, and there were very superior houses now in the lane where the pi-dogs had howled (one was occupied by the Secretary General of the National Reform Council which at that moment was governing Sierra Leone). It took me quite a while to recognize my old home, brightly painted with a garden where the mud had been. The little office had become a kitchen, the sitting-room which had been bleak with PWD furniture was gay with the abstract paintings of a Sierra Leone young woman. I went upstairs and looked into the bedroom where the rats had swung – there were still rats, the owner said – and I stopped on the stairs where I had watched for so long a fly's copulation. The image brought back the boredom of my adolescence, a youth playing at Russian roulette ... perhaps that had been a stage towards this barren hermitage on the Brookfield flats.

The Brookfield church was unchanged, where my friend Father Mackie used to preach in Creole: the same bad statue of St Anthony over the altar, the same Virgin in the butterfly blue robe. At Midnight Mass I could have believed myself back in 1942 if in that year I had not missed the Mass. A fellow Catholic, the representative of the rival secret service, SOE, had come to dine with me tête-à-tête and we were soon too drunk on Portuguese wine to stagger to the church. Now the girl in front of me wore one of the surrealist Manchester cotton dresses which are rarely seen since Japanese trade moved in. The word 'soupsweet' was printed over her shoulder, but I had to wait until she stood up before I could confirm another phrase: 'Fenella lak' good poke.' Father Mackie would have been amused, I thought, and what better description could there be of this poor lazy lovely coloured country than 'soupsweet'?

It was with some shame that my companion, Mario Soldati, and I moved out of the old City Hotel for the conventional comfort of the new luxury Paramount built up the hill behind the former police station where I used to come every day to collect my cables from the Commissioner. The old man would not have approved this change in Freetown, and I remembered the morning in the rains when he went out of his mind under the pressure of overwork, the strain of controlling corrupt officers, the badgering of MI5 bureaucrats from home. He was not a drinking man, but in his knowledge and humanity he was more akin to the inhabitants of the City Hotel than I was now. I had been spoilt for the communal douche and the bare bedroom. They treated me with great charity when I left, they gave me a warm welcome whenever I returned for a drink, but I felt the guilt of a beach-comber *manqué*: I had failed at failure. How could they tell that for a writer as much as for a priest there is no such thing as success?

1968

MORE ABOUT PENGUINS
AND PELICANS

For further information about books available from Penguins please write to Dept EP, Penguin Books Ltd, Harmondsworth, Middlesex, UB7 0DA.

In the U.S.A.: For a complete list of books available from Penguins in the United States write to Dept CS, Penguin Books, 625 Madison Avenue, New York, New York 10022.

In Canada: For a complete list of books available from Penguins in Canada write to Penguin Books Canada Ltd, 2801 John Street, Markham, Ontario L3R 1B4.

In Australia: For a complete list of books available from Penguins in Australia write to the Marketing Department, Penguin Books Australia Ltd, P.O. Box 257, Ringwood, Victoria 3134.

GRAHAM GREENE IN PENGUINS

BRIGHTON ROCK

Set in the pre-war Brighton underworld, this is the story of a teen-age gangster, Pinkie, and Ida, his personal Fury who relentlessly brings him to justice.

THE POWER AND THE GLORY

This poignant story set during an anti-clerical purge in one of the southern states of Mexico 'starts in the reader an irresistible emotion of pity and love' – *The Times*

THE COMEDIANS

In this novel, Graham Greene makes a graphic study of the committed and the uncommitted in the present-day tyranny of Haiti.

THE QUIET AMERICAN

This novel makes a wry comment on European interference in Asia in its story of the Franco–Vietminh war in Vietnam.

THE HEART OF THE MATTER

Scobie – a police officer in a West African colony – was a good man but his struggle to maintain the happiness of two women destroyed him.

THE END OF THE AFFAIR

This frank intense account of a love-affair and its mystical after-math takes place in a suburb of war-time London.

GRAHAM GREENE IN PENGUINS

MAY WE BORROW YOUR HUSBAND?
AND OTHER COMEDIES OF THE SEXUAL LIFE

This collection of short stories holds some of Greene's saddest observations on the hilarity of sex.

THE MINISTRY OF FEAR

In this his most phantasmagoric study, the story, largely set in the London 'blitz', passes 'through twilit corridors of horror' – *Observer*

A BURNT-OUT CASE

Philip Toynbee described this novel, set in a leper colony in the Congo, as being 'perhaps the best that he has ever written'.

IT'S A BATTLEFIELD

The unforgettable sense of menace of Greene's seedy London settings tightens as each episode leads on to the deadly irony of the climax.

LOSER TAKES ALL

Bertram, a conspicuously unsuccessful accountant, is wafted by another man's whim to Monte Carlo. Inevitably he goes to the casino – and loses. Then suddenly his system starts working . . .

LIONEL DAVIDSON IN PENGUINS

THE NIGHT OF WENCESLAS

'Invited' to Prague on what seems to be an innocent business trip, young Nicholas Whistler finds himself trapped – between the Cold War and the hot clutches of the amorous and statuesque Vlasta.

THE ROSE OF TIBET

Charles Houston should never have been in Tibet in the first place; he only went there to find his missing brother. But the Chinese invade, and he must get out fast – with Chinese soldiers and the cruel Himalayan winter on his heels.

MAKING GOOD AGAIN

Lionel Davidson plunges into the aftermath of the Second World War. A claim for reparations sends James Raison into a whirlpool of conflicting identity and age-old hate.

THE SUN CHEMIST

As the oil crisis overturns the economies of the West, Igor Druyanov is on the trail of the philosopher's stone, a formula for synthetic oil left by the great Chaim Weizmann on his death-bed. And the political consequences of such a formula, as the reader will understand, are enormous . . .

V. S. NAIPAUL IN PENGUINS

'It is time . . for him to be quite simply recognized as this country's most talented and promising young writer' – Anthony Powell in the *Daily Telegraph*

THE MIMIC MEN

Living in a run-down London suburb, Ralph Singh, a disgraced colonial minister exiled from the Caribbean island of his birth, is writing his biography. When he comes to politics he finds himself caught up in the upheaval of empire, in the turmoil of too-large events which move too fast . . .

A HOUSE FOR MR BISWAS

Mohun Biswas wants success, a house and a portion of land of his own. As he moves from job to job, acquiring a wife and four children, the odds against him lengthen and his ambition becomes more remote.

THE MYSTIC MASSEUR

Ganesh, who cured the Woman Who Couldn't Eat and the Man Who Made Love to His Bicycle, becomes involved in a local scandal. But he manages to keep some surprises in reserve . . .